BLUE LABYRINTH

DOUGLAS PRESTON and LINCOLN CHILD are the number one bestselling co-authors of the celebrated Pendergast novels, as well as the Gideon Crew books. Preston and Child's *Relic* and *The Cabinet of Curiosities* were chosen by readers in a National Public Radio poll as being among the one hundred greatest thrillers ever written, and *Relic* was made into a number one box office hit movie. Readers can sign up for their monthly newsletter, The Pendergast File, at www.PrestonChild.com and follow them on Facebook.

PRESTON & CHILD

'A collision between past and present that
will leave you breathless.'
LEE CHILD

'If you're willing to surrender to Preston and Child's
fiendish imaginations, you might devour the Pendergast
books the way kids do Halloween candy... There's
nothing else like them.'
WASHINGTON POST

'Preston and Child have done it again! *White Fire*
continues their white hot streak of bestselling suspense...
the most eccentric and ruthlessly clever FBI agent in
the business... Simply brilliant!'
LISA GARDNER

'Solid research, clear swift prose and enough twists to
fill a jar of pretzels. Sit back, crack open the book and
get ready for the ride of your life.'
DAVID BALDACCI

'I've read every Pendergast thriller.'
R.L. STINE

INTERNATIONAL BESTSELLERS

Also by Douglas Preston and Lincoln Child

Agent Pendergast Novels

Relic

Reliquary

The Cabinet of Curiosities

Still Life with Crows

Brimstone

Dance of Death

The Book of the Dead

The Wheel of Darkness

Cemetery Dance

Fever Dream

Cold Vengeance

Two Graves

White Fire

Blue Labyrinth

Gideon Crew Novels

Gideon's Sword

Gideon's Corpse

The Lost Island

Other Novels

Mount Dragon

Riptide

Thunderhead

The Ice Limit

PRESTON & CHILD

BLUE LABYRINTH

HEAD of ZEUS

First published in the USA in 2014 by Grand Central Publishing,
a division of Hachette Book Group, Inc.

First published in the UK in 2014 by Head of Zeus Ltd. This paperback edition
first published in the UK in 2015 by Head of Zeus Ltd

9 7 5 3 1 2 4 6 8

A catalogue record for this book is available from the British Library

Paperback ISBN: 9781784081102
eBook ISBN: 9781781859407

Printed and bound in the UK by Clays Ltd, St Ives Plc

Head of Zeus Ltd
Clerkenwell House
45-47 Clerkenwell Green
London EC1R 0HT
WWW.HEADOFZEUS.COM

I

The stately Beaux-Arts mansion on Riverside Drive between 137th and 138th Streets, while carefully tended and impeccably preserved, appeared to be untenanted. On this stormy June evening, no figures paced the widow's walk overlooking the Hudson River. No yellow glow from within flowed through the decorative oriel windows. The only visible light, in fact, came from the front entrance, illuminating the drive beneath the building's porte cochere.

Appearances can be deceiving, however—sometimes intentionally. Because 891 Riverside was the residence of FBI Special Agent Aloysius Pendergast—and Pendergast was a man who valued, above all, his privacy.

In the mansion's elegant library, Pendergast sat in a leather wing chair. Although it was early summer, the night was blustery and chill, and a low fire flickered on the grate. He was leafing through a copy of the *Manyōshū*, an old and celebrated anthology of Japanese poetry, dating to AD 750. A small *tetsubin*, or cast-iron teapot, sat on a table beside him, along with a china cup half-full of green tea. Nothing disturbed his concentration. The only sounds were the occasional crackle of settling embers and rumble of thunder from beyond the closed shutters.

Now there was a faint sound of footsteps from the reception hall beyond and Constance Greene appeared, framed in the library doorway. She was wearing a simple evening dress. Her violet eyes and dark hair, cut in an old-fashioned bob, offset the paleness of her skin. In one hand she held a bundle of letters.

"The mail," she said.

Pendergast inclined his head, set the book aside.

Constance took a seat beside Pendergast, noting that, since returning from what he called his "Colorado adventure," he was at last looking like his old self. His state of mind had been a cause of uneasiness in her since the dreadful events of the prior year.

She began sorting through the small stack of mail, putting aside the things that would not interest him. Pendergast did not like to concern himself with quotidian details. He had an old and discreet New Orleans law firm, long in the employ of the family, to pay bills and manage part of his unusually extensive income. He had an equally hoary New York banking firm to manage other investments, trusts, and real estate. And he had all mail delivered to a post office box, which Proctor, his chauffeur, bodyguard, and general factotum, collected on a regular basis. At present, Proctor was preparing to leave for a visit to relatives in Alsace, so Constance had agreed to take over the epistolary matters.

"Here's a note from Corrie Swanson."

"Open it, if you please."

"She's attached a photocopy of a letter from John Jay. Her thesis won the Rosewell Prize."

"Indeed. I attended the ceremony."

"I'm sure Corrie appreciated it."

"It is rare that a graduation ceremony offers more than an anesthetizing parade of platitudes and mendacity, set to the tiresome refrain of 'Pomp and Circumstance.'" Pendergast took a sip of tea at the recollection. "This one did."

Constance sorted through more mail. "And here's a letter from Vincent D'Agosta and Laura Hayward."

He nodded for her to scan it. "It's a thank-you note for the wedding gift and once again for the dinner party."

Pendergast inclined his head as she put the letter aside. The month before, on the eve of D'Agosta's wedding, Pendergast had hosted a private dinner for the couple, consisting of several courses he had prepared himself, paired with rare wines from his cellar. It was this gesture, more than anything, that had convinced Constance that Pendergast had recovered from his recent emotional trauma.

She read over a few other letters, then put aside those of interest and tossed the rest on the fire.

"How is the project coming, Constance?" Pendergast asked as he poured himself a fresh cup of tea.

"Very well. Just yesterday I received a packet from France, the Bureau Ancestre du Dijon, which I'm now trying to integrate with what I've already collected from Venice and Louisiana. When you have the time, I do have a couple of questions I'd like to ask about Augustus Robespierre St. Cyr Pendergast."

"Most of what I know consists of oral family history—tall tales, legends, and some whispered horror stories. I'd be glad to share most of them with you."

"Most? I was hoping you'd share them all."

"I fear there are skeletons in the Pendergast family closet, figurative and literal, that I must keep even from you."

Constance sighed and rose. As Pendergast returned to his book of poetry, she walked out of the library, across the reception hall lined with museum cabinets full of curious objects, and through a doorway into a long, dim space paneled in time-darkened oak. The main feature of the room was a wooden refectory table, almost as long as the room itself. The near end of the table was covered with journals, old letters, census pages, yellowed photographs and engravings, court transcripts, memoirs, reprints from newspaper microfiche, and other documents, all arranged in neat stacks. Beside them sat a laptop computer, its screen glowing incongruously in the dim room. Several months before, Constance had taken it upon herself to prepare a genealogy of the Pendergast family. She wanted both to satisfy her own curiosity and to help draw Pendergast out of himself. It was a fantastically complex, infuriating, and yet endlessly fascinating undertaking.

At the far end of the long room, beyond an arched door, was the foyer leading to the mansion's front door. Just as Constance was about to take a seat at the table, a loud knock sounded.

Constance paused, frowning. They rarely entertained visitors at 891 Riverside Drive—and never did one arrive unannounced.

Knock. Another rap resounded from the entryway, accompanied by a low grumble of thunder.

Smoothing down her dress, Constance walked down the length of the room, through the archway, and into the foyer. The heavy front door was solid, with no fish-eye lens, and she hesitated a moment. When no third rap came, she undid the upper lock, then the lower, and slowly opened the door.

There, silhouetted in the light of the porte cochere, stood a young man. His blond hair was wet and plastered to his head. His rain-spattered features were fine and quintessentially Nordic, with a high-domed forehead and chiseled lips. He was dressed in a linen suit, sopping wet, which clung to his frame.

He was bound with heavy ropes.

Constance gasped, began to reach out to him. But the bulging eyes took no notice of the gesture. They stared straight ahead, unblinking.

For a moment, the figure remained standing, swaying ever so slightly, fitfully illuminated by flashes of lightning—and then it began to fall, like a tree toppling, slowly at first and then faster, before crashing facedown across the threshold.

Constance backed up with a cry. Pendergast arrived at a run, followed by Proctor. Pendergast grasped her, pulled her aside, and quickly knelt over the young man. He gripped the figure by the shoulder and turned him over, brushing the hair from his eyes, and feeling for the pulse that was so obviously absent beneath the cold flesh of the neck.

"Dead," he said, his voice low and unnaturally composed.

"My God," Constance said, her own voice breaking. "It's your son Tristram."

"No," Pendergast said. "It's Alban. His twin."

For just a moment longer he knelt by the body. And then he leapt to his feet and, in a flash of feline motion, disappeared into the howling storm.

2

Pendergast sprinted to Riverside Drive and paused at the corner, scanning north and south along the broad avenue. The rain was now coming down in sheets, traffic was light, and there were no pedestrians. His eye lit upon the closest vehicle, about three blocks south: a late-model Lincoln Town Car, black, of the kind seen on the streets of Manhattan by the thousands. The license plate light was out, leaving the details of the New York plate unreadable.

Pendergast ran after it.

The vehicle did not speed up, but continued at a leisurely pace down the drive, at each cross street moving through one set of green lights after another, steadily gaining distance. The lights turned yellow, then red. But the vehicle continued on, running a yellow and a red, never accelerating, never slowing.

He pulled out his cell phone and punched in a number as he ran. "Proctor. Bring the car. I'm headed south on Riverside."

The Town Car had almost disappeared, save for a faint pair of taillights, wavering in the downpour, but as the drive made the slow curve at 126th Street even those disappeared.

Pendergast continued on, pursuing at a dead run, his black suit jacket whipping behind him, rain stinging his face. A few blocks ahead, he saw the Town Car again, stopped at another light behind two other vehicles. Once again, he pulled out his phone and dialed.

"Twenty-Sixth Precinct," came the response. "Officer Powell."

"This is SA Pendergast, FBI. In pursuit of a black Town Car, New York license plate unidentified, traveling southbound on Riverside at One Hundred Twenty-Fourth. Operator is suspect in a homicide. Need assistance in motor vehicle stop."

"Ten-four," came the dispatcher. And a moment later: "We have a marked unit in the area, two blocks over. Keep us posted on location."

"Air support as well," Pendergast said, still at a dead run.

"Sir, if the vehicle operator is only a suspect—"

"This is a priority target for the FBI," Pendergast said into the phone. "Repeat, a *priority target*."

A brief pause. "We're putting a bird in the air."

As he put the phone away, the Town Car suddenly veered around the cars idling at the red light, jumped the curb and crossed the sidewalk, tore through a set of flower beds in Riverside Park, churning up mud, then headed the wrong way down the exit ramp to the Henry Hudson Parkway.

Pendergast called dispatch again and updated them on the vehicle's location, followed it up with another call to Proctor, then cut into the park, leapt over a low fence, and sprinted through some tulip beds, his eyes locked on the taillights of the car careening down the off-ramp onto the parkway, the screech of tires floating back to his ears.

He vaulted the low stone wall on the far side of the drive, then half ran, half slid down the embankment, scattering trash and broken glass in an attempt to cut the vehicle off. He fell, rolled, and scrambled to his feet, chest heaving, soaked with rain, white shirt plastered to his chest. He watched as the Town Car pulled a U-turn and came blasting down the exit helix toward him. He reached for his Les Baer, but his hand closed over an empty holster. He looked quickly around the dark embankment, then—as brilliant light slashed across him—was forced to roll away. Once the car had passed, he rose again to his feet, following the vehicle with his eyes as it merged into the main stream of traffic.

A moment later a vintage Rolls-Royce approached and braked rapidly to the curb. Pendergast opened the rear door and jumped in.

"Follow the Town Car," he told Proctor as he strapped himself in.

The Rolls accelerated smoothly. Pendergast could hear faint sirens from behind, but the police were too far back and would no doubt get hung up in traffic. He plucked a police radio from a side compartment. The chase accelerated, the Town Car shifting lanes and dodging cars at speeds that approached a hundred miles an hour even as they entered a construction area, concrete barriers lining both shoulders of the highway.

There was a lot of chatter on the police radio, but they were first in pursuit. The chopper was nowhere to be seen.

Suddenly a series of bright flashes came from the traffic ahead, followed instantly by the report of gunshots.

"Shots fired!" Pendergast said into the open channel. He understood immediately what was happening. Ahead, cars veered wildly right and left, panicking, along with the flashes of additional shots. Then a *crump, crump, crump* sounded as multiple vehicles piled into each other at highway speed, causing a chain reaction that quickly filled the road with hissing, ruined metal. With great expertise, Proctor braked the Rolls and steered into a power slide, trying to maneuver it past the chain reaction of collisions. The Rolls hit a concrete barrier at an angle, was deflected back into the lane, and was hit from behind by a driver who rammed into the pileup with a deafening crash of metal. In the backseat, Pendergast was thrown forward, stopped hard by his seat belt, then slammed back. Partially stunned, he heard the sound of hissing steam, screams, shouts, and the screeching of brakes and additional crashes as cars continued to rear-end each other, mingling with a rising chorus of sirens and now, finally, the *thwap* of helicopter blades.

Shrugging off a coating of broken glass, Pendergast struggled to collect his wits and remove the seat belt. He leaned forward to examine Proctor.

The man was unconscious, his head bloody. Pendergast fumbled for the radio to call for help, but even as he did so the doors were pulled open and paramedics were pushing in, hands grasping at him.

"Get your hands off me," Pendergast said. "Focus on him."

Pendergast shrugged free and exited into the sweeping rain, more glass falling away as he did so. He stared ahead at the impenetrable tangle of cars, the sea of flashing lights, listening to the shouts of paramedics and police and the thud of the useless, circling chopper.

The Town Car was long gone.

3

As a classics major from Brown University and a former environmental activist, Lieutenant Peter Angler was not a typical officer of the NYPD. However, there were certain traits he shared with his fellow cops: he liked to see his cases solved clean and fast, and he liked to see perps behind bars. The same single-minded drive that had motivated him to translate Thucydides's *Peloponnesian War* during his senior year in 1992, and to sink nails into old-growth redwoods to frustrate chain-saw loggers later that same decade, also caused him to rise through the ranks to Lieutenant–Commander Detective Squad at the young age of thirty-six. He organized his investigations like military campaigns, and made sure that the detectives under his supervision performed their duty with thoroughness and precision. The results that such a strategy obtained were a source of lasting pride to Angler.

Which was precisely why this current case gave him such a bad feeling.

Admittedly, the case was less than twenty-four hours old. And his squad could not be blamed for the lack of progress. Everything had been handled by the book. The first responders had secured the location, taken statements, held the witnesses until the technical investigators arrived. Those investigators, in turn, had thoroughly processed the scene, surveying and searching and collecting evidence. They had worked closely with the crime scene unit, with the latents team, the forensic investigators, photographers, and the M.E.

No—his dissatisfaction lay with the unusual nature of the crime itself . . . and, ironically, with the father of the deceased: a special agent in the FBI. Angler had read a transcript of the man's statement, and it was remarkable for its brevity and lack of helpful information. While not exactly hindering the CSU, the agent had been curiously unwilling to allow them any more access to his residence than had been necessary beyond the perimeter of the crime scene—even to the point of refusing to let an officer use a bathroom. The FBI was not officially on the case, of course, but Angler had been prepared to give the man courtesy access to the case files, if he'd wished it. But the agent had made no such request. If Angler hadn't known better, he would almost have assumed this man Pendergast didn't want his son's murderer to be caught.

Which was why he'd decided to interview the man himself, in— he glanced at his watch—precisely one minute.

And precisely one minute later, the agent was ushered into his office. The man who did the ushering was Sergeant Loomis Slade, Angler's aide-de-camp, personal assistant, and frequent sounding board. Angler took in the salient details of his visitor with a practiced glance: tall, lean, blond-white hair, pale-blue eyes. A black suit and a dark tie of severe pattern completed the ascetic picture. This was anything but your typical FBI agent. Then again, given his residences— an apartment in the Dakota, a veritable mansion on Riverside Drive where the body had been dumped—Angler decided he shouldn't be surprised. He offered the agent a chair, then sat back down behind his desk. Sergeant Slade sat in a far corner, behind Pendergast.

"Agent Pendergast," he said. "Thank you for coming."

The man in the black suit inclined his head.

"First of all, let me offer my condolences on your loss."

The man did not reply. He did not look bereaved, exactly. In fact, he betrayed no expression at all. His face was a closed book.

Angler's office was not like that of most lieutenants in the NYPD. Certainly, it had its share of case files and stacks of reports. But the walls displayed, instead of commendations and photo ops with brass, a dozen framed antique maps. Angler was an avid cartographic collector. Normally, visitors to the office were immediately drawn to the page from LeClerc's French Atlas of 1631, or Plate 58 from Ogilby's Britannia Atlas, showing the road from Bristol to Exeter, or—his pride and joy—the yellowed, brittle fragment from the Peutinger Table, as copied by Abraham Ortelius. But Pendergast gave the collection not even a passing glance.

"I'd like to follow up on your initial statement, if you don't mind. And I ought to say up front that I will have to ask some awkward and uncomfortable questions. I apologize in advance. Given your own law enforcement experience, I'm sure you'll understand."

"Naturally," the agent replied in a mellifluous southern accent, but with something hard behind it, metallic.

"There are several aspects to this crime that, frankly, I find baffling. According to your statement, and that of your—" a glance at the report on his desk—"your ward, Ms. Greene, at approximately twenty minutes past nine last evening, there was a knock on the front door of your residence. When Ms. Greene answered it, she found your son, his body bound with thick ropes, on your doorstep. You ascertained he was dead and chased a black Town Car south on Riverside Drive while calling nine-one-one. Correct?"

Agent Pendergast nodded.

"What gave you the impression—initially, at least—that the murderer was in that car?"

"It was the only vehicle in motion at the time. There were no pedestrians in sight."

"It didn't occur to you that the perpetrator could have been hiding somewhere on your grounds and made good his escape by some other route?"

"The vehicle ran several lights, drove over a sidewalk and through a flower bed, entered the parkway on an exit ramp, and made an illegal U-turn. In other words, it gave a rather convincing impression of trying to elude pursuit."

The dry, faintly ironic delivery of this statement irritated Angler.

Pendergast went on. "May I ask why the police helicopter was so dilatory?"

Angler was further annoyed. "It wasn't late. It arrived five minutes after the call. That's pretty good."

"Not good enough."

Seeking to regain control of the interview, Angler said, rather more sharply than he intended: "Getting back to the crime itself. Despite a careful canvassing of the vicinity, my detective squad has turned up no witnesses beyond those on the West Side Highway who saw the Town Car itself. There were no signs of violence, no drugs or alcohol in your son's system; he died of a broken neck perhaps five hours before you found him—at least, that's the preliminary assessment, pending the autopsy. According to Ms. Greene's statement, it took her about fifteen seconds to answer the summons. So we have a murderer—or murderers—who takes your son's life, binds him up—not necessarily in that order—props him against your front door while in a state of rigor mortis; rings your doorbell; gets back into the Town Car; and manages to get several blocks before you yourself could effect pursuit. How did he, or they, move so quickly?"

"The crime was flawlessly planned and executed."

"Well, perhaps, but could it also be that you were in shock—perfectly understandable, given the circumstances—and that you reacted less quickly than indicated in your statement?"

"No."

Angler considered this terse answer. He glanced at Sergeant Slade—as usual, silent as a Buddha—and then back again at Pendergast. "Then we have the, ah, dramatic nature of the crime itself. Bound with ropes, planted at your front door—it displays certain hallmarks of a gangland-style killing. Which brings me to my main line of questioning, and again, excuse me if some of these are intrusive or offensive. Was your son involved in any mob activity?"

Agent Pendergast returned Angler's gaze with that same featureless, unreadable expression. "I have no idea what my son was involved in. As I indicated in my statement, my son and I were estranged."

Angler turned a page of the report. "The CSU, and my own

detective squad, went over the crime scene with great care. The scene was remarkable for its lack of obvious evidence. There were no latents, either full or partial, save those of your son. No hair or fiber, again save that of your son. His clothes were brand new—and of the most common make—and on top of that, his deceased body had been carefully washed and dressed. We retrieved no bullet casings from the highway, as the shots must have been fired from within the vehicle. In short, the perps were familiar with crime scene investigation techniques and were exceptionally careful not to leave evidence. They knew exactly what they were doing. I'm curious, Agent Pendergast—speaking from a professional capacity, how would you account for such a thing?"

"Again, I would merely repeat that this was a meticulously planned crime."

"The leaving of the body at your doorstep suggests the perpetrators were sending you a message. Any idea what that message might be?"

"I am unable to speculate."

Unable to speculate. Angler looked at Agent Pendergast more searchingly. He'd interviewed plenty of parents who had been devastated by the loss of a child. It wasn't uncommon for the sufferers to be numb, in shock. Their answers to his questions were often halting, disorganized, incomplete. But Pendergast wasn't like that at all. He appeared to be in complete possession of his faculties. It was as if he did not want to cooperate, or had no interest in doing so.

"Let's talk about the, ah, mystery of your son," Angler said. "The only evidence he is, in fact, your son is your statement to that effect. He is in none of the law enforcement databases we've checked: not CODIS, not IAFIS, not NCIC. He has no record of birth, no driver's license, no Social Security number, no passport, no educational record, and no entry visa into this country. There was nothing in his pockets. Pending the DNA check against our database, from all we've learned it appears your son, essentially, never existed. In your statement, you said he was born in Brazil and was not a U.S. citizen. But he's not a Brazilian citizen, either, and that country has no record of him. The town you indicate he grew up in doesn't seem to exist, at least officially. There's no evidence of his exit from Brazil or entry into this country. How do you explain all this?"

Agent Pendergast slowly crossed one leg over the other. "I can't. Again, as I mentioned in my statement, I only became aware of my son's existence—or the fact that I had a son—some eighteen months ago."

"And you saw him then?"

"Yes."

"Where?"

"In the Brazilian jungle."

"And since then?"

"I have neither seen nor communicated with him."

"Why not? Why haven't you sought him out?"

"I told you: we are—were—estranged."

"Why, exactly, were you estranged?"

"Our personalities were incompatible."

"Can you say anything about his character?"

"I hardly knew him. He took delight in malicious games; he was an expert at taunting and mortification."

Angler took a deep breath. These non-answers were getting under his skin. "And his mother?"

"In my statement you will see that she died shortly after his birth, in Africa."

"Right. The hunting accident." There was something odd about that as well, but Angler could only deal with one absurdity at a time. "Might your son have been in some kind of trouble?"

"I have no doubt of it."

"What kind of trouble?"

"I have no idea. He was eminently capable of managing even the worst trouble."

"How can you know he was in trouble without knowing what sort?"

"Because he had strong criminal tendencies."

They were just going around and around. Angler had the strong feeling Pendergast was not only uninterested in helping the NYPD catch his son's killer, but was probably withholding information, as well. Why would he do that? There was no guarantee the body was even that of his son. True, there was a remarkable resemblance. But the only identification was Pendergast's own. It would be interesting to see if the victim's DNA returned any hits in the database. And it would be simple to compare his DNA with Pendergast's—which, since he was an FBI agent, was already on file.

"Agent Pendergast," he said coldly. "I must ask you again: Do you have any idea, any suspicion, any clue, as to who killed your son? Any information about the circumstances that might have led to his death? Any hint of why his body would be deposited on your doorstep?"

"There is nothing in my statement that I am able to expand upon."

Angler pushed the report away. This was only the first round. In no way was he finished with this man. "I don't know what's stranger here—the specifics of this killing, your non-reaction to it, or the non-background of your son."

Pendergast's expression remained absolutely blank. "O brave new world," he said, "that has such people in't."

"'Tis new to thee," Angler shot back.

At this, Pendergast showed the first sign of interest of the entire interview. His eyes widened ever so slightly, and he looked at the detective with something like curiosity.

Angler leaned forward and put his elbows on his desk. "I think we're done for the present, Agent Pendergast. So let me close by saying simply this: *You* may not want this case solved. But it *will* be solved, and I'm the man who's going to do it. I will take it as far as it leads, if necessary to the doorstep of a certain uncooperative FBI agent. Is that understood?"

"I would expect no less." Pendergast rose, stood, and—nodding to Slade as he opened the door—exited the office without saying another word.

Back at the Riverside Drive mansion, Pendergast strode purposefully through the reception hall and into the library. Moving toward one of the tall bookcases full of leather-bound volumes, he pulled aside a wooden panel, exposing a laptop computer. Typing quickly, using passwords when necessary, he first accessed the NYPD file servers, then the database of open homicide cases. Jotting down certain reference numbers, he moved next to the force's DNA database, where he quickly located the forensic test results for DNA samples collected from the supposed Hotel Killer, who had traumatized the city with brutal murders in upscale Manhattan hotels a year and a half earlier.

Even though he was logged in as an authorized user, the data was locked and would not allow for alteration or deletion.

Pendergast stared at the screen for a moment. Then, plucking his cell phone from his pocket, he dialed a long-distance number in River Pointe, Ohio. It was answered on the first ring.

"Well," came the soft, breathless voice. "If it isn't my favorite Secret Agent Man."

"Hello, Mime," Pendergast replied.

"How can I be of assistance today?"

"I need some records removed from an NYPD database. Quietly, and without a trace."

"Always happy to do what I can to subvert our boys in blue. Tell me: does this have anything to do with—what was that name again—Operation Wildfire?"

Pendergast paused. "It does. But please, Mime: no further questions."

"You can't blame me for being curious. But never mind. Do you have the necessary reference numbers?"

"Let me know when you're ready."

"I'm ready now."

Slowly and distinctly, eyes on the screen, fingers on the laptop's trackpad, Pendergast began reciting the numbers.

4

It was six thirty that evening when Pendergast's cell phone rang. The screen registered UNKNOWN NUMBER.

"Special Agent Pendergast?" The voice was anonymous, monotonal—and yet familiar.

"Yes."

"I am your friend in need."

"I'm listening."

A dry chuckle. "We met once before. I came to your house. We drove beneath the George Washington Bridge. I gave you a file."

"Of course. Regarding Locke Bullard. You're the gentleman from—" Pendergast stopped himself before mentioning the man's place of employment.

"Yes. And you are wise to leave those pesky government acronyms out of unprotected cell phone conversations."

"What can I do for you?" Pendergast asked.

"You should ask instead: What can *I* do for *you*?"

"What makes you think I need help?"

"Two words. Operation Wildfire."

"I see. Where shall we meet?"

"Do you know the FBI firing range on West Twenty-Second Street?"

"Of course."

"Half an hour. Firing bay sixteen." The connection went dead.

*   *   *

Pendergast entered through the double doors of the long, low building at the corner of Twenty-Second Street and Eighth Avenue, showed his FBI shield to the woman at the security barrier, descended a short flight of stairs, showed his shield again to the range master, picked up several paper targets and a pair of ear protectors, and entered the range proper. He walked along the forward section, past agents, trainees, and firearms instructors, to firing bay 16. There were protective sound baffles between every two firing bays, and he noticed that both bay 16 and the one beside it, 17, were empty. The report of gunfire from the other bays was only partially muffled by the baffles, and—always sensitive to sound—Pendergast fitted the hearing protection over his ears.

As he was laying out four empty magazines and a box of ammunition on the little shelf before him, he sensed a presence enter the bay. A tall, thin, middle-aged man in a gray suit, with deep-set eyes and a face rather lined for his age, had entered it. Pendergast recognized him immediately. His hair was perhaps a little thinner than the only other time Pendergast had seen him—some four years before—but in every other way he looked unchanged, bland, still surrounded with an air of mild anonymity. He was the sort of person that, if you passed him on the street, you would be unable to furnish a description even moments later.

The man did not return Pendergast's glance, instead pulling a Sig Sauer P229 from his jacket and placing it on the shelf of bay 17. He did not don hearing protection, and with a discreet motion—still not looking Pendergast's way—he made a motion for the agent to remove his own.

"Interesting choice of venue," Pendergast said, looking downrange. "Rather less private than a car under the approach to the George Washington Bridge."

"The very lack of privacy makes it even more anonymous. Just two feds, practicing at a firing range. No phones to tap, no wires to record. And of course, with all this racket, no chance for eavesdropping."

"The range master's going to remember the appearance of a CIA operative at an FBI range—especially since you fellows usually don't carry concealed weapons."

"I have my share of alternative identities. He won't remember anything specific."

Pendergast opened the box of ammo and began loading the magazines.

"I like your custom 1911," the man said, glancing at Pendergast's weapon. "Les Baer Thunder Ranch Special? Nice-looking piece."

"Perhaps you'd care to tell me why we're here."

"I've been keeping something of an eye on you since our first meeting," the man said, still without making eye contact. "When I learned of your involvement in initiating Wildfire, I grew intrigued. A low-profile but intense monitoring operation, by certain members of both the FBI and CIA, for the location of a youth who may or may not be calling himself Alban, who may or may not be in hiding in Brazil or adjoining countries, who speaks Portuguese, English, and German fluently, and who above all things should be considered exceptionally capable and extremely dangerous."

Instead of replying, Pendergast clipped a target—a marksman bull's-eye with a red central X—to the rail and, pressing the OUT button on the baffle to his left, ran it out the full twenty-five yards. The man beside him clipped on an FBI qualification target—a gray bottle-like shape, without scaling or marking—and ran it out to the end of bay 17.

"And just today I get wind of an NYPD report in which you state that your son—also named Alban—was left on your doorstep, dead."

"Go on."

"I don't believe in coincidence. Hence, this meeting."

Pendergast picked up one of the magazines, charged his weapon. "Please don't think me rude if I ask you to get to the point."

"I can help you. You kept your word on the Locke Bullard case and saved me a lot of trouble. I believe in reciprocation. And like I said, I've kept track of you. You're a rather interesting person. It's entirely possible that you could be of assistance to me again, down the road. A partnership, if you will. I'd like to bank that."

Pendergast didn't respond.

"Surely you know you can trust me," the man said over the muffled, yet omnipresent, sound of gunfire. "I'm the soul of discretion—as are you. Any information you give me stops with me. I may have resources you wouldn't otherwise have access to."

After a moment, Pendergast nodded once. "I'll accept your offer. As for background, I have two sons, twins, whose existence I only learned of a year and a half ago. One of those sons—Alban—is, or was, a sociopathic killer of a most dangerous type. He's the so-called Hotel Killer, a case that remains open and unsolved by the NYPD. I wish the case to remain so, and have taken steps to ensure that it shall. Shortly after I became aware of his existence, he disappeared into the jungles of Brazil and was neither seen nor heard from until he appeared on my doorstep last night. I always believed that he would surface one day . . . and that the results would be catastrophic. For that reason, I initiated Operation Wildfire."

"But Wildfire never received any hits."

"None."

The nameless man charged his own weapon, racked a bullet into the chamber, took aim with both hands, and discharged the entire magazine into the qualification target. Every shot landed within the gray bottle. The sound was deafening within the baffled space.

"Until yesterday, who knew that Alban was your son?" the man asked as he ejected his magazine.

"Only a handful of people—most of them family or house help."

"And yet someone not only located and captured Alban, but also managed to kill him, leave him on your doorstep, and then escape practically undetected."

Pendergast nodded.

"In short, our perp was able to do what the CIA and FBI could not, plus a lot more."

"Exactly. The perpetrator has great ability. He may well be in law enforcement himself. Which is why I have no faith the NYPD will make any headway on this case."

"I understand Angler's a good cop."

"Alas, that's the problem. He's just good enough to become a gross impediment to my own effort to find the killer. Better that he were incompetent."

"Which is why you're being so unhelpful?"

Pendergast said nothing.

"You've no idea why they killed him, or what their message to you was?"

"That's the essential horror of it: I have absolutely no clue as to either the messenger or the message."

"And your other son?"

"I've arranged for him to be in protective custody abroad."

The man loaded another magazine into the Sig, released the slide, emptied the magazine into the target, and pressed the button to reel the target in. "And what are your feelings? About the murder of your son, I mean."

Pendergast did not answer for a long time. "In the parlance of the day, the best answer would be: I am *conflicted*. He is dead. That is a good outcome. On the other hand... he was my son."

"What are your plans when—or if—you find the responsible party?"

Again, Pendergast did not reply. Instead he raised the Les Baer in his right hand, left hand behind his back, in an unsupported stance. Briskly, shot after careful shot, he emptied the magazine into the target, then quick-changed to a fresh magazine, shifted the gun into his left hand, turned to face the target once again, this time from the other way, and—much faster now—again fired all seven rounds. Then he pressed the in button on the wall of the baffle to reel back the target.

The CIA operative looked over. "You tore the bull's-eye completely out. One-handed, and a bladed stance, no less—using both strong and weak hands." There was a pause. "Was that your answer to my question?"

"I was merely taking advantage of the moment to hone my skills."

"You don't need honing. In any case, I'll put my resources to work immediately. As soon as I find out anything, I'll let you know."

"Thank you."

The operative nodded. Then, fitting his earmuffs to his head, he put the Sig Sauer to one side and began refilling his own magazines.

5

Lieutenant Vincent D'Agosta began climbing the broad, granite steps of the main entrance to the New York Museum of Natural History. As he did so, he glanced up through the noon light at the vast Beaux-Arts façade—four city blocks long, in the grand Roman style. This building held very bad memories for him...and it seemed like an unpleasant twist of fate that he would find himself entering it again, now of all times.

Just the night before, he had returned from the best two weeks of his life: a honeymoon, with his new bride Laura Hayward, at the Turtle Bay Resort on the fabled North Shore of Oahu. They'd spent the time sunbathing, walking the miles of pristine beach, snorkeling Kuilima Cove—and, of course, getting to know each other even more intimately. It had been, quite literally, paradise.

So it had been a nasty shock to report to work that morning—a Sunday, no less—and find himself assigned as lead detective on the murder of a technician in the Museum's Osteology Department. Not only was he saddled with a case the minute he got back...but he'd have to conduct his investigation in a building that he'd really, really wished he never had to enter again.

Nevertheless, he was determined to bring closure to this case and bring the perp to justice. It was exactly the kind of bullshit killing that gave New York a bad name—a random, senseless, vicious murder of some poor guy who happened to be in the wrong place at the wrong time.

He stopped to catch his breath—damn, he'd have to go on a diet after the past two weeks of poi, kalua pig, opihi, haupia, and beer. After a moment, he continued up the stairs and passed through the entrance into the vastness of the Great Rotunda. Here he paused again to pull out his iPad and refresh himself on the details of the case. The murder had been discovered late the previous evening. All the initial crime scene work had been completed. D'Agosta's first task would be to re-interview the security guard who had discovered the body. Then he had a date with the public relations director who—knowing the Museum—would be more concerned with neutralizing bad press than solving the crime. There were another half a dozen names on his list of interviewees.

He showed his shield to one of the guards, signed in, got a temporary ID, then made his way across the echoing expanse, past the dinosaurs, past another checkpoint, through an unmarked door, and down a series of labyrinthine back corridors to Central Security—a journey he remembered all too well. A uniformed guard sat, alone, in the waiting area. As D'Agosta entered, he jumped to his feet.

"Mark Whittaker?" D'Agosta asked.

The man nodded rapidly. He was short—about five foot three—and portly, with brown eyes and thinning blond hair.

"Lieutenant D'Agosta, homicide. I know you've been over all this before, and I'll try not to take up more of your time than necessary." He shook the man's limp, sweaty hand. In his experience, private security guards were one of two types—wannabe cops, resentful and pugnacious, or mild-mannered door shakers, cowed and intimidated by the real McCoy. Mark Whittaker was definitely of the latter breed.

"Can we chat at the crime scene?"

"Sure, yes, of course." Whittaker seemed eager to please.

D'Agosta followed him on another lengthy journey back out of the bowels and into the public areas of the Museum. As they walked through the winding corridors, D'Agosta couldn't help glancing at the exhibits. It had been years since he'd set foot in this place, but it didn't seem to have changed much. They were walking through the darkened, two-story African hall, past a herd of elephants, and from there into the Hall of African Peoples, Mexico and Central America, South America, hall after echoing hall of cases full of birds, gold, pottery, sculpture, textiles, spears, clothing, masks, skeletons, monkeys . . . He found himself panting and wondering how the hell it was he could hardly keep up with this fat little guard.

They made their way into the Hall of Marine Life and Whittaker finally came to a stop at one of the more distant alcoves, which had been sealed off with yellow crime scene tape. A Museum guard stood before the tape.

"The Gastropod Alcove," D'Agosta said, reading the name off a brass plaque that stood beside the opening.

Whittaker nodded.

D'Agosta showed his shield to the guard, ducked under the tape, and motioned Whittaker to follow. The space beyond was dark and the air dead. Glass cabinets covered the three walls of the alcove, stuffed full of shells of all sizes and shapes, from snails to clams to whelks. Waist-high display cases, sporting still more shells, stood before the cabinets. D'Agosta sniffed. This had to be the least-visited place in the entire damn Museum. His eye fell on a queen conch, pink and shiny, and for a moment he was transported back to one particular evening on the North Shore of Hawaii, the sand still warm from the just-departed sun, Laura lying beside him, the creamy surf curling around their feet. He sighed and hauled himself back to the present.

He glanced below one of the display cases, where a chalk outline and several evidence tags were visible, along with a long, long rivulet of dried blood. "When did you find the body?"

"Saturday night. About eleven ten."

"And you came on duty at what time?"

"Eight."

"This hall was part of your normal shift?"

Whittaker nodded.

"When does the Museum close on Saturdays?"

"Six."

"How often do you patrol this hall, after hours?"

"It varies. The rotation can be anywhere from half an hour to every forty-five minutes. I have a card I have to swipe as I go along. They don't like us to make our rounds on a regular schedule."

D'Agosta took out of his pocket a floor plan of the Museum he had grabbed on the way in. "Could you draw on here your rounds of duty or whatever you call it?"

"Sure." Whittaker fumbled a pen out of his pocket and drew a wandering line on the map, encompassing much of the floor. He handed it back to D'Agosta.

D'Agosta scrutinized it. "Doesn't look like you normally go into this particular alcove."

Whittaker paused for a moment, as if this might be a trick question. "Not usually. I mean, it's a cul-de-sac. I walk past it."

"So what made you look into it at eleven PM last night?"

Whittaker dabbed at his brow. "The blood had run out into the middle of the floor. When I shone my light in, the . . . the beam picked it up."

D'Agosta recalled all the blood from the SOC photographs. A reconstruction of the crime indicated that the victim, an older technician named Victor Marsala, had been bludgeoned over the head with a blunt instrument in this out-of-the-way alcove, his body stuffed beneath the display case, minus watch, wallet, and pocket change.

D'Agosta consulted his tablet. "Any special events going on yesterday evening?"

"No."

"No sleepovers, private parties, IMAX shows, after-hours tours? Things of that nature?"

"Nothing."

D'Agosta already knew most of this, but he liked to go over familiar ground with a witness, just in case. The coroner's report indicated that the time of death had been around ten thirty. "In the forty minutes leading up to your discovery of the body, did you see anyone or anything unusual? A tourist after hours, claiming to be lost? A Museum employee out of his or her normal working area?"

"I didn't see anything odd. Just the usual scientists and curators working late."

"And this hall?"

"Empty."

D'Agosta nodded out past the alcove, toward a discreet door in the far wall with a red EXIT sign over it. "Where does that lead?"

Whittaker shrugged. "Just the basement."

D'Agosta considered. The South American gold hall wasn't far away, but it hadn't been touched, nothing had been stolen or disturbed. It was possible Marsala, on his way out after completing a late-night assignment, had disturbed some bum, taking a catnap in this desolate corner of the Museum, but D'Agosta doubted the story was even that exotic. What was unusual about the case was that the killer had apparently managed to leave the Museum without notice. The only way out at that time of the night was through a heavily guarded checkpoint on the lower level. Was the killer a Museum employee? He had a list of everyone working late that night, and it was surprisingly long. Then again, the Museum was a big place with a staff of several thousand.

He asked Whittaker a few more perfunctory questions, then thanked him. "I'm going to look around, you can head back on your own," he said.

He spent the next twenty minutes poking around the alcove and adjoining areas, regularly referring to the crime scene photos on his tablet. But there was nothing new to see, nothing to find, nothing that appeared to have been overlooked.

Fetching a sigh, D'Agosta stuffed the iPad back into his briefcase and headed off in the direction of the public relations department.

6

Observing an autopsy ranked low on the list of Lieutenant Peter Angler's favorite activities. It wasn't that he had a problem with the sight of blood. In his fifteen years on the force, he'd seen more than his share of dead bodies—shot, stabbed, bludgeoned, run over, poisoned, pancaked on the sidewalk, cut in pieces on the subway tracks. Not to mention his own injuries. And he was no shrinking violet: he'd drawn his gun in the line of duty a dozen times and used it twice. He could deal with violent death. What made him uneasy was the cold, clinical way in which a corpse was systematically taken apart, organ by organ, handled, photographed, commented on, even joked about. That and, of course, the smell. But over the years he'd learned to live with the task, and he approached it with stoic resignation.

There was something about this autopsy, however, that gave it a particularly macabre cast. Angler had seen a lot of autopsies—but he'd never seen one that was being keenly observed by the victim's own father.

There were five people in the room—living people, anyway: Angler; one of his detectives, Millikin; the forensic pathologist in charge of the autopsy; the assisting diener, short and shriveled and hunched like Quasimodo—and Special Agent Aloysius Pendergast.

Of course, Pendergast had no official status here. When Pendergast made his bizarre request, Angler had considered denying him

access. After all, the agent had been uncooperative in the investigation to date. But Angler had done some checking up on Pendergast
and learned that—while he was known in the Bureau for his unorthodox methods—he was also held in awe for his remarkable success
rate. Angler had never seen a dossier so full of both commendations
and censures. So in the end he decided it simply wasn't worth trying
to bar the man from the autopsy. After all, it *was* his son. And besides,
he had a pretty good sense that Pendergast would have found a way
to be present, no matter what he said.

The pathologist, Dr. Constantinescu, also seemed to know of
Pendergast. Constantinescu looked more like a kindly old country
doctor than a medical examiner, and the presence of the special agent
had thrown him for a loop. He was as tense and nervous as a cat in a
new house. Time and again, as he'd murmured his medical observations into the hanging mike, he'd paused, glanced over his shoulder at
Pendergast, then cleared his throat and begun again. It had taken him
almost an hour to complete the external examination alone—which
was remarkable, given the almost total absence of evidence to discover, collect, and label. The removal of the clothing, photography,
X-rays, weighing, toxicity tests, noting of distinguishing marks, and
the rest of it had gone on forever. It was as if the pathologist was afraid
of making the slightest mistake, or had a strange reluctance to get on
with the work. The diener, who didn't seem to be in on the story, was
impatient, rocking from one foot to the other, arranging and rear-
ranging instruments. Throughout it all Pendergast stood motionless,
somewhat back from the others, the gown like a shroud around him,
eyes moving from Constantinescu to the body of his son and back
again, saying nothing, expressing nothing.

"No obvious external bruises, hematomas, puncture wounds, or
other injuries," the pathologist was saying into the microphone. "Initial external examination, along with X-ray evidence, indicates that
death resulted from a crushing injury to the cervical vertebrae C3
and C4, along with possible lateral rotation of the skull, transecting
the spinal column and inducing spinal shock."

Dr. Constantinescu stepped back from the mike, cleared his

throat yet again. "We, ah, we're about to commence with the internal examination, Agent Pendergast."

Still Pendergast remained motionless, save perhaps for the slightest inclination of his head. He was very pale; his features were as set as any Angler had seen on a man. The more he got to know this Pendergast, the less he liked him. The man was a kind of freak.

Angler turned his attention back to the body lying on the gurney. The young man had been in excellent physical condition. Staring at the corpse's sleek musculature and lines graceful even in death, he was reminded of certain depictions of Hektor and Achilles in Black Figure pottery paintings attributed to the Antiope Group.

We're about to commence with the internal examination. The body wasn't going to be beautiful much longer.

At a nod from Constantinescu, the diener brought over the Stryker saw. Firing it up, the pathologist moved it around Alban's skull—as it cut bone, the saw made a distinct, grinding whine that Angler hated—and removed the top of the head. This was unusual: in Angler's experience, usually the brain was the last of the organs to be removed. Most autopsies began with the standard Y-incision. Perhaps it had something to do with the cause of death being a broken neck. But Angler felt a more likely cause was the other observer in the room. He stole a glance toward Pendergast. The man looked, if anything, even paler, his face more closed than ever.

Constantinescu examined the brain, carefully removed it, placed it on a scale, and murmured some more observations into the mike. He took a few tissue samples, handed them to the diener, and then—without looking over this time—spoke to Pendergast. "Agent Pendergast . . . are you planning on an open casket viewing?"

For a moment, silence. And then Pendergast replied. "There will be no viewing—or funeral. When the body is released I'll make the necessary arrangements to have it cremated." His voice sounded like a knife blade scraping against ice.

"I see." Constantinescu replaced the brain in the skull cavity, and hesitated. "Before continuing, I should like to ask a question. The X-rays appeared to show a rounded object in the . . . deceased's stomach. And yet there are no scars on the body to indicate old gun-shot wounds or surgical procedures. Are you aware of any implants the body might have contained?"

"I am not," Pendergast said.

"Very well." Constantinescu nodded slowly. "I will make the Y-incision now."

When nobody spoke, the pathologist took up the Stryker saw again, making cuts in the left and right shoulders and angling them down so they met at the sternum, then completing the incision in a single line to the pubis with a scalpel. The diener handed him a set of shears and Constantinescu completed the opening of the chest cavity, lifting away the severed ribs and flesh and exposing the heart and lungs.

Behind Angler's shoulder, Pendergast remained rigid. A certain odor began to spread through the room—an odor that always stayed with Angler, much like the whine of the Stryker.

One after the other, Constantinescu removed the heart and the lungs, examined them, weighed them on the scale, took tissue samples, murmured his observations into the mike, and placed the organs in plastic bags for returning to the body during the final, reconstitution phase of the autopsy. The liver, kidneys, and other major organs were given the same treatment. Then the pathologist turned his attention to the central arteries, severing them and making quick inspections. The man was working rapidly now, the polar opposite of his dawdling with the preliminaries.

Next came the stomach. After inspection and weighing, photographing and tissue sampling, Constantinescu reached for a large scalpel. This was the part Angler really hated: examination of the stomach contents. He moved a little farther away from the gurney.

The pathologist hovered over the metal basin in which the stomach lay, working on it with gloved hands, now and then using the scalpel or a pair of forceps, the diener leaning in close. The smell in the room grew worse.

Suddenly there came a noise: a loud clink of something hard in the steel container. The pathologist audibly caught his breath. He murmured to the diener, who handed him a fresh pair of forceps. Reaching into the metal basin that held the stomach and its contents, Constantinescu lifted something with the forceps—something roundish, slick with opaque fluids—and turned to a sink, where he carefully rinsed it off. When he turned back, Angler saw to his vast surprise that what lay between the forceps was a stone, irregular in shape and just a little larger than a marble. A deep-blue stone—a precious stone.

In his peripheral vision, he saw that Pendergast had, finally, reacted.

Constantinescu held the stone up in the forceps, staring at it, turning it this way and that. "Well, well," he murmured.

He put it into an evidence bag and proceeded to seal it. As he did so, Angler found that Pendergast had stepped to his side, staring at the stone. Gone was the remote, unreadable expression, the distant eyes. There was now a sudden hunger in them, a need, that almost pushed Angler back.

"That stone," Pendergast said. "I must have it."

Angler wasn't quite sure he'd heard correctly. "*Have* it? That stone is the first piece of hard evidence we've come across."

"Exactly. Which is why I must be given access to it."

Angler licked his lips. "Look, Agent Pendergast. I realize it's your son who's on that gurney, and that this can't be easy for you. But this is an official investigation, we have rules to obey and procedures to follow, and with evidence so short here you must know that—"

"I have resources that can help. I need that stone. I must have it." Pendergast stepped closer, skewering Angler with his gaze. "*Please.*"

Angler had to consciously keep from retreating before the intensity of Pendergast's gaze. Something told him that *please* was a word Pendergast used rather infrequently. He stood silent a moment, torn between conflicting emotions. But the exchange had one strong effect on Angler—he was now persuaded that Pendergast actually did want to find out what had happened to his son. He suddenly felt sorry for the man.

"It needs to be logged as evidence," he said. "Photographed, fully described, cataloged, entered into the database. Once all that is complete, you may sign it out from Evidence, but only with the chain-of-custody protocols strictly observed. It must be returned within twenty-four hours."

Pendergast nodded. "Thank you."

"Twenty-four hours. No longer."

But he found himself speaking to Pendergast's back. The man was moving swiftly toward the door, the green gown flapping behind him.

7

The Osteology Department of the New York Museum of Natural History was a seemingly endless warren of rooms tucked under broad rooftops, reachable only by a massive set of double doors at the end of a long corridor containing the Museum's fifth-floor offices, and thence by a gigantic, slow-moving freight elevator. When D'Agosta had stepped into that elevator (and found himself sharing the space with the carcass of a monkey stretched out on a dolly), he realized why the department was situated so far from the public spaces of the Museum: the place stank—as his father would have said—like a whorehouse at low tide.

The freight elevator boomed to a stop, the doors opened, top and bottom, and D'Agosta stepped out into the Osteology Department, looked around, and rubbed his hands together impatiently. His next scheduled interview was with Morris Frisby, the chair of both the Anthropology and Osteology Departments. Not that he held out much hope for the interview, because Frisby had just returned this morning from a conference in Boston, and had not been in the Museum at the time of the technician's death. More promising was the youth shuffling over to meet him, one Mark Sandoval, an Osteology technician who'd been out for a week with a bad summer cold.

Sandoval closed the main Osteology door behind them. He looked as if he was still sick as a dog: his eyes were red and swollen, his face pale, and he was dabbing at his nose with a Kleenex. At least, D'Agosta thought, the guy was spared the terrible smell. Then again, he was probably used to it.

"I'm ten minutes early for my meeting with Dr. Frisby," D'Agosta said. "Mind showing me around? I want to see where Marsala worked."

"Well..." Sandoval swallowed, glanced over his shoulder.

"Is there a problem?" D'Agosta asked.

"It's..." Another glance over the shoulder, followed by a lowering of voice. "It's Dr. Frisby. He's not too keen on..." The voice trailed off.

D'Agosta understood immediately. No doubt Frisby was a typical Museum bureaucrat, jealous of his petty fiefdom and gun-shy about adverse publicity. He could picture the curator: tweed jacket trailing pipe dottle, pink razor-burned wattles quivering in fussy consternation.

"Don't worry," D'Agosta said. "I won't quote you by name."

Sandoval hesitated another moment and then began leading the way down the corridor.

"I understand you were the person who worked most closely with Marsala," D'Agosta said.

"As close as anybody could, I suppose." He still seemed a little on edge.

"He wasn't popular?"

Sandoval shrugged. "I don't want to speak ill of the dead."

D'Agosta took out his notebook. "Tell me anyway, if you don't mind."

Sandoval dabbed at his nose. "He was...well, a hard guy to get along with. Had something of a chip on his shoulder."

"How so?"

"I guess you could say he was a failed scientist."

They walked past what looked like the door of a gigantic freezer. "Go on."

"He went to college, but he couldn't pass organic chemistry—and without that, you're dead meat as far as a PhD in biology goes. After college he came to work here as a technician. He was really good at working with bones. But without an advanced degree he could only go so far. It was a real sore point. He didn't like the scientists ordering him around, everyone had to walk on eggshells with him. Even me—and I was the closest thing to a friend Victor had here. Which isn't saying much."

Sandoval led the way through a doorway on the left. D'Agosta found himself in a room full of huge metal vats. Overhead, a row of gigantic vents were busily sucking out the air, but it didn't seem to help—the smell was much stronger.

"This is the maceration room," Sandoval said.

"The what?"

"The maceration room." Sandoval dabbed at his nose with the Kleenex. "See, one of the main jobs here in Osteology is to receive carcasses and reduce them to bones."

"Carcasses? As in human?"

Sandoval grinned. "In the old days, sometimes. You know, donations to medical science. Now it's all animals. The larger specimens are placed in these maceration vats. They're full of warm water. Not sterile. Leave a specimen in a vat long enough, it liquefies, and when you pull the plug all you have left are the bones." Sandoval pointed to the nearest soup-filled vat. "There's a gorilla macerating in that one at the moment."

Just then, a technician came in pushing the dolly with the monkey on it. "And that," said Sandoval, "is a snow monkey from the Central Park Zoo. We've a contract with them—we get all their dead animals."

D'Agosta swallowed uncomfortably. The smell was really getting to him now, and the spicy fried Italian sausages he'd had for breakfast weren't sitting all that well.

"That was Marsala's primary job," Sandoval said. "Overseeing the maceration process. He also worked with the beetles, of course."

"Beetles?"

"This way." Sandoval walked back out into the main corridor, passed several more doors, then stepped into another lab. Unlike the maceration room, this space was full of small glass trays, like aquariums. D'Agosta walked up to one and peered within. Inside, he saw what appeared to be a large, dead rat. It was swarming with black beetles, busily engaged in gorging themselves on the carcass. He could actually hear the noise of their munching. D'Agosta stepped back quickly with a muttered curse. His breakfast stirred dangerously in his stomach.

"Dermestid beetles," Sandoval explained. "Carnivorous. It's how we strip the flesh from the bones of smaller specimens. Leaves the skeletons nicely articulated."

"Articulated?" D'Agosta asked in a strangled voice.

"You know—wiring the bones together, mounting them on metal frames for display or examination. Marsala cared for the beetles, watched over the specimens that were brought in. He did the degreasing, too."

D'Agosta didn't ask, but Sandoval explained anyway. "Once a specimen is reduced to bones, it's immersed in benzene. A good soaking turns them white, dissolves all the lipids, gets rid of the odor."

They returned to the central hallway. "Those were his main responsibilities," Sandoval said. "But as I told you, Marsala was a whiz with skeletons. So he was often asked to articulate them."

"I see."

"In fact, the articulation lab was the place Marsala made his office."

"Lead the way, please."

Dabbing at his nose again, Sandoval continued down the seemingly endless corridor. "These are some of the Osteology collections," he said, gesturing at a series of doors. "The bone collections, arranged taxonomically. And now we're entering the Anthropology collections."

"Which are?"

"Burials, mummies, and 'prepared skeletons'—dead bodies collected by anthropologists, often from battlefields during the Indian wars—and brought back to the Museum. Something of a lost art. We've been forced to return a lot of these to the tribes in recent years."

D'Agosta glanced into an open doorway. He could make out row after row of wooden cabinets with rippled glass doors, within which lay innumerable sliding trays, each with a label affixed to it.

After passing another dozen or so storage rooms, Sandoval

showed D'Agosta into a lab full of workbenches and soapstone-topped tables. The stench was fainter here. Skeletons of various animals sat on metal frames atop the benches, in various stages of completion. A few desks were pushed up against the far wall, computers and a variety of tools sitting on them.

"That was Marsala's desk," Sandoval said, pointing at one.

"Did he have a girlfriend?" D'Agosta asked.

"Not that I know of."

"What did he do in his off hours?"

Sandoval shrugged. "He didn't talk about it. He more or less kept to himself. This lab was practically his home—he worked long hours. Didn't have much of an outside life, it seemed to me."

"You say he was a prickly guy, hard to work with. Was there anyone in particular that he clashed with?"

"He was always getting into spats."

"Anything that really stood out?"

Sandoval hesitated. D'Agosta waited, notebook in hand.

"There was one thing," Sandoval said at last. "About two months back, a curator of mammalogy came in with a suite of extremely rare, almost extinct bats he'd collected in the Himalayas. Marsala put them in some of the dermestid beetle trays. Then he...messed up. He didn't check them as frequently as he should have, left them too long. That wasn't like Marsala at all, but at the time he seemed to have something on his mind. Anyway, if you don't take the specimens out of the trays in time, they can be ruined. The hungry beetles chew through the cartilage and the bones get disarticulated and then they eat the bones themselves. That happened to the bat specimens. The bat scientist—he's a little crazy, like a lot of curators—went nuts. Said some terrible things to Marsala in front of the whole Osteology staff. Really pissed Marsala off, but he couldn't do anything about it, because he was the one at fault."

"What was the name of this mammalogy curator?"

"Brixton. Richard Brixton."

D'Agosta wrote down the name. "You said Marsala had something else on his mind. Any idea what it was?"

Sandoval thought a moment. "Well, around that time he'd started working with a visiting scientist on some research."

"Is that uncommon?"

"On the contrary—it's very common." Sandoval pointed out the door toward a room across the hall. "That's where visiting scientists examine bones. They're coming in and out all the time. We get scientists from all over the world. Marsala didn't usually work with them, though—his attitude problem and all that. In fact, this was the first scientist he'd worked for in almost a year."

"Did Marsala say what kind of research it was?"

"No. But at the time, he'd seemed pretty pleased with himself. As if he anticipated a feather in his cap or something."

"You recall this scientist's name?"

Sandoval scratched his head. "I think it was Walton. But it might have been Waldron. They have to sign in and out, get credentialed. Frisby keeps a list. You could find out that way."

D'Agosta looked around the room. "Anything else I should know about Marsala? Anything unusual, or odd, out of character?"

"No." Sandoval blew his nose with a mighty honk.

"His body was found in the Gastropod Alcove off the Hall of Marine Life. Can you think of any reason why he should have been in that section of the Museum?"

"He never went there. Bones—this lab—was all he cared about. That's not even on the way out."

D'Agosta made another notation.

"Any other questions?" Sandoval asked.

D'Agosta glanced at his watch. "Where can I find Frisby?"

"I'll take you there." And Sandoval led the way out of the lab and up the corridor—heading back into the foulest section of the department.

8

Dr. Finisterre Paden backed away from the X-ray diffraction machine he had been hunched over, only to find himself ricocheting off what appeared to be a pillar of black cloth. He recoiled with a sharp expostulation and found himself staring up at a tall man clad in a black suit, who had somehow materialized behind him and must have been hovering, inches away, as he worked.

"What on *earth*?" Paden said furiously, his small, portly frame jiggling with affront. "Who let you in here? This is my office!"

The man did not react, and continued gazing down at him with eyes the color of white topaz and a face so finely modeled that it could have been carved by Michelangelo.

"Look here, who are you?" Paden asked, regaining his curatorial equilibrium. "I'm trying to get some work done and I can't have people barging in!"

"I'm sorry," said the man in a soothing voice, taking a step back.

"Well, so am I," said Paden, somewhat mollified. "But this is really an imposition. And where's your visitor's badge?"

The man reached into his suit and removed a brown leather wallet.

"That's no badge!"

The wallet fell open, revealing a dazzle of blue and gold.

"Oh," said Paden, peering closely. "FBI? Good Lord."

"The name is Pendergast, Special Agent A. X. L. Pendergast. May I sit down?"

Paden swallowed. "I suppose so."

With a graceful flourish, the man parked himself in the only chair in the office other than Paden's and crossed his legs, as if readying himself for a long stay.

"Is this about the murder?" Paden asked breathlessly. "Because I wasn't even in the Museum when that happened. I don't know anything about it, never met the victim. On top of that, I've no interest in gastropods. In my twenty years here, never been in that hall, not even once. So if that's what..."

His voice trailed off as the man slowly raised a delicate hand. "It isn't about the murder. Won't you sit, Dr. Paden? It is your office, after all."

Paden took a wary seat at the worktable, folded and unfolded his arms, wondering what this was about, why Museum security hadn't notified him, and if he should answer questions or perhaps call a lawyer. Except he had no lawyer.

"Really, Dr. Paden, I do ask your forgiveness for the sudden intrusion. I have a small problem I need your help with—informally, of course."

"I'll do what I can."

The man extended one hand, closed. Like a magician, he opened it slowly to reveal a blue stone. Paden, relieved that it was a mere identification problem, took the stone and examined it. "Turquoise," he said, turning it over. "Tumbled." He took a loupe off the worktable, placed it in his eye, and looked more closely. "It appears to be natural stone, not stabilized and certainly not reconstituted, oiled, or waxed. A fine, gemmy specimen, of an unusual color and composition. Most unusual, in fact. I'd say it's worth a fair amount of money, perhaps more than a thousand dollars."

"What makes it so valuable?"

"Its color. Most turquoise is sky blue, often with a greenish cast. But this stone is an unusually deep, deep blue, almost in the ultraviolet spectrum. That, along with its surrounding golden matrix, is very rare."

He removed the loupe, held the stone back out to the FBI agent. "I hope I've been of assistance."

"Indeed you have," came the honeyed return, "but I was hoping you might tell me where it came from."

Paden took it back, examined it for a longer period of time. "Well, it's certainly not Iranian. I'd guess it's American—southwestern. Startling deep-azure color with a golden spiderweb matrix. I would say this most likely comes from Nevada, with Arizona or Colorado as outside possibilities."

"Dr. Paden, I was told you were one of the world's foremost experts on turquoise. I can see already that I was not deceived."

Paden inclined his head. He was surprised to meet someone from law enforcement as insightful, and as gentlemanly, as this fellow.

"But you see, Dr. Paden, I need to know the exact *mine* it came from."

As he spoke, the pale FBI agent looked at him most intensely. Paden smoothed his hand over his bald pate. "Well, Mr., ah, Pendergast, that's a horse of a different color."

"How so?"

"If I can't recognize the source mine from an initial visual examination—and in this case I can't—then testing of the specimen would be required. You see—" and here Paden drew himself up as he launched into his favorite subject—"turquoise is a hydrous phosphate of copper and aluminum, which forms by the percolation of water through a rock with many cavities and empty spaces, usually volcanic. The water carries dissolved copper sulfides and phosphorous, among other things, which precipitate in the interstices as turquoise. Southwestern turquoise almost invariably occurs where copper sulfide deposits are found among potassium feldspar bearing porphyritic intrusives. It can also contain limonite, pyrites, and other iron oxides." He rose and, moving fast on stubby legs, walked to a massive cabinet, bent over, and pulled open a drawer. "Here you see a small but exquisite collection of turquoise, all from prehistoric mines. We use it to help archaeologists identify the source of prehistoric turquoise artifacts. Come, take a look."

Paden waved the agent over, then took the turquoise sample from him and rapidly compared it with others in the drawer. "I don't see anything close to a match here, but turquoise can vary in appearance even from one part of a mine to another. And this is only a small sampling. Take this piece of Cerrillos turquoise, for example, from the Cerrillos mines south of Santa Fe. This rare piece comes from the famed prehistoric site known as Mount Chalchihuitl. It's ivory with a pale-lime matrix, of great historical value, even if it isn't the finest quality. And here we have examples of prehistoric turquoise from Nevada—"

"How terribly interesting," Pendergast said smoothly, stemming the flow of words. "You mentioned testing. What sort of testing would be necessary?"

Paden cleared his throat. It had been mentioned to him more than once that he had a tendency to run on. "What I'll have to do is analyze your stone—turquoise and matrix—using various means. I'll start with proton-induced X-ray emission analysis, in which the stone is bombarded with high-speed protons in a vacuum, and the resulting X-ray emission analyzed. Fortunately, here at the Museum we have an excellent mineralogy lab. Would you care to see it?" He beamed at Pendergast.

"No, thank you," said Pendergast. "But I'm delighted you're willing to do the work."

"But of course! This is what I do. Mostly for archaeologists, of course, but for the FBI—I am at your service, Mr. Pendergast."

"I almost forgot to mention to you my little problem."

"Which is?"

"I need the work done by noon tomorrow."

"What? Impossible! It will take weeks. A month, at least!"

A long pause. "But would it be *physically possible* for you to complete the analysis by tomorrow?"

Paden felt his scalp prickle. He wasn't sure that this man was quite as pleasant and easygoing as he seemed at first. "Well." He cleared his throat. "It's physically possible, I suppose, to get some preliminary results by then, but it would mean working nonstop for the next twenty hours. And even then I might not succeed."

"Why not?"

"It would all depend on whether this particular type of turquoise has been analyzed before, with its chemical signature recorded in the database. I've done quite a lot of turquoise analyses for archaeologists, you see. It helps them figure out trade routes and so forth. But if this piece comes from a newer mine, we might never have analyzed it. The older the mine, the better the chance."

A silence. "May I ask you, Dr. Paden, to kindly undertake this task?"

Paden smoothed his pate again. "You're asking me to stay up for the next twenty hours, working on your problem?"

"Yes."

"I have a wife and children, Mr. Pendergast! Today's a Sunday— normally I wouldn't even be here. And I am not a young man."

The agent seemed to take this in. Then, with a languid motion, he reached into his pocket and removed something, again holding it in his closed hand. He reached out and opened the hand. Inside was nestled a small, glittering reddish-brown cut stone of about a carat. Instinctively, Paden reached out to take it, screwed the loupe into his eye, and examined it, turning it this way and that. "Oh my. Oh my, my. Strongly pleochroic..." He grabbed a small, handheld UV light from the table and switched it on. The stone instantly changed color, becoming a brilliant neon green.

He looked up, his eyes wide. "Painite."

The FBI agent bowed his head. "I was not deceived in thinking you were a most excellent mineralogist."

"Where in heaven's name did you get this?"

"My great-grand-uncle was a collector of oddities, which I inherited along with his house. I plucked this from his collection, as an inducement. It's yours—provided you accomplish the task at hand."

"But this stone must be worth . . . good heavens, I hesitate to even put a price on it. Painite is one of the rarest gemstones on earth!"

"My dear Dr. Paden, the information on what mine that turquoise came from is far more precious to me than that stone. Now: can you do it? And," he added dryly, "are you sure your wife and children won't object?"

But Paden was already on his feet, placing the turquoise in a ziplock bag and thinking ahead to the many chemical and mineralogical tests he would need to perform. "Object?" he said over his shoulder as he departed into the inner sanctum of his laboratory. "Who the hell cares?"

9

After three wrong turns and two stops to ask directions, Lieutenant D'Agosta finally managed to find his way out of the maze of the Osteology Department and down to the ground floor. He crossed the Great Rotunda toward the entrance, walking slowly, deep in thought. His meeting with the chief curator, Morris Frisby, had been a waste of time. None of the other interviews had shed much light on the murder. And he had no idea how the perp effected egress from the Museum.

He'd been wandering the Museum since early that morning, and now both his feet and the small of his back ached. This was looking more and more like a typical piece-of-shit New York City murder case, random and brainless—and as such, a pain in the ass to clear. None of the day's leads had panned out. The consensus was that Victor Marsala had been an unpleasant person but a good worker. Nobody at the Museum had reason to kill him. The only possible suspect—Brixton, the bat scientist, who'd had a row with Marsala two months before—had been out of the country at the time of the murder. And besides, a weenie like that just wasn't the type. Members of D'Agosta's team had already interviewed Marsala's neighbors in Sunnyside, Queens. They all labeled him as quiet, a loner who kept to himself. No girlfriend. No parties. No drugs. And quite possibly no friends, except perhaps the Osteology technician, Sandoval. Parents lived in Missouri, hadn't seen their son in years. The body had been found in an obscure, rarely visited section of the Museum, missing wallet, watch, and pocket change. There was little doubt in D'Agosta's mind: this was just another robbery gone bad. Marsala resisted and the dumb-ass perp panicked, killed him, and dragged him into the alcove.

To make matters worse, there was no lack of evidence—if anything, D'Agosta and his team were already drowning in it. The crime scene was awash in hair, fiber, and prints. Thousands of people had tramped through the hall since it was last mopped and the cases wiped down, leaving their greasy traces everywhere. He had a brace of detectives reviewing the Museum's security videos, but so far they'd found nothing suspicious. Two hundred employees had worked late last night—so much for taking weekends off. D'Agosta could see it now, all too plainly: he'd beat his head against the case for another week or two, wasting his time in vain dead-end investigations. Then the case would be filed and slowly grow cold, another squalid unsolved homicide, with its megabytes of interview transcripts, digitized photos, and SOC analyses washing around the NYPD's database like dirty water at the base of a pier, serving no purpose other than dragging down his clearance rate.

As he turned toward the exit and quickened his step, he spied a familiar figure: the tall form of Agent Pendergast, striding across the polished marble floor, black suit flapping behind him.

D'Agosta was startled to see him—particularly here, in the Museum. He hadn't seen Pendergast since the private dinner party the FBI agent had hosted the month before in celebration of his impending wedding. The meal, and the wines, had been out of this world. Pendergast had prepared it himself with the help of his Japanese housekeeper. The food was unbelievable . . . At least until Laura, his wife, had deconstructed the printed menu the following day, and they realized they had eaten, among other things, fish lips and intestine soup (*Sup Bibir Ikan*) and cow's stomach simmered with bacon, cognac, and white wine (*Tripes à la Mode de Caen*). But perhaps the best part of the dinner party was Pendergast himself. He had recovered from the tragedy that had befallen him eighteen months before, and returned from a subsequent visit to a ski resort in Colorado having lost his pallor and skeletal gauntness, and now he looked fit both physically and emotionally, if still his usual cool, reserved self.

"Hey, Pendergast!" D'Agosta hurried across the Rotunda and seized his hand.

"Vincent." Pendergast's pale eyes lingered on D'Agosta for a moment. "How good to see you."

"I wanted to thank you again for that dinner. You really went out of your way, and it meant a lot to us. Both of us."

Pendergast nodded absently, his eyes drifting across the Rotunda. He seemed to have something on his mind.

"What are you doing here?" D'Agosta asked.

"I was...consulting with a curator."

"Funny. I was just doing the same thing." D'Agosta laughed. "Like old times, eh?"

Pendergast didn't seem to be amused.

"Look, I wonder if I could ask you a favor."

A vague, noncommittal look greeted the question.

D'Agosta plowed ahead gamely. "No sooner do I get back from my honeymoon than Singleton dumps this murder case on me. A technician in the Osteology Department here was found last night, head bashed in and stuffed into an out-of-the-way exhibit hall. Looks like a robbery that escalated into homicide. You've got such a great nose for these things that I wonder if I could just share a few details, get your take..."

During the course of this mini-speech, Pendergast had grown increasingly restive. Now he looked at D'Agosta with an expression that stopped him in midsentence. "I'm sorry, my dear Vincent, but I fear that at present I have neither the time nor the interest to discuss a case with you. Good day." And with the shortest of nods, he turned on his heel and strode briskly in the direction of the Museum's exit.

IO

Deep within the stately German Renaissance confines of the Dakota, at the end of a succession of three interconnected and very private apartments, beyond a sliding partition of wood and rice paper, lay an *uchi-roji*: the inner garden of a Japanese teahouse. A path of flat stones wound sinuously between dwarf evergreens. The air was full of the scent of eucalyptus and the song of unseen birds. In the distance sat the teahouse itself, small and immaculate, barely visible in the simulacrum of late-afternoon light.

This near-miracle—a private garden, in exquisite miniature, set down within the fastness of a vast Manhattan apartment building—had been designed by Agent Pendergast as a place for meditation and rejuvenation of the soul. He was now sitting on a bench of carved *keyaki* wood, set just off the stone path and overlooking a tiny goldfish pond. He remained motionless, gazing into the dark waters, where orange-and-white fish moved in desultory fashion, mere shadows.

Normally, this sanctuary afforded him relief from the cares of the world, or at least a temporary oblivion. But this afternoon, no peace was to be found.

A chirp came from the pocket of his suit jacket. It was his cell phone, its number known to less than half a dozen people. He glanced at the incoming call and saw UNKNOWN NUMBER displayed.

"Yes?"

"Agent Pendergast." It was the dry voice of the unnamed CIA operative he had met with at the firing range two days before. On prior occasions, the man's voice had contained a trace of wryness, as if detached from the workaday goings-on of the world. Today the irony was absent.

"Yes?" Pendergast repeated.

"I'm calling because I knew you'd want to hear the bad news sooner rather than later."

Pendergast gripped the phone a little tighter. "Go on."

"The bad news is that I have no news at all."

"I see."

"I've deployed some serious assets, expended a great deal of currency, and called in favors both locally and abroad. I've had several undercover operatives risk exposure, on the chance that certain foreign governments might be hiding information related to Operation Wildfire. But I've come up empty-handed. No sign that Alban ever surfaced in Brazil or elsewhere abroad. No records of his entering the country—I've had facial-recognition server farms at both Customs and Homeland Security working on it, without a hit. No local or federal law enforcement bread-crumb trails that have led anywhere."

Pendergast took this in without a word.

"It's still possible something will surface, of course—some nugget from an unexpected quarter, some database we overlooked. But I've exhausted everything in the standard bag of tricks—and then some."

Still Pendergast said nothing.

"I'm sorry," came the voice over the cell phone. "It's...it's more than a little mortifying. In my job, with the tools at my disposal, one gets used to success. I fear I may have seemed overconfident at our last meeting, raised your hopes."

"There's no need to apologize," Pendergast said. "My hopes were not raised. Alban was formidable."

There was a brief silence before the man spoke again. "One thing you might want to know. Lieutenant Angler, the NYPD's lead investigator on your son's homicide...I took a look at his internal reports. He's got a decided interest in you."

"Indeed?"

"Your lack of cooperation—and your behavior—aroused his curiosity. Your appearance at the autopsy, for example. And your interest in that lump of turquoise, which you convinced the NYPD to loan you and which is now, I understand, overdue. You may be heading for a problem with Angler."

"Thank you for the advice."

"Don't mention it. Again, I'm sorry I don't have more. I still have eyes on the ground. If there's any way I can be of further assistance, call the main number at Langley and ask for Sector Y. Meanwhile, I'll let you know of any change in status."

The line went dead.

Pendergast sat for a moment, staring at the cell phone. Then he slipped it back into his pocket, stood up, and made his way down the stone walkway and out of the tea garden.

In the large kitchen of the apartment's private quarters, Pendergast's housekeeper, Kyoko Ishimura, was at work chopping scallions. As the FBI agent passed through, she glanced over and—with a deaf person's economy of gesture—indicated there was a telephone message waiting. Pendergast nodded his thanks, then continued down the hall to his office, stepped inside, picked up the phone, and—without taking a seat at the desk—retrieved the message.

"Um, ah, Mr. Pendergast." It was the rushed, breathy voice of Dr. Paden, the mineralogist at the Museum. "I've analyzed the sample you left me yesterday with X-ray diffraction, brightfield microscopy, fluorescence, polarization, diascopic and episcopic illumination, among other tests. It is most definitely natural turquoise: hardness 6, refractive index is 1.614 and the specific gravity is about 2.87, and as I mentioned earlier there is no indication of stabilization or reconstitution. However, the sample exhibits some, ah, curious phenomena. The grain size is most unusual. I've never seen such semi-translucence embedded in a large spiderweb matrix. And the color . . . it doesn't come from any of the well-known mines, and there is no record of its chemical signature in the database . . . In short, I, ah, fear it is a rare sample from a small mine that will prove difficult to identify, and that more time than I expected will be needed, perhaps a lot more time, so I'm hoping that you will be patient and won't ask for the return of the painite while I . . ."

Pendergast did not bother to listen to the rest of the message. With a jab of his finger, he deleted it and hung up the phone. Only then did he sit down behind his desk, put his elbows on the polished surface, rest his chin on tented fingers, and stare off into space, seeing nothing.

Constance Greene was seated in the music room of the Riverside Drive mansion, playing softly on a harpsichord. It was a gorgeous instrument, made in Antwerp in the early 1650s by the celebrated Andreas Ruckers II. The beautifully grained wood of the case had been edged in gilt, and the underside of the top was painted with a pastoral scene of nymphs and satyrs cavorting in a leafy glade.

Pendergast himself had little use for music. But—while Constance's own taste was by and large limited to the baroque and early classical periods—she was a superb harpsichordist, and Pendergast had taken enjoyment in acquiring for her the finest period instrument available. Other than the harpsichord, the room was simply and tastefully furnished. Two worn leather armchairs were arranged before a Persian carpet, bookended by a brace of identical standing Tiffany lamps. One wall had a recessed bookcase full of sheet music of seventeenth- and eighteenth-century composers in urtext editions. The opposite wall held half a dozen framed pages of faded handwritten scores, original holographs of Telemann, Scarlatti, Handel, and others.

Not infrequently, Pendergast would glide in, like a silent specter, and take a seat in one of the chairs while Constance was playing. This time, Constance glanced up to see him standing framed in the doorway. She arched an eyebrow, as if to ask whether she should cease playing, but he simply shook his head. She continued with the Prelude no. 2 in C-sharp Minor from Bach's *Well-Tempered Clavier*. As she worked her way effortlessly through the short piece, wickedly fast and dense with ostinato passages, Pendergast did not take his accustomed seat, but instead roamed restlessly around the room, plucking a book of sheet music from the bookcase, leafing through it idly. Only when she was done did he move over to one of the leather armchairs and sit down.

"You play that piece beautifully, Constance," he said.

"Ninety years of practice tends to improve one's technique," she replied with a ghost of a smile. "Any further word about Proctor?"

"He'll pull through. He's out of the ICU. But he'll need to spend a few more weeks in the hospital, and then a month or two more in rehabilitation."

A brief silence settled over the room. Then Constance rose from the harpsichord and took a seat in the opposite armchair. "You're troubled," she said.

Pendergast did not immediately reply.

"Naturally, it's about Alban. You haven't said anything since—since that evening. How are you doing?"

Still Pendergast said nothing, continuing to leaf idly through the book of sheet music. Constance, too, remained silent. She, more than anyone, knew that Pendergast intensely disliked discussing his feelings. But she also sensed instinctively that he had come to ask her advice. And so she waited.

At last, Pendergast closed the book. "The feelings I have are those that no father would ever wish for. There's no grief. Regret—perhaps. Yet I'm also conscious of a sense of relief: relief that the world will be spared Alban and his sickness."

"Understandable. But . . . he *was* your son."

Abruptly, Pendergast flung the volume aside and stood up, pacing back and forth across the carpet. "And yet the strongest sensation I feel is bafflement. How did they do this? How did they capture and kill him? Alban was, if anything, a *survivor*. And with his special gifts . . . it must have taken enormous effort, expenditure, and planning to get him. I've never seen such a well-executed crime, one that left only the evidence meant to be left and no more. And most puzzling of all—*why?* What is the message being conveyed to me?"

"I confess I'm as mystified as you are." Constance paused. "Any results from your inquiries?"

"The only real evidence—a piece of turquoise found in Alban's stomach—is resisting identification. I just had a call about it from Dr. Paden, a mineralogist at the Museum of Natural History. He doesn't seem confident of success."

Constance watched the FBI agent as he continued to pace. "You mustn't brood," she said at last in a low voice.

He turned, made a dismissive motion with one hand.

"You need to throw yourself into a fresh case. Surely there are plenty of unsolved homicides awaiting your touch."

"There is never a shortage of jejune murders out there, unworthy of mental application. Why should I bother?"

Constance continued to watch him. "Consider it a distraction. Sometimes I enjoy nothing more than playing a simple piece written for a beginner. It clears the mind."

Pendergast wheeled toward her. "Why waste my time with some trifle, when the great mystery of Alban's murder is staring me in the face? A person of rare ability seeks to draw me into some sort of malevolent game of his own devising. I don't know my opponent, the name of his game—or even the rules."

"And that's exactly why you should immerse yourself in something totally different," Constance said. "While awaiting the next development, take up some small conundrum, some simple case. Otherwise . . . you'll lose your equilibrium."

These last five words were spoken slowly, and with conviction.

Pendergast's gaze drifted to the floor. "You're right, of course."

"I suggest this because—because I care for you, and I know how obsessive and unhappy this bizarre case could make you. You've suffered enough."

For a moment, Pendergast remained still. Then he glided forward, bent toward her, took her chin in one hand, and—to her great astonishment—kissed her gently.

"You are my oracle," he murmured.

II

Vincent D'Agosta sat at the table in the small area he had claimed as his forward office in the New York Museum of Natural History. It had taken a heavy hand to pry it loose from the Museum's administration. Grudgingly they had given up a vacant cubby deep within the Osteology Department, which was thankfully far from the reeking maceration tanks.

Now D'Agosta listened as one of his men, Detective Jimenez, summarized their review of the Museum's security tapes for the day of the murder. In a word: zip. But D'Agosta put on a show of listening intently—he didn't want the man to think his work wasn't appreciated.

"Thank you, Pedro," D'Agosta said, taking the written report.

"What next?" Jimenez asked.

D'Agosta glanced at his watch. It was quarter past four. "You and Conklin knock off for the day, go out and have a cold one, on me. We'll be holding a status meeting in the briefing room tomorrow morning at ten."

Jimenez smiled. "Thank you, sir."

D'Agosta watched his departing form. He'd have given just about anything to join the guys in hoisting a few. But no: there was something he had to do. With a sigh, he flipped quickly through the pages of Jimenez's report. Then, putting it aside, he pulled his tablet from his briefcase and began preparing a report of his own—for Captain Singleton.

Despite his team's best efforts, and two days during which more than a hundred man-hours of investigative work had been expended, not a single decent lead had surfaced in the murder of Victor Marsala. There were no eyewitnesses. The Museum's security logs had picked up nothing unusual. The big question was how the damn perp had gotten out. They'd been beating their heads against that question from the beginning.

None of the enormous amount of forensic evidence they'd gathered was proving relevant. There appeared to be no good motive for murder among Marsala's co-workers, and those who bore even the faintest grudge against him had ironclad alibis. His private life was as boring and law abiding as a damn bishop's. D'Agosta felt a prickling of personal affront that, after all his time on the job, Captain Singleton should toss him an assignment like this.

He began drafting his interim report for Singleton. In it, he summarized the steps the investigation had taken, the persons interviewed, the background checks on Marsala, the forensic and SOC data, the analysis of the Museum's security tapes, and the statements of the relevant security guards. He pointed out that the next step, should Singleton decide to authorize it, would be an expansion of the interview process beyond the Osteology Department. It would mean the wholesale interviewing, cross-correlation, and background examination of all the Museum staff who had worked late that evening—in fact, perhaps the entire Museum staff, whether they had worked late or not.

D'Agosta guessed Singleton wouldn't go for that. The expense in time, manpower, and cost was too high, given the small chance a lead would turn up. No: he would likely assign a reduced force to the case, let it move to the back burner. In time, that force, too, would be reassigned. Such was the way of the cold case.

He finished the report, read it over quickly, transmitted it to

Singleton, and then shut down his tablet computer. When he looked up, he saw—with a sudden shock—that Agent Pendergast was seated in the lone chair across from the tiny desk. D'Agosta had neither seen nor heard him come in.

"Jesus!" D'Agosta said, taking a deep breath to recover from the surprise. "You just love creeping up on people, don't you?"

"I admit to finding it amusing. Most people are about as aware of their surroundings as a sea cucumber."

"Thanks, I appreciate that. So what brings you here?"

"You, my dear Vincent."

D'Agosta looked at him intently. He had heard, the day before, about the murder of Pendergast's son. In retrospect, D'Agosta understood why Pendergast had been so short with him in the Museum's rotunda.

"Look," he began a little awkwardly, "I was really sorry to hear about what happened. You know, when I approached you the other day, I didn't know about your son, I'd just returned from my honeymoon and wasn't up on departmental business—"

Pendergast raised a hand and D'Agosta fell silent. "If anyone should apologize, it should be me."

"Forget it."

"A brief explanation is in order. Then I would deem it appropriate if the subject was not raised again."

"Shoot."

Pendergast sat forward in his chair. "Vincent, you know I have a son, Alban. He was deeply sociopathic. I last saw him a year and a half ago, when he disappeared into the Brazilian jungle after perpetrating the Hotel Killings here in New York."

"I didn't hear that."

"Since then, he never surfaced . . . until his corpse was placed upon my doorstep four nights ago. How this was effected and who did it, I have no idea. A Lieutenant Angler is investigating, and I fear he is inadequate to the task."

"Know him well. He's a damned good detective."

"I have no doubt he is competent—which is why I had an associate with excellent computer skills delete all DNA evidence of the Hotel Killer from the NYPD files. You may recall that you once made an official report that Alban and the Hotel Killer were one and the same. Luckily for me, that report was never taken seriously. Be that as it may, it would not do to have Angler run my son's DNA against the database and come up with a hit."

"Jesus Christ, I don't want to hear any more."

"In any case, Angler is up against a most unusual killer and will not succeed in finding him. But that is my concern, not yours. Which brings me to why I'm here. When last we spoke, you had a case you wished to solicit my advice on."

"Sure. But you must have more important things to do—"

"I would be glad of the diversion."

D'Agosta stared at the FBI agent. He was as gaunt as usual, but he seemed perfectly composed. The ice-chip eyes returned the look, regarding him coolly. Pendergast was the strangest man he'd ever met, and God only knew what was going on below the surface.

"Okay. Great. I warn you, though, it's a bullshit case." D'Agosta went over the details of the crime: the discovery of the body; the particulars of the scene; the mass of forensic evidence, none of which seemed germane; the reports of the security guards; the statements of the curators and assistants in the Osteology Department. Pendergast took it all in, utterly motionless save for the occasional blink of his silvery eyes. Then a shadow appeared in the cubicle, and Pendergast's eyes shifted.

D'Agosta looked over his shoulder, following Pendergast's gaze, and saw the tall, heavyset form of Morris Frisby, head of the department. When D'Agosta had first interviewed him, he had been surprised to find not the slope-shouldered, nearsighted curator he'd expected, but a man who was powerful and feared by his staff. D'Agosta had felt a little intimidated himself. The man was wearing an expensive pin-striped suit with a red tie, and he spoke with a crisp, upper-class New York accent. At well over six feet in height, he dominated the tiny space. He looked from D'Agosta to Pendergast and back, radiating irritation at the continued presence of the police in his domain.

"You're still here," he said. It was a statement rather than a question.

"The case hasn't been solved," said D'Agosta.

"Nor is it likely to be. This was a random crime committed by someone from the outside. Marsala was in the wrong place at the wrong time. The murder has nothing to do with the Osteology Department. I understand you've been repeatedly interviewing my staff, all of whom have a great deal of work, important work, on their plates. Can I assume that you'll be finishing up your investigation in short order and allowing my staff to continue their work in peace?"

"Who is this man, Lieutenant?" Pendergast asked mildly.

"I am Dr. Morris Frisby," he said crisply, turning to Pendergast. He had dark-blue eyes with very large whites, and they focused on a person like klieg lights. "I am the head of the anthropology section."

"Ah, yes. Promoted after the rather mysterious disappearance of Hugo Menzies, if I'm not mistaken."

"And who might you be? Another policeman in mufti?"

With a languid motion, Pendergast reached into his pocket, removed his ID and shield, and waved them at Frisby *à la distance*.

Frisby stared. "And how is it the feds have jurisdiction?"

"I am here merely out of idle curiosity," said Pendergast breezily.

"A busman's holiday, I presume. How nice for you. Perhaps you can tell the lieutenant here to wrap up his case and cease his pointless interruptions of my department's time and taxpayer dollars, not to mention the occupation of our departmental space."

Pendergast smiled. "My idle curiosity might lead to something more official, if the lieutenant feels his work is being hindered by an officious, small-minded, self-important bureaucrat. Not you, of course. I speak in general terms only."

Frisby stared at Pendergast, his large face turning an angry red.

"Obstruction of justice is a serious thing, Dr. Frisby. For that reason I'm so glad to hear from the lieutenant how you've been extending your full cooperation to him and will continue to do so."

Frisby remained rigid for a long moment. And then he turned on his heel to leave.

"Oh, and Dr. Frisby?" Pendergast continued, still in his most honeyed tone.

Frisby did not turn around. He merely paused.

"You may continue your cooperation by digging up the name and credentials of the visiting scientist who recently worked with Victor Marsala and giving them to my esteemed colleague here."

Now Frisby did turn back. His face was almost black with rage. He opened his mouth to speak.

Pendergast beat him to it. "Before you say anything, Doctor, let me ask you a question. Are you familiar with game theory?"

The chief curator did not answer.

"If so, you would be aware that there is a certain subset of games known to mathematicians and economists as zero-sum. Zero-sum games deal with resources that neither increase nor decrease in amount—they only shift from one player to the other. Given your present frame of mind, were you to speak now, I'm afraid you might say something rash. I would feel it incumbent to offer a rejoinder. As a result of this exchange, you would be mortified and humiliated, which—as dictated by the rules of game theory—would increase my influence and status at your expense. So I'd suggest the most prudent course of action would be for you to remain silent and go about securing the information I asked for with all possible haste."

While Pendergast had been speaking, an expression quite unlike any D'Agosta had ever seen before crept slowly over Frisby's face. He said nothing, merely swayed a little, first backward, then forward, like a branch caressed by a breeze. Then he gave what might have been the smallest of nods and disappeared around the corner.

"Ever so obliged!" Pendergast said, leaning over in his seat and calling after the curator.

D'Agosta had watched this exchange without a word. "You just put your boot so far up his ass, he'll have to eat his dinner with a shoehorn."

"I can always count on you for a suitable bon mot."

"I'm afraid you made an enemy."

"I've had long experience with this Museum. There is a certain subset of curators who behave in their little fiefdoms like a liege lord. I tend to be severe with such people. An annoying habit, but very hard to break." He rose from his chair. "And now, I'd very much like to have a word with that Osteological technician you mentioned. Mark Sandoval."

D'Agosta heaved himself to his feet. "Follow me."

12

They found Sandoval down the hall in one of the storage rooms. He was puttering about, opening drawers full of bones, examining them, and taking notes. His nose was still red and his eyes were puffy—the summer cold was proving tenacious.

"This is Special Agent Pendergast of the FBI," D'Agosta said. "He'd like to ask you a few questions."

Sandoval looked around nervously, as if worried someone might see them—probably Frisby. "Here?"

"Yes, here," said Pendergast as he took in the surroundings. "What a charming place. How many sets of human remains are in this room?"

"About two thousand, give or take."

"And where do they hail from?"

"Oceania, Australia, and New Zealand."

"And how many in the full collection?"

"About fifteen thousand, if you combine the Osteology and Anthropology collections."

"Mr. Sandoval, I understand that one element of your job is to assist visiting scientists."

"It's our primary responsibility, actually. We get a steady stream of them."

"But not Victor Marsala's job—even though he was a technician."

"Vic didn't have the right temperament. Sometimes, distinguished visiting specialists can be, well, difficult—or worse."

"What does your assistance involve?"

"Usually, scientists come to the Museum wishing to research a particular specimen or collection. We're like the bone librarians: we retrieve the specimens, wait until they've been examined, then put them back."

"Bone librarian—a most apt description. How many visiting scientists do you help in, say, any given month?"

"It varies. Six to ten, perhaps."

"It varies on what?"

"On how complicated or extensive the person's requirements are. If you have one visiting scientist with a very detailed list of objectives, you may have to work with him exclusively for weeks. Or you may get a string who just want to look at a femur here, a skull there."

"What qualifications do you require of these visiting scientists?"

Sandoval shrugged. "They have to have some sort of institutional affiliation and a cogent plan of research."

"No particular credentials?"

"Nothing specific. A letter of introduction, a formal request on university letterhead, proof of university or medical school affiliation."

Pendergast idly adjusted his shirt cuffs. "It's my understanding that, though he did it infrequently, Marsala did in fact work with a visiting scientist on a project some two months ago."

Sandoval nodded.

"And he mentioned to you that the project was of particular interest to him?"

"Er, yes."

"And what did he say about it?"

"He sort of hinted the scientist might be able to help him out in some way."

"And Marsala worked with this scientist exclusively?"

"Yes."

"In what possible way could the work of an external scientist benefit Mr. Marsala, who was admittedly very skilled at bone articulation but whose main duties were to oversee the maceration vats and the dermestid beetles?"

"I don't know. Maybe he was planning to give Vic a junior authorship line in the paper he would publish."

"Why?"

"For his help. Being a bone librarian isn't all cut and dried. Sometimes you get unusual requests that aren't all that specific, and you have to use your own specialized knowledge."

D'Agosta listened to this exchange with increasing mystification. He'd expected Pendergast to immerse himself in the forensic aspects of the case. But as usual, the FBI agent seemed to have gone off on a tangent with no apparent relation to the case at hand.

"Mr. Sandoval, do you know which specimens this particular scientist asked to examine before he departed?"

"No."

"Can you find out for us?"

"Of course."

"Excellent." Pendergast gestured toward the door. "In that case: after you, Mr. Sandoval."

They moved out of the storage room, through a maze of passageways, to a computer terminal in what looked like the main laboratory: a space full of tables and workstations, with several half-articulated skeletons laid out on trays of green baize.

D'Agosta and Pendergast leaned over Sandoval as the technician, seated at a terminal, accessed the Museum's Osteological and Anthropological databases. The lab fell silent save for Sandoval's tapping of keys. Then there was the whisper of a printer and Sandoval grabbed a piece of paper from it. "It seems Marsala only checked out one specimen for the scientist," he said. "Here's the summary."

D'Agosta leaned in closer, reading the accession record aloud. "Date of most recent access: April twenty. Hottentot, male, approximately thirty-five years of age. Cape Colony, formerly Griqualand East. Condition: excellent. No disfiguring marks. Cause of death:

dysentery, during the Seventh Frontier War. Date: 1889. Procured by N. Hutchins. AR: C-31234-rn.''

"That is the original record, of course," Sandoval said. "*Hottentot* is now considered derogatory. The correct term is Khoikhoi."

"This record says the body was sent to the Museum in 1889," said Pendergast. "If memory serves, however, the Seventh Frontier War ended in the late 1840s."

Sandoval hemmed and hawed for a moment. "The body was probably disinterred before being sent to the Museum."

There was another silence in the lab.

"It was common enough practice in the early days," Sandoval added. "They dug up graves to get a desired specimen. Not anymore, of course."

Pendergast pointed to the accession number. "May we see the specimen, please?"

Sandoval frowned. "Why?"

"Humor me."

Yet another silence.

Pendergast inclined his head. "I would simply like to familiarize myself with the processes involved in locating and retrieving a specimen."

"Very well. Follow me."

Scribbling the accession number on a slip of paper, Sandoval led them back out into the central hallway, and then even farther down its length, penetrating deep into the seemingly endless labyrinth of collections. It took a while, searching through old wooden cabinets with brass fixtures and rippled glass doors, to locate the specimen. At last Sandoval stopped before one cabinet in particular. The desired accession number, handwritten in faded copperplate, was affixed to a large tray on one of the upper shelves of the cabinet, tucked into a corner. Sandoval cross-checked the number and slid the tray off the shelf. He carried it back to the examination lab and laid it on a fresh section of green baize. He handed D'Agosta and Pendergast pairs of thin latex gloves. And then, donning a pair of gloves himself, he removed the top from the tray.

Inside lay a jumble: ribs, vertebrae, countless other bones. An unusual odor wafted up: to D'Agosta it smelled of musk, old roots, and mothballs, with the faintest overlay of decay.

"These bones are awfully clean for having been buried in the earth for forty years," he said.

"It used to be that skeletons received by the Museum were thoroughly cleaned," Sandoval replied. "They didn't realize back then that the dirt itself was a valuable part of the specimen and should be preserved."

Pendergast glanced into the tray for a minute. Then, reaching in, he carefully removed the skull, minus the jaw. He held it out in front of him—for all the world, D'Agosta thought, like Hamlet standing in the grave of Yorick.

"Interesting," he murmured. "Most interesting indeed. Thank you, Mr. Sandoval." Then he returned the skull to the tray, nodded to the technician that the interview was concluded, and—removing his gloves—led D'Agosta back down the passageway toward the land of the living.

13

The Executive Dining Room—or the EDR, as it was commonly known—was located on the second-to-top floor of One Police Plaza. It was where the police commissioner, the deputy commissioner, and other departmental princelings held court during the lunch hour. D'Agosta had been inside only once—for a celebratory luncheon the day he and two dozen others had made lieutenant—and while the room itself looked like a time capsule of cheesy early 1960s interior decor, the views of Lower Manhattan offered by the floor-to-ceiling windows were stunning.

As he waited in the capacious anteroom outside the EDR, however, D'Agosta wasn't thinking about the view. He was watching the faces filing out, looking for Glen Singleton. It was the third Wednesday of the month—the day when the chief lunched with all departmental captains—and he knew Singleton would be among them.

All at once he spied the well-dressed, well-groomed form of Singleton. Quickly, D'Agosta threaded his way through the throng until he reached the captain's side.

"Vinnie." Singleton looked surprised to see him.

"I heard you wanted to see me," D'Agosta said.

"I did. You didn't have to hunt me down, though. It could've waited."

D'Agosta had checked with Singleton's secretary and learned the captain had a full afternoon. "No problem. What's up?"

They had been walking in the general direction of the elevator, but now Singleton stopped. "I read your report on the Marsala killing."

"Oh?"

"Fine job, under the circumstances. I've decided to put Formosa in charge, and I'm giving you that Seventy-Third Street homicide instead. You know, the jogger who got her throat slashed fighting off a mugger. It looks like a solid case with several eyewitnesses and good forensics. You can handpick your men from the Museum case to transfer over."

This was basically what D'Agosta had expected to hear. It was also why he had tracked Singleton down to the Executive Dining Room—he wanted to catch the captain before things went too far. Formosa... he was one of the newest lieutenants on the force, still wet behind the ears.

"If it's just the same to you, sir," he said, "I'd like to stay on the Museum case."

Singleton frowned. "But your report. It's not a good case, really. The lack of hard evidence, lack of witnesses..."

Over Singleton's shoulder, D'Agosta saw his new bride, Laura Hayward, emerge from the Executive Dining Room, her lovely figure framed through the tall windows by the Woolworth Building. She saw him, smiled instinctively, began to come over, noticed he was talking to Singleton, and satisfied herself with a wink before heading to the elevator bank.

D'Agosta looked back at Singleton. "I know it's a heartbreaker, sir. But I'd like just another week with it."

Singleton stared at him curiously. "This reassignment isn't a slap on the wrist, if that's what you're thinking. I'm giving you a decent, solvable, high-profile case that will help your clearance."

"I wasn't thinking that, Captain. I read about the jogger murder, I know it would be a hell of an assignment."

"Then why stay with the Marsala homicide?"

The day before, he'd been ready—eager—to slough it off onto some other poor sap. "I'm not sure, sir," he replied slowly. "Not exactly. It's just that I hate walking away from a case. And sometimes you get a sixth sense, a hunch, that something's about to break. You probably know the feeling yourself, Captain."

It was a hunch, D'Agosta realized, that happened to be named Pendergast.

Singleton looked at him another moment—a long, appraising moment. Then the ghost of a smile appeared on his face and he nodded. "I do indeed," he said. "And I'm a great believer in hunches. All right, Vinnie—you can stay on the case. I'll give the jogger homicide to Clayton."

D'Agosta swallowed just a little painfully. "Thank you, sir."

"Good luck. Keep me informed." And with another nod, Singleton turned away.

14

As Pendergast entered the cluttered Museum office, Dr. Finisterre Paden quickly ushered him to the chair reserved for visitors.

"Ah, Agent Pendergast. Please have a seat." The diffident tone of his phone message two days earlier was gone. Today the man was all smiles. He seemed pleased with himself.

Pendergast inclined his head. "Dr. Paden. I understand you have some new information for me?"

"I do. I do, indeed." The mineralogist rubbed his chubby hands together. "I must confess, Mr. Pendergast—you will keep this between ourselves, I trust?—to feeling a degree, the very slightest degree, of chagrin." He unlocked a drawer, reached inside, took out a soft cloth, unwrapped it to reveal the stone, then gave it a brief, almost caressing touch.

"Beautiful. How utterly beautiful." The mineralogist seemed to recollect himself, and he passed the stone over to Pendergast. "In any case, since the stone was not immediately recognizable to me, or included in the obvious sources, I resorted to researching its chemical signature, refractive index, and other such avenues of attack. The fact is, I . . . ahem, not to put too fine a point on it . . . didn't see the forest for the trees."

"I'm not quite sure I follow you, Dr. Paden."

"I should have been focusing on the *appearance* of the stone, rather than its chemical qualities. I told you from the start that your specimen was of a most unusual color, and that its spiderweb matrix is the most valuable of all. But you may recall I also told you that this deep-indigo turquoise is found in only three states. And that is true—save for one exception."

He reached over to his color laser printer, plucked a sheet from its bin, and handed it to Pendergast.

The agent gave it a quick glance. The sheet appeared to contain an item from a jeweler's catalog, or perhaps an auction listing. There were a few paragraphs of descriptive text, along with a photograph of a precious stone. While it was significantly smaller than the stone found in Alban's stomach, in all other respects it appeared almost identical.

"The only azure American turquoise found outside of those three states," Paden said almost reverently. "And the only azure turquoise with a golden spiderweb matrix that I've ever encountered."

"Where did it come from?" Pendergast asked in a very low voice.

"From an obscure mine in California, known as the Golden Spider. It's a very old mine, played out over a hundred years ago, and it wasn't in any of the obvious books or catalogs. Even so, the stone is so unusual I feel I should have recognized it. But the mine was small, you see, with a very low output—the estimate is that no more than fifty or sixty pounds of top-grade turquoise was mined from it. It was that obscurity—and the California location—that tripped me up."

"Where in California?" Pendergast asked, his voice even quieter.

"On the edge of the Salton Sea, northeast of Anza-Borrego and south of Joshua Tree National Park. A most unusual location, especially from a mineralogical perspective, because the only—"

Up until this point, Pendergast had been sitting motionless in the chair. Now, quite suddenly, he was in swift movement, rising and flitting out of the office, black suit jacket flapping, the printout clutched in one hand, a brief murmur of thanks floating back toward the startled curator.

15

The Evidence and Property Storage Room of the NYPD's Twenty-Sixth Precinct was not really a room in the conventional sense at all, but rather a rambling warren of nooks, cubbyholes, and niches, sealed off from the rest of the precinct basement by thick wire mesh. The building was old, and the basement smelled strongly of mold and niter. Lieutenant Peter Angler sometimes felt that, were they to institute a search, they would find behind some wall the bricked-up skeleton that had inspired Poe to write "The Cask of Amontillado."

He stood now, waiting, at the large window set into the wire mesh labeled EVIDENCE DEPOSIT. He could hear faint, invisible bangings and scrapings from the spaces beyond. Another minute, and Sergeant Mulvahill emerged from the dimness, a small evidence container held in both hands.

"This is it, sir," he said.

Angler nodded, then walked a few steps down the corridor and entered the Report Writing Room. Closing the door behind him, he waited for Mulvahill to place the container in the pass-through locker set into the common wall. He signed the chit and sent it back through. Then he took the evidence container to the nearest table, sat down with the container before him, removed its top, and looked inside.

Nothing.

Actually, *nothing* was a slight exaggeration. There were some samples of Alban Pendergast's clothing; a bit of dirt from the heel of one shoe, enclosed in a tiny ziplock bag. There were also several badly mangled rounds that had been pried out of car frames, but these were still being analyzed by ballistics.

Yet the only real evidence—the piece of turquoise—was not there. Just a small, empty plastic container that had held it... until Pendergast checked it out.

In his bones, Angler had known the stone would not be there. But he'd hoped against hope Pendergast would have returned it. Staring into the evidence container, he felt a slow burn coming on. Pendergast had promised to return it within twenty-four hours... which had lapsed two days before. Angler had been unable to reach the man; his numerous calls remained unreturned.

But as upset as he was with Pendergast, Angler was even more upset with himself. The FBI agent had practically pleaded for the turquoise—at the autopsy of his own son, no less—and in a moment of weakness, against his better judgment, Angler had relented. And the result? Pendergast had betrayed his trust.

What the hell was he doing with the stone?

A faint blur of black registered in the corner of his vision, and Angler turned to see Pendergast himself—as if conjured into life by his own thoughts—standing in the doorway of the Report Writing Room. Wordlessly, as Angler watched, the FBI agent came forward, reached into his pocket, and handed him the turquoise.

Angler stared at it closely. It was the same piece—at least, it appeared to be. He opened the plastic container, put the deep blue stone in it, closed it again, and placed it in the evidence box. And then he looked back at Pendergast.

"What am I supposed to say about this?" he asked.

Pendergast returned the stare with a pleasant expression. "I was hoping you might thank me."

"*Thank* you? You kept this forty-eight hours longer than I stipulated.

You didn't return my calls. Agent Pendergast, the chain-of-custody rules are in place for a reason, and this is highly unprofessional."

"I'm well aware of the chain-of-custody rules," Pendergast said. "As are you—and you allowed me to borrow that stone in spite, not because, of them."

Angler took a deep breath. He prided himself on not losing his cool, and he'd be damned if this marble-like apparition dressed in black, this Sphinx, was going to goad him into it. "Tell me why you kept it as long as you did."

"I was trying to locate its source."

"And did you?"

"The results are not yet conclusive."

Not yet conclusive. Answers didn't come any vaguer than that. Angler paused a moment. Then he decided to try a different tack. "We're taking a new direction in our hunt for your son's killer," he said.

"Indeed?"

"We're going to track, as best we can, Alban's movements in the days and weeks leading up to the murder."

Pendergast listened silently to this. And then, with a faint shrug, he turned to leave.

Despite himself, Angler found his irritation spilling over. "That's your reaction? A shrug?"

"I'm rather in a hurry, Lieutenant. Again, you have my gratitude for indulging me with the turquoise. And now, if you don't mind, I must be going."

Angler wasn't done with him. He followed him toward the door. "I'd like to know what the hell is going on inside your head. How can you be so damned... *uninterested*? Don't you want to know who killed your son?"

But Pendergast had disappeared around the corner of the Report Writing Room. Angler stared at the empty doorway with narrowed eyes. He could hear Pendergast's light, rapid footsteps echoing down the stone hallway toward the staircase that led up to the first floor.

Finally—once the footsteps had retreated beyond audibility—he turned around, closed the evidence container, knocked on the common wall of the Evidence Storage Room to alert Mulvahill, then placed the container back in the pass-through locker.

And then once again, almost despite himself, his gaze drifted back to the empty doorway.

16

The attractive thirtyish woman with the glossy, shoulder-length brown hair separated herself from the crowd milling around the Museum's Great Rotunda, trotted up the broad central stairway to the second floor, then walked down the echoing marble corridor toward a door flanked by painted images of Anasazi petroglyphs, tastefully illuminated. She paused, took a deep breath, then stepped through the doorway. Beyond, a maître d' standing behind a small wooden podium looked up expectantly.

"I have a lunch reservation for two," the woman said. "Name of Green. Margo Green."

The man consulted his screen. "Ah yes, Dr. Green. Welcome back. Your party's already here."

Margo followed the man as he threaded a path between linen-covered tables. She glanced around. The room, she knew, had a curious history. Originally, it had been the Anasazi Burial Hall, full of dozens of Native American mummies, still in their original flexed positions, along with countless blankets, pots, and arrowheads, snagged from Arizona's Mummy Cave and other prehistoric grave-yards in the late nineteenth century. Over time the hall became con-troversial, and in the early 1970s a large group of Navajos journeyed to New York to picket the Museum, protesting what they considered tomb desecration. The hall was quietly closed and the mummies removed. And so it had remained for decades until just two years before, when some forward-thinking staffer realized the space was perfect for an upscale restaurant catering to donors, Museum members, and curators with important guests. It was named Chaco, and it retained the charming old murals that had decorated the original hall, painted to resemble the inside of a kiva of an ancient Anasazi pueblo, sans the mummified remains. One ersatz adobe partition that had made up the far wall had been removed, however, revealing huge windows overlooking Museum Drive, now aglow in brilliant sunlight.

Margo glanced toward the windows gratefully.

Lieutenant Vincent D'Agosta was rising from a table directly before her. He looked almost the same as when she'd last seen him—a little thinner, fitter, even less hair. The way his present image kept faithful to her memory touched her with a strange mixture of gratitude and melancholy.

"Margo," he said, giving her a handshake that turned into a slightly awkward embrace. "Great to see you."

"Likewise."

"You're looking wonderful. I'm really glad you could make it on short notice."

They sat down. D'Agosta had called her out of the blue just the day before, asking if they could meet somewhere in the Museum. She'd suggested Chaco.

D'Agosta looked around. "The place sure has changed since you and I first met. How many years ago was that, anyway?"

"The time of the Museum killings?" Margo thought a moment. "Eleven years. No, twelve."

"Unbelievable."

A waiter brought them menus, the covers emblazoned with a silhouette of Kokopelli. D'Agosta ordered an iced tea, and she did likewise. "So. What have you been up to all this time?"

"I'm now working at a nonprofit medical foundation on the East Side. The Pearson Institute."

"Oh yeah? Doing what?"

"I'm their ethnopharmacologist. I evaluate indigenous botanical remedies, looking for potential drugs."

"Sounds fascinating."

"It is."

"Still teaching?"

"I got burned out on that. There's a potential here to help thousands, instead of one classroom."

D'Agosta picked up the menu again, perused it. "Found any wonder drugs?"

"The biggest thing I've worked on so far is a compound in the bark of the ceiba tree that might help with epilepsy and Parkinson's. The Maya use it for treating dementia in old people. Problem is, it takes forever to develop a new drug."

The waiter returned, and they gave their orders. D'Agosta looked back at her. "On the phone, you mentioned you visit the Museum regularly."

"Two or three times a month, at least."

"Why is that?"

"The sad fact is that the natural habitats of these botanicals I study are being logged, burned, or plowed under at a terrifying rate. God knows how many potential cures for cancer have already gone extinct. The Museum has the finest ethnobotanical collection in the world. Of course, they didn't have me in mind when they assembled it—they were simply gathering up local medicines and magical remedies from tribes around the world. But it's perfectly geared to my research. There are plants in the Museum's collections that simply can't be found in nature anymore." She stopped, reminding herself that not everyone shared her passion for the work.

D'Agosta folded his hands together. "Well, as it happens, your being a regular here works out perfectly for me."

"How so?"

He leaned forward slightly. "You heard about the recent homicide here, right?"

"You mean Vic Marsala? I used to work with him when I was a graduate student in the Anthro Department. I was one of the few people he actually got along with." Margo shook her head. "I can't believe anyone would kill him."

"Well, I'm in charge of the investigation. And I need your help."

Margo didn't reply.

"It seems Marsala was working with a visiting scientist not long before his death. Marsala helped this scientist locate and examine a specimen in the anthropology collections—the skeleton of a Hottentot male. Agent Pendergast's been helping me with the case, and he seemed to be interested in the skeleton."

"Go on," Margo said.

D'Agosta hesitated. "It's just that . . . well . . . Pendergast vanished. Left town night before last, leaving no word where he can be reached. You know how he is. On top of that, we discovered just yesterday that the credentials of the visiting scientist working with Marsala were fake."

"Fake?"

"Yeah. False accreditation. Claimed to be Dr. Jonathan Waldron, a physical anthropologist with a university outside Philly, but the real Waldron knows nothing about it. I interviewed him myself. He's never even been to the Museum."

"How do you know he isn't the killer, and is just claiming to know nothing about it?"

"I showed his photograph to the Anthropology staff. Totally different person. He's a foot shorter and twenty years older."

"Bizarre."

"Yeah. Why would somebody pretend to be somebody else just to look at a skeleton?"

"You think this phony scientist killed Marsala?"

"I don't think anything yet. But it's a damned good lead, first one I've got. So . . ." He hesitated. "I was wondering if you'd be willing to have a look at the skeleton yourself."

"Me?" Margo asked. "Why?"

"You're an anthropologist."

"Yes, but my specialty is ethnopharmacology. I haven't done any physical anthropology since graduate school."

"I'll bet you can still run circles around most of the anthropologists here. Besides, I can trust you. You're here, you know the Museum—but you're not on staff."

"My research keeps me pretty busy."

"Just a look. On the side. I'd really appreciate your opinion."

"I really can't see what an old Hottentot skeleton would have to do with a murder."

"I don't know, either. But it's my only lead so far. Look, Margo, do this for me. You knew Marsala. Please help me solve his murder."

Margo sighed. "If you put it that way, how can I say no?"

"Thank you." D'Agosta smiled. "Oh, and lunch is on me."

17

Clad in faded jeans, a denim shirt with studded buttons, and old cowboy boots, Agent A. X. L. Pendergast surveyed the Salton Sea from the thick cover of ripgut grass at the fringes of the Sonny Bono National Wildlife Refuge. Brown pelicans could be seen hovering over the dark waters, wheeling and crying. It was half past ten in the morning, and the temperature stood at a comfortable 109 degrees.

The Salton Sea was not a sea at all, but rather an inland lake. It had been created by accident at the turn of the twentieth century, when an ill-conceived network of irrigation canals was destroyed by heavy rains, sending the water of the Colorado River flooding into the Salton Sink, submerging the town of Salton and eventually creating a lake covering almost four hundred square miles. For a time the region was fertile, and a series of resorts and vacation towns sprang up along the shores. But as the waters receded and grew increasingly salty, the towns were left high and dry, the vacationers stopped coming, and the resorts went bankrupt. Now the area—with its barren desert hills and salt-encrusted shores, fringed by wrecked trailer parks and abandoned 1950s resorts—looked like the world after nuclear armageddon. It was a land that had been depopulated, skeletonized, burned to white, a brutal landscape where nothing lived—save thousands upon thousands of birds.

Pendergast found it most appealing.

He put up his powerful binoculars and walked back out to his car—a 1998 pearl-colored Cadillac DeVille. He drove back to Route 86 and began making his way up the Imperial Valley, following the western edge of the sea. Along the way, he stopped at roadside stands and sad-looking "antiques" shops, where he spent time examining the merchandise, asking about collectibles and dead pawn Indian jewelry, passing out his card, and occasionally buying something.

Around noon, he pointed the Caddy down an unmarked back road, drove a couple of miles, and parked at the foot of the Scarrit Hills, a series of naked ridges and peaks stripped to the bone by erosion and devoid of life. Plucking the binoculars from the passenger seat, he exited the car and trekked up the nearest rise, slowing as he approached the summit. Ducking behind a large rock, he fitted the binoculars to his eyes and slowly peered over the crest.

To the east, the foothills ran down to the desert floor and, perhaps a mile away, the bleak shores of the Salton Sea itself. Wind devils crawled across the salt flats, whipping up cyclones of dust.

Below him, halfway between the hills and the shore, a bizarre structure rose from the desert floor, weather-beaten and dilapidated. It was a vast, sprawling mélange of concrete and wood, once painted in garish colors but now bleached almost white, studded with gables, minarets, and pagodas, like some fantastical cross between a Chinese temple and an Asbury Park amusement parlor. This was the former Salton Fontainebleau. Sixty years before, it had been the most lavish resort on the Salton Sea, known as "Las Vegas South," frequented by movie stars and mobsters. An Elvis film had been shot on its beaches and capacious verandas. The Rat Pack had sung in its lounges, and people like Frank Costello and Moe Dalitz had cut deals in its back rooms. But then the waters of the sea had receded from the resort's elegant piers, the increasing salinity had killed the fish, which washed up in stinking, rotting piles, and the resort had been abandoned to the sun, winds, and migrating birds.

From his place of concealment, Pendergast examined the old resort with minute attention. The weather had scoured the paint from the boards, and most of the windows were mere black openings. In a few spots, the vast roof had collapsed, leaving yawning holes. Here and there, elaborate balconies listed to one side, weakened by years of desuetude. There was no sign of recent activity. The Fontainebleau was untouched, undisturbed, isolated, not even worth the attention of teenage gangs or graffiti artists.

Now Pendergast aimed his binoculars half a mile to the north, beyond the resort. Here, an ancient, gullied track led to a dark opening in the hillside, its ragged maw barred by an ancient wooden door. This was the entrance to the Golden Spider Mine—the site from which the piece of turquoise found in Alban's digestive system had been extracted. Pendergast surveyed the entrance, and the approach to it, with extreme care. Unlike the Fontainebleau, the old turquoise mine had evidently been the site of recent activity. He could see fresh tire tracks going up the old road, and in front of the mine the crust had been disturbed, broken, exposing a lighter shade of salt. An effort had been made to erase both the tracks and prints, but ghost images of them were nevertheless evident from the vantage point of the hilltop.

This was no accident, no coincidence. Alban had been killed and the turquoise planted in his body for one reason: to lure Pendergast to this godforsaken place. The reason why was deeply mysterious.

Pendergast had allowed himself to be lured. But he would not allow himself to be surprised.

He continued to examine the mine entrance for a long time. Then, finally, he pointed the binoculars still farther to the north, scanning the surrounding landscape. Some two miles beyond the Fontainebleau, atop a small rise of land, were the gridded streets, broken streetlights, and abandoned houses of what had once been a town. Pendergast scrutinized it carefully. Then he spent another hour scouring the landscape both north and south, looking for anything else that might indicate recent activity.

Nothing.

He retreated down the hill to his car, got in, and drove in the direction of the abandoned development. As he approached, a large, weather-beaten sign, barely readable, welcomed him to the town of Salton Palms. The ghostly illustration below appeared to show a bikini-clad woman on water skis, waving and smiling.

Reaching the outskirts of the decrepit neighborhood, Pendergast parked and strolled into Salton Palms in a desultory fashion, his cowboy boots making a hollow sound on the cracked asphalt streets, kicking up plumes of snow-like dust. Salton Palms had once been a hamlet of modest second homes. Now the homes were in ruins—wind-scoured, doors missing, burned, others collapsed. A ruined marina, tilted at a crazy angle, sat, beached and rotting, hundreds of yards from the current shoreline. A lone tumbleweed was affixed into the crust of salt, festooned with salt crystals like some gigantic snowflake.

Pendergast wandered slowly through the disarray, glancing around at the rusty swing sets in the grassless backyards, the ancient barbecue grills and cracked kiddie pools. An old toy pedal car from the '50s lay on its side in the middle of the street. In the shade of a breezeway lay the skeleton of a dog, salt-encrusted, its collar still attached. The only sound was the faint moaning of the wind.

On the southern outskirts of Salton Palms, away from the other structures, stood an improvised shack with a tar-paper roof—dingy, rimed with salt, cobbled together from pieces of abandoned houses. An ancient but operable pickup truck, more rust than metal, stood beside it. Pendergast stared at the shack for a long, appraising moment. Then, with an easy, loping stride, he began to approach it.

Other than the pickup truck, there was no evident sign of life. The shack seemed to be without electricity or running water. Pendergast glanced around again, then rapped on the piece of corrugated metal that served as a rude door. When there was no reply, he rapped again.

There was the faintest sound of movement within. "Go 'way!" a hoarse voice rang out.

"Pardon me," Pendergast said through the door, the accent of the Old South replaced by a mild Texas twang, "but I wonder if I might have just a minute of your time?"

When this produced no discernible result, Pendergast plucked a business card from one of the breast pockets of his shirt. It read:

William W. Feathers
Dealer in Collectibles, Dead Pawn,
Western Artifacts, and Cowboy High Style
eBay reselling my specialty

He slid it beneath the piece of corrugated metal. For a moment, it remained in place. Then it quickly disappeared. And then the hoarse voice spoke again. "What you want?"

"I was hoping you might have a few things for sale."

"Don't got nothin' right now."

"People always say that. They never know what they have until I show them. I pay top dollar. Ever watch *Antiques Roadshow?*"

No response.

"Surely you've rustled up some interesting things around here, combed this old town for collectibles. Maybe I can buy some off you. 'Course, if you aren't interested, I'll just have a look around some of these old houses myself. Having come all this way, I mean."

Still nothing for perhaps a minute. And then the door creaked open and a grizzled, bearded face appeared, hovering like a ghostly balloon in the darkness of the interior, creased with suspicion.

Immediately, Pendergast took the opportunity to put his foot inside the door with a jolly greeting, pumping the man's hand enthusiastically as he pushed his way in, with a show of bluff good-fellowship, showering the man with thanks and not giving him an opportunity to get in a single word.

The inside of the shack was rank and stifling. Pendergast looked around quickly. A rumpled pallet lay in one corner. Beneath the lone window sat a cookstove, atop which was a cast-iron skillet. Two sawn-off sections of tree trunk substituted for chairs. Everything was a whirlwind of disorder: clothes, blankets, bric-a-brac, empty tin cans, ancient road maps, driftwood, broken tools, and innumerable other items lay scattered around the tiny abode.

Something glinted faintly amid the ruin. Breaking off his hand-shaking, Pendergast bent down to seize it with a cry of delight. "You see what I mean—just look at this! Why, heck, what's this doing on the ground? This should be in a display case!"

It was a piece of a squash blossom necklace, dented and scratched, of cheap pot silver, missing its precious stone. But Pendergast cradled it as reverently as if it were a stone tablet from God. "I can get sixty bucks for this on eBay, no sweat!" he crowed. "I handle the entire transaction, take the photo, do the write-up, deal with the mailing and the collection, everything. All I ask is a small commission. I make you a payment to get the ball rolling, and then, if I make more on eBay, I keep ten percent. Did I say sixty? Let's make that seventy." And without further ado, he pulled out a roll of money.

The rheumy eyes of the shack's resident went from Pendergast's face to the huge wad. They stayed there as Pendergast peeled off seven $10 bills and proffered them. There was the slightest hesitation, and then the old man's trembling hand reached up and snatched away the money, as if it might fly off at any moment, and stuffed it into the pockets of his dungarees.

With a big Texas smile Pendergast made himself at home, easing himself down onto a tree trunk. His host, with an uncertain expression on his ancient face, did likewise. The man was short and skinny, with long, tangled white hair and whiskers, stubby hands, and incredibly dirty fingernails. His face and arms were dark from long days in the sun. Suspicion still burned in his eyes, tempered somewhat by the sight of money.

"What's your name, friend?" Pendergast asked. He kept the bank-roll casually gripped in his hand.

"Cayute."

"Well, Mr. Cayute, allow me to introduce myself. Bill Feathers, at your service. You've got some nice little things here. I'm sure we'll be able to come to terms!" Pendergast picked up an old metal road sign for State Highway 111, propped up on two cinder blocks, being used as a small table. The paint was peeling and its surface was peppered with buckshot. "For example, this. You know, they hang these on the

walls of steak houses. Big demand. I'll bet I can turn this around for—
oh, I don't know—fifty bucks. What do you say?"

The gleam in the eyes grew brighter. After a minute, Cayute gave
a quick, ferret-like nod. Pendergast duly peeled off five more bills and
handed them over.

Then he beamed. "Mr. Cayute, I can see that you're a man of
business. I calculate this will be a most productive exchange for both
of us."

18

Within fifteen minutes, Pendergast had purchased five more utterly worthless items for a grand total of $380. This had had the effect of mollifying the highly suspicious Cayute. A pint bottle of Southern Comfort, produced from a back pocket of Pendergast's jeans and freely offered, had the additional effect of lubricating the old codger's tongue. He was a squatter, it seemed, who had spent some time in the area as a boy and then, when he'd fallen on hard times, had drifted back to Salton Palms after it had been abandoned. He used the "bungalow" as his base while foraging for things to sell.

With patience and tact, Pendergast inquired into the history of the town and the nearby Salton Fontainebleau, and was rewarded— in fits and starts—with anecdotes of the casino's triumph and long, sad decline. It seemed Cayute had been a busboy in the Fontainebleau's poshest restaurant, at the zenith of its glory days.

"My Lord," said Pendergast, "that must have been a sight to see."

"More'n you can imagine," Cayute replied in his gravelly voice, draining the pint bottle and putting it to one side, like a collectible itself. "Everybody came there. All them Hollywood hotshots. Why, Marilyn Monroe signed her autograph on my shirt cuff while I was bussing her table!"

"No!"

"Accidentally laundered," Cayute said sadly. "Think of what that'd be worth today."

"Darn shame." A pause. "How long has it been since the resort was boarded up?"

"Fifty, fifty-five years."

"Seems a tragedy, such a beautiful building and all."

"They had everything. Casino. Swimming pool. Promenade. Boat dock. Spa. Animal garden."

"Animal garden?"

"Yep." The man picked up the empty bottle of Southern Comfort, eyed it wistfully, replaced it. "Built it up out of a natural hole in the ground beneath the hotel. Just outside the cocktail lounge, it was. All jungle-like. They had real live lions and black panthers and Siberian tigers down there. In the evenings, all the big shots would gather 'round the balcony above with their drinks and watch them animals."

"How interesting." Pendergast rubbed his chin thoughtfully. "Anything of value still inside? I mean, that is, have you explored the interior?"

"Stripped. Totally."

Something else caught Pendergast's eye, peeping out from beneath a tattered Sears, Roebuck catalog at least half a century old that lay on the floor, its spine broken. He picked it up and held it to the improvised window for a better look. It was a raw fragment of turquoise, veined in black.

"What a beautiful stone. Lovely markings. Perhaps we can come to terms on this, as well." He glanced at Cayute. "I understand there's an old mine nearby. The Golden Spider, if memory serves. Is that where you got this from?"

The old man shook his grizzled head. "Don't never go in there."

"Why not? I should think that would be the perfect place to search for turquoise."

"'Cause of the stories."

"Stories?"

Cayute's face screwed up into a strange expression. "Folks said the place was haunted."

"You don't say."

"It ain't a big mine, but there's some purty deep shafts. Lot of rumors."

"What rumors?"

"One I heard was that the mine's owner hid a fortune in turquoise somewhere inside. He died, the story went, and the location of the fortune died with him. Every now and then somebody would hunt around inside, but they never found nothin'. Then some twenty years back, a treasure hunter went exploring inside. Some floorboards had rotted out and he fell through them, down a shaft. Broke both legs. Nobody heard him bawlin' for help. Died of the thirst and the heat, down there in the dark."

"How awful."

"Folk say that if you go in there now, you can still hear him."

"Hear him? You mean, footsteps?"

Cayute shook his head. "No. More of a dragging sound, like, and crying out for help."

"Dragging. Of course, because of the broken legs. What an awful story."

Cayute said nothing, just looked wistfully again at the empty bottle.

"I guess that legend doesn't seem to deter everybody," Pendergast said.

Cayute's eyes darted toward him. "What's that?"

"Oh, I was wandering around outside the mine entrance earlier. I saw footprints, tire tracks. Recent."

As quickly as the eyes had moved toward Pendergast, they moved away again. "Wouldn't know anything about that."

Pendergast waited for an elaboration, but none was forthcoming. Finally, he shifted on his improvised chair. "Really? I'm surprised to hear that. You've got such a good view of the mine from your residence here." As he spoke, Pendergast casually removed the thick bankroll from his pocket.

Cayute didn't respond.

"Yes, I'm surely surprised. The place can't be more than a mile or so away." And he slowly flipped through the tens, exposing twenties and fifties beneath.

"Why you so interested?" Cayute asked, suddenly suspicious again.

"Well, turquoise is a specialty of mine. And so is—not to put too fine a point on it—treasure hunting. Just like the fellow in that story of yours." Pendergast leaned in conspiratorially, put a finger to one side of his nose. "If there's activity at the Golden Spider, that would be of interest to me."

The old scavenger looked uncertain. He blinked his bloodshot eyes: once, twice. "They paid me not to say nothin'."

"I can pay, too." Pendergast opened the bankroll, drew off a fifty, then another. "You can earn twice—and no one will know."

Cayute looked hungrily at the money but didn't say anything. Pendergast drew off two more fifties and proffered them. Another hesitation, and then quickly—before he could think better of it—the old man snatched the bills and stuffed them into his pocket along with the others.

"It was a few weeks back," he said. "They came in a couple of trucks, all sorts of hustle and bustle. Parked outside the mine entrance and began uncrating equipment. I figured they were reopening the mine, so I walked over and said howdy. Offered to sell 'em an old map of the mine I got."

"And?"

"Not the most amiable of folks. Said that they were inspecting the mine for . . . for structural integrity, I think it was. Didn't hardly seem like it, though."

"Why not?"

"Didn't look like no inspectors to me. And because of the equipment they were taking inside. Never seen anything like it before in my life. Hooks, ropes, and something like a . . . like a . . ." Cayute gestured with his hands. "Like one of them things a diver gets into."

"A shark cage?"

"Yeah. Only bigger. They didn't want my map, said they already had one. Then they told me to mind my own business and gave me a fifty to shut up about it." The old man plucked at Pendergast's sleeve. "You ain't going to tell nobody about what I seen, are you?"

"'Course not."

"Promise?"

"It'll be our secret." Pendergast rubbed his chin. "What happened then?"

"They drove off after a couple of hours. Came back again, just yesterday. It was late. One truck this time, two fellers inside. They parked some ways off and got out."

"Yes?" Pendergast prompted.

"There was a full moon, I could see it real clear. One swept away all the tracks with a rake, and the other broomed the dust all around. They walked backward, like, sweeping up the tracks and everything, all the way back to the truck. Then they got in and drove away again."

"Could you describe these men any further? What they looked like?"

"They was rough. Didn't get a good look. I've already said more than I should. Remember your promise."

"Fear not, Mr. Cayute." Pendergast's expression seemed to go far away for a moment. "What was that you said about a map of the mine?"

The venal gleam returned to the bleary old eyes, tempering the agitation and perpetual suspicion. "What about it?"

"I might be interested in acquiring it."

Cayute remained motionless for a time. Then, without getting up from his improvised stool, he rummaged around in the litter at his feet, finally producing a faded, flyspecked roll of paper, torn and badly soiled. Wordlessly, he unrolled the map and showed it to Pendergast without offering it to him.

Pendergast bent in for a close look. Then, equally wordlessly, he peeled off four more fifties and showed them to Cayute.

The transaction was quickly completed. Then, rolling the map up and rising from his seat, Pendergast shook the leathery old hand. "Thanks and good day, Mr. Cayute," he said, stuffing his purchases into his pockets and tucking the map and road sign beneath one arm. "Pleasure doing business with you. Don't bother to get up—I'll find my own way out."

19

D'Agosta perched on a desk in the central laboratory of the Osteology Department, Margo Green standing beside him, arms folded, drumming the fingers of one hand restlessly against her elbow. D'Agosta was watching with suppressed irritation as the technician, Sandoval, worked at his terminal, alternately tapping on his keyboard and peering at the screen. Everything in the Museum happened so damn slowly, he wondered how they ever got anything done.

"I threw away the scrap of paper with that accession number," Sandoval said. "I didn't think you'd need to see it again." He seemed put out having to go through the process again—or perhaps it was just the thought of Frisby walking in and seeing the NYPD taking up more of his time.

"I wanted Dr. Green to have a look at the specimen as well," D'Agosta said, giving the slightest emphasis to the word *doctor*.

"Got it." Another few taps and, with a low whine, a piece of paper spooled out from the nearby printer. Sandoval handed it to D'Agosta, who shared it with Margo. She scanned it.

"This is the summary," she said. "Can I see the details, as well?"

Sandoval blinked at her a minute. Then he turned back to the keyboard, in no hurry, and resumed his tapping. Several more sheets emerged from the printer, and he handed them to Margo. She looked them over.

The room was chilly—like the rest of the Museum—but D'Agosta noticed that a few beads of sweat had sprung out on her forehead and she seemed pale. "Are you feeling all right, Margo?"

Margo gave him a dismissive wave, a fleeting smile. "And this is the only specimen that Vic showed the fake scientist?"

Sandoval nodded as Margo continued to glance through the accession record. "Hottentot, male, approximately thirty-five years of age. Complete. Preparator: Dr. E. N. Padgett."

At this, Sandoval chuckled. "Oh. *Him.*"

Margo glanced at him briefly and returned her attention to the sheets.

"See anything interesting?" D'Agosta asked.

"Not really. I see it was acquired in the usual way—the usual way back then, that is." More flipping of pages. "It seems the Museum contracted with an explorer in South America to supply skeletons for their Osteological collections. The field notes of the explorer—a man named Hutchins—are included here." Silence while Margo read a little farther. "My guess is this Hutchins was little better than a grave robber. He probably learned about a Hottentot funeral ceremony, spied on it, and then in the dead of night robbed the grave, prepared and shipped the skeleton back to the Museum. This supposed cause of death—dysentery, contracted during the Seventh Frontier War—was likely a ruse to make the transaction palatable to the Museum."

"You don't know that," Sandoval said.

"You're right. I don't. But I've examined enough anthropological accession records to know how to read between the lines." She put the paperwork down.

D'Agosta turned to Sandoval. "Would you mind getting the skeleton now?"

Sandoval sighed. "Right." He got up from the desk, picked up the sheet containing the accession record number, and made for the hallway. Halfway to the open door, he glanced over his shoulder. "You want to come?"

D'Agosta made a move to follow him, but Margo put a restraining hand on his forearm. "We'll wait in the examination room across the hall."

Sandoval shrugged. "Suit yourself." He disappeared around the corner.

D'Agosta followed Margo down the hallway to the room where specimens were examined by visiting scientists. He was beginning to wish that he'd taken Singleton up on his offer of the jogger case. It was damn annoying that Pendergast vanished the way he did, without even saying why he thought the skeleton was important. It hadn't occurred to D'Agosta until it was too late how much he'd been banking on the FBI agent's assistance. And to top it off, he was starting to drown in reams of interview transcripts, evidence reports, and logs. All cases were full of useless paperwork, but this one—thanks to the size of the Museum and the number of its employees—was unique. Already, the empty office next to his at police headquarters was piling up with the spillover paperwork.

He watched as Margo put on a pair of latex gloves, glanced at her watch, and proceeded to pace back and forth. She gave every appearance of being agitated.

"Margo," he said, "if this is a bad time, we can always come back later. I told you, it's more a hunch than anything else."

"No," she replied. "It's true, I'm due back at the institute soon—but that isn't the problem." She paced a moment longer, then—seeming to come to some decision—stopped and turned toward him. Her green eyes, so clear and intent, looked into his, and for a minute D'Agosta felt himself transported back, all those many years, to when he'd first questioned her about the Museum murders.

She held his gaze a long moment. Then she sank into one of the chairs surrounding an examination table. D'Agosta did the same.

Margo cleared her throat, swallowed. "I'd appreciate your not telling anyone this."

D'Agosta nodded.

"You know what happened to me, back then."

"Yeah. The Museum killings, the subway murders. It was a bad time."

Margo looked down. "It's not that. It's what...what happened to me...afterward."

For a moment, D'Agosta didn't understand. And then it hit him like a load of bricks. *Oh Christ*, he thought. He'd totally forgotten about what had happened to Margo when she returned to the Museum to edit their scientific journal, *Museology*. How she'd been stalked like an animal in the darkened halls, terrorized, ultimately stabbed and nearly killed by a vicious and maniacal serial killer. It had taken her many months in a clinic to regain her health. He hadn't considered how that might have affected her.

Margo remained silent for a moment. Then she began to speak again, a little haltingly. "Since then, it's been...difficult for me to be in the Museum. Ironic, isn't it, since my research can only be done here?" She shook her head. "I was always so brave. Such a tomboy. Remember how I insisted on accompanying you and Pendergast down into the subway tunnels—and beneath? But everything's different now. There are only a few places I can go inside the Museum... without a panic attack. I can't go too far into the collection areas. Stuff has to be brought out to me. I've memorized all the closest exits, how to get out in a hurry if I have to. I need people around me when I work. And I never stay past closing time—after dark. Just being here, on an upper floor, is difficult."

As he listened, D'Agosta felt even worse for asking her help—he felt like a complete fool. "What you're going through is normal."

"It's worse. I can't stand dark places. Or the dark at all. I keep the lights in my apartment burning all night. You should see my electric bill." She gave a sour laugh. "I'm a mess. I think I've got a new syndrome: *museumophobia*."

"Listen," D'Agosta interrupted, taking her hand. "Maybe we should forget about this damn skeleton. I'll find somebody else who can—"

"No way. I may be psycho, but I'm not a coward. I'll do this. Just don't ask me to go down there." She pointed down the hall, deeper into the collections, where Sandoval had retreated. "And don't *ever* ask me—" she tried to keep her voice light, but a quaver of fear underscored it—"to go into the basement."

"Thank you," said D'Agosta.

At that moment footsteps sounded in the hallway. Sandoval reappeared, the familiar-looking collection tray held in both hands. He carefully laid it on the table between them.

"I'll be at my desk," he said. "Let me know when you're finished."

He left, closing the door behind him. D'Agosta watched as Margo pulled the gloves tighter onto her hands, then took a folded sheet of cotton from a nearby drawer, smoothed it out on the table's surface, and began plucking bones from the tray and placing them on the cloth. A procession of bones emerged: ribs, vertebrae, arm and leg bones, skull, jaws, and many small bones he couldn't identify. He remembered how Margo had bounced back from the trauma of the Museum murders, how she'd begun working out, gotten a handgun license, learned how to use a weapon. She seemed so together. But he'd seen the same thing happen to cops, and he hoped to hell this wasn't making things worse...

He forgot his train of thought as he looked at Margo. She was sitting beside him, having suddenly gone still, a pelvis held in both gloved hands. The look on her face had changed. The distant, preoccupied expression was gone, replaced by puzzlement.

"What is it?" he asked.

Instead of answering, she turned the pelvis around in her hands, peering close. Then she carefully laid it on the cotton, picked up the lower jaw, and examined it intently, viewing it from one angle and another. At last she put it down and glanced over at D'Agosta.

"A Hottentot male, age thirty-five?"

"Yeah."

Margo licked her lips. "Interesting. I'll need to come back when I have more time, but I can tell you one thing already: this skeleton is about as much a Hottentot male as I am."

20

The sun had been burning in the noonday sky when Pendergast drove away from Salton Palms in his pearl-colored Cadillac. When he returned again, it was after midnight.

He stopped three miles short of the ghost town. Turning off the headlights, he drove well off the road and hid the car behind a stand of stunted Joshua trees. He shut off the motor and sat motionless in the driver's seat, considering the situation.

Most aspects remained shrouded in mystery. However, he now knew two particulars. Alban's death had been an elaborate device to lure him to this place—the Golden Spider Mine. And the mine itself had been carefully prepared for him. Pendergast had no doubt that the mine entrance, even now, was under close observation. They were waiting for him.

Pendergast retrieved two rolled-up pieces of paper, which he smoothed open on his lap. One was the map of the Golden Spider Mine he had purchased from Cayute. The other contained old construction blueprints of the Salton Fontainebleau.

Pulling a hooded flashlight from the glove compartment, he first turned his attention to the map of the mine. It was a relatively small mine, with a central passage that appeared to slope downward at a shallow angle, heading southwestward away from the lake. About half a dozen smaller passages angled off from the central one, some straight, others crooked, following the veins of turquoise. Some ended in deep shafts. Pendergast had already committed all this to memory.

He moved the beam of his flashlight to the far edge of the map. At the back end of the mine, a corkscrew passage led off from the main works, narrowing as it went, finally terminating half a mile away in a steep, almost vertical climb: an air shaft, perhaps, or more likely a back entrance that had gone unused. Its lines were faded and worn, as if even the cartographer had forgotten about it by the time the map was complete.

Now Pendergast overlaid the diagram of the mine with the blueprints of the old hotel. He looked back and forth between one and the other, trying to set in his mind the relative positions of the Golden Spider and the Salton Fontainebleau. The blueprints were arranged by floor, and clearly showed the guest suites, capacious lobby, dining rooms, kitchen, casino, spas, ballrooms—and a curious circular construction between the cocktail lounge and the rear promenade labeled ANM. GRDN.

Animal garden, Cayute had said. *Built it up out of a natural hole in the ground beneath the hotel. Had real live lions and black panthers and Siberian tigers down there.*

Once again, Pendergast compared the blueprints with the map with extreme care. The resort's animal garden was situated precisely over the back entrance to the Golden Spider Mine.

Pendergast turned off the flashlight and sat back. It made perfect sense: what better place to construct a subterranean animal garden than in a forgotten, disused section of a long-abandoned mine?

His mysterious hosts had busily prepared the mine for his arrival and taken pains to conceal their tracks. The mine was, without doubt, a trap—but a trap *with a back door.*

While the cooling engine ticked quietly, Pendergast considered how to proceed. Under cover of darkness, he would reconnoiter and enter the resort, locate the back entrance to the mine, and approach the trap from the rear. He would learn the nature of the trap and, if necessary, retask it for his own purposes or disable it. Then, the following day, he would drive up to the main entrance of the mine, without any attempt at disguise, seemingly unaware of the trap inside. And in this way, he would lay his hands on his host or hosts. Once they were in his power, he had no doubt he could encourage them to reveal what lay behind this expensive and absurdly elaborate scheme . . . and who had killed his son to set it in motion.

Of course, he had to admit to the possibility that there might be something he had overlooked; some unknown complication that would force him to revise his plans. But he had been very careful in his surveillance and his preparations, and this strategy seemed to offer the greatest chance of success by far.

He spent another fifteen minutes poring over the hotel blueprints, committing every last hallway and closet and staircase to memory. The animal garden itself was in the basement, its beasts kept at a safe distance from the spectators above. It was accessible through a small suite of rooms comprising a grooming area and several handling and veterinary rooms. Pendergast would have to pass through these rooms to access the garden itself—and thereby reach the back entrance to the mine.

Taking his Les Baer .45 from the glove compartment, Pendergast checked it and snugged it into his waistband. Blueprints in hand, he exited the car, quietly closed the door, and waited in the darkness, all his senses on alert. The half-moon was partially obscured by wispy clouds, providing just enough light for his preternaturally sharpened senses to see by. Gone were the jeans, denim shirt, and cowboy boots: he now wore black pants, black rubber-soled shoes, and a black turtleneck under a black utility vest.

All was utterly still. He waited another moment, carefully scanning the landscape. Then he stuffed the blueprints into his vest and began moving silently northward, in the concealing shadow of the Scarrit Hills.

After fifteen minutes, he veered eastward and climbed up the rearward side of the hill. From the rocks at the summit he examined the lines of the Salton Fontainebleau, its gables and minarets looking even more spectral in the faint moonlight. Beyond lay the dark, dank, motionless surface of the Salton Sea.

Pulling the binoculars from his utility vest, Pendergast surveyed the area, from south to north, with extreme care. All was silent and still, the landscape as dead as the sea that it surrounded. To the north, he could just make out the small black declivity that led into the main entrance of the mine. Even now, unseen eyes, hidden somewhere in the ruins of Salton Palms, were probably surveilling it, awaiting his arrival.

He spent another ten minutes, concealed in the rocks, binoculars constantly roaming. Then, as clouds thickened before the moon, he crept over the crest of the hill and made his way down the far side, careful to remain in the darkness behind the ruins of the Fontaine-bleau, where he could not be seen by anyone watching the mine entrance. As he inched forward, black against the night-dark sand, the huge resort loomed up until it blotted out the sky.

A broad veranda ran along the rear of the resort. Pendergast flitted up to it, paused, and carefully climbed its stairs to the quiet protest of desiccated wood. With each step he took, blooms of fine dust rose in small mushroom clouds. It was like walking on the lunar surface. From the vantage point of the veranda, he glanced left and right along its length, back at the short set of stairs he had climbed, down at the railing. There was nothing to see but his own footprints. The Fontainebleau slept in undisturbed silence.

Now he approached a set of double doors leading into the resort. He trod as lightly as a cat, testing the floorboards with each step. The doors were closed, and had once been locked, but long-ago vandals had ripped one door from its hinges, and it hung open.

Beyond lay a large common room of some kind, perhaps used for afternoon tea. It was very dark. Pendergast stood motionless just within the doorway, giving his eyes time to adjust. There was a strong smell of dry rot, salt, and rat urine. A huge stone fireplace dominated one wall. Wing chairs and skeletonized sofas were arranged around the room, springs protruding from their rotten fabric. Leather banquettes with their tables ran along the far edge of the room, the once-soft seats now cracked, split, and spewing cotton. A few broken and faded photographs of the Salton Sea in its 1950s heyday—motorboats, water-skiers, fishermen in waders—adorned the walls among many empty, pale rectangles, the rest having long been stolen. Everything was covered in a fine mantle of dust.

Pendergast crossed the room, stepped beneath an archway, and emerged into a central passage. There was a huge staircase here that swept up to the floors above, where the guest rooms and suites were located. Ahead lay the dim outlines of the main lobby, with its thick wooden columns and seaside murals only partially visible. He stood for a moment in the silence, getting his bearings. The resort's blueprints were tucked into his vest, but he did not need them—the layout was imprinted on his mind. A spacious corridor led down to the left, presumably to the spa and the ballrooms. To his right was a low archway leading into the cocktail lounge.

Set into a nearby wall was a broken glass display case, containing a single sheet of mimeographed paper, curled and faded. Pendergast approached it and—peering close in the faint moonlight—scanned its contents.

Welcome to the fabulous Salton Fontainebleau!
"The In Place on the Inland Sea"

Saturday, October 5, 1962
Today's Activities:

6 AM – Health swim with Ralph Amandero, two-time
      Olympic contender

10 AM – Water-skiing competition

2 PM – Inline motor boat races

4 PM – "Miss Salton Sea" pageant

8:30 PM – Dancing in the Grand Ballroom, Verne Williams
      Orchestra, starring Jean Jester

11 PM – "The Jungle Comes Alive" animal viewing,
      with free cocktail service

Pendergast turned toward the arch leading into the lounge. The windows of the lounge were shuttered, and although several slats were drooping or had fallen away, the glass shattered, the room was still very dark. Pendergast reached into a pocket of his vest, pulled out a pair of night-vision goggles with a third-generation image intensifier, fitted them to his head, and turned them on. Instantly his surroundings bloomed into clarity, chairs and walls and chandeliers all outlined in ghostly green. Pendergast turned a dial on the goggles, adjusting the brightness of the image tube, then moved across the lounge.

It was large, with a stage in one corner and a long, semicircular bar dominating the far wall. Round tables were arranged around the rest of the room. Broken cocktail glasses lay on the floor and on the tables, their contents long since evaporated into tarry deposits. The bar itself, although the liquor was gone, displayed neatly arranged rows of napkins and jars full of swizzle sticks, all covered with a fine layer of dust. The marbled mirror behind the bar had shattered, dully glittering shards lying on the bar and floor. It was a testament to the remote bleakness of the Salton Fontainebleau—or, perhaps, the vague sense of restless unease, such as a haunted house might exude—that vandals, or scavengers like Cayute, had not completely preyed upon it. Instead the old hotel remained for the most part a time capsule of the Rat Pack generation, abandoned to the vagaries of the elements.

One wall of the lounge was supplied with a picture window, which had survived the passage of time with only a few cracks in it, but so covered with a hoarfrost of salt that it was almost opaque. Pendergast walked over to it, wiped a spot clear with a paper napkin, and peered through. Beyond lay a circular enclosure, lounge chairs arranged around its circumference, as around an indoor swimming pool, except that where the pool would normally be was a yawning black hole lined with brick, surrounded by a protective iron railing. It was about fifteen feet across and looked like the maw of an oversize well. Peering closely with the night-vision goggles, Pendergast thought he could make out, within the blackness of the hole, the plastic, warped upper leaves of several fake palm trees.

The animal garden. It was not hard to imagine high rollers and Hollywood stars rubbing shoulders here half a century earlier, under the starry night, highballs in hand, laughter and the clinking of glasses mingling with the roar of wild beasts as they sipped their drinks and looked down at the animals roaming below.

Pendergast mentally reviewed the hotel blueprints and the map of the Golden Spider Mine. The animal garden was situated directly over the rear entrance to the mine, utilizing the tunnel as a place for the animals to roam under the sight of the guests.

Turning away from the window, he lifted up the hinged bar and stepped into the bartender's station. He walked past the empty shelves that had once held innumerable bottles of fine cognac and vintage champagne, being careful not to tread on broken glass, until he reached a cobwebbed door with a single round window set into it. He pressed against the door and it opened with a soft creak, the cobwebs parting softly. He heard the faintest skittering of rodents. A smell of stuffiness, rancid grease, and droppings reached his nostrils.

Beyond lay a warren of kitchens, storage rooms, and food preparation areas. Pendergast moved silently through them, looking this way and that with the goggles, until he located the door that opened onto a concrete stairway leading down.

The service spaces of the resort's basement were spare and functional, like the lower decks of a passenger ship. Pendergast made his way past a boiler room and several storage areas—one full of rotting deck chairs and beach umbrellas, another with rack after rack of moth-eaten maids' uniforms—until he reached a door of solid metal.

Once again he paused to mentally reconstruct the layout of the hotel. This door led to the animal handling area: housing, veterinary care, feeding. And beyond that would be the animal garden itself— and the rear entrance to the mine.

Pendergast tried to open the door, but the metal had rusted over long years of disuse and would not budge. He tried again, exerting more pressure, until it opened an inch with a disturbing screech of iron. Reaching into his equipment vest, he removed a small pry bar and applied it to half a dozen spots around the edge of the door, working the rust loose, with the help of a spray of marine super-penetrating oil. This time, when he tried the handle, the door yielded just enough for him to squeeze through.

Beyond lay a corridor tiled in white porcelain. Open doors lay on either side, pools of darkness even in the night-vision goggles. Pendergast moved forward carefully. Even now, all these years later, the musk of wild animal and big-game scat freighted the air. To the left was a room containing four large, iron-barred cages with feeding doors. This opened to another room, a tiled veterinary area for examinations and, it appeared, minor surgical procedures. A little farther on, the hallway ended in another metal door.

Pendergast stopped, staring at the door through his goggles. Beyond, he knew, was the handling room. Here was where the animals would have been sedated if the need arose, for special handling, cleaning, emergency removal from the garden, or medical treatment. As best he could make out from the blueprints, the room acted as a kind of air lock, a staging area between the subterranean garden and the controlled atmosphere of the handling areas.

The blueprints did not indicate precisely how the animal garden had been constructed over the rear entrance to the mine: not shown was whether the mine had been sealed or whether it was open to the animal garden itself. Either way, he was ready; if it had been sealed, he had the means to break through—chisels, hammer, lock picks, pry bar, and lubricant.

This second metal door was rusted, too, but not as badly, and Pendergast was able to open it without much difficulty. He stood in the doorway and inspected the room beyond. It was small and extremely dark, clad in porcelain tile, cross-ties and restraint fixtures on the walls, with some closed vents in the ceiling. It had been sealed so well from the outside elements that it appeared to be in much better shape than the rest of the ruin—indeed, almost new. The walls were clean and almost gleamed in the sickly light of his goggles...

Suddenly a terrific blow to his neck sent him sprawling to the floor. He fell, stunned, and as his head cleared he saw his attacker standing between him and the door: tall, well muscled, wearing camos and night-vision goggles, aiming a .45.

Pendergast slowly removed his hand from his vest, leaving the Les Baer in its holster. He rose quietly as he saw the door shutting behind the man as if of its own accord, locking with an audible click. Giving every sign of complete submission and cooperation, he kept his hands in sight, moving slowly, as he recovered from the surprise of being waylaid. The extreme emptiness of the place, the dust and the age, had lulled him into a false sense of isolation.

Quickly, his preternatural sharpness of senses returned.

The man had said nothing. He hadn't moved. But Pendergast could see his frame relaxing ever so slightly, his sense of extreme readiness softening as Pendergast continued to convey by his body language that he was under the man's control.

"What's going on?" he asked, a submissive whine in his voice, the Texas accent back in force. "Why'd you hit me?"

The man said nothing.

"I'm just an artifact collector, checking the place out." Almost groveling, Pendergast ducked his head and took a step closer, as if to genuflect in front of the man. "Please don't shoot me."

He ducked his head again, fell to his knees with a repressed sob. "Please."

The pry bar on his vest—given a touch of assistance—fell to the tiled floor with a clatter. And in this millisecond of distraction, Pendergast rose up in one explosive movement, striking the man's right wrist, cracking it and sending the gun flying.

But instead of lunging for his gun, the man pivoted on the sole of one foot and sent the other foot, karate-style, slamming into Pendergast's chest so fast he could not pull his own weapon. He was again knocked to the floor, but this time—cognizant of his attacker, no longer caught unaware—he spun over just in time to fend off another brutal kick and flipped to his feet, just managing to lean away from a roundhouse punch. He jammed his heel into the inside of the man's right knee as he sprang back, hearing the popping of tendons. His attacker staggered, delivered a cross punch. Pendergast feinted away, then drew him in with a pull counter; as the man delivered the punch into air, Pendergast jerked back and responded with a blow to his face, his fingers in the kung fu "tiger hand" position. The man reared back, the blow missing him by less than an inch, while simultaneously sinking a fist into Pendergast's stomach, almost knocking the wind from him.

It was the most peculiar of battles, conducted in pitch black, in utter silence, with singular intensity and ferocity. The man said nothing, made no sound save for the occasional grunt. He moved so quickly that he gave Pendergast no time to extract his Les Baer. The man was possessed of excellent fighting skills, and for an eternity of sixty seconds they seemed equally matched. But Pendergast had a superior range of martial arts moves, along with highly unusual self-defense techniques he had learned at a certain Tibetan monastery. At last, using one of these latter moves called a Crow Beak—a lightning-like sword-slash of two hands held together as if in prayer—he knocked the goggles from his adversary's face. This gave him an instant advantage, and he used it to land a flurry of blows that brought the man to his knees, gasping. In another moment Pendergast had his .45 out, trained on the man. He gave him a brief search, pulling out a knife, which he tossed away.

"FBI," he said. "You're under arrest."

The man did not reply. Indeed, he hadn't spoken a word throughout the entire encounter.

"Open the door."

Silence.

Pendergast spun the man around, zip-tied his hands behind his back, sought out a loop of pipe, found one, and further zip-tied him to that. "Very well. I'll open it myself."

Again, the man said nothing, giving no indication he had even heard. He just sat on the floor, tied to the pipe, face blank.

As Pendergast went to the door to fire a few rounds into the lock, something strange happened. The room began to fill with a distinct scent: the delicate, sweet smell of lilies. Pendergast glanced around for the source of the odor. It seemed to come from the vent in the ceiling directly above where he had tied the assailant—a vent that had previously been closed, but was now open, a mist descending with a whisper of air. Pendergast's assailant, blinded by the loss of his goggles, stared about in fear as the cloud of mist cloaked his face and body, and he began to cough and shake his head.

Quickly Pendergast aimed at the lock, pulled the trigger. The sound was explosive in the confined space, the round deflected by the metal—a major surprise. But even as he prepared to fire again, he felt his limbs get heavy, his movements begin to grow sluggish. A strange sensation flooded his head—a feeling of *fullness* and a sense of well-being, serenity, and lassitude. Black spots danced before the green field of his vision. He swayed, caught himself, swayed again, dropped the gun. Just as blackness overtook him and he sank to the floor, he heard the ceiling grate begin to close again. And with it came the whispered words:

"You have Alban to thank for this ..."

Later—he did not know how much later—Pendergast swam slowly up from dark dreams and broke the surface into consciousness. He opened his eyes to a green haze. For a moment, he was disoriented, unsure of what he was looking at. Then he realized he was still wearing the goggles, and the green object was the ceiling vent... and everything came back to him.

He rose to his knees, and then—painfully—to his feet. He was sore from the fight but otherwise felt oddly strong, refreshed. The smell of lilies was gone. His opponent was crumpled on the floor, still unconscious.

Pendergast took stock. He surveyed the room through his goggles, far more intently this time. Porcelain tiles rose four feet up the walls, above which was stainless steel. Although there was the closed grate in the ceiling, and nozzles set high up in the walls, the drain in the floor had been sealed with cement.

It reminded Pendergast of another, very different, kind of room that had once been used for unspeakably barbaric purposes.

The silence, the darkness, and the strange quality of the room chilled him. He reached into his pocket, fumbled for his cell phone, began to dial.

As he did so, there was another audible click; the lock snapped free and the metal door swung ajar, revealing the short corridor beyond, empty of anything save his own footsteps in the dust.

21

Lieutenant D'Agosta showed up promptly at one PM. As he closed the door quietly behind him, Margo gestured toward a chair.

"What have you got?" he asked as he sat down, glancing curiously at the bone-littered table before him.

She took a seat beside him, flipping open her laptop. "Remember what the accession record said? A Hottentot male, aged approximately thirty-five?"

"How could I forget? He haunts my dreams."

"What we actually have here is the skeleton of a Caucasian woman, most likely American, and probably not a day under sixty."

"Jesus. How do you know that?"

"Take a look at this." Margo reached over, carefully picked up the pelvic bone. "The best way to sex a skeleton is to examine its pelvis. See how wide the pelvic girdle is? That's designed for giving birth. In a male pelvis, the spread of the ilia would be different. Also, note the bone density, the way the sacrum is tilted back." She replaced the pelvis on the table, picked up the skull. "Take a look at the shape of the forehead, the relative lack of eyebrow ridges—additional indicators of sex. Then, can you see how both the sagittal suture and the coronal suture are fully fused: here, and here? That would argue for somebody over the age of forty. I examined the teeth under a stereozoom, and the wear indicates someone even older—at least sixty, perhaps sixty-five."

"Caucasian?"

"That's not quite so cut and dried, but you can frequently tell a skeleton's racial heritage from its skull and jawbone." She turned the skull over in her hands. "Note the shape of the nasal cavity—triangular—and the gentle slope of the eye socket. Those are consistent with European ancestry." She pointed to the sinus at the bottom of the skull. "See this? The arch of the maxilla is parabolic. If this was a so-called Hottentot, it would be hyperbolic in shape. Of course, you'd need to do DNA sequencing to be absolutely sure—but I'd bet the family Bible this was a white lady in her sixties."

Through the window set into the closed door of the examination room, Margo could see somebody walk past in the corridor beyond, then stop and turn. Dr. Frisby. He looked through the window at her, then at D'Agosta, his expression turning to a scowl. Frisby looked back at her once more, then turned away and disappeared down the corridor. She shivered. She'd never liked the guy and wondered what D'Agosta had done to apparently antagonize him.

"And the American part?" D'Agosta asked.

Margo looked back at him. "That's more a guess. The teeth are evenly worn and well maintained. Good bone health, no apparent diseases. Chemical tests could tell you more definitively—there are isotopes in teeth that can indicate where a person lived and, often, what his diet was."

D'Agosta whistled. "You learn something new every day."

"Another thing. The accession record says the skeleton is complete. But it's now missing a long bone."

"Clerical error?"

"Never. A 'complete' notation was unusual. Not something you'd normally mistake, and the long bone is one of the biggest in the body."

The examination room fell silent. Margo began returning the bones to their tray while D'Agosta looked on, slumped in the chair, a thoughtful expression on his face.

"How in hell did this skeleton end up here? Does the Museum have little old lady collections?"

"No."

"Any idea how old it is?"

"Based on the look of the dental work, I'd say late nineteenth century. But we'd have to do radiocarbon dating to be positive. That could take weeks."

D'Agosta digested this. "Let's make sure the mislabeling wasn't a mistake, and that the missing bone didn't end up nearby. I'll ask our pal Sandoval to pull all the skeletons from the surrounding drawers and those with adjacent accession numbers. You wouldn't mind coming back and seeing if any of those look more like, um, a thirty-five-year-old Hottentot?"

"Glad to. There are other tests I'd like to run on this skeleton, anyway."

D'Agosta laughed. "If Pendergast was around, you can bet he'd say something like: *That bone is critical to solving this case.*" He stood up. "I'll give you a call to set up the next session. Keep this under wraps, will you? Especially from Frisby."

As Margo was making her way back down the central passage of Osteology, Frisby seemed to materialize out of the dim dustiness of a side corridor to walk alongside her.

"Dr. Green?" He looked straight ahead as he walked beside her.

"Yes, hello, Dr. Frisby."

"You were talking to that policeman."

"Yes." She tried to sound relaxed.

Frisby continued to look straight ahead. "What did he want?"

"He asked me to examine a skeleton."

"Which one?"

"The one Vic Marsala pulled for that, ah, visiting scientist."

"He asked *you* to examine it? Why *you*?"

"I've known the lieutenant a long time."

"And what did you find?"

This was rapidly becoming an inquisition. Margo tried to stay calm. "According to the accession label, a Hottentot male, added to the collection in 1889."

"And just what possible bearing could a hundred-and-twenty-five-year-old skeleton have on Marsala's murder?"

"I couldn't say, sir. I was just helping the police at their request."

Frisby snorted. "This is intolerable. The police are barking up the wrong tree. It's as if they're looking to draw my department deeper into this pointless murder case, into scandal and suspicion. All this poking around—I've had a bellyful of it." Frisby stopped. "Did he ask you for any other assistance?"

Margo hesitated. "He mentioned something about examining a few other skeletons from the collection."

"I see." Now at last Frisby looked at her. "I believe you've got some high-level research privileges around here."

"Yes, and I'm very thankful for that."

"What would happen if those privileges were rescinded?"

Margo looked at him steadily. This was outrageous. But she was not going to lose her cool. "It would deep-six my research. I might lose my job."

"What a shame that would be." He said nothing else, only turned and strode down the corridor, leaving Margo standing there, staring at his tall, brisk, receding form.

22

The third-floor suite of the Palm Springs Hilton was dimly lit, the curtains drawn across the picture windows overlooking the swimming pool and cocktail cabana, shimmering in the late-morning sun. In a far corner of the suite, Agent Pendergast was reclining in an armchair, a pot of tea on a table beside him. His legs were crossed at the ankles on a leather ottoman, and he was speaking into his cell phone.

"He's being held in lieu of bail at the Indio jail," he said. "There was no identification on his person, and his fingerprints aren't in any database."

"Did he say why he attacked you?" came the voice of Constance Greene.

"He's been as silent as a Trappist monk."

"You were both knocked out by some anesthetizing agent?"

"So it would seem."

"To what purpose?"

"That is still a mystery. I've been to the doctor, I'm in perfect health—save for the injuries inflicted during the struggle. There's no trace of any poison or ill effects. No needle marks or anything to indicate I was interfered with while unconscious."

"The person who attacked you must have been in league with whoever administered the sedative. It seems strange he would have anesthetized his own associate."

"The entire sequence of events is strange. I believe the man was duped as well. Until he talks, his motive remains obscure. There is one thing, however, that is quite clear. And it is much to my discredit."

He paused.

"Yes?"

"All of this—the turquoise, the Golden Spider Mine, the Salton Fontainebleau, the ineffectually erased tire tracks, the map of the mine itself, and possibly the old man I spoke to—was a setup. It was carefully orchestrated to lure me into that particular animal handling room where that gas could be administered. That room was built years ago for the very purpose of administering anesthetic gas to dangerous animals."

"So what's to your discredit?"

"I thought I was one step ahead of them, when in reality they were always several steps ahead of me."

"You say *they*. Do you really believe that Alban could have been involved, somehow?"

Pendergast did not answer at once, and then repeated, in a low voice, *"You have Alban to thank for this.* A rather unambiguous statement, don't you think?"

"Yes."

"This complex arrangement at the Salton Fontainebleau, over-engineered as if to compensate for any possible failure, has all the tricky hallmarks of something Alban would delight in setting up. And yet—it was his murder that set the trap in motion."

"A strange kind of suicide?" asked Constance.

"I doubt it. Suicide is not Alban's style."

The line lapsed into silence before Constance spoke again. "Have you told D'Agosta?"

"I haven't informed anybody, especially Lieutenant D'Agosta. He already knows more about Alban than is good for him. As for the NYPD in general, I have no faith that they can be of any assistance to me in this matter. If anything, I fear they would trod about, doing damage. I'll go back to the Indio jail this afternoon to see if I can get anything out of this fellow." A pause. "Constance, I'm terribly chagrined I fell into this trap to begin with."

"He was your son. You weren't thinking clearly."

"That's neither comfort nor excuse." And with that, Pendergast ended the call, slipped the cell phone into a pocket of his suit jacket, and remained unmoving, a vague, thoughtful figure in a darkened room.

23

Terry Bonomo was the NYPD's crack Identi-CAD expert. He was also a wiseass in the true Jersey-Italian tradition and, consequently, one of D'Agosta's favorite people on the force. Just sitting in forensics, among the computers and displays and charts and lab equipment, D'Agosta felt his spirits rise. It felt good to be away from the musty, dim confines of the Museum. It also felt good to actually be doing something. Of course he *had* been doing things, trying to identify the visiting "professor"—while his forensic team scoured the bones and tray for latents, DNA, hair, and fiber. But creating a composite sketch of the phony Dr. Waldron's face was different. It would be a major step forward. And nobody was better at facial composites than Terry Bonomo.

D'Agosta leaned over Bonomo's shoulder and watched as he worked with the complex software. Across the table sat Sandoval, the Osteology tech. The job could have been done in the Museum, but D'Agosta always preferred to bring witnesses down to headquarters for this kind of work. Being in a police station was intimidating and helped a witness focus. And Sandoval—who looked a little paler than usual—was clearly concentrating.

"Hey, Vinnie," Bonomo said in his booming New Jersey accent. "You recall the time I was putting together a portrait of a suspected murderer—using the testimony of the murderer himself?"

"That was legendary," D'Agosta said with a chuckle.

"Jesus H. Christopher. The guy thought he was being cute, pretending to be a witness to a murder rather than the killer. His idea was to put together a bullshit portrait, throw us off. But I began to smell a rat almost as soon as we started." Bonomo worked while he talked, tapping away at the keys and moving around the mouse. "Lots of witnesses have bad memories. But this clown—he was giving us the exact opposite of what he looked like. He had a big nose—so he said the bad guy's was small. His lips? Thin. So the perp had thick lips. His jaw? Narrow. Perp had a big jaw. He was bald—so the perp had long full hair."

"Yeah, I'll never forget when you caught on and started putting in the opposite of what he said. When you were done, there was our perp, staring up at us from the screen. By trying to be clever, he'd fed us his own ugly mug."

Bonomo brayed a laugh.

D'Agosta watched him working on a facial rough, based on Sandoval's answers, as a new window popped up here, an additional layer was created there. "That's quite a program," he said. "Improved since the last time I was in here."

"They're always upgrading it. It's like Photoshop with a single purpose. Took me three months to master it, and then they redid it. Now I've got the sucker nailed. You remember the old days, with all those little cards and the blank face templates?"

D'Agosta shuddered.

Bonomo hit a final key with a flourish, then swiveled the laptop around so Sandoval could see it. A large central window held a digital sketch of a man's face, with other smaller windows surrounding it. "How close is that?" he asked Sandoval.

The tech stared at it for a long time. "It looks sort of like him."

"We're just getting started. Let's go feature by feature. We'll start with the eyebrows."

Bonomo clicked on a window containing a catalog of facial features and selected BROWS. A horizontal scroll of small boxes containing representations of eyebrows appeared. Sandoval picked the best match, and then a bunch more appeared, all variations on that, and Sandoval picked the best match again. D'Agosta watched as Bonomo went through the exhaustive process of winnowing down the look of the suspect's eyebrows: shape, thickness, taper, distance between, on and on. Finally, when both Bonomo and Sandoval appeared satisfied, they moved on to the eyes themselves.

"So what's this perp supposed to have done?" Bonomo asked D'Agosta.

"He's a person of interest in the murder of a lab technician at the Natural History Museum."

"Yeah? Of interest how?"

D'Agosta recalled Bonomo's incurable curiosity about the details behind the faces he had to create. "He used a phony identity to access the Museum's collections, and perhaps kill a technician. The identity actually belonged to this college professor in Bryn Mawr, Pennsylvania. Doddering old fart with trifocals. He almost soiled his underwear when he learned someone had stolen his identity and was now wanted for questioning in a murder."

Bonomo let out another loud bray. "I can just see it."

D'Agosta hovered as Bonomo went through the interminable process of sharpening the nose, lips, jaw, chin, cheekbones, ears, hair, skin color and pigment, and a dozen other features. But he had a good witness in Sandoval, who had seen the fake scientist on more than one occasion. Finally, Bonomo clicked a button and the Identi-CAD program brought up a series of computer-generated variations of the final face from which Sandoval could choose. Some shading and blending, a few additional tweaks, and then Bonomo sat back with an air of satisfaction like that of an artist completing a portrait.

The computer seemed to have frozen. "What's it doing now?" D'Agosta asked.

"Rendering the composite."

A few minutes passed. Then the computer gave a chirrup and a small window appeared on the screen that read RENDERING PROCESS COMPLETE. Bonomo clicked a button and a nearby printer stirred into life, spooling out a sheet containing a grayscale image. Bonomo plucked it from the tray, glanced over it, then showed it to Sandoval.

"That him?" he asked.

Sandoval looked at the picture in amazement. "My God. That's the guy! Unbelievable. How'd you do that?"

"You did it," said Bonomo, clapping him on the shoulder.

D'Agosta peered over Bonomo's picture at the sheet. The facial portrait it contained was almost photographic in its clarity.

"Terry, you're the man," he murmured.

Bonomo beamed, then printed half a dozen more copies and passed them over.

D'Agosta squared up the sheets on the edge of the table and put them in his case. "Email me the image, okay?"

"Will do, Vinnie."

As D'Agosta left with Sandoval in tow, he thought that now it was just a question of trying to match this sketch to the twelve thousand people who came and went from the Museum on the day of the murder. That was going to be fun.

24

Interrogation Room B of the California State Holding Facility at Indio was a spacious room with beige cinder-block walls and a single table with four chairs: three on one side, one on the other. A boom mike descended from the ceiling, and video cameras sprouted from two corners. Along the far wall ran a dark rectangle of one-way glass.

Special Agent Pendergast sat in the center of the three chairs. His hands rested on the table, fingers interlocked. The room was perfectly silent. His pale eyes were fixed at some faraway point in space, and he remained as still as a marble statue.

Now sounds of footsteps echoed in the corridor outside. There was a rolling noise as a security bolt was drawn back, then the door opened inward. Pendergast glanced over to see John Spandau, senior corrections officer, enter the room.

Pendergast rose, a little stiff from the previous day's struggle, and extended his hand. "Mr. Spandau," he said.

Spandau smiled faintly, nodded. "He's ready if you are."

"Has he said anything?"

"Not a word."

"I see. Bring him in, by all means."

Spandau stepped back out into the corridor. There was a brief murmur of conversation. Then Pendergast's attacker from the Salton Fontainebleau entered, wearing an orange jumpsuit, escorted by two prison guards. The man had a cast on one wrist and a brace on one knee, and he walked slowly, with a limp. He was in cuffs and leg-chains. The guards directed him to the lone chair on the far side of the table, sat him down.

"Do you want us to be present?" Spandau asked.

"No, thank you."

"They'll be right outside if you need anything." Spandau nodded to the guards, then all three men left the interrogation room. There was the sound of the security bolt sliding home, then a key being turned in a lock.

Pendergast's gaze rested on the closed door for a moment. Then he sat down and turned to regard the man opposite the table. The man returned the look. His face was absolutely impassive. He was tall and muscular, with a broad face, high forehead, and heavy brows.

For a long time, the two men just stared at each other without speaking. Finally, Pendergast broke the silence. "I'm in a position to help you," he said. "If you'll let me."

The man did not reply.

"You're a victim, just as much as I am. You were as surprised as I was when the sedative agent was injected into that room." His tone was gentle, understanding, almost deferential. "You've been made into—in the parlance of the day—a 'fall guy' or 'stooge.' Not very agreeable. Now, I don't know why you undertook this job, why you agreed to attack me, or how you were to be compensated. I only know that it must have *been* a job, not any personal grievance, because I've never seen you before in my life. You were set up, played, used—and then thrown to the wolves." He paused. "I told you that I could help. And I will—if you tell me who you are and who you're working for. That's all I want from you: two names. I shall do the rest."

The man merely looked back at him with the same impassive expression.

"If you are maintaining your silence out of some misguided sense of loyalty, let me clarify: *you have already been sacrificed.* Do you under-stand? Whoever your puppeteer is—whoever has been guiding your actions—clearly meant from the very beginning for you to be incapacitated as well as myself. So why remain silent?"

Still, silence.

"Let me tell you a story. One of my fellow agents put a mobster in jail seven years ago for extortion and blackmail. The mobster was given many opportunities to provide the names of his bosses in exchange for leniency. But he remained a loyal soldier. He did the whole stretch, all seven years of his sentence. This man was released just two weeks ago. The first thing he did was go home to his family, who greeted him with tears of joy. Less than an hour later, he was shot to death by the very mobsters he'd gone to prison to protect. They acted to make sure his mouth stayed closed... *despite* his seven years of loyal silence."

As Pendergast spoke, the man blinked infrequently, but made no other movement.

"Are you keeping silent out of the hope you will be rewarded? That will never happen."

Nothing. Now Pendergast fell silent for a time, staring appraisingly at the man across the table. At last, he spoke again.

"Perhaps you are protecting your family. Perhaps you fear that, if you speak, they will be killed."

The man did not respond to this, either.

Pendergast rose. "If this is the case, then the only hope for your family and for you is to speak. We can protect them. Otherwise, both you and they will be lost—utterly. Trust me: I've seen it happen many times."

Something flashed in the man's eyes—perhaps.

"Good day."

With this, he called for the guards. The door was unlocked, the bolt thrust back, and the guards entered, along with Spandau. Pendergast remained standing while the two guards led the prisoner away.

Pendergast hesitated. "I'll be heading back to New York. Will you arrange for me to obtain his mug shots, fingerprints, DNA, and the medical report from the admitting doctor?"

"Of course."

"You've been most cooperative." He paused. "Tell me, Mr. Spandau—you are something of a wine connoisseur, are you not?"

The man looked back at him with veiled surprise. "What makes you say that?"

"A pamphlet detailing Bordeaux futures on your desk, which I noticed yesterday."

Spandau hesitated. "I am a bit of an enthusiast, I admit."

"You're familiar, then, with Château Pichon Longueville Comtesse de Lalande."

"Sure."

"Do you like it?"

"I've never tasted it." Spandau shook his head. "Nor will I, on a correction officer's salary."

"Pity. It just so happens that this morning I was able to procure a case of the 2000 vintage. An excellent year, quite drinkable already. I've arranged for it to be delivered to your home."

Spandau frowned. "I don't understand."

"I would take it as a great personal favor if you could call me right away should our friend start to talk. All for a good cause—solving this case."

Spandau considered this in silence.

"And if you could arrange for a transcript to be made of what he says—officially, of course—that would be simply icing on the cake. It's possible I might be of assistance. Here's my card."

Spandau remained still another moment. And then a smile spread across his normally unemotional features. "Agent Pendergast," he said, "I believe it would be my pleasure."

25

Leaving the prison, Pendergast drove south from Indio. It was late afternoon when he pulled his car off the main road and parked beneath the cruel ridgeline of the Scarrit Hills.

He climbed to the crest and gazed eastward. Between him and the dead shore of the Salton Sea lay the Fontainebleau, its gaudy, ragged lines dwarfed by the bleak expanse. All was still. From horizon to horizon, stretching to infinity, there was not the slightest sign of life. He had only the faint moaning of the wind for company.

Now Pendergast looked northward, toward the gullied track that led to the Golden Spider Mine. The ill-disguised tire tracks he had noted the day before were gone, leaving nothing but an apparently unbroken crust of salt.

He walked down the far side of the foothills and approached the resort, just as he had done the night before. His footprints raised plumes of salt dust as he walked. And yet there was no sign of his tracks from the previous evening—the steps leading up to the veranda, and the veranda itself, appeared to have lain untouched for decades.

He turned away from the Salton Fontainebleau and walked the half mile north to the main entrance of the Golden Spider Mine. Its ancient door was half-buried in a wash of salt. Miniature salt dunes, formed by dust devils, were scattered along the gullied approach.

It was as it had appeared from the ridgeline: the salt crust seemed undisturbed.

Pendergast scrutinized the entrance from a variety of angles, walking first here, then there, pausing now and then to stare with an appraising eye. And then he knelt and very carefully examined the crust beneath his feet, taking a tiny whisk from a pocket of his suit jacket and brushing the surface—gently, gently—gradually exposing the lighter-colored salt underneath. And now he saw, finally, the faintest traces of activity, so skillfully erased that there would be no way to deconstruct or glean any information from them. He stared for a long time, marveling at the obvious effort, before rising again.

The wind cried and moaned, stirring his hair and ruffling the lapels of his jacket. For the briefest of moments, the dry air was touched by a pleasing scent of lilies.

Turning away from the mine, Pendergast continued north, walking the two miles to the outskirts of the ghost town of Salton Palms. It looked just as it had the day before: broken streetlights, ruined houses, gaping windows, rusting birdbaths, empty swimming pools. But the cobbled-together shack with the tar-paper roof that had stood at the south edge of town was gone.

Pendergast walked over to where it had been—where, just the day before, he had knocked on the rude door and spoken to Cayute. Now there was nothing but dirt and patches of desiccated grass.

It was as if everything—the resort, the mine—had sat here, unvisited, untouched, for years. As if the old man and his worthless possessions had never existed.

It was as if it had all been a dream.

For a brief moment Pendergast swayed, a trifle unsteadily, as the wind worried and tugged at his ankles. And then he turned southward and began the trek back through the salt, dust, and sand to his rental car.

26

Yes," said the junior curator. "Sure, I remember him. He was working with Marsala, maybe two months ago. He and Marsala seemed like buddies, which was kind of unusual."

"That guy on the screen look like him?" asked Bonomo.

"Almost exactly. Except..." The curator stared at the laptop screen. "I think his forehead was a little broader. Around the temples, maybe."

Bonomo worked his magic with the Identi-CAD program. "Like this?"

"A little broader still," the curator said, conviction growing in his voice. "And higher."

More magic. "This?"

"Yes. That's perfect."

"Perfect? Really?"

"Really."

"We aim to please!" Bonomo said with his trademark bray of laughter.

D'Agosta watched this exchange with amusement. They had been making the rounds of the Osteology Department, speaking with everyone who remembered seeing the "scientist" Marsala had assisted. This had allowed Bonomo to tweak the portrait he'd created the day before, making it an even better match. D'Agosta felt optimistic enough to begin a software review of the security video feeds again, with portrait in hand. He was interested in two dates in particular: the day Marsala died, and the day he signed out the specimen for the visitor.

D'Agosta checked the junior curator's name off his list, and they continued down the hall. Spotting another Osteology worker who'd seen the fake scientist, D'Agosta introduced her to Bonomo, and looked on as the police technician showed her the composite portrait and asked for her feedback. Bonomo had cut quite a swath through the dusty, quiet Museum, talking loudly, cracking jokes, making wiseass remarks and laughing at the top of his lungs. This had given D'Agosta a measure of secret joy, especially when Frisby had popped his head out of his office more than once, glowering. He hadn't said anything—what could he say? This was police business.

Out of the corner of his eye, D'Agosta caught sight of Margo Green. She was coming down the corridor from the main entrance to Osteology. Their eyes met, and she gestured toward a nearby storeroom.

"What's up?" D'Agosta said, following her inside and closing the door behind them. "Ready to examine those additional specimens?"

"Already done. Not a Hottentot to be found. The missing long bone didn't turn up in any nearby trays, either. But I've done further analysis of the female skeleton, as promised. I wanted to give you an update."

"Shoot."

To D'Agosta, Margo seemed a little breathless. "I've been able to confirm most of my initial conclusions about the bones. Further examination, and in particular the ratio of oxygen and carbon isotopes present in the skeleton, indicate a diet and geographic location consistent with a late-nineteenth-century woman, roughly sixty years of age, living in an urban American environment, probably New York or vicinity."

From the corridor beyond came another bark of laughter from Bonomo that almost shook the walls.

"A little louder," Margo said, "and your friend out there could channel Jimmy Durante."

"He's a bit obnoxious, but he's the best at what he does. Besides, it's fun to watch Frisby get his knickers in a twist."

At the mention of Frisby's name, Margo's face darkened.

"How are you managing?" D'Agosta asked. "I mean, being in here like this. I know it's not easy for you."

"I'm doing all right."

"Is Frisby giving you a hard time?"

"I can handle it."

"Do you want me to have a word with him?"

"Thanks, but it wouldn't help. There's nothing to be gained and everything to lose from a confrontation. The Museum can be a real snake's den. If I keep a low profile, everything should be fine." She paused. "Look, there's something else I wanted to talk to you about."

"Yeah?"

Despite the fact they were alone, Margo lowered her voice. "Do you remember when we had Sandoval check the accession record for that skeleton?"

D'Agosta nodded. He couldn't imagine where this was leading.

"And when we got to the name of the preparator—Dr. Padgett—Sandoval said: *Oh. Him.*"

"Go on."

"At the time, it struck me as strange. So today I asked Sandoval about it. Like many Museum workers, he loves to collect old Museum rumors and gossip. Anyway, he told me that this Padgett—an Osteological curator here many years ago—happened to have a wife who disappeared. There was some sort of scandal. Her body was never found."

"Disappeared?" D'Agosta asked. "How? What kind of scandal?"

"He didn't know," Margo said.

"You thinking what I'm thinking?"

"Probably—and it's creeping the heck out of me."

27

Lieutenant Peter Angler sat at a scuffed desk, heaped with paper, in the rambling offices of the Transportation Security Administration. Outside the room's lone window, a steady stream of jets screamed by on JFK's runway 4L-22R. It was almost as noisy inside: the TSA offices were awash in ringing phones, clacking keyboards, slamming doors, and—not infrequently—voices raised in anger or protest. Directly across the hall, a heavyset man from Cartagena was being subjected— visible past a door that was more than ajar—to a body cavity search.

What was that line of Sophocles from *Oedipus Rex*? "How awful a knowledge of the truth can be." Angler looked quickly back at the paperwork strewn across the desk.

With little else to go on, several of his men were checking into the many ways Alban could have entered the country. He had one hard fact: before showing up dead on a doorstep in New York City, Alban's last reported location had been Brazil. And so Angler had dispatched teams to the local airports, Penn Station, and the Port Authority bus terminal, searching for any evidence on his movements.

Angler reached for a stack of paper. Passenger manifests: lists of people who had entered the country from Brazil over the last several months, via flights into JFK. It was one of many such manifests, and it was an inch thick. Searching for any evidence? They were wallowing in "evidence"—all of it apparently useless, a distraction. His men were examining these same manifests, looking for known criminals that Alban might have associated with, checking for anything remotely out of place or suspicious.

He himself was simply checking—paging through the lists, hour after hour, waiting for something, anything, to catch his attention.

Angler knew he didn't think like the average cop. He was right-brained: always searching for that intuitive leap, that strange connection, that a more orthodox, logical approach would overlook. It had served him well on more than one occasion. And so he kept turning the pages and reading the names, not even knowing what he was looking for. Because the one thing they did know was that Alban did not enter the country under his own name.

Howard Miller
Diego Cavalcanti
Beatriz Cavalcanti
Roger Taylor
Fritz Zimmermann
Gabriel Azevedo
Pedro Almeida

As he did so, he had the fleeting sense—not for the first time in this case—that somebody had made this journey before him. It was just little things: the slight disorder among papers that had no reason to be disordered, file drawers that looked like they'd recently been pawed through, and a few people who had vague recollections of someone else asking similar questions six months or a year ago.

But who could it have been? Pendergast?

At the thought of Pendergast, Angler felt a familiar irritation. He'd never before met such a character. If the man had been the slightest bit cooperative, maybe all this pawing through paper wouldn't be necessary.

Angler shook this line of reflection away and returned to the manifests. He was experiencing a touch of indigestion, and he wasn't going to let thoughts of Pendergast make it worse.

Dener Goulart
Matthias Kahn
Elizabeth Kemper
Robert Kemper
Nathalia Rocha
Tapanes Landberg
Marta Berlitz
Yuri Pais

Suddenly he stopped. One of the names—Tapanes Landberg—
stood out.

Why? Other odd names had jumped out at him before...and
proven to be nothing. What was it about this one that stirred something in his right brain?

He paused to consider. What had Pendergast said about his son?
He'd said so little that all of it had stayed in Angler's mind. *He was eminently capable of managing even the worst trouble.* There was something
else, too; something that had stood out: *He took delight in malicious
games; he was an expert at taunting and mortification.*

Games. Taunting and mortification. Interesting. What meaning,
exactly, was hiding behind the veil of those words? Had Alban been a
trickster? Did he like his little jokes?

Taking a pencil, Angler—slowly, lips pursed—began doodling
with the name Tapanes Landberg in the top margin of the manifest.

Tapanes Landberg
Tapanes Bergland
Sada Plantenberg
Abrades Plangent

Abrades Plangent. On a whim, Angler removed the letters that
made up Alban from this name. He found himself left with:

rdesPagent

Shifting to the bottom margin, he rearranged these letters.

dergaPenst
Pendergast

Angler glanced at the manifest details. The flight had been Air Brazil, Rio de Janeiro to New York.

The person who entered Kennedy Airport from Brazil came in with a name that was an anagram of Alban Pendergast.

For the first time in several days, Peter Angler smiled.

28

The Microforms Reading Room on the first floor of the New York Public Library's main building was brightly lit, packed with machines for reading microfilm and microfiche, and too warm for comfort. As he took a seat beside Margo, D'Agosta loosened his tie and unbuttoned the top button of his shirt. He watched as she loaded a reel of microfilm onto their machine and threaded it through the mechanism and onto the takeup spindle.

"Christ," D'Agosta said. "You'd think they would have digitized all this by now. So what are we looking at?"

"The *New-York Evening Independent*. It was quite comprehensive for its time, but verged toward more sensationalist stories than the *Times*." She glanced at the microfilm box. "This spool covers the years 1888 to 1892. Where do you suggest we start?"

"The skeleton entered the collection in '89. Let's start there." D'Agosta tugged his tie down a little farther. Damn, it was hot in here. "If this guy got rid of his wife, he wouldn't wait around to dispose of her body."

"Right." Margo nudged the big dial on the front of the microfilm machine into forward. Old newspaper pages scrolled up the screen, first slowly, then more quickly. The machine made a whirring noise. D'Agosta glanced over at Margo. She seemed a different person when outside the Museum—more at ease.

He couldn't shake the feeling that, while this might be an interesting exercise, in the end it wouldn't move his own case forward—even if Padgett had killed his wife and stuffed her bones in the collection. He found himself freshly annoyed at Pendergast for the way he'd stopped by the Museum, asked just enough questions to raise D'Agosta's own hopes for the case—and then disappeared without a word. That had been five days ago. D'Agosta had begun to leave increasingly testy messages for Pendergast, but so far they had borne no fruit.

Margo slowed the machine again as they reached 1889. Page after page passed: stories about New York politics, colorful or lurid foreign events, gossip and crime and all the attendant hustle and bustle of a city still growing at flank speed. And then, in late summer, something of interest appeared:

GENERAL LOCAL NEWS

~ ~ ~ ~ ~

Elevated Railway Stock Released—Man Arraigned on Suspicion of Wife's Disappearance—New Opening at the Garrick Theatre—Sugar Ring Collapses—Stinson in jail following libel suit

~ ~ ~ ~ ~

Special to the New-York Evening Independent.

NEW YORK, AUG. 15.—Consolidated Steel has just announced a tender offer of new stock for the sale of steel to be used for the elevated railway being considered for Third Avenue—The New-York Metropolitan Police have arrested a Dr. Evans Padgett of the New York Museum in connection with the recent disappearance of his wife—The Garrick Theatre will be debuting a new version of Othello, with Julian Halcomb as The Moor, this Friday next—The notorious Sugar Ring has been rumored recently to be on the brink…

"My God," Margo murmured. "So he *did* kill his wife."
"It's just an arrest," D'Agosta told her. "Let's keep going."
Margo moved through the next several issues. About a week later, another related notice appeared. It had become more important now and was given its own story.

MUSEUM SCIENTIST ACCUSED OF UXORICIDE
BODY OF WIFE SOUGHT IN WIDENING SCANDAL.

SUSPECT TALKED ABOUT MURDERING WIFE IN DAYS PRIOR TO HER DISAPPEARANCE—UNCOMMUNICATIVE UNDER EXAMINATION—MUSEUM'S PRESIDENT DENIES INSTITUTION'S INVOLVEMENT

NEW YORK, AUG. 23.—Dr. Evans Padgett was officially arraigned today in connection with the disappearance and presumed murder of his wife, Ophelia Padgett. Mrs. Padgett had been known by friends and neighbors as suffering from a wasting and painful disease, along with increasing signs of mental disturbance. Dr. Padgett first came under suspicion when colleagues at the New York Museum of Natural History, where he is a curator, told police that he had referred on several occasions to his desire to end his wife's life. Said colleagues reported that Dr. Padgett had claimed a certain patent medicine or nostrum was responsible for his wife's present condition, and made veiled allusions to "relieving her of her misery." Since his arrest, Padgett himself has made no statement to either police or to the prosecuting bodies, but rather has maintained a resolute silence. He is presently in custody at The Tombs awaiting trial. When asked for comment, the president of the Museum said only that he would have no words on the distressing events beyond observing that the institution itself obviously had no role in the disappearance.

D'Agosta scoffed. "Even back then, the Museum was more concerned with protecting its reputation than helping solve a crime." He paused. "Wonder what this patent medicine was. Probably loaded with cocaine or opium."

"The condition doesn't sound like your standard drug addiction. Wasting...that was nineteenth-century-speak for terminal. Now, that's interesting..." She paused.

"What?"

"It's just that one of the tests I conducted on the skeleton did show some anomalous mineralization. Perhaps Ophelia Padgett was suffering from a bone disorder or other degenerative condition."

D'Agosta watched as she moved forward through the newspaper's later issues. There were one or two brief mentions of the upcoming trial; another brief dispatch stating the trial was under way. And then, on November 14, 1889:

Dr. Evans Padgett, of Gramercy-Lane, who had been accused of murdering his wife, Ophelia, was today acquitted of all charges laid against him by the presiding judge in the King's Courtroom at 2 Park Row. Although certain eyewitnesses came forth to describe Padgett's veiled statements about ending his wife's existence, and circumstantial evidence was presented by the attorney for the State of New York, Dr. Padgett was declared exonerated because no *corpus delicti* could be found, despite the most diligent search by the Manhattan constabulary forces. Padgett was set free by the bailiff and allowed to leave the Court a free man as of noon on this day.

"No *corpus delicti*," D'Agosta said. "Of course there was no body. The old guy had it macerated in the Osteology vats and then stuck the bones into the collection, labeling them Hottentot!"

"The science of forensic anthropology wasn't very advanced in 1889. Once she was reduced to a skeleton, they'd never have been able to identify her. The perfect crime."

D'Agosta slumped in his chair. He felt a lot more tired now than when he'd entered the room. "But what the hell does it mean? And why would this phony scientist steal one of her bones?"

Margo shrugged. "It's a mystery."

"Great. Instead of solving a week-old murder, we've uncovered a century-old one."

29

Where did we come from? How did our lives begin? How did we end up on this speck of dust called Earth, surrounded by the countless other specks of dust that make up the universe? In order to answer these questions, we have to go back billions of years, to a time before that universe existed. To a time when there was nothing—nothing but darkness . . .

D'Agosta turned from the gentle curve of the one-way glass and rubbed his bleary eyes. He'd heard the presentation five times already and could probably recite the damn thing by heart.

Stifling a yawn, he looked around the dim confines of the Museum's video security room. Actually, it wasn't really the video security room—the actual name of the room was Planetarium Support. It housed the computers, software, and banks of NAS drives and image servers that drove the fulldome video at the heart of the Museum's planetarium. The room was tucked into a corner of the sixth floor, hard by the upper section of the planetarium's dome—hence the curved glass in the far wall. As far as D'Agosta could make out, while the Museum had been quite proactive in installing security cameras, it hadn't occurred to anyone that they might actually need to be viewed at some later date. Hence, the monitors for viewing archival security images had been retrofitted into Planetarium Support, and the technology for playing back those images was borrowed from the planetarium computers—no doubt some bean counter's idea of economizing resources.

The problem was, during visiting hours the room's lights had to be dimmed to a point where they were almost completely off—otherwise, the glow would bleed out through the one-way glass in the planetarium's dome and spoil the illusion for the tourists in their seats below. The video monitors for examining the security footage all faced away from that single window. And it was cramped: D'Agosta and two of his detectives, Jimenez and Conklin, had to sit practically in each other's laps while working the three available security playback workstations. D'Agosta had been sitting here in the dark for hours now, staring at the grainy little screen, and a nasty headache was beginning to form just behind his eyeballs. But something drove him on: a tickle of fear that, unless the videotapes scored a hit, the case was going to go cold again.

All of a sudden the dark room filled with a brilliant explosion of light: in the planetarium beyond and below the window, the Big Bang had just taken place. D'Agosta should have remembered this—after all, he'd heard the intro start up just the minute before—but once again it took him by surprise and he jumped. He shut his eyes, but it was too late: already, he could see stars dancing crazily behind his shut eyelids.

"God*damn* it!" he heard Conklin say.

Now thunderous music intruded into the cramped space. He sat motionless, eyes closed, until the stars went away and the music decreased slightly in volume. Then he opened his eyes again, blinked, and tried to focus on the screen before him.

"Anything?" he asked.

"No," said Conklin.

"Nada," said Jimenez.

He'd known it was a silly question even as he asked it—the moment they saw something, they'd sing out. But he'd asked anyway, in the crazy hope that simply by articulating it he might force something to happen.

The tape he was watching—a view of the main entrance to the Hall of Marine Life, five PM to six PM, Saturday, June 19, the day Marsala had been murdered—came to an end without showing anything of interest. He moused the window closed, rubbed his eyes again, drew a line through the corresponding entry on a clipboard that sat between him and Jimenez, then pulled up the security program's main menu to select another, as-yet-unwatched video. With a distinct lack of enthusiasm, he chose the next video in the series: Hall of Marine Life, main entrance camera, six PM to seven PM, once again from June 12. He began running through the video stream, first at true speed, then at double speed, then—as the hall became completely empty—at eight times speed.

Nothing.

Crossing out this video entry in turn, he selected, for a change of pace, a camera that covered the southern half of the Great Rotunda, four PM to five PM. With a practiced hand he cued the digital feedback to its beginning, switched the display to full-screen mode, then started the playback at normal speed. A bird's-eye view of the Rotunda flickered into life, streams of people moving from right to left across the screen. Closing time was drawing near, and they were heading for the exits in droves. He rubbed his eyes and peered closer, determined to concentrate despite the lousy conditions. He could make out the guards at their stations, the docents with their flags-on-a-stick weaving their way through the crowds, the volunteers at the information desk beginning to put away maps and flyers and donation requests for the night.

A thunderous roar from the planetarium beyond the far wall. Shouts and applause arose from the audience: the formation of the earth was taking place, all jets of flame and coronas of color and balls of fire. Deep-bass organ notes vibrated D'Agosta's chair to a point where he almost fell out of it.

Shit. He shoved himself away from the screen with a brutal push. Enough was enough. Tomorrow morning, he'd go back to Singleton, eat crow, kiss ass, grovel, do whatever he had to do in order to be reassigned to that Upper East Side slasher murder.

Suddenly he froze. And then he scrambled back to the video screen, staring at it intently. He watched for perhaps thirty seconds. Then, fingers almost trembling with eagerness, he clicked the REWIND button, then watched the video play back, eyes just inches from the screen. Then he played it back again. And again.

"Mother of God," he whispered.

There he was—the fake scientist.

He glanced at the printout of Bonomo's facial reconstruction—taped to the side of Jimenez's monitor—and then back to the screen. It was unmistakably him. He was wearing a lightweight trench coat, dark slacks, and slip-on rubber sneakers: the kind that made no noise when you walked. Not exactly standard attire for a scientist. D'Agosta watched as he came through the entrance doors, glanced around—apparently noting the location of the cameras—paid admission, then made his way through the security station and strolled across the Rotunda—against the exiting traffic—before disappearing out of view. D'Agosta played it back yet again, marveling at the man's coolness, the almost insolent slowness of his walk.

Christ. This is it. He turned in excitement to announce his discovery when he noticed a dark figure standing behind him.

"Pendergast!" he said in surprise.

"Vincent. I understand from Mrs. Trask that you, ah, have been asking after me. Urgently." Pendergast looked around, his pale eyes taking in the room. "Box seats to the cosmos—how stimulating. What, pray tell, is going on?"

In his exhilaration, D'Agosta forgot his earlier annoyance at the agent.

"We found him!"

"God?"

"No, no—the fake Dr. Waldron! Right here!"

A look of what might have been impatience flitted across Pendergast's face. "The fake who? I'm lost."

Jimenez and Conklin crowded around the monitor as D'Agosta explained. "Remember, the last time you were here, you wondered about the visiting scientist Victor Marsala worked with? Well, his credentials were false. And now look: I've got eyes on him, entering the Museum at four twenty PM, on the very afternoon of the day Marsala was murdered!"

"How interesting," said Pendergast, in a bored voice, already edging toward the door. He seemed to have lost all interest in the case.

"We did a facial composite," said D'Agosta, "and here he is. Compare this guy on screen to the composite." D'Agosta plucked the composite from the side of Jimenez's monitor and held it toward him. "It's a match. Take a look!"

"Delighted to hear the case is proceeding well," said Pendergast, moving closer to the door. "I'm afraid my attention is now fully occupied on something else, but I'm sure things are in excellent hands—"

He paused as his eye fell on the portrait D'Agosta held out toward him. His voice died away, and he froze. A great stillness took hold while the agent's features went as pale as death. He reached out, took the sheet, and stared at it, the paper making a rattling sound. Then he sank into an empty chair set against the wall, still clutching the paper and staring at it with great intensity.

"Bonomo did a damn good job," D'Agosta said. "Now all we have to do is track down the son of a bitch."

For a moment, Pendergast did not reply. When he did, his voice was low, sepulchral, as if emanating from the grave. "Remarkable indeed," he said. "But there is no need to track him down."

This stopped D'Agosta. "What do you mean?"

"I made this gentleman's acquaintance recently. Quite recently, in fact." And the hand holding the facial composite dropped very slowly as the sheet of paper slid to the dusty floor.

30

Lieutenant D'Agosta had never been in the gun room of Pendergast's Riverside Drive mansion before. There were many rooms he'd never seen—the place seemed to go on forever. However, this room was a particularly welcome surprise. His father had been an avid collector of vintage firearms, and D'Agosta had picked up the interest to a somewhat lesser degree. As he looked around, he saw that Pendergast owned some rare pieces indeed. The room was not large, but was luxuriously appointed, with rosewood walls and a matching coffered ceiling. Two huge tapestries, obviously very old, hung opposite each other. The rest of the walls were taken up by recessed cabinets, with locked glass doors, that held an astonishing variety of classic weaponry. None of the guns seemed to be more recent than World War II. There was a Lee-Enfield .303 and a Mauser Model 1893, both in pristine condition; a rare Luger chambered in .45; a .577 Nitro Express elephant gun by Westley Richards with an inlaid ivory stock; a Colt .45 single-action revolver straight out of the Old West, with seven notches on its handle; and many other rifles, shotguns, and handguns D'Agosta didn't recognize. He moved from cabinet to cabinet, peering inside and whistling appreciatively under his breath.

The room's only furniture was a central table, around which half a dozen chairs were arranged. Pendergast sat at the head of the table, fingertips tented, his index fingers tapping against each other, cat's eyes staring into nowhere. D'Agosta glanced from the weapons to the FBI agent. He'd been annoyed at Pendergast's cryptic refusal to explain who the man was, but he reminded himself that the agent did things in his own eccentric way. So he had swallowed his impatience and accompanied Pendergast from the Museum back to his mansion.

"Quite a collection you got here," D'Agosta said.

It look Pendergast a moment to glance toward him; an even longer moment to answer. "The collection was assembled by my father," he said. "Aside from my Les Baer, my own taste runs in other directions."

Margo came into the room. A moment later, Constance Greene entered. Despite having a last name similar to Margo's, Constance couldn't have been more different. She was wearing an old-fashioned evening dress with bands of white lace at both the throat and wrists, which, D'Agosta thought, made her look like a character in a film. He admired her rich mahogany-colored hair. She was a beauty. A forbidding, even scary beauty.

When she saw D'Agosta, she gave him a nod.

D'Agosta smiled back. He didn't know why Pendergast had assembled everyone like this, but no doubt he was about to learn.

Pendergast gestured for everyone to take a seat. As he did so, the faintest rumble of thunder from outside penetrated the thick walls. The big thunderstorm they'd been predicting for a couple of days had arrived.

The FBI agent looked first at D'Agosta, then at Margo, his eyes like silver coins in the dim light. "Dr. Green," he said to Margo. "It is nice to see you again after all this time. I wish it could have been under more pleasant circumstances."

Margo smiled an acknowledgment.

"I have asked you here," Pendergast went on, "because it is now a certainty that the two murders we have been investigating as separate affairs are, in fact, linked. Vincent, I have kept certain information from you because I did not want to involve you any more than necessary in my son's murder investigation. I've put you in an awkward enough position with the NYPD already. But now the time has come to share what I know."

D'Agosta inclined his head. It was true: Pendergast, through no fault of his own, had burdened him with a terrible secret. But that was, as his grandmother used to say, *acqua passata*, water under the bridge. At least he hoped so.

The agent turned to Margo. "Dr. Green, I know that I can count on your discretion—nevertheless, I must ask you and everyone here to keep what is spoken of within these walls absolutely confidential."

There were murmurings of agreement.

Pendergast, D'Agosta noticed, seemed uncharacteristically restless, his fingers tapping on the table. Normally he was as motionless as a cat.

"Let us review the facts," Pendergast began. "Exactly eleven days ago this evening, my son, Alban, was found dead on the doorstep of this house. A piece of turquoise was found in his digestive tract. I traced the turquoise to an obscure mine on the shores of the Salton Sea in California. A few days ago, I visited that mine. An ambush awaited me: I was attacked."

"Who the hell could get the drop on you?" D'Agosta asked.

"An interesting and as yet unanswered question. As I managed to subdue my attacker, we were both subjected to a paralyzing agent of some kind. I blacked out. Once I regained consciousness, I apprehended my assailant and he was incarcerated. The man has remained absolutely silent, his identity as yet unknown."

He glanced back at D'Agosta. "Let us now turn to your case: the death of Victor Marsala. The prime suspect appears to be a gentleman who posed as a scientist and examined a curious skeleton in the Museum's collection. With Margo's assistance, you were able to determine three additional items of interest. First: a bone was missing from the skeleton."

"The right femur," Margo said.

"Evidently our ersatz scientist made off with this bone, for reasons unknown. He later killed Marsala."

"Perhaps," said D'Agosta.

"Second: the skeleton in the collection did not match its accession label. Instead of being a young Hottentot male, it was an elderly American woman—most likely the remains of the wife of a Museum curator who was put on trial for killing her in 1889. He was acquitted: there was no body. Now you have found the body." Pendergast looked around the table. "Have I missed anything of importance so far?"

D'Agosta stirred. "Yeah—just how are these two murders connected?"

"That leads to my third point: the man who attacked me at the Salton Sea, and the man you are searching for in connection with Victor Marsala's death—this would-be 'visiting scientist'—are *one and the same*."

D'Agosta felt himself go cold. *"What?"*

"I recognized him immediately from your most excellent composite image."

"But what's the connection?"

"What indeed? When we know that, my dear Vincent, we will be well on the way to solving both cases."

"I'll have to go interview him in Indio, of course," D'Agosta said.

"Naturally. Perhaps you'll be more successful than I was." Pendergast shifted restlessly and turned to Margo. "And now, perhaps, you could fill in for us the details of your own inquiry?"

"You've pretty much covered it," Margo said. "I have to assume the curator, a man named Padgett, snuck his wife's corpse into the Museum, macerated it in the Osteology vats, and then placed it in the collections with a false accession record."

Across the table, Constance Greene had drawn her breath in sharply. All heads turned toward her.

"Constance?" Pendergast asked.

But Constance was looking at Margo. "Did you say a Dr. Padgett?" These were the first words she had spoken since the conference began.

"Yes. Evans Padgett. Why?"

For a moment, Constance did not reply. Then she passed a hand over the lacework at her throat. "I've been doing archival research into the background of the Pendergast family," she said in her deep, strangely antique voice. "I recognize that name. He was one of the first people to publicly accuse Hezekiah Pendergast of peddling a poisonous patent medicine."

Now it was Pendergast's turn to appear startled.

D'Agosta was growing increasingly confused. "Wait. Who the heck is Hezekiah Pendergast? I'm totally lost."

The room fell silent. Constance continued to look at Pendergast. For what seemed like ages, the FBI agent did not respond. Then he gave an almost imperceptible nod. "Please proceed, Constance."

"Hezekiah Pendergast," Constance continued, "was the great-great-grandfather of Aloysius—and a first-rate mountebank. He began his career as a snake-oil salesman for traveling medicine shows and, over time, devised his own 'medicine': Hezekiah's Compound Elixir and Glandular Restorative. He was a shrewd marketer, and during the late 1880s sales of the nostrum quickly exploded. The elixir was inhaled—not uncommon in those days—using a special kind of atomizer he called a Hydrokonium. An old-fashioned nebulizer, really, but he patented the device and sold it along with the elixir. Together they helped restore the wealth of the Pendergast family, which at the time had been in decline. As I recall, the elixir was called a 'pleasant physic for all bilious complaints' that could 'make the weak strong and the neurasthenic calm' and 'perfume the very air one breathes.' But as use of Hezekiah's elixir spread, rumors began to rise: of madness, homicidal violence, and painful, wasting death. Lone voices—such as Dr. Padgett's—rose in protest, only to be ignored. Some medical doctors decried the elixir's poisonous effects. But there was no public outcry until an issue of *Collier's* magazine exposed the compound as an addictive and lethal blend of chloroform, cocaine, noxious botanicals, and other toxic ingredients. Production ceased around 1905. Ironically, one of the final victims was Hezekiah's own wife—named Constance Leng Pendergast, but always known to the family as Stanza."

A freezing silence descended on the room. Pendergast had resumed looking into space, fingers drumming lightly on the table, his expression unreadable.

It was Margo who broke the silence. "One of the newspaper articles we uncovered mentioned that Padgett blamed his wife's sickness on a patent medicine. When I did the isotope analysis of her bones, I got some anomalous chemical readings."

D'Agosta glanced at Constance. "So you're saying that Padgett's wife was a victim of this patent medicine—this elixir formulated and sold by Pendergast's ancestor—and that he killed her to end her pain and suffering?"

"That's my guess."

Pendergast stood up from his chair. All eyes swiveled toward him. But he simply smoothed his shirtfront and then sat down again, his fingers trembling ever so slightly.

D'Agosta was about to say something, then stopped. A connection among all these facts was starting to assemble itself in his mind—but one so bizarre, so terrible, that he could not bring himself to seriously consider it.

At that moment, the door opened quietly and Mrs. Trask entered. "There's a call for you, sir," she told Pendergast.

"Please take a message."

"Pardon me, but it's from Indio, California. The man said it can't wait."

"Ah." Pendergast rose again and began to make his way toward the door. Halfway across the room, he stopped.

"Ms. Green," he said, turning to Margo. "What we've discussed here is of the most sensitive nature. I hope you won't think it amiss if I ask you to promise not to divulge it to anyone else."

"As I said, you can rely on me. You already asked us to practically swear an oath of secrecy tonight."

Pendergast nodded. "Yes," he said. "Yes, of course." And with a brief look at each of the three still arrayed around the table, he followed Mrs. Trask out of the room and shut the door behind him.

31

As they approached the town of Indio from Interstate 10 East, D'Agosta looked curiously out of the window of the State Department of Corrections vehicle. He'd been to California only once before, as a kid of nine, when his parents had taken him to visit Disneyland. He remembered only fleeting images of palm trees, sculptured pools, clean wide boulevards adorned with flower-filled planters, the Matterhorn, and Mickey Mouse. But this, the backside of the state, was a revelation. It was all brown and desiccated, hot as hell, with weird bushes, stunted cactus-like trees, and barren hills. How anyone could live in such a godforsaken desert was beyond him.

Beside him in the rear of the car, Pendergast shifted.

"You've already tried to get the guy to talk once—got any fresh ideas?" D'Agosta asked.

"I learned something, ah, "fresh" in the telephone call I received last night. It was from the senior corrections officer at the Indio jail. It seems our friend in custody *has* begun to talk."

"No kidding." D'Agosta looked back out the window. Typical of Pendergast to withhold this particular nugget of information until the last minute. Or was it? On the red-eye flight out he had seemed silent and irritable, which D'Agosta had assumed was due to lack of sleep.

The California State Holding Facility at Indio was a long, low, drab-looking affair that—had it not been for the guard towers and the three rings of walls topped with razor wire—would have looked like a series of Costcos strung together. A few sad clumps of palm trees stood outside the wire, limp in the relentless sun. They entered the main gate, were buzzed through a series of security checkpoints, and finally arrived at the official entrance. There they got out of the car. D'Agosta blinked in the sunlight. He had been up for seven hours already, and the fact that it was only nine AM California time was more than a little disorienting.

A narrowly built, dark-haired man was waiting for them just inside. As Pendergast approached, the man extended his hand. "Agent Pendergast. Nice to see you again."

"Mr. Spandau. Thank you for contacting me so promptly." Pendergast turned to make the introductions. "John Spandau, senior corrections officer. This is Detective Lieutenant D'Agosta of the NYPD."

"Lieutenant." Spandau shook D'Agosta's hand in turn and they started down the corridor.

"As I mentioned on the phone last night," Pendergast told Spandau, "the prisoner is also the suspect in a recent murder in New York that the lieutenant is investigating." They paused to pass through another security checkpoint. "The lieutenant would like to question him first."

"Very well. I told you he was talking, but he isn't making much sense," said Spandau.

"Anything else of note?"

"He's gotten restless. Pacing his cell all night. Not eating."

D'Agosta was ushered into a typical interrogation room. Pendergast and Spandau left to take up positions in an adjoining space that overlooked the room through one-way glass.

D'Agosta waited, standing. A few minutes later, the security bolt was drawn back and the door opened. Two security guards entered, a man in a prison jumpsuit between them. He had a cast on one wrist. D'Agosta waited as the guards sat him down in the lone chair on the table's far side, then took up positions beside the door.

He turned his attention to the man across the table. He was

well built, and of course the face was familiar. This man did not look particularly like a criminal, but that didn't surprise D'Agosta: the man had had the stones to pose as a scientist, and had done so convincingly enough to fool Marsala. That took both intelligence and self-confidence. But the look was oddly offset by the man's facial expression. The charismatic features so recognizable from Bonomo's reconstruction seemed to be compromised by some kind of mysterious inner dialogue. His red-rimmed eyes drifted around the room—sluggishly, like an addict's—without settling on the man across from him. His manacled hands were crossed protectively over his chest. D'Agosta noticed he was rocking back and forth in his chair, ever so faintly.

"I'm Lieutenant Vincent D'Agosta, NYPD homicide," D'Agosta began, pulling out his notebook and placing it before him. The man had already been Mirandized, so he didn't need to go through all that. "This interview is being recorded. Would you mind stating your name, for the record?"

The man said nothing, merely rocking subtly back and forth. His eyes were looking around with more purpose now, the brows furrowed, as if searching for something forgotten—or, perhaps, lost.

"Excuse me, hello?" D'Agosta tried to get his attention.

The man's eyes finally settled on him.

"I'd like to ask you some questions about a homicide that took place two weeks ago in the New York Museum of Natural History."

The man looked at him placidly, then his eyes drifted away.

"When were you last in New York?"

"The lilies," the man replied. His voice was surprisingly high and musical for such a large man.

"What lilies?"

"The lilies," the man said in a tone of wistfulness combined with pained reverie.

"What about the lilies?"

"The *lilies*," the man said, his eyes snapping back to D'Agosta, startling him.

This was nuts. "Does the name Jonathan Waldron ring a bell?"

"The smell," the man said, the wistful tone in his voice increasing. "That lovely smell, the scent of lilies. It's gone. Now...it smells terrible. *Awful*."

D'Agosta stared at the man. Was he faking? "We know you stole the identity of Professor Jonathan Waldron to gain access to a skeleton in the Museum of Natural History. You worked with a technician in the Osteology Department of the Museum by the name of Victor Marsala."

The man went abruptly silent.

D'Agosta leaned forward, clasped his hands together. "I'm going to get to the point. I think you killed Victor Marsala."

The rocking stopped. The man's eyes drifted away from D'Agosta.

"In fact, I *know* you killed him. And now that we've got your DNA, we're going to look for a match with DNA from the crime scene. And we're going to find it."

Silence.

"What'd you do with the leg bone you stole?"

Silence.

"You know what I think? I think you'd better get yourself an attorney, pronto."

The man had gone still as a statue. D'Agosta took a deep breath.

"Listen," he said, increasing the menacing tone. "You're being held here because you assaulted a federal officer. That's bad enough. But *I'm* here because the NYPD are going to extradite you to the fine Empire State for murder one. We've got eyewitnesses. We've got you on video. If you don't start cooperating, you're going to be so far up shit creek that not even Lewis and Clark could paddle you back. Last chance."

The man was now looking around the room as if he'd forgotten D'Agosta was even there.

A great weariness settled over D'Agosta. He hated interrogations like this, with the repeated questions and mulish suspects—and this guy seemed loony, to boot. He was sure they had their man—they were just going to have to build the case without a confession.

The door slid open, and D'Agosta looked up to see the dark figure of Pendergast standing in the hallway. He gave a gesture as if to say: *Mind if I try?*

D'Agosta picked up his notebook and stood up. *Sure*, his answering shrug said, *knock yourself out.*

He went into the observation room next door and took a seat beside Spandau. He watched as Pendergast made himself comfortable in one of the chairs opposite the suspect. He seemed to spend an interminable amount of time adjusting his tie, buttoning his jacket, examining his cufflinks, adjusting his collar. At last, he sat forward, elbows on the desk, fingertips resting lightly on the scuffed wood. For a moment the fingertips drummed a nervous tattoo, then—as if recollecting himself—he curled them into his palms. He stared across the table, gaze resting lightly on his attacker. And then—just when D'Agosta thought he would burst from pent-up impatience—Pendergast began to speak in his dulcet, gracious accent.

"In the parts I come from, it is seen as unbearably rude not to refer to somebody by his proper name," he began. "The last time we met, you seemed unwilling to supply that name—a name that I know is not Waldron. Have you changed your mind?"

The man looked back at him but did not reply.

"Very well. Since I abhor rudeness, I shall confer on you a name of my choosing. I shall call you Nemo, which, as you may know, is Latin for 'no one.'"

This did not elicit any result.

"I don't wish to waste as much time on this visit as I did on my last, Mr. Nemo. So let us be brief. Are you willing to tell me who hired you?"

Silence.

"Are you willing to tell me why you were hired, or the purpose of that bizarre trap?"

Silence.

"If you do not wish to provide names, are you at least willing to tell me what the intended outcome of all this was to be?"

Silence.

Pendergast examined his gold watch with an idle gesture. "I hold the key to whether you will be tried in state or federal court. By talking or not talking to me, you can choose between Rikers Island or the Florence Administrative Maximum Facility in Colorado. Rikers is a hell on earth. ADX Florence is a hell that not even Dante could have imagined." He peered at the man with a peculiar intensity. "The furniture in each cell is made of poured concrete. The shower is on a timer. It goes off three times a week, at five AM, for exactly three minutes. From the window, you can see only cement and sky. You get one hour of 'exercise' a day in a concrete pit. ADX Florence has fourteen hundred remote-controlled steel doors and is surrounded by pressure pads and multiple rings of twelve-foot razor-wire fences. There your very existence will vanish from the tablets of history. If you don't talk to me right now, you truly will become 'no one.'"

Pendergast stopped speaking. The man shifted in his seat. D'Agosta, watching through the one-way glass, was now convinced the guy was crazy. No sane man could have resisted that line of questioning.

"There are no lilies in ADX Florence," Pendergast said quietly.

D'Agosta exchanged a puzzled glance with Spandau.

"Lilies," the man said, slowly, as if tasting the word.

"Yes. Lilies. Such a lovely flower, don't you think? With such a delicate, exquisite aroma."

The man hunched forward. Pendergast had finally gotten his attention.

"But then, the scent is gone, isn't it?"

The man seemed to tense. He shook his head slowly, from side to side.

"No—I'm wrong. The lilies are still there; you said as much. But something's wrong with them. They've gone off."

"They stink," the man muttered.

"Yes," Pendergast said, his voice a curious mixture of empathy and mockery. "Nothing smells worse than a rotting flower. What a stench it produces!"

Pendergast had suddenly raised his voice.

"*Get it out of my nose!*" the man screamed.

"I can't do that," Pendergast said, his voice abruptly dropping to a whisper. "You won't have lilies in your cell at ADX Florence. But the stink will remain. And it will grow as the rottenness increases. Until you—"

With a sudden, animal cry, the man leapt out of his chair and across the table at Pendergast, his cuffed hands like talons, his eyes wide with murderous fury, flecks of foam and spittle flying from his mouth as he screeched. With a swift dodge, like a bullfighter, Pendergast rose out of his chair and sidestepped the attack; the two guards came forward, Tasers at the ready, and zapped the man. It took three shots to subdue him. In the end he lay draped across the table, twitching spasmodically, tiny wisps of smoke rising toward the microphone and ceiling lights. Pendergast stood to one side, examining the man with a clinical eye, then turned and strolled out of the room.

A moment later Pendergast entered the observation room, flicking a piece of lint off the shoulder of his suit with a look of irritation. "Well, Vincent," he said. "I don't see much point in our remaining here any longer. What is the expression? I'm afraid our friend is, ah, 'bird-shit' crazy?"

"Bat-shit crazy."

"Thank you." He turned to Spandau. "Once again, Mr. Spandau, I thank you for your invaluable assistance. Please let me know if his ravings grow lucid."

Spandau shook the proffered hand. "I will."

As the two left the prison, Pendergast took out his cell phone and began to dial. "I'd worried we might have to take the red-eye back to New York," he said. "But our friend proved so unforthcoming we may catch an earlier flight. I'll just check, if you don't mind. We aren't going to get anything else out of him now—or, I fear, ever."

D'Agosta took a deep breath. "Mind telling me what the hell just happened in there?"

"What do you mean?"

"All those crazy questions. About flowers, lilies. How'd you know he'd react that way?"

Pendergast stopped dialing and lowered the phone. "It was an educated guess."

"Yeah, but *how*?"

There was a pause before Pendergast replied. When he did, it was in a low tone indeed. "Because, my dear Vincent, our prisoner is not the only one who has begun smelling flowers of late."

32

Pendergast slipped into the music room of the Riverside Drive mansion so abruptly that Constance, startled, stopped playing the harpsichord. She stopped to watch as he made his way to the sideboard, put down a large sheaf of papers, removed a bulbous glass, poured himself a large measure of absinthe, fitted a slotted spoon over the glass, placed a cube of sugar within, dribbled ice water over it from a carafe, and then picked up the papers and went straight to one of the leather armchairs.

"Don't stop playing on my account," he said.

Constance, taken aback by his terse tone, resumed playing the Scarlatti sonata. Even though she could only see him out of the corner of her eye, she sensed something was amiss. He took a hasty gulp of the absinthe and placed the glass down with a rattle, then took another, downing a good portion of the drink. One foot tapped against the Persian carpet, unevenly, out of time with the music. He leafed through the papers—which appeared to be an extensive assortment of old scientific treatises, medical journals, and news clippings—before putting them aside. On his third gulp of the drink, Constance stopped playing—it was a fiendishly difficult piece, and demanded absolute concentration—and turned to face him.

"I assume the trip to Indio was a disappointment," she said.

Pendergast, who was staring now at one of the framed holographs, nodded without looking at her.

"The man remained silent?"

"On the contrary, he was most prolix."

Constance smoothed down her skirt front. "And?"

"It was all gibberish."

"What did he say, exactly?"

"As I said, gibberish."

Constance folded her arms. "I would like to know exactly what he said."

Pendergast turned to her, his pale eyes narrowing. "You're rather insistent this evening."

Constance waited.

"The man spoke of flowers."

"Lilies, by any chance?"

A hesitation. "Yes. As I have repeatedly said, it was meaningless rubbish."

Again, Constance fell silent. Neither spoke for several minutes. Pendergast continued to play with his glass, finished it off, rose, and returned to the side table. He reached for the absinthe bottle again.

"Aloysius," she began. "The man may have spoken rubbish—but it was not meaningless rubbish."

Ignoring her, Pendergast began preparations for a second drink.

"There's something I need to talk to you about—a matter of some delicacy."

"Well, pray be about it, then," Pendergast said, pouring the absinthe into the reservoir at the bottom of the glass and placing the slotted spoon on top.

"Where's the bloody sugar?" he muttered to himself.

"I've been researching your family history. During our meeting in the gun room yesterday the name of a Dr. Evans Padgett came up. Are you familiar with that name?"

Pendergast placed the cube and began dribbling the ice water. "I'm not fond of drama. Out with it."

"Dr. Padgett's wife was poisoned by your great-great-grandfather's elixir. The man in the Indio jail is suffering from the same symptoms as Padgett's wife—and as everyone else who took Hezekiah's patent medicine."

Pendergast gripped the absinthe glass and took a long drink.

"The person who apparently murdered the Osteological technician at the Museum—and who attacked you—stole a long bone from Padgett's wife. Why? Perhaps because he was working for someone who was trying to reconstruct the elixir. Clearly, there must have been residues in the bone."

"What rot," said Pendergast.

"I fear not. My research into the elixir has been thorough. All the victims spoke of smelling lilies at first—that was part of the elixir's sales pitch. When they first began taking the elixir, the smell was fleeting, accompanied by a feeling of well-being and mental alertness. With time, the scent became constant. Heavier. With additional doses of elixir, the smell of lilies began to go off, as if they were rotting. The victim became irritable, restless, unable to sleep. The feeling of well-being was replaced by anxiety and manic behavior, with periods of sudden listlessness. At this point, additional doses of the elixir were useless—in fact, they only served to accelerate the victim's suffering. Ungovernable rages became common, interspersed with periods of extreme lethargy. And then the pain set in: headaches and joint pain, until it became almost impossible to move without excruciating suffering. In—" Constance hesitated. "In the end, death was a release."

As she was speaking, Pendergast put down the glass and stood up. He began pacing about the room. "I'm well aware of my ancestor's wrongdoing."

"There's another thing: the elixir was administered in vapor form. You didn't take it as pills or drops. It had to be inhaled."

More pacing.

"Surely you can see where this is headed," said Constance.

Pendergast brushed this away with a dismissive gesture.

"Aloysius, for God's sake, you've been poisoned with the elixir. Not only that—but by what was evidently a very concentrated dose!"

"You are growing shrill, Constance."

"Have you begun to smell lilies?"

"It is a common enough flower."

"After our conference yesterday, I asked Margo to do a follow-up investigation. She discovered that somebody—no doubt using a false name—did research into Hezekiah's elixir at both the New York Public Library and the New-York Historical Society."

Pendergast halted. He sat back down in the armchair and picked up his glass. Leaning back in the chair, he took a quick swig before setting it down.

"Forgive my being blunt. But somebody has taken revenge on you for your ancestor's sins."

Pendergast did not seem to hear. He tossed the last of the absinthe down and began to prepare another one.

"You've got to get help now, or you'll end up like that man in California."

"There is no *help* for me," said Pendergast with sudden savagery, "save what I can do for myself. And I will thank you not to interfere with my investigations."

Constance rose from the piano bench and took a step toward him. "Dear Aloysius. Not so long ago, in this very room, you called me your oracle. Allow me to play that part. You're growing ill. I can see it. We can help you—all of us. Self-delusion will be fatal—"

"Self-delusion?" Pendergast issued a peal of harsh laughter. "There's no self-delusion here! I'm acutely aware of my condition. Don't you think I've tried my utmost to find a way to remedy the situation?" He snatched up the pile of papers and dashed them into a corner of the room. "If my ancestor Hezekiah, whose own wife was dying as a result of his elixir, could not find a cure ... then how can I? What I cannot abide is your meddling. It's true, I did call you my oracle. But now you're becoming my albatross. You're a woman with an idée fixe, as you demonstrated so dramatically when you precipitated your late paramour into the Stromboli volcano."

A change came over Constance. Her body went rigid. Her fingers flexed—once only. Sparks flashed in her violet eyes. The very air darkened around her. The change was so abrupt, and with such an undercurrent of menace, that Pendergast, in raising his glass for another sip, was startled and inadvertently jostled his arm, slopping the drink onto his hand.

"If any other man were to have said that to me," she told him in a low voice, "he would not live out this night." Then she pivoted on her heel and left the room.

33

There's someone to see you, Lieutenant."

Peter Angler, looking up from the pile of printouts that sat on his desk, raised an inquiring eyebrow at his assistant, Sergeant Slade, who stood in the doorway.

"Who is it?"

"The prodigal son," Slade said with a thin smile as he stepped aside. A moment later, the lean, ascetic form of Special Agent Pendergast appeared in the doorway.

Angler did a good job of concealing his surprise. Wordlessly, he motioned Pendergast to a chair. There was a different look to the man today, Angler sensed; he wasn't quite sure what it was, but he thought it had to do with the cast of the man's eyes, which seemed unusually bright in what was otherwise a pallid face.

He leaned back in his chair, away from the printouts. He'd done enough wooing of this man; he would let the FBI agent speak first.

"I wanted to congratulate you, Lieutenant, on your inspired discovery," Pendergast began. "It would never have occurred to me to search for an anagram of my son's name in the passenger manifests from Brazil. It was just like Alban to make a game of it."

Of course it wouldn't, Angler thought; that was not the way Pendergast's mind worked. He wondered, idly, if Alban Pendergast had perhaps been more intelligent than his father.

"I find myself curious," Pendergast went on. "What day did Alban fly into New York, exactly?"

"It was June fourth," Angler replied. "On an Air Brazil flight from Rio."

"June fourth," Pendergast repeated, almost to himself. "A week before he was murdered." He glanced back at Angler. "Naturally, once you had found the anagram, you went back and checked earlier manifests?"

"Naturally."

"And did you find anything else?"

For a moment, Angler considered being evasive and giving Pendergast a taste of his own medicine. But he wasn't that kind of a cop. "Not yet. That investigation is still ongoing. There are a huge number of manifests to check, and not all of them—especially the foreign airlines—are as in order as one might wish."

"I see." Pendergast seemed to ponder something for a moment. "Lieutenant, I wish to apologize for, ah, being less forthcoming on past occasions than perhaps I should have been. At the time, I felt that I might make more progress on my son's murder if I pursued the case on my own."

In other words, you figured me for the bumbling idiot you presume most of the force to be, Angler thought.

"In that I may have been mistaken. And so in order to rectify the situation, I wanted to place before you the facts to date—as far as I know them."

Angler made a slight gesture with his hand, turning his palm up, asking Pendergast to proceed. In the shadows at the rear of the office, Sergeant Slade remained standing—perfectly silent, as was his wont—taking everything in.

Pendergast briefly and succinctly recited to Angler the story of the turquoise mine, the ambush, and its link to the murder of the technician at the Museum of Natural History. Angler listened with growing surprise and irritation, even anger, at all that Pendergast had withheld. At the same time, the information might be very useful. It would open the case up to fresh lines of investigation—that is, if it could be relied upon. Angler listened impassively, taking care not to betray any reaction.

Pendergast finished his story and fell silent, looking at Angler, as if expecting a reply. Angler gave him none.

After a long moment, Pendergast rose. "In any case, Lieutenant, that is the progress of the case, or cases, to date. I offer this to you in the spirit of cooperation. If I can help in any other way, I hope you'll let me know."

Now at last Angler shifted in his chair. "Thank you, Agent Pendergast. We will."

Pendergast nodded courteously and left the office.

Angler sat in his chair, leaning away from the desk, for a moment. Then he turned to Slade and gestured for him to come forward. Sergeant Slade shut the door and took the chair vacated by Pendergast.

Angler regarded Slade for a moment. He was short, dark, and saturnine, and an exceptionally shrewd judge of human nature. He was also the most cynical man Angler had ever known—all of which made him an exceptional counselor.

"What do you think?" he asked.

"I can't believe the son of a bitch held out on us like that."

"Yes. So why this, now? Why, after doing his best to give me only the merest scraps of information—why come here on his own volition and spill all his secrets?"

"Two possibilities," Slade said. "A, he wants something."

"And B?"

"He isn't."

"Isn't what?"

"Isn't spilling all his secrets."

Angler chuckled. "Sergeant, I like the way your mind works." He paused. "It's too pat. This sudden volte-face, this open and apparently friendly offer of cooperation—and this story about a turquoise mine, a trap, and a mysterious assailant."

"Don't get me wrong," said Slade, popping a piece of licorice toffee into his mouth—he was never without a pocketful—and tossing the crumpled wrapper into the garbage can. "I believe his story, as cockamamie as it sounds. It's just there's more that he isn't saying."

Angler looked down at his desk and thought for a moment. Then he glanced back up. "So what does he want?"

"He's fishing. Wants to know what we've uncovered about his son's movements."

"Which means he doesn't already know everything about his son's movements."

"Or maybe he does. And by pretending to show an interest, he wants to point us in the wrong direction." Slade smiled crookedly as he chewed.

Angler sat forward, pulled a sheet of paper toward him, scribbled a few notations in shorthand. He liked shorthand not only because it was quick, but because it had fallen into such disuse that it made his notes almost as secure as if they had been encrypted. Then he pushed the sheet away again.

"I'll send a team to California to check out this mine and interview the man in the Indio jail. I'll also call D'Agosta and get all the case files on his Museum investigation. In the meantime, I want you to quietly—*quietly*—dig up everything on Pendergast you can find. History, his record of arrests and convictions, commendations, censures—whatever. You've got some FBI buddies. Take them out for drinks. Don't ignore the rumors. I want to know this man inside and out."

Slade gave a slow smile. This was the kind of job he liked. Without another word, he stood up and slipped out the door.

Angler sat back in his chair again, put his hands behind his head, and gazed up at the ceiling. He mentally reviewed all his previous dealings with Pendergast: the initial meeting in this very office, where Pendergast had been so remarkable in his lack of cooperation; the autopsy; the later encounter in the evidence room, where Pendergast had, perversely, seemed to show little or no interest in the hunt for his son's murderer; and now once again in this office, where Pendergast had abruptly become the soul of forthrightness. This sudden reversal smacked to Angler of a common theme in many of the Greek myths he knew so well: betrayal. Atreus and Thyestes. Agamemnon and Clytemnestra. And now, as he stared at the ceiling, he realized that—while over the past weeks he had felt irritation and doubt toward Pendergast—all that time, another emotion had been slowly developing within him:

Dark suspicion.

34

In a dun-colored room on the top floor of the U.S. consulate in Rio de Janeiro, Special Agent Pendergast paced restlessly. The room was small and spartan, containing only a single desk, a few chairs, and the obligatory photos of the president, vice president, and secretary of state, all lined up neatly on one of the walls. The air conditioner wheezed and shuddered in the window. The flight from New York, and the rushed arrangements that made it possible, had tired him, and now and then he paused to grasp the back of a chair and take a few deep breaths. Then he would resume his pacing, occasionally glancing out the room's single window, which looked down upon a hillside crowded with uncountable ramshackle structures, their roofs an identical beige but the walls a riot of conflicting colors, bright in the morning sun. Beyond lay the glittering waters of Guanabara Bay and, beyond that, Sugarloaf.

The door opened and two figures walked in. The first was the man he recognized as the CIA agent from Sector Y, wearing a muted business suit. He was accompanied by a shorter, heavyset man wearing a uniform sporting a variety of epaulets, badges, and medals.

The CIA agent gave no appearance of ever having met Pendergast before. He walked up to him, hand extended. "I'm Charles Smith, assistant to the consul-general, and this is Colonel Azevedo of ABIN, the Brazilian Intelligence Agency."

Pendergast shook both their hands, then the men all took seats. Pendergast had not offered his own credentials. He apparently did not need to. He observed Smith glancing over the desktop as if he was unfamiliar with it. He may well have been; he wondered how long ago the man had taken this undercover assignment.

"Being somewhat familiar with your situation," Smith said, "I asked Colonel Azevedo to kindly put himself at our disposal."

Pendergast nodded his thanks. "I am here," Pendergast told them, "concerning Operation Wildfire."

"Of course," Smith said. "Perhaps you might fill in Colonel Azevedo on the details."

Pendergast turned to the colonel. "The purpose of Operation Wildfire was to use both American and foreign assets to watch for any sign of the reemergence of a person of interest to Langley—and to myself personally—who disappeared in the Brazilian jungle eighteen months ago."

Azevedo nodded.

"The murdered corpse of this same person appeared two weeks ago on my doorstep in New York. A message had been sent. I'm here to find out who sent the message, why it was sent, and what the message is."

Azevedo looked surprised; Smith did not.

"This man flew from Rio to New York, using a false passport issued by Brazil, on June fourth," Pendergast continued. "He was using the name of Tapanes Landberg. Is that name familiar to you, Colonel?"

The man indicated it was not.

"I need to trace his movements here over the last year and a half." Pendergast passed the back of a hand across his forehead. "Many manhours, and a great detail of classified technology, went into the search for this person. And yet Operation Wildfire scored no hits—not one. How is such a thing possible? How could this man have evaded detection here in Brazil over the course of eighteen months—or at least for the time he was here?"

Colonel Azevedo finally spoke. "Such a thing is possible." Considering his brawn, the man's voice was mild, almost soft, and he spoke perfect, almost accent-less English. "If we assume this man has been in Brazil—a likely possibility, given what you say—there are only two places he could have hidden: the jungle . . . or a *favela*."

"*Favela*," Pendergast repeated.

"Yes, *Senhor* Pendergast. You have heard of them? They are one of our great social problems. Or rather, social plagues. Fortified slums, run by drug dealers and sealed off from the rest of the city. They pirate water and electricity from the grid, make their own laws, enforce their own iron discipline, protect their borders, kill rival gang members, oppress their occupants. They are like corrupt, petty fiefdoms, states within a state. In a *favela*, there are no police, no security cameras. A man who needed to could disappear in there—and many men have. Until a few years ago, there were countless *favelas* scattered around Rio. But now, with the Olympics coming, the government has begun to act. BOPE and the Unidade de Polícia Pacificadora have begun invading the *favelas*, and—one by one—are pacifying them. This work will continue until all the *favelas* have been dealt with." Azevedo paused. "All but one, that is—one that neither the military nor the UPP will touch. It is named Cidade dos Anjos—City of Angels."

"And why will it receive special treatment?"

The colonel smiled grimly "It is the largest, most violent, and most powerful of all the *favelas*. The drug lords who lead it are ruthless and fearless. More to the point: the year before last, they invaded a military base and made off with thousands of weapons and ammunition. Fifty-caliber machine guns, grenades, RPGs, mortars, rocket launchers—even surface-to-air missiles."

Pendergast frowned. "That would seem all the more reason to clear it out."

"You are looking on the situation as an outsider. The *favelas* only make war on each other—not on the general populace. To invade the Cidade dos Anjos now would be a bloody, bloody business, with great loss of life to our military and police. No other *favela* will challenge them. And in time, all the other *favelas* will be gone. So why disturb the natural order of things? Better the enemy that you know than the enemy you don't."

"This person of interest vanished into the jungle eighteen months ago," Pendergast said. "But I doubt he would have stayed there long."

"Well then, Mr. Pendergast," the CIA agent said. "It appears we have one possible answer to how your Mr. Tapanes Landberg maintained his invisibility." This was followed by a faint smile.

Pendergast rose from his chair. "Thank you both."

Colonel Azevedo looked at him appraisingly. "*Senhor* Pendergast, I fear to speculate what your next move will be."

"My diplomatic brief disallows me from accompanying you," the CIA agent said.

To this, Pendergast simply nodded, then turned toward the door.

"If it were any other place, we would assign you a military escort," the colonel said. "But not if you go in there. All I can offer you is advice: settle your affairs before you enter."

35

Pendergast lay, fully dressed, on the king-size bed in his suite of rooms in the Copacabana Palace Hotel. The lights were off and, although it was just noon, the room was very dark. The faintest roar of surf from Copacabana Beach filtered through the closed windows and shuttered blinds.

As he lay there, quite still, a trembling washed over him, almost a palsy, that shook his frame with increasing violence. He squeezed his eyes tightly shut and balled his hands into fists, trying through sheer force of will to make this sudden, unexpected attack pass. After a few minutes the worst of the trembling began to lessen. It did not, however, go entirely away.

"I will master this," Pendergast murmured under his breath.

At first—when he'd initially noted the symptoms—Pendergast had held out hope that a way could be found to reverse them. When he found no answer in the past, he began searching the present, in the hope of uncovering the methods of his tormentor. But the more he comprehended the diabolical complexity of the plot to poison him, and the more he reflected on the story of his ancestor Hezekiah and his doomed wife, the more he had realized such hope was a cruel delusion. What drove him forward now was a burning need to see this investigation—which seemed ever more likely to be his final investigation—through . . . while he still had time.

He forced his thoughts back to that morning's meeting—and the words of the Brazilian colonel. *There are only two places he could have hidden,* he'd said of Alban. *The jungle . . . or a favela.*

Other words came into Pendergast's head, unbidden. They were the parting words Alban had given him—on that day, eighteen months ago, when he had walked, with an almost insolent lack of hurry, into the Brazilian forest. *I have a long and productive life ahead of me. The world is now my oyster—and I promise you it'll be a more interesting place with me in it.*

Pendergast held the image of that parting in his head, recalling every detail to the utmost extent of his intellectual rigor.

He knew, of course, that his son had begun those eighteen months in the jungles of Brazil—he'd seen him melt into the unbroken line of trees with his own eyes. But as he'd told the colonel, he was also certain that Alban would not have stayed there. There would not have been enough to occupy him, to keep him entertained—and, most important, to allow him to plan his various schemes. He had not returned to the town of his birth, Nova Godói—that was now in the hands of the Brazilian government, under a kind of military receivership. Besides, nothing was left for Alban there anymore: the complex had been destroyed, its scientists and soldiers and young leaders now dead, in prison, rehabilitated, or scattered to the winds. No—the more Pendergast considered the matter, the more certain he was that, sooner rather than later, Alban would have emerged from the jungle—and slipped into a *favela.*

It would be the perfect place for him. No police to worry about, no security cameras, no surveillance or intelligence operatives shadowing him. With his keen intelligence, criminal genius, and sociopathic outlook, he might well have something to offer the drug lords who ran the *favela.* All this would give Alban the time and space he needed to develop his plans for the future.

The world is now my oyster—and I promise you it'll be a more interesting place with me in it.

Pendergast was equally certain which *favela* Alban would have chosen. Always the biggest and best for him.

But these answers simply led to other questions. What had happened to Alban within the City of Angels? What strange journey brought Alban from the *favela* to his doorstep? And what was the connection between him and the attack at the Salton Sea?

I fear to speculate what your next move will be. The next move was obvious, of course.

Pendergast took several deep, shuddering breaths. Then he raised himself from the bed and placed his feet on the floor. The room rocked around him and the trembling turned into a painful, racking muscle spasm that slowly released. He had begun taking a regimen of self-prescribed drugs, including atropine, chelators, and glucagon, along with painkillers to keep him going during the fits that were beginning to plague him on a steadily increasing basis. But he was shooting blindly in the dark—and so far they had done little good.

He felt his body preparing to spasm again. This would not do—not for what he had next in mind.

He waited until the second spasm was over, then made his way to a desk pushed against the far wall. His toilet kit and duty holster lay upon it, the latter containing his Les Baer .45. Next to it rested several spare magazines.

He sat down at the desk and pulled the weapon from its holster. He'd had no difficulty bringing it into Brazil; he'd checked in with the TSA at Kennedy Airport, following standard protocol, and he had carry permits for several foreign countries. It had not passed through a scanner; it had not been x-rayed.

Not that it would matter if it had.

Steadying his fingers, Pendergast lifted the gun and—reaching into the barrel—pulled out a small rubber plug with his fingernails. Upending the gun, he carefully let a miniature syringe and several hypodermic needles slide out of the barrel and onto the table. He fitted one of the needles to the syringe and placed it to one side.

Next, he turned his attention to one of the spare magazines. He removed the top round, and—taking a miniature set of pliers from his coat pocket—carefully pried the bullet from its casing. Spreading out a piece of writing paper from inside the desk, he carefully turned the casing over and let its contents drain onto the paper. Instead of gunpowder, a fine white powder streamed out.

Pendergast pushed the empty shell and useless round away with the back of his hand. Reaching for his toilet kit and pulling it toward him, he fumbled inside and pulled out two vials of prescription pills. One contained a schedule 2 semi-synthetic opioid used for relief of pain; the other, a muscle relaxant. Taking two pills from each bottle, he placed them on the sheet of paper and, using a spoon from a nearby room service tray, ground each into fine powder.

There were now three small mounds on the sheet of paper. Pendergast mixed them together carefully, scooped the powder into the spoon. Taking a lighter from his toilet kit, he held it beneath the spoon and flicked it into life. Under heat, the mixture began to darken, bubble, and liquefy.

Pendergast let the lighter drop to the desk and held the spoon with both hands as another painful spasm racked his body. He waited a minute, allowing the toxic, dangerous mixture to cool. Then he dipped the needle into the liquid and filled the syringe.

He let the empty spoon fall to the table with a quiet sigh; the hardest part was over. Now he reached one last time into his toilet kit and removed a length of elastic. Rolling back one sleeve, he tied the rubber around his upper arm, made a fist, pulled the rubber tight with his teeth.

A vein sprang into view in the inside of his elbow.

Holding the elastic carefully between his teeth, he lifted the syringe with his free hand. Timing his movements between the spasms of his limbs, he inserted the needle into the vein. He waited a moment, then parted his teeth slightly, releasing the elastic. Slowly, judiciously, he slid the plunger home.

He let his eyes drift shut and sat there for several minutes, the needle drooping from his arm. Then, opening his eyes again, he plucked out the syringe and put it aside. He took a shallow breath, cautiously, like a bather testing the temperature of water.

The pain was gone. The spasms had abated. He was weak, disoriented—but he could function.

Dreamily, like an old man awakened from sleep, he rose from the chair. Then he shrugged into his holster, put on his jacket. He carefully removed his FBI shield and ID and locked them in the in-room safe, keeping his passport and wallet. With a final glance around, he exited the hotel suite.

36

The entrance to the City of Angels lay at the end of a narrow dog-leg on a street in Rio's Zona Norte. At first glance, the *favela* beyond did not look much different from the neighboring region of Tijuca. It consisted of drab boxes of concrete, three and four stories tall, crammed tightly together, above a warren of streets almost medieval in their crookedness and complexity. The closest buildings were gray in color, but the colors changed to green and then to terra-cotta as the vast shantytown climbed the steep slopes stretching away to the north, trailing a thousand plumes of smoke from cooking fires, hazy and wavering in the hot sun. It was not until Pendergast noticed the two youths lounging on empty gasoline drums, wearing shorts and Havaianas flip-flops, machine guns slung over their bare shoulders—lookouts, checking everyone who came and went—that he realized he was at the gates into an entirely different part of Rio de Janeiro.

He paused in the alleyway, swaying ever so slightly. The drugs he had taken—while necessary for endurance—had dulled his mind and slowed his reaction time. In his condition, it would have been too risky to attempt a disguise. Pendergast could speak only a few words of Portuguese, and in any case he never would have been able to master the patois, which varied from *favela* to *favela*. If the drug dealers or their guards in the Cidade dos Anjos took him for an undercover cop, he would be immediately killed. His only option was no disguise at all: to stand out like a sore thumb.

He approached the youths, who watched him, unmoving, through slitted eyes. Overhead, the electrical wires and cable TV lines that crossed and recrossed the street were so dense they cast the street into perpetual gloom, sagging under their own weight like some huge and ominous web. It was oven-hot in the fetid street, the air stinking of garbage, dog feces, and acrid smoke. As he approached, the youths—while not rising from their perches on the gasoline drums—let their machine guns slide down off their shoulders and into their hands. Pendergast made no attempt to pass them, but instead walked up to the older of the two.

The boy—he couldn't have been more than sixteen—eyed the agent up and down with a combination of curiosity, hostility, and scorn. In the sweltering heat, wearing his black suit, white shirt, and silk tie, Pendergast looked like a visitor from another planet.

"Onde você vai, gringo?" he asked in a menacing tone. As he did so, the other youth—taller, with his head shaved bald—slid off his own drum, raising his machine gun and casually aiming it at Pendergast.

"Meu filho," Pendergast said. "My son."

The youth snickered and exchanged a glance with his compatriot. No doubt this was a common sight: the father looking for his wayward son. The shaved one appeared in favor of shooting Pendergast without asking any further questions. Instead, the shorter youth—who seemed nominally in charge—overruled this. With the barrel of his gun, he gestured for Pendergast to raise his hands. Pendergast complied, and the bald youth frisked him. His passport was removed, then his wallet. The small amount of money in the wallet was taken out and immediately divided. When the lookout found the Les Baer .45, an argument broke out. The shorter youth grabbed the gun from the bald one and shook it in Pendergast's face, asking angry questions in Portuguese.

Pendergast shrugged. *"Meu filho,"* he repeated.

The argument continued, and a small knot of curious onlookers gathered. It appeared as if the bald one would get his way, after all. Reaching into a secret inner pocket of his suit jacket, Pendergast extracted a wad of bills—one thousand reais—and offered it to the shorter lookout.

"*Meu filho,*" he said yet again, in a quiet, non-threatening voice.

The youth stared at the money, but did not take it.

Pendergast again reached into his pocket, drew out another thousand reais, and added it to the wad he was proffering. Two thousand reais—a thousand dollars—was a lot of money in a community such as this.

"*Por favor,*" he said, waving the money gently in front of the lookout. "*Deixe-me entrar.*"

With a sudden grimace, the youth snatched the money away. "*Porra,*" he muttered.

This elicited another outburst from his shaven-headed companion, who was evidently in favor of simply shooting Pendergast and taking the money. But the shorter one silenced him with a volley of curses. He handed the passport and wallet back to Pendergast, keeping the gun.

"*Sai da aqui,*" he said, waving Pendergast on dismissively. "*Fila da puta.*"

"*Obrigado.*" As Pendergast walked past the makeshift guard post he saw, out of the corner of his eye, the shaven-headed youth detach himself from the assembled group and disappear down a back alley.

Pendergast wandered up the central street of the *favela,* which quickly split into a confusing labyrinth of ever-narrower roads that crossed and recrossed, turned at odd angles, and—occasionally—dead-ended abruptly. People eyed him silently as he passed by, some with curiosity, others with suspicion. Now and then he stopped to ask someone, "*meu filho,*" but this was greeted with a quick, silent shake of the head and a hurrying past, as if to avoid the mutterings of a madman.

Working through the dullness of the drugs, Pendergast pushed his senses to take in everything. He needed to understand. The alleyways were relatively clean, with the occasional chicken or slinking, emaciated dog. Besides the two guards he saw no weapons, drug dealing, or open criminality. Indeed, the *favela* seemed to display more order than the city outside. The buildings were decorated in a wild profusion of garishly colored posters and handbills, much of it peeling off and fluttering. The sound was almost overwhelming. From open windows poured Brazilian funk music, conversation, or loud argument; the occasional expostulation of *"Caralho!"* or some other invective. The air smelled overpoweringly of frying meat. Mopeds and rusted bicycles passed by infrequently—there were almost no cars. At each intersection there was at least one *barzinho*—a corner bar with grubby plastic tables, a dozen men inside gathered around an ancient TV with bottles of Cerveja Skol in their hands, cheering on the inevitable soccer game. Their voices rose from every point when a goal was scored.

Pendergast stopped, took his bearings as best he could, then started climbing the mountain face that the Cidade dos Anjos was spread across. As he ascended the winding streets, the character of the buildings changed. The three-story concrete structures began being replaced by shacks and shantyhouses of remarkable decrepitude, slats and sections of wood wired or tied together and covered—if they were covered at all—with roofs of corrugated iron. Now garbage appeared, strewn about, and the smell of bad meat and rotting potatoes lingered in the air. Adjoining buildings leaned against each other, apparently for support. Laundry hung in every direction from an impossible tangle of crisscrossing lines, dangling limply in the tremendous heat. Passing a small, improvised soccer field in a vacant lot, surrounded by the remains of a chain-link fence, Pendergast could make out, far below, the stately outlines of the high-rise apartment buildings of Rio's Zona Norte. They were a mere mile or two away, but from his vantage point they could have been a thousand.

As the pitch grew steeper, the surrounding landscape changed to a confusing welter of terraces, rickety public staircases of badly poured concrete and wooden lathe, and narrow switchback lanes. Dirty children peered at him through barbed wire and broken slats. There was less music here, less shouting, less life. The stillness of poverty and despair infected the muggy air. Lashed-together structures rose up all around, each at its own level and angle, with seeming disregard to the surrounding buildings: a three-dimensional maze of back alleys and passageways and common spaces and tiny plazas. Still, Pendergast mumbled to all he passed the same pathetic phrase: *"Meu filho. Por favor. Meu filho."*

As he passed a small, grimy upholstery store, a dented and scarred Toyota Hilux four-door pickup stopped in front of him with a screech. It was barely narrower than the alleyway itself and effectively blocked his progress. While the driver stayed behind the wheel, three young men in khaki pants and brightly colored knit shirts burst out from the other three doors. Each carried an AR-15, and each had his weapon trained on Pendergast.

One of the men stepped quickly up to him while the other two held back. *"Pare!"* he demanded. "Stop!"

Pendergast stopped. There was a tense moment of stasis. Pendergast took a step forward, and one of the men stopped him with a rifle butt, pushing him back. The other two closed in, pointing their own weapons at Pendergast's head.

"Coloque suas maos no carro!" the first man yelled, spinning Pendergast around and pushing him against the pickup. While the other two covered him, the man frisked Pendergast for weapons. Then he opened the nearest rear door of the pickup.

"Entre," he said roughly.

When Pendergast did nothing but blink in the bright sunlight, the man took him by the shoulders and propelled him into the rear seat. The other two followed, one on each side, weapons still pointed. The first man slid into the front passenger seat; the driver put the pickup into gear, and they shot away down the dingy street, raising a cloud of dust that completely obscured their departure.

37

One of the duty cops stuck his head into D'Agosta's office. "Loo? You've got a call waiting. Somebody named Spandau."

"Can you take a message? I'm in the middle of something here."

"He says it's important."

D'Agosta looked over at Sergeant Slade, sitting in his visitor's chair. He was, if anything, grateful for the interruption. Slade, Angler's errand boy, had stopped in at Angler's request to "liaise" on their two cases, the Museum murder and the dead body on Pendergast's doorstep. Just how much Angler knew about what the two cases had in common, D'Agosta wasn't sure . . . the man was playing his cards close. And so was Slade. But they wanted copies of all the case files—everything—and they wanted them now. D'Agosta didn't like Slade . . . and it wasn't just the disgusting licorice toffee he was so fond of. For some reason, he reminded D'Agosta of the toady of a schoolboy who, if he saw you doing something wrong, would tell the teacher as a way of currying favor. But D'Agosta also knew Slade to be clever and resourceful, which only made it worse.

D'Agosta held the phone up. "Sorry. I'd better take this. Might be a while. I'll check in with you later."

Slade glanced at him, at the duty cop, and stood up. "Sure." He left the office, trailing an aroma of licorice behind him.

D'Agosta watched him walk away and lifted the phone to his ear. "What's going on? Has our boy recovered his marbles?"

"Not exactly," came Spandau's matter-of-fact tone down the line.

"What is it, then?"

"He's dead."

"*Dead?* How? I mean, the guy looked sick, but not *that* sick."

"One of the guards found him in his cell, not half an hour ago. Suicide."

Suicide. This case was a ball-buster. "Jesus, I can't believe this." Frustration put an edge to his voice that he didn't intend. "Didn't you have a suicide watch on him?"

"Of course. The full works: padded cell, leather restraints, fifteen-minute rotations. Just after the last check, he struggled out of the restraints—broke a collarbone in the process—bit off the big toe of his left foot, and then . . . choked on it."

For a moment, D'Agosta was shocked into silence.

"I tried calling Agent Pendergast," Spandau went on. "When I couldn't reach him, I called you."

It was true: Pendergast had vanished into thin air again. It was infuriating—but D'Agosta wasn't going to think about that now. "Okay. Did he ever get lucid?"

"Just the opposite. After you left, what little lucidity he had vanished. He kept raving, saying the same things over and over."

"What things?"

"You heard some of it. He kept mentioning a smell—rotting flowers. He stopped sleeping, was making a racket day and night. He'd been complaining about pain, too; not a localized pain, but something that seemed to affect his whole body. After you left, it grew worse. The prison doctor did some tests, administered meds, but nothing seemed to help. They couldn't diagnose it. In the last twenty-four hours, he really started to go downhill. Nonstop raving, moaning, crying. I was making arrangements to have him transferred to the facility hospital when word of his death reached me."

D'Agosta fetched a deep breath; let out a long, slow sigh.

"The autopsy is scheduled for later today. I'll send you the report when I get it. Is there anything else you'd like me to do?"

"If I think of something, I'll let you know." And as an after-thought: "Thanks."

"I'm sorry I didn't have better news for you." And the line went dead with a click.

D'Agosta leaned back in his chair. As he did so, his eyes moved slowly—unwillingly—to the stack of files that covered his desk, all of which had to be copied for Slade.

Great. Just frigging great.

38

The Hilux, horn blaring, forced its way through the twisting alley-ways of the *favela* like an elephant through a cane break. Sidewalk vendors had no choice but to retreat inside their building fronts; pedestrians and bicyclists either veered away down alleys or shrank into doorways. On more than one occasion, the rearview mirrors of the pickup scraped against buildings on either side. Pendergast's abductors said nothing, merely covering him with their AR-15s. Always the vehicle climbed, moving determinedly up the switch-backs, past the structures that spread across the flanks of the hillside like a multicolored fungus.

At last they stopped at a small compound at the very highest point of the *favela*. Yet another armed man rolled open an improvised chain-link gate, and the Hilux drove into a small parking area. All four men got out of the pickup. One of them gestured with his rifle for Pendergast to do the same.

The agent complied, blinking in the harsh sunlight. The seemingly endless cluster of ramshackle sheds and improvised houses sprawled down the hillside below, eventually yielding to the more orderly streets of Rio proper and, beyond, the sparkling azure of Guanabara Bay.

The compound consisted of three buildings, functionally iden-tical, different from the rest of the *favela* only in that they were in better repair. Several large, ragged holes in the central building had been patched over with cement and repainted. A generator stood in the courtyard, grinding away. At least a dozen cables of various colors looped overhead, fixed to various points on the roofs. Two of the men gestured for Pendergast to enter the central building.

The interior was dark, cool, and spartan. With the barrels of their semi-automatic weapons, the guards prodded him down a tiled corridor, up two flights of stairs, and into a large room that was clearly an office. Like the rest of the house, it was almost monastic in its lack of decor. There was a desk of some nondescript wood—flanked by more guards carrying more AR-15s—and a few hard wooden chairs. A crucifix hung on one of the painted cinder-block walls and a large flat-panel television on another. It was tuned to a soccer game, the sound muted.

Behind the desk sat a man perhaps thirty years old. He was dark-skinned, with unruly wavy hair and three days' growth of beard. He wore shorts, a tank top, and a pair of the ubiquitous Havaianas. A thick platinum chain hung around his neck, and a gold Rolex was strapped to one wrist. Despite the relative youth and informal dress, he radiated confidence and authority. As Pendergast entered, the man regarded him with glittering black eyes. He took a long pull from a bottle of Bohemia beer that sat on his desk. Then he turned to Pendergast's abductors and spoke to them in Portuguese. One of them frisked Pendergast, removed the wallet and passport, and laid them on the desk.

The man glanced at them without bothering to examine either. "*Pasporte.*" He frowned. "*Só isso?* That's all?"

"*Sim.*"

Pendergast was searched again, more thoroughly this time. The remainder of the wad of reais was recovered and placed on the desk in turn. But when they were done, Pendergast indicated with his chin something they'd missed in the hem of his jacket.

They searched it, found the crackle of a folded piece of paper. With a curse, one of them opened a flick knife and cut open the hem, removing a photograph. It was one taken of Alban after his death, retouched slightly to make it more life-like. They spread it open and laid it on the desk, next to the wallet and passport.

When the man saw the photograph, his entire expression changed from one of irritated boredom to shock and surprise. He snatched up the photograph and stared at it.

"*Meu filho,*" Pendergast repeated.

The man stared at him, stared at the photo, stared back at him with a searching expression. Only now did he pick up the other objects, first the passport, then the wallet, and examined each one carefully. At last, he turned to one of the guards. "*Guarda a porta,*" he said. "*Niguen pode entrar.*"

The guard walked over to the office door, shut and locked it, then stood before it, weapon at the ready.

The man behind the desk looked up at Pendergast again. "So," he said in accented but excellent English. "You are the man who fearlessly enters the Cidade dos Anjos dressed like an undertaker, carrying a gun, and wandering about telling everyone that you are looking for your son."

Pendergast did not reply. He merely stood before the desk, swaying slightly.

"I am amazed you survived. Perhaps because it was such a crazy thing to do, they assumed you were harmless. Now—" he tapped the photograph—"I realize you are anything but harmless."

The man picked up the passport and the photograph and stood up. A large handgun could be seen shoved into the waistband of his shorts. He came around the desk and placed himself directly before Pendergast.

"You don't look well, *cada,*" he said, apparently taking note of Pendergast's pallor, the beading of sweat on his temples. He took another look at the passport and the photograph. "Nevertheless, a remarkable resemblance," he said more to himself than to anyone else.

A minute passed in silence.

"When did you last see your son?" he asked.

"Two weeks ago," Pendergast replied.

"Where?"

"Dead. On my doorstep."

A look of shock, or pain, or perhaps both, briefly distorted the young man's expression. Another minute passed before he spoke again. "And why are you here?"

A pause. "To find out who killed him."

The man nodded. This was a motive he could understand. "And that is why you wander our *favela*, asking everyone about him?"

Pendergast passed a hand over his eyes. The drugs were starting to wear off, and the pain was returning. "Yes. I need to . . . know what he was doing here."

The room fell into a silence. Finally, the man sighed. *"Caralho,"* he muttered.

Pendergast said nothing.

"And you seek revenge on his killer?"

"I only seek information. What happens after that . . . I don't know."

The man seemed to consider this a moment. Then he gestured toward one of the chairs. "Please. Take a seat."

Pendergast sank into the nearest chair.

"My name is Fábio," the man continued. "When my scouts reported that a strange man had come into my city, mumbling about his son, I thought little of it. But when they described a man tall of carriage, hands like nervous white spiders, skin as pale as marble, eyes like silver conchas—I had to wonder. And yet how could I be sure? I apologize for the manner in which you were brought to this place, but . . ." He shrugged. Then he stared sharply at Pendergast. "What you say—it is really true? It is hard to believe a person such as him could be murdered."

Pendergast nodded.

"Then it is as he feared," the man named Fábio said.

Pendergast looked across the desk. He knew that this was precisely how the drug lords of Rio dressed; how they lived; how they were armed. He struggled to recall the words of Colonel Azevedo: *The Cidade dos Anjos is the largest, most violent, and most powerful of the favelas. The drug lords who lead it are not only ruthless, but fearless.*

"All I want is information," said Pendergast.

"And you shall have it. In fact, it is my duty to give it to you. I will tell you the story. The story of your son. Alban."

39

Taking a seat again behind his desk, Fábio drained his bottle of Bohemia and placed it to one side. It was immediately replaced with a fresh one. He picked up the photograph from the desk, touching it lightly with his fingertips in a gesture that was almost a caress. Then he put it back and looked up at Pendergast.

Pendergast nodded.

"Prior to his death, when did you last see your son alive?"

"Eighteen months ago, in Nova Godói. He disappeared into the jungle."

"Then I will begin the story at that point. At first, your son—Alban—lived with a small tribe of Indians, deep in the Amazon rain forest. It was a difficult time for him, and he spent it recovering, and—what is the word?—regrouping. He had plans for himself; plans for the world. And plans for you, *rapiz*." At this, Fábio nodded significantly.

"It did not take Alban long to understand he could not further his plans from the middle of the jungle. He came to Rio and quickly melted into our *favela*. This he accomplished with no difficulty. You know as well as I, *o senhor*, he is—was—a master of disguise and deception. And he spoke perfect Portuguese as well as many dialects. There are hundreds of *favelas* in Rio, and he chose his well. A perfect place to find shelter, without fear of discovery."

"The Cidade dos Anjos," Pendergast said.

Fábio smiled. "Correct, *rapiz*. It was a different place then. He killed someone here—a drifter, a loner—and stole his home and identity. He turned himself into a Brazilian citizen named Adler, twenty-one years old, and he fit himself into the life of the *favela* with ease."

"That sounds like Alban," Pendergast said.

For a moment, Fábio's eyes flashed. "Do not judge him, *cada*, until you have heard his story. Until you have lived in a place like this." And he stretched out one arm as if to encompass the entire *favela*. "He took on an occupation—that of importer-exporter—that would give him reason to travel the world."

He twisted the top off the bottle of beer, took a pull. "At that time, the City of Angels was run by a gangster known as O Punho—The Fist—and his posse. O Punho got his nickname from the very personal and brutal ways he used to kill his enemies. Alban—Adler—was unimpressed by O Punho and his gang. Their disorganized ways of doing business were contrary to the sense of order that had been bred into him. Bred almost from birth. Correct, *senhor*?" And he gave Pendergast a knowing smile.

"Adler amused himself by considering how he would be much better at organizing and running the *favela* if he were in command. But he took no action then, as he had other, more pressing things on his mind. And then everything changed."

Fábio went silent. Pendergast sensed that the man was waiting for him to speak.

"You seem to know a great deal about my son," he said.

"He was . . . my friend."

Pendergast controlled his reaction to this.

"Alban met a girl, the daughter of a Norwegian diplomat. Her name was Danika Egland, but she was known to all as the Anja das *Favelas*."

"The Angel of the *Favelas*," Pendergast said.

"She was given this name for the way she fearlessly entered them to administer medicine, give away food and money—and to preach education and independence for the oppressed. The *favela* leaders distrusted her, of course. But they had to put up with her because of her immense popularity among their citizens and her powerful father. Danika made a strong impression on Adler. She had poise, courage, and a beauty that was very…that was very…" And Fábio made a series of gestures around Pendergast's own face.

"Nordic," said Pendergast.

"That is the word. But at that time, as I say, Adler was preoccupied with other things. He spent much time doing research."

"Researching what, exactly?"

"I do not know. But the documents he read were old. Scientific, chemical formulae. And then he went to America."

"When was this?" Pendergast asked.

"A year ago."

"Why did he go?"

For the first time, Fábio's confident look faltered.

"You are reluctant to speak of it. You said Alban had plans. Those plans had to do with me, did they not? Vengeance?"

Fábio did not reply.

"There is no reason to deny it now. He was planning to kill me."

"I do not know the details, *o senhor*. But, yes, I believe it had something to do with…perhaps not just killing you. Something worse. He played his cards close, that one."

Into the silence that followed came a series of metallic clicks; one of the guards was fooling with his AR-15.

Fábio began again. "When Adler returned, he was different. A weight seemed to have been lifted from him. He turned his attention to two things: the leadership of the *favela*, and Danika Egland. She was older than he was, twenty-five. He admired her—was drawn to her. And she to him." He shrugged his shoulders. "Who knows how these things happen, *cada*? One day, they realized they were in love."

Upon hearing this latter word, Pendergast exhaled sharply through his nose in what might have been a scoff.

"The girl's father knew of her work in the *favelas* and disapproved strongly. He feared for her life. She kept the love affair secret from her family. The Anja would not move in with Adler at first, but she spent many nights in his house, far from her father's mansion in a gated community downtown. And then Adler learned that Danika was pregnant."

"Pregnant," Pendergast repeated in a low murmur.

"They wed in secret. Meanwhile, Adler had become obsessed with taking over the *favela* himself. He believed that, with his leadership, it could become something quite different from a disorganized slum. He believed he could turn it into something lean, efficient, organized."

"I'm not surprised," said Pendergast. "The *favela* was a perfect place from which to organize and launch his plan of domination. A replacement for what was destroyed at Nova Godói. A state within a state—with him as leader."

Again, Fábio's eyes flashed. "I do not pretend to know what was then in his head, *senhor*. All I can tell you is that, in very little time, he put together a clever plan for a coup of Cidade dos Anjos. But someone betrayed his plan to O Punho and his gang. The Fist knew that the Angel of the *Favelas* was Adler's lover and wife. He decided to act. One night, he and his men surrounded Adler's house and torched it. Burned to the ground. Adler himself happened to be away . . . but his wife and unborn child died in the blaze."

Pendergast waited in the silence to hear the rest of the story, willing his own pain away. Alban's wife and unborn child, burned alive . . .

"I have never seen a man so utterly consumed with bloodlust. But in a silent way, an inner way, his outward appearance as if nothing had happened. But I knew Adler, and I could see his entire being was bent on vengeance. He went to the fortified compound of O Punho. He went heavily armed but alone. I was sure he would die. But there he unleashed such an orgy of violence as I have never heard of or even imagined. He killed The Fist and all his henchmen. In one night, he single-handedly murdered the entire leadership of the *favela*. From their compound, the blood ran down through the street gutters more than half a mile. It was a night the *favela* will never forget."

"Naturally," said Pendergast. "He wished to mold the *favela* into something infinitely greater—and infinitely worse—than it already was."

A look of surprise came over Fábio's face. "No. No, you do not understand at all. This is what I was getting to. Something in him changed when his wife and child were killed. I do not say I understand it myself. Something *inside* him changed."

Evidently, Pendergast's disbelief was all too clear, because Fábio continued in great earnestness. "I believe that it was the goodness of his wife, and her brutal end, that changed him. He suddenly understood what was right and what was wrong in this world."

"No doubt," said Pendergast sarcastically.

Fábio stood up from his desk. "It is true, *rapiz*! And the proof of it lies all around you. Yes, Adler took control of the City of Angels. But he *remade* it. All for the better! Gone are the cruelty, the drugs, the hunger, the tyranny of gangs. Of course it looks poor to you. And of course we have arms—all kinds of arms. We still need to defend ourselves against a violent and uncaring world—rival gangs, the military, the corrupt politicians who spend billions building soccer and Olympic stadiums while the people starve. There is little violence inside the Cidade dos Anjos. We are on the path of transformation. We ..." Fábio searched for a word. "We take care of our people. We *empower* them. Yes—that is the term he used. People can live here, free of the corruption, crime, taxes, and police brutality that plague the rest of Rio. We still have our problems, but thanks to Adler things are getting better."

All of a sudden Pendergast felt his force of will begin to weaken. His head suddenly swam, and pain shot through his bones. He took a deep breath. "How do you know all this?" he finally asked.

"Because I was your son's lieutenant in the *new* City of Angels. I am the man who stood at his right hand. I knew him better than all but Danika."

"And why have you told me all this?"

Fábio eased himself back into his seat and hesitated a moment before answering. "I told you, *senhor*—I have a duty. Three weeks ago, Adler left the *favela* a second time. He told me he was going to Switzerland, and then to New York."

"Switzerland?" Pendergast said, suddenly alarmed.

"After Danika's death, Adler—Alban—made me promise that— if something were ever to happen to him—I was to track down his father and tell him the story of his redemption."

"Redemption!" Pendergast said.

Fábio went on. "But he never got around to telling me your name or explaining how I could get in touch with you. He was gone three weeks...I heard nothing. And now you have come, telling me he is dead." Fábio took another long pull at the bottle of beer. "I have told you the story he wanted me to tell. I have now done my duty."

There was a long pause in which neither man spoke.

"You do not believe me," Fábio said.

"This house of Alban's," Pendergast replied. "The one that was burned. What was its address?"

"Thirty-One, Rio Paranoá."

"Will you have your men take me there?"

Fábio frowned. "It is nothing but a ruin."

"I ask nevertheless."

After a moment, Fábio nodded.

"And this O Punho of whom you speak. Where did he live?"

"Why, here, of course." Fábio shrugged as if this should have been obvious. "Anything else, *senhor*?"

"I would like my sidearm back."

Fábio turned to one of his guards. "*Me da a arma.*" A minute later, Pendergast's Les Baer was produced.

Pendergast slipped it into his suit jacket. Slowly—very slowly— he retrieved his wallet, passport, the photograph, and the wad of money from the desk. And then, with a final nod of thanks to Fábio, he turned and followed the armed men out of the office and down the stairs to the steamy street outside.

40

D'Agosta entered the Museum's video security room at exactly quarter to two in the afternoon. Jimenez had asked to see him, and D'Agosta hoped the meeting wouldn't take more than fifteen minutes: he'd timed it so he arrived between planetarium shows, and he wasn't sure he could take yet another eighty-decibel tour of the cosmos.

Jimenez and Conklin were sitting at a small table, tapping on laptops. D'Agosta walked over to them, navigating through the racks of equipment in semi-darkness.

"What's up?" he asked.

Jimenez straightened up. "We're done."

"Yeah?"

"We've run through all the security tapes covering the Museum's entrance from June twelfth, the day of Marsala's murder, back to April sixth. That's a week before any eyewitnesses recall seeing the murderer in the Museum, but we went the extra week, just to be safe." He gestured toward his laptop. "We have the sighting of him that you found initially, entering the Museum late on the afternoon of June twelfth. We have tapes of him entering and exiting the Museum on April twentieth, and another entrance and exit set on April fourteenth."

D'Agosta nodded. The April 20 date matched with the date the

Padgett skeleton had been most recently accessed. And no doubt April 14 was the date that the murderer, under the guise of a visiting scientist, first met with Marsala to arrange for the examination. June 12 was the day of the murder.

He sank into a chair beside them. "Good job," he said. And he meant it. It was a boring slog, peering at video after grainy video, feeling your eyes slowly going dry and bleary, to the sound of the Big Bang. They'd found two prior dates on which the murderer had visited the Museum and his entrance on the day of the murder. But they still hadn't found him leaving the Museum *after* the murder.

A part of him wondered why he'd even bothered having his men complete this exercise. The suspected murderer was dead—a suicide. It wasn't like they were gathering evidence in preparation for a trial. It was the old-fashioned cop in him, he supposed: dotting every *i* and crossing every *t*.

Suicide. The image of the killer, there at the Indio Holding Facility, had stayed with him. The way he'd rambled on about the stink of rotting flowers, his agitation and incoherence. Not to mention the way he'd jumped so homicidally at Pendergast. Those weren't easy things to forget. And Christ almighty, killing yourself by biting off your own toe and choking on it? A man would really have to want to check out to do something like that. It didn't seem consistent with the ersatz Professor Waldron, a man who'd clearly been calm and intelligent and rational enough to fool Victor Marsala and other Museum staff into believing he was a scientist.

D'Agosta sighed. Whatever had happened to the man since Marsala's murder, one fact remained: on June 12, the day of the murder, he'd definitely been in his right mind. He'd been clever enough to lure Marsala into an out-of-the-way location, kill him quickly and efficiently, and disguise the murder as a piece-of-shit robbery gone bad. And most of all, he'd somehow managed to get out of the Museum afterward without being seen by any of the cameras.

Maybe it didn't matter, but how the hell had he done that?

Mentally, D'Agosta reviewed his tour of the murder scene with Whittaker, the security guard. It had been in the Gastropod Alcove, at the far end of the Hall of Marine Life, near a basement exit and not far from the South American gold hall . . .

Suddenly D'Agosta sat up in the chair.

Of course.

He couldn't believe how stupid he'd been. He stood up, pacing back and forth, then wheeled toward Jimenez.

"Marsala was murdered on a Saturday night. What time does the Museum open on Sundays?"

Jimenez rooted through some papers on the desk, found a folded guide to the Museum. "Eleven o'clock."

D'Agosta moved over to one of the security playback workstations and sat down. Beyond and below, the three o'clock planetarium show was starting up, but he paid it no attention. He moused through a series of menus on the workstation screen, consulted a long list of files, then selected the one he was interested in: the video feed of the Great Rotunda, southern perspective, eleven AM to noon, Sunday, June 13.

The familiar bird's-eye view swam into life on the screen. As Jimenez and Conklin came up behind him, D'Agosta began playing the video stream at normal speed, then—once his eyes had accustomed themselves to the blurry images—at double speed, then four times speed. As the hour progressed at an accelerated pace before them, the streams of people entering the Museum and passing through the security stations thickened and swelled, moving left to right across the little screen.

There. A lone figure, heading right to left, in the opposite direction, like a swimmer fighting the tide. D'Agosta paused the security feed, noted the timestamp: eleven thirty-four AM. Half an hour before D'Agosta had entered the Museum to open the case. He zoomed in on the figure, then began running the video again, once more at normal speed. There could be no mistake: the face, the clothing, the insolently slow walk—it was the murderer.

"Damn," Conklin murmured over D'Agosta's shoulder.

"There was an exit leading to the basement, just beyond the Gastropod Alcove," D'Agosta explained. "That basement is a maze of levels and tunnels and storage areas. Video coverage would be spotty, at best. He hid there overnight, waited for the Museum to open the next morning, and then just blended in with the crowd on his way out."

He sat back from the workstation. So they'd tied off this particular loose end, at least. The murderer's ingress and egress of the Museum were now documented.

D'Agosta's cell phone began to ring. He plucked it from his pocket and glanced at it. It was a number he didn't know, Southern California area code. He pressed the ANSWER button.

"Lieutenant D'Agosta," he said.

"Lieutenant?" came the voice from the other end of the country. "My name's Dr. Samuels. I'm the pathologist with the Department of Corrections here at Indio. We've been doing the autopsy on the recent John Doe suicide, and we've come across something of interest. Officer Spandau thought I ought to give you a call."

"Go on," he said.

Normally, D'Agosta prided himself on his professionalism as a police officer. He didn't lose his temper; he kept his weapon holstered; he didn't use profanity with civilians. But as the coroner continued, D'Agosta forgot this last personal maxim.

"Son of a fucking *bitch*," he muttered, phone still pressed to his ear.

41

The Toyota Hilux turned a corner and came to a screeching stop. The guard sitting in the rear seat opened the door and got out—semi-automatic rifle now pointed toward the ground—and gestured for Pendergast to get out as well.

Pendergast eased himself out of the pickup. The guard nodded at the building directly before them. It had, like those around it, once been a narrow three-story building, but now it was little more than a burned-out hulk, roofless, its upper story caved in, heavy streamers of black soot soiling the stucco above the empty windowsills. The charred remains of the front door were studded with several ragged holes, as if would-be rescuers had tried to punch their way in with battering rams.

"*Obrigado,*" Pendergast said. The guard nodded, got back into the pickup, and the vehicle moved away.

Pendergast stood in the narrow alley for a moment, watching the vehicle recede into the distance. Then he scanned the surrounding buildings. They resembled the other sections of the Cidade dos Anjos he had seen—haphazardly constructed, wedged tightly together, painted in gaudy colors, rooflines rising and falling crazily with the topography of the mountainside. A few people glanced curiously out of windows at him.

He turned back to the house. While there was no street sign—there were no street signs anywhere in the *favela*—the ghostly remains of the number 31 could be seen painted over the ruined door. Pendergast pushed the door open—a lock lay on the tiled floor just inside, rusted and covered with soot—stepped slowly in, then closed the door behind him as best he could.

The interior was stifling and, even now, smelled strongly of charred wood and melted plastic. He looked around, giving his eyes time to adjust to the dimness, trying to ignore the pain that washed over him in slow waves. There was a tiny packet of painkillers in a hidden pocket of his jacket—something those who had frisked him had missed—and for a moment he considered chewing and swallowing several, but then rejected the idea. It would not do for what lay ahead.

For now, the pain would have to stay.

He navigated the first floor. The layout of the narrow house resembled the shotgun shacks of the Mississippi Delta. There was a living room, with a table burned to a heap of scorched sticks, a burnt sofa popping open with black springs. A polyester rug had melted into the concrete floor. Beyond lay a small kitchen, with a two-burner enamel stove, a scratched and dented cast-iron sink, some drawers and shelving, all open. The floor was covered with broken crockery, glassware, and cheap, half-melted cutlery. Smoke and fire had left strange, menacing patterns over the walls and ceiling.

Pendergast stood in the doorway of the kitchen. He tried to imagine his son, Alban, entering the house and striding into this room; greeting his wife; engaging in small talk; laughing, discussing their unborn child and plans for the future.

The image refused to form in his head. It was inconceivable. After a moment or two he abandoned the attempt.

There was so much that made no sense. A pity his mind was not clearer. He recalled the details of Fábio's story. Alban hiding out in a *favela*, killing some loner and stealing his identity—that he could well believe. Alban, sneaking back into the States, setting in motion some plan of revenge against his father—he could readily believe that, as well. Alban staging a coup and taking over the *favela* for his own evil purposes. Most believable of all.

You have Alban to thank for this . . .

But Alban, loving father and family man? Alban, secretly married to the Angel of the *Favelas*? This he could not see. Nor could he see Alban as benevolent slum leader, ridding it of tyranny and ushering in an age of peace and prosperity. Surely Alban had deceived Fábio as he had deceived everyone else.

And there was the other thing Fábio had said—that before he had gone to America for the second time, Alban had planned to stop off in Switzerland.

Recalling this, Pendergast felt a chill despite the oppressive heat of the ruined house. There was only one reason he could think for Alban to go to Switzerland. But how could he possibly know that his brother, Tristram, was at a boarding school there, under an assumed name? Immediately Pendergast knew the answer: it would be a simple matter for a man of Alban's gifts to discover Tristram's whereabouts.

. . . And yet Tristram *was* safe. Pendergast knew this for a fact, because, in the wake of Alban's death, he had made additional arrangements to ensure Tristram's security.

What had been going through Alban's mind? What had been his plan? The answers—if there were any answers to be had—might lie in these very ruins.

Pendergast made his way back to the front of the house and the concrete staircase. It was badly charred, missing its railing. He ascended it carefully, one hand trailing against the wall, the blackened treads squeaking ominously under his feet.

The second floor was in far worse shape than the first. The acrid stench was stronger here. In places, the third floor had collapsed into the second during the conflagration, causing a dangerous welter of carbonized furniture and charred, splintered beams. In several spots, the roof yawned open, revealing skeletal beams and the blue Brazilian sky above. Slowly picking his way through the rubble, Pendergast determined that the floor had once held three rooms: an office or study of some kind; a bathroom; and a small bedroom that—based on the once-pleasant wallpaper and the ribs of a crib it contained—had been intended as a nursery. Despite the scorched walls and cracked and hanging ceiling, this room had fared better than the others.

The bedroom of Danika—of Danika and Alban—must have been on the third floor. Nothing remained of it. Pendergast stood in the half-light of the nursery, musing. This room would have to do.

He waited there, motionless, for five minutes, then ten. And then—grimacing in pain—he slowly lay down on the floor, ignoring the layer of ash, coal, and dirt that covered the tiles. He folded his hands across his chest and let his eyes flit across the walls and ceilings for a moment before closing them and going utterly still.

Pendergast was one of a tiny handful of practitioners of an esoteric mental discipline known as Chongg Ran, and one of only two masters of it outside of Tibet. With years of training, extensive study, near-fanatical intellectual rigor, and a familiarity with other cerebral exercises such as those in Giordano Bruno's *Ars Memoriae*, and the *Nine Levels of Consciousness* described in the rare seventeenth-century chapbook by Alexandre Carêem, Pendergast had developed the ability to place himself in a state of pure concentration. From this state—utterly removed from the physical world—he could merge in his mind thousands of separate facts, observations, suppositions, and hypotheses. Through this unification and synthesis, he was able to re-create scenes from the past and put himself among places and people that had vanished long ago. The exercise often led to startling insights unobtainable any other way.

The problem at present was the intellectual rigor, the need to clear his mind of distraction, before proceeding. In his current state, this would be exceedingly difficult.

First, he had to isolate and compartmentalize his pain while simultaneously keeping his mind as clear as possible. Shutting everything out, he began with a problem in mathematics: integrating $e^{-(x^2)}$, e raised to the power of minus x squared.

The pain remained.

He moved on to tensor calculus, working out two problems in vector analysis simultaneously in his head.

Still the pain remained.

Another approach was necessary. Breathing shallowly, keeping his eyes gently but completely closed, careful to keep his mind from acknowledging the pain that coursed through his limbs, Pendergast allowed a tiny, perfect orchid to form in his imagination. For a minute it floated there, rotating slowly in perfect blackness. He then allowed the orchid to languorously fall into its component parts: petals, dorsal sepal, lateral sepal, ovary, post-anterior lobe.

He focused his attention on a single part: the labellum. Willing the rest of the flower to vanish into the blackness, he let the labellum grow and grow until it filled the entire field of his mental vision. And still it grew, expanding with geometric regularity, until he could see past the enzymes and strands of DNA and electron shells into its very atomic structure—and still deeper, to the particles at the subatomic level. For a long moment, he looked on with detachment as the deepest and most profound elements of the orchid's structure moved in their strange and unfathomable courses. And then—with a great effort of will—he stilled the entire atomic engine of the flower, forcing all the countless billions of particles to hang suspended, motionless, in the black vacuum of his imagination.

When he finally let the labellum vanish from his mind, the pain was gone.

Now, still within his mind, he left the would-be nursery, descended the stairs, passed through the closed front door, and found himself on the street. It was night, perhaps six months, perhaps nine months earlier.

Suddenly the house from which he had just exited exploded in flame. As he watched—disembodied, unable to act, powerless to do anything but observe—accelerants quickly carried the flames through the third floor of the residence. Down a back alley, he saw two dark figures racing away.

Almost immediately the crackle of flames became mingled with the sounds of a woman's screams. A crowd had gathered, shouting, crying hysterically. Several men tried to force open the locked front door with improvised battering rams. It took them at least a minute, and by the time they succeeded the screams had stopped and the third floor of the house was already collapsing into a fiery labyrinth of beams and glowing ceiling tiles. Nevertheless, several of the men—Pendergast recognized Fábio among them—ran into the building, quickly forming a bucket brigade.

Pendergast watched the frantic activity, a spectral composite of intellect and memory. Within half an hour the fire was out—but the damage had been done. He now saw a new figure come running up the Rio Paranoá. It was a figure he recognized: his son, Alban. But it was an Alban that Pendergast had never seen before. Instead of the usual haughty, scornful, bored visage, this Alban was frantic with worry. He looked as if he had run a long way. Gasping with breath, he pushed through the crowds, forcing his way toward the door of number 31.

He was met in the doorway by his lieutenant, Fábio. His face was a mess of soot and sweat. Alban tried to push his way past but Fábio barred the doorway, shaking his head violently, pleading with Alban in a low, fast voice not to attempt to enter.

At last, Alban staggered back. He placed one hand on the plaster façade for support. To Pendergast, watching from his mind's eye, it seemed as if Alban's world was about to fall asunder. He tore at his hair; he struck the smoke-blackened wall, emitting a half moan, half wail of despair. It was an expression of grief as profound as any Pendergast had ever seen—and never would have expected from Alban.

And then—quite suddenly—Alban changed. He grew calm, almost preternaturally so. He glanced up at the ruined house, still smoking, its ruined upper floors dropping glowing embers. He turned to Fábio, asked him pointed questions in a low, urgent tone. Fábio listened, nodded. And then the two turned and melted away down a side alley.

For a moment the scene playing out in Pendergast's head vanished. When it became visible again, the location had changed. He was now outside the compound at the very summit of the Ciudad dos Anjos: the gated, fenced complex from which he had come not an hour before. Now, however, it looked more like an armed camp than a residence. There were two guards patrolling the fence; dogs with handlers wearing heavy leather gloves moved back and forth across the courtyard beyond. The windows of the upper story of the central building were brilliantly lighted; talk and harsh laughter floated down from them. From his vantage point in the shadows across the street, Pendergast saw the silhouette of a large, heavyset man move briefly before one of the windows. O Punho—The Fist.

Pendergast glanced over his shoulder, down at the *favela* that sprawled over the flanks of the mountainside. A faint glow rose out of a crabbed warren of streets about half a mile below: Alban's house was still smoldering.

And now there came a new sound: the low throb of an engine. Pendergast saw a battered jeep, its headlights out, approach, then pull over to the side of the road about a quarter mile away. A single figure got out of the driver's seat: Alban.

Pendergast squinted through the darkness of his mind's eye for a clearer look. Alban had a large pack slung over his shoulder, and a weapon in each hand. He shrank against the façade of the nearest house, and then—making sure he wasn't spotted—moved rapidly up the darkened street to the gated entrance to the compound.

And then something surprising happened. Just as he reached it, Alban stopped, turned, and looked directly at Pendergast.

Of course, Pendergast could not be seen. His corporeal form was not there, but rather in the ruined nursery, and all this was a creation inside his own mind. And yet the piercing, strangely knowing gaze of Alban disconcerted him, threatened to dissolve the already-fragile memory crossing...

...Then Alban looked away. He crouched, checking his weapons: twin TEC-9s, each equipped with silencers and thirty-two-round magazines.

One of the guards outside the fence had turned away and was lighting a cigar. Alban crept swiftly forward and waited for the other guard to come to his location. In a peculiar way he seemed to anticipate the man's movement. As the guard strolled along, Alban removed a knife from his belt, waited for the guard to pause and ignite his lighter, and then slit his throat just as the man was concentrating on touching the flame to the tip of the cigarette. A wet sigh of air was the only sound as he let the man's body down gently and the second guard, his cigarillo now lit, turned back. The guard reached for his weapon but Alban—again with his preternatural gift of foresight—anticipated his movements by seizing the barrel and twisting the weapon from the guard's hands even as he buried the knife in his heart.

Satisfying himself that both guards were dead, Alban retreated once more to his initial vantage point. Removing the bulky pack and placing it on the ground, he pulled out something long and villainous looking. As he fitted the pieces together, Pendergast recognized an RPG-7 grenade launcher.

Alban paused, preparing himself. Then, reslinging the pack over his shoulder and tucking the TEC-9s into his waistband, he approached the compound again. As Pendergast watched out of the darkness of memory, Alban positioned himself some distance from the gate, balanced the grenade launcher on his shoulder, sighted it in, and fired.

There was a huge explosion, followed by a tremendous boiling cloud of orange flame and smoke. In the distance, Pendergast could hear shouts, barking, and a clattering rain of metal as pieces of the fence began falling all around. Dogs and their human handlers came running out of the smoke. Slinging the RPG over his other shoulder and plucking the TEC-9s from his waistband, Alban dispatched one team after another with bursts of automatic fire, even before they emerged from the cloaking smoke.

When no more guards came, Alban reached into the pack, pulled out another rocket-propelled grenade, and fitted it to the RPG-7. He moved cautiously through the ruins of the fence, smoke still drifting here and there in thick pockets, weapons at the ready. Pendergast followed.

The courtyard was empty. There was much activity and consternation in the central building. Seconds later a stream of machine-gun fire came from an upper window. But Alban had positioned himself in cover, outside the field of fire. Aiming his RPG again, he fired a grenade at the windows of the upper floor. They flew apart in a storm of glass, cinder block, and wood. As the thunder echoed away, screams of pain could be heard within. Alban fitted another grenade into the launcher; fired again.

Now armed men began boiling out of the buildings to the left and right. Dropping the RPG, Alban began firing at them in controlled bursts from the TEC-9s, moving from one pool of darkness to another, one cover to another, avoiding their volleys even before they started.

Within minutes, the deadly ballet was over. A dozen more men lay dead, their bodies draped in doorways or splayed over the cobbles of the courtyard.

And now Alban approached the central building, automatic handguns at the ready. He entered the front door. Pendergast followed. Alban glanced around briefly, hesitating, before stealthily moving up the staircase.

At the top of the stair, a man burst out of a darkened room, handgun raised, but with that strange sixth sense of his Alban had anticipated the move and his own weapon was already raised; he fired even before the man had fully appeared, the fatal rounds ripping through the door frame to kill the man as he emerged. Alban paused to eject the magazines of the TEC-9s, slap two more home. And then he crept up the stairway to the third floor.

The office—the office Pendergast had visited himself, just an hour before, but at the same time half a year later—lay in ruins. Furniture was burning; two grenade entry holes punctured the walls. Alban moved to the center of the office, weapons at the ready, and slowly looked around. At least four bloody figures lay motionless: some sprawled across overturned chairs, one actually pinned to the wall by a massive splinter of blown-apart wooden furniture.

A heavyset man lay across the desk, rivulets of blood running from his mouth and nose. O Punho. He twitched slightly. Alban turned toward him and let a stream of at least a dozen bullets stitch their way through the gang lord's body. There was a dreadful convulsing; a gargling sound; and then nothing. Blood ran across the floor and streamed out the hole in the side of the building.

Alban paused, listening. But all was silent. O Punho's lieutenants and personal guards—all of them—were dead.

For a moment Alban remained standing amid the blood and the devastation. And then—very slowly—he crumpled onto the floor, sinking into the running sheets of blood.

Watching him, Pendergast recalled the words of Fábio. *You do not understand at all. Something in him changed when his wife and child were killed.*

From the doorway, in his mind's eye, Pendergast watched his son: sunken to the floor, silent and motionless, the blood wicking into his clothes, surrounded by ruination of his own causing. Had Fábio been telling the truth? Was this more than mere violent retribution that Pendergast was now witnessing? Was it possible this was remorse? Or a kind of justice? Had Alban learned what evil—*true* evil—really was? Was he changing?

Suddenly the walls of the ruined office flickered; went black briefly; came back into view in his mind's eye; flickered again. Desperately, Pendergast tried to keep the memory crossing alive in his head: to observe his son, to learn the answer to his questions. But then the pain burst through again, all the worse for having been suppressed, and the entire tableau—the burning compound, the bloody bodies, and Alban—vanished from Pendergast's mind.

For a moment, Pendergast simply lay where he was in the burnt nursery, motionless. Then he opened his eyes and—with difficulty—raised himself to his feet. He dusted himself off, looked around with wavering eyes. As if in a dream, he left the nursery, made his way down the staircase, and stepped out of dimness into the bright sunlight of the grimy street.

42

Margo Green took a seat at a large conference table in a forensic suite on the tenth floor of One Police Plaza. The suite was an odd combination of computer lab and medical examination room: terminals and workstations stood cheek by jowl with gurneys, light boxes, and sharps disposal cases.

Across the table sat D'Agosta. He had summoned her from the Museum, where she'd been spending her off afternoon analyzing the anomalous compound found in the bones of Mrs. Padgett and dodging Dr. Frisby. Beside him sat a tall, thin Asian man. Next to him was Terry Bonomo, the department's Identi-CAD expert, with his ubiquitous laptop. He was swiveling back and forth in his seat and grinning at nothing in particular.

"Margo," D'Agosta said. "Thanks for coming. You already know Terry Bonomo." He gestured at the other man. "This is Dr. Lu of Columbia Medical School. His expertise is plastic surgery. Dr. Lu, this is Dr. Green, an ethnopharmacologist and anthropologist currently working at the Pearson Institute."

Margo nodded at Lu, who smiled in return. His teeth were dazzlingly white.

"Now that you're both here, I can put the call through." D'Agosta reached for a phone at the center of the table, pressed its SPEAKER button, and made a long-distance call. It was answered on the third ring.

"Hello?"

D'Agosta leaned toward the speaker. "Is this Dr. Samuels?"

"Yes."

"Dr. Samuels, this is Lieutenant D'Agosta, NYPD. I have you on speakerphone with a plastic surgeon from Columbia Medical and an anthropologist connected with the New York Museum of Natural History. Could you please share with them what you told me yesterday?"

"Certainly." The man cleared his throat. "As I told the lieutenant, I'm a pathologist with the Indio Department of Corrections here in California. I was undertaking the autopsy on the John Doe suicide—the man suspected in the murder of the employee at your Museum—when I noticed something." He paused. "I first established the mode of death, which, as you know, was rather unusual. As I was completing a gross examination of the corpse, I noticed some unusual healed scars. They were inside the mouth, along both the upper and lower gingival sulcus. At first I thought they might be the result of an old beating or car accident. But as I examined them, I could see the scars were too precise for that. I found a similar, symmetrical set of scars on the other side of the mouth. At this point, I realized they were the result of surgery: specifically, reconstructive facial surgery."

"Cheek and chin implants?" Dr. Lu said.

"Yes. X-rays and CAT scans bore this out. In addition, the imaging showed plates—titanium, as it turned out—fixed to the jawbone."

Dr. Lu nodded thoughtfully. "Were there any other scars? On the skull or the hip, or inside the nose?"

"When we shaved the head, we found no scars. But yes, there were intranasal incisions, and a scar on the hip, just above the iliac crest. The images I forwarded to Lieutenant D'Agosta document everything."

"Did the autopsy turn up any anomalous findings, chemical or otherwise?" D'Agosta asked. "The man was in obvious pain before he killed himself. And he was acting more than a little crazy. He might have been poisoned."

There was a pause. "I wish we could say with certainty. There were some very unusual compounds present in the blood that we're still trying to analyze. The man was on the verge of renal failure; it's possible those compounds could have caused that."

"If you come up with anything definitive, please relay it to me via the lieutenant," Margo said. "Also, I'd appreciate it if you could analyze the skeleton for the presence of unusual compounds as well."

"Will do. Oh, and one other thing—the man dyed his hair. It wasn't black, but dirty blond."

"Thank you, Dr. Samuels. If there's anything else, we'll be in touch." D'Agosta ended the conference call with the press of a button.

There was a large manila envelope on the table, and now D'Agosta slid it in Lu's direction. "Doctor? I wonder if you could give us the benefit of your expertise."

The plastic surgeon opened the envelope, pulled out the contents, and quickly arranged them in two piles. Margo saw that one pile contained a mug shot and morgue photographs; the other, colored X-rays and CAT scans.

Lu sorted through the photos of the man Margo recognized as the phony Professor Waldron. He held up one close-up and displayed it to the group: Margo made out the inside of a mouth, the upper gums, soft palate, and uvula clearly visible. "Dr. Samuels was correct," Lu said, tracing his finger against a faint line just above the gum. "Notice this intraoral incision—technically named, as Dr. Samuels told you, the upper gingival sulcus."

"And its significance?" D'Agosta asked.

Lu put down the photograph. "There are basically two kinds of plastic surgery. The first is skin work. Face-lifts, eye bag removal— procedures that make you look younger. The second kind is bony work. This is much more invasive, and is used in cases of trauma. Say you were in a car accident and had your face crushed. Bony work would attempt to correct the damage." He waved a hand at the photographs. "Most of the procedures done to this man involved bony work."

"And this bony work—could it be used to alter a person's appearance?"

"Definitely. In fact, since there's no evidence of prior trauma, I would guess that all the procedures done to this man were to alter his facial appearance."

"Just how many operations would it take to accomplish that?"

"If the operation was sufficient to change the bony orientation— a midface advancement, for example—just one. The patient would look completely different, especially with dyed hair."

"But it sounds as if this man had several procedures."

Lu nodded, then picked up and showed them another picture. Margo recognized it, with some disgust, as a close-up of the inside of a hairy nose. "See the intranasal incision? It's well hidden, but visible if you know what to look for. The doctor used that incision to introduce silicone into the nose, no doubt to make it look taller." He flipped through the other pictures. "The upper intraoral incisions, where the gum meets the sulcus, would be used to alter the cheeks—you make a cut on either side, make a pocket in the bone, slip in the implants. The lower intraoral incision, on the other hand, would have been used to add silicone to the chin, make it protrude."

Terry Bonomo had his laptop open and was furiously typing notes as the surgeon spoke.

Margo watched D'Agosta shift in his chair. "So our friend here had his cheeks altered, his chin altered, and the height of his nose changed." He glanced significantly in Bonomo's direction. "Anything else?"

"Samuels mentioned titanium plates." Lu reached for the X-rays, stood up, and walked over to a series of X-ray light boxes fixed to one wall. He snapped them on, fastened the X-rays to the glass, and examined them.

"Ah, yes," he said. "The face was restructured by advancing the jaw."

"Can you explain that, please?" Bonomo asked.

"It's called a LeFort osteotomy. You essentially break and realign the face. Using the same incision in the upper gingival sulcus, you go right down to the bone, make a complete cut so it becomes mobile, and then push out the jaw. Pieces of bone from other areas of the body are added to fill up the space—usually from the patient's skull or hip. In the case of this person, there is a scar above the iliac crest, so clearly the extra bone was taken from the hip. Once this is completed, titanium plates are used to fix the maxilla in position. You can see one of them, here." He pointed to an X-ray.

"Jesus H. Christopher," said Bonomo. "Sounds painful."

"Any idea how long ago these procedures might have been done?" Margo asked.

Lu turned back to the X-rays. "It's hard to tell. "The maxilla is fully healed—you can see the callus, here. The titanium plates haven't been removed, but then again, that's common. I would say at least a few years ago, maybe more."

"I count four procedures," D'Agosta said. "And you say these would have been enough to change the man's looks completely?"

"Just the LeFort osteotomy would have done the job."

"And based on the photographic, CAT scan, and X-ray evidence here, can you reverse-engineer these changes? Show us what the guy looked like before all this work?"

Lu nodded. "I can try. The fractures in the medulla, and the size of the incisions in the mucosa, are clear enough. We can work backward from there."

"Great. Please work with Terry Bonomo here and see if we can't get an image of this guy's original face." D'Agosta turned to the ID expert. "Think you can do this?"

"Hell, yeah," Bonomo said. "If the doc here can give me specifics, it's a cinch to modify the facial biometrics. I've already got wireframe and three-D composites of the perp's head loaded into the software; now I just need to take my standard operating procedure and run it backward, so to speak."

While Margo looked on, Dr. Lu took a seat beside Bonomo and together—hunched over the laptop—they began refiguring the face of the killer, essentially undoing the work some anonymous plastic surgeon had done years ago. Now and then Lu returned to the autopsy photographs, or the X-ray and CAT scan images, as they painstakingly adjusted various parameters in the cheeks, chin, nose, and jaw.

"Don't forget the dirty-blond hair," D'Agosta said.

Twenty minutes later, Bonomo hit a key on the laptop with a dramatic flourish. "Let's give it a moment to render the image."

Margo heard the laptop give a chirrup about thirty seconds later.

Bonomo swiveled the laptop toward Dr. Lu, who examined it a moment, then nodded. And then Bonomo turned the laptop all the way around so Margo and D'Agosta could see it.

"My God," D'Agosta murmured.

Margo was shocked. The plastic surgeon was right—the image looked like a completely different man.

"I want you to model that from several angles," D'Agosta told Bonomo. "Then download the rendered images into the departmental database. We'll run the facial-recognition software against it, see if the face is anywhere out there." He turned to Lu. "Doctor, thanks so much for your time."

"My pleasure."

"Margo, I'll be back." And without another word, he stood up and walked out of the forensic suite.

In less than twenty minutes, D'Agosta was back. His face was slightly flushed, and he was out of breath.

"Goddamn," he told her. "We've got a hit. Just like that."

43

Pendergast pulled into the visitors' parking lot of the Sanatorium de Piz Julier and killed the engine. The lot was, as he expected, empty: the convalescence spa was remote, tiny, and selective. In fact, at the moment it had only one patient in residence.

He got out of the car—a twelve-cylinder Lamborghini Gallardo Aventador—and walked slowly to the far end of the lot. Beyond and far below, the green skirts of the Alps stretched down to the Swiss resort town of St. Moritz, from this distance almost too perfect and beautiful to be real. To its south reared the Piz Bernina, the tallest mountain of the eastern Alps. Sheep were grazing peacefully on its lower flanks, tiny dots of white.

He turned back and headed toward the sanatorium, a red-and-white confection with gingerbread molding and brimming flower boxes beneath the windows. While he was still rather weak and unsteady on his feet, the most severe symptoms of the pain and mental confusion he had experienced in Brazil had eased, at least temporarily. He'd even scrapped his plans to hire a driver and rented a car instead. He knew the Lamborghini was flashy and not at all his style, but he told himself the speed and technical handling the mountain roads required would help clear his mind.

Pendergast stopped at the front door and rang the bell. An unobtrusive security camera set above the door swiveled in his direction.

Then a buzzer sounded, the door sprang open, and he entered. Beyond lay a small lobby and nurse's station. A woman in a white uniform with a small cap on her head sat behind it.

"*Ja?*" the woman said, looking up at him expectantly.

Pendergast reached into his pocket, gave her his card. She reached into a drawer, took out a folder, glanced at a photograph that lay within, then back at Pendergast.

"Ah yes," the woman said, replacing the folder and switching to accented English. "*Herr* Pendergast. We have been expecting you. Just one minute, please."

She picked up the phone that sat on her desk and made a brief call. A minute later, a door in the wall behind her buzzed open and two more nurses appeared. One of them gestured for Pendergast to approach. Passing through the interior door, he followed the two women down a cool hallway, punctuated by windows through which streamed brilliant morning sunlight. With its taffeta curtains and colorful Alpine photos, the place appeared bright and cheerful. And yet the bars on the windows were of reinforced steel, and weapons could be seen bulging beneath the crisp white uniforms of the two nurses.

Near the end of the hall, they stopped before a closed door. The nurses unlocked it. Then they opened the door, stepped back, and gestured for Pendergast to enter.

Beyond lay a large and airy room, its windows—also open, also barred—giving out on a beautiful view of the lake far below. There was a bed, a writing table, a bookshelf full of books in English and German, a wing chair, and a private bath.

At the table, silhouetted in a beam of sunlight, sat a young man of seventeen. He was studiously—even laboriously—copying something from a book into a journal. The sun gilded his light-blond hair. His gray-blue eyes moved from the book to the journal and back again, so intent on his work he remained unaware anyone had entered. Silently, Pendergast took in the patrician features, the lean physique.

His sense of weariness increased.

The youth looked up from his work. For a brief moment, his face was a mask of incomprehension. Then he broke into a smile. "Father!" he cried, leaping from the chair. "What a surprise!"

Pendergast allowed himself to return his son's embrace. This was followed by an awkward silence.

"When can I get out of this place?" Tristram finally asked. "I hate it here." He spoke in an oddly formal, schoolboy English, with a German accent softened by a touch of Portuguese.

"Not for a while, I'm afraid, Tristram."

The youth frowned and played with a ring on the middle finger of his left hand—a gold ring set with a beautiful star sapphire.

"Are you being treated well here?"

"Well enough. The food's excellent. I go on hikes every day. But they hover over me all the time. I have no friends and it is boring. I liked the École Mère-Église better. Can I go back there, Father?"

"In a little while." Pendergast paused. "Once I have taken care of certain things."

"What things?"

"Nothing you need be concerned about. Listen, Tristram, I need to ask you something. Has anything unusual happened to you since we last met?"

"Unusual?" Tristram echoed.

"Out of the ordinary. Letters you've received, perhaps? Telephone calls? Unexpected visits?"

At this, a blank look came over Tristram. He hesitated for a moment. Then, silently, he shook his head.

"No."

Pendergast looked at him closely. "You're lying."

Tristram said nothing, his eyes fixed on the ground.

Pendergast took a deep breath. "I don't quite know how to tell you this. Your brother is dead."

Tristram started. "Alban? *Tot?*"

Pendergast nodded.

"How?"

"Murdered."

The room went very still. Tristram stared, shocked, and then his gaze dropped to the floor again. A single tear gathered tremulously in the corner of one eye, then rolled down his cheek.

"You feel sad?" Pendergast asked. "After the way he treated you?"

Tristram shook his head. "He was my brother."

Pendergast felt deeply affected by this. *And he was my son.* He wondered why he felt so little sorrow for Alban's death; why he lacked his son's compassion.

He found Tristram looking back at him with those deep-gray eyes. "Who did it?"

"I don't know. I'm trying to find out."

"It would take a lot . . . to kill Alban."

Pendergast said nothing. He felt uncomfortable with Tristram's eyes on him so intently. He had no idea how to be a father to this boy.

"Are you ill, Father?"

"I am merely recovering from a bout of malaria brought on by my recent travels—nothing more," he said hastily.

Another silence fell over the room. Tristram, who had been hovering over his father during this exchange, now went back to his writing desk and sat down. He appeared to be struggling with some inner conflict. Finally, his gaze turned back to Pendergast.

"Yes. I lied. There is something I have to tell you. I promised him, but if he's dead . . . I think you must know."

Pendergast waited.

"Alban visited me, Father."

"When?"

"A few weeks ago. I was still at Mère-Église. I was taking a walk in the foothills. He was there, ahead of me, on the trail. He told me he had been waiting for me."

"Go on," Pendergast said.

"He looked different."

"In what way?"

"He was older. Thinner. He looked sad. And the way he spoke to me—it was not like the old way. There was no . . . no . . ." He moved his hands, uncertain of the word to use. "*Verachtung.*"

"Disdain," said Pendergast.

"That is it. There was no disdain in his voice."

"What did he discuss with you?"

"He said he was going to the United States."

"Did he say why?"

"Yes. He said that he was going to . . . right a wrong. Undo some terrible thing he himself had put into motion."

"Were those his exact words?"

"Yes. I didn't understand. Right a wrong? Write a wrong? I asked him what he meant and he refused to explain."

"What else did he say?"

"He asked me to promise not to tell you of his visit."

"That's it?"

Tristram paused. "There was something else."

"Yes?"

"He said he had come to ask my forgiveness."

"Forgiveness?" Pendergast repeated, hugely surprised.

"Yes."

"And what did you say to that?"

"I forgave him."

Pendergast rose to his feet. With something like a throb of despair, he realized the mental confusion, the pain, was beginning to return. "*How* did he ask for your forgiveness?" he asked harshly.

"He wept. He was almost crazy with grief."

Pendergast shook his head. Was this remorse real, or some cruel game Alban was practicing on his simple twin brother? "Tristram," he said. "I moved you here for your own safety, after your brother was murdered. I'm trying to find the killer. You'll have to stay here until I've solved the case and . . . taken care of things. Once that happens, I hope you won't want to return to Mère-Église. I hope you'll want to come back to New York—and live with . . ." He hesitated. "Family."

The young man's eyes widened, but he did not speak.

"I'll remain in contact, either directly or through Constance. If you need anything, please write and let me know." He approached Tristram, kissed him lightly on the forehead, then turned to leave.

"Father?" Tristram said.

Pendergast glanced back.

"I know malaria well. Back in Brazil, many *Schwächlinge* died of malaria. You don't have malaria."

"What I have is my own business," he said sharply.

"And is it not my business, too, as your son?"

Pendergast hesitated. "I'm sorry. I didn't mean to speak to you like that. I'm doing what I can about my . . . affliction. Good-bye, Tristram. I hope to see you again soon."

With that, he hastily let himself out of the room. The two nurses, who had been waiting outside, relocked the door and then escorted him back down the corridor of the sanatorium.

44

Thierry Gabler took his seat on the outdoor terrace of Café Remoire and opened his copy of *Le Courrier* with a sigh. It took less than a minute for a waitress to come bustling up with his usual order: a glass of Pflümli, a small plate of cold cured meats, and a few slices of brown bread.

"*Bonjour, Monsieur* Gabler," she said.

"*Merci*, Anna," Gabler replied with what he hoped was a winning smile. She walked away, and he followed the sway of her hips with a long, lingering gaze. Then he turned his attention to the Pflümli, picked up the glass, and took a sip, sighing with quiet satisfaction. He had retired from his job as a civil servant the year before, and taking in an aperitif at a sidewalk café in the late afternoons had become something of a ritual. He particularly liked the Café Remoire: while it didn't have a view of the lake, it was one of the few truly traditional cafés left in Geneva, and—given its location, centrally situated on the Place du Cirque—it was an ideal spot to enjoy the bustle of the city.

He took another sip of the eau-de-vie, folded the newspaper neatly onto page three, and glanced around. At this time of day, the café was bustling with the usual assortment of tourists, businessmen, students, and small knots of gossiping wives. The street itself was busy, cars rushing by, people walking hurriedly here and there. The Fêtes de Genève was not far away, and already the city's hotels were filling with people anticipating the world-famous fireworks display.

He delicately folded a piece of cured meat onto a slice of bread, raised it to his lips, and was about to take a bite when all of a sudden— with a loud screech of brakes—a car nosed to the curb not four feet from where he was seated on the café's terrace. Not just any car, either. This vehicle looked like something from a future century: slung very low, it was at once sleek and angular, seemingly sculpted from a single chunk of flame-colored garnet. The massive rims of its wheels came up to the top of the dashboard, itself barely visible behind smoked black glass. Gabler had never seen a vehicle like it. Unconsciously, he put his piece of bread down as he stared. He could make out the Lamborghini badge on the car's evil-looking snout, where the grille should have been.

Now the driver's door opened vertically, gullwing-style, and a man got out, heedless of the oncoming traffic: an approaching car almost hit him and it sheared away into the passing lane, honking angrily. The driver took no notice. He slammed the car door, then made for the entrance to the café. Gabler stared at him. He was as unusual looking as his vehicle: dressed in a severely tailored black suit, with a white shirt and expensive tie. He was pale—paler than any man Gabler had ever seen. His eyes were dark and bruised looking, and his walk was both deliberate and unsteady, like a drunk trying to pass himself off as sober. Gabler saw the man briefly speaking to the patroness inside. Then he emerged again and took a seat on the terrace a few tables down. Gabler took another sip of Pflümli, and then remembered the bread-and-meat he'd made for himself and took a bite of it, all the time trying not to stare openly at this stranger. Out of the corner of his eye he saw the man being served what looked like an absinthe, which had only recently been legalized in Switzerland.

Gabler picked up his newspaper and addressed himself to page three, now and then allowing himself a glance at the man a few tables down the terrace. He sat still as stone, paying attention to nothing or nobody, pale eyes staring into the distance, rarely blinking. Now and then he lifted the glass of absinthe to his lips. Gabler noticed that the man's hand was shaking, and that the glass rattled whenever it was returned to the table.

In short order, the glass was emptied; another was ordered. Gabler ate his bread, drank his Pflümli, and read his copy of Le Courrier, and eventually the odd-looking stranger was forgotten in favor of the long-established activities of his typical afternoon.

And then something happened that attracted his attention. From down the Place du Cirque, Gabler spied a traffic officer slowly making his way toward them. He had a ticket book in hand, and was examining each parked car in turn. Now and then, when he came to an illegally parked vehicle, or one whose time had expired on the meter, he would pause, smile with private satisfaction, fill out a ticket, and slip it beneath a wiper blade.

Gabler glanced at the Lamborghini. Geneva's parking rules were both byzantine and strict, but the vehicle was clearly improperly parked.

Now the officer was nearing the café's terrace. Gabler watched, certain that the black-clad man would rouse himself and move his car before the meter man got there. But no: he remained where he was, now and then sipping his drink.

The officer reached the Lamborghini. He was a rather short, rotund figure, with a reddish face and thick white hair curling out from beneath his cap. The car was so obviously parked illegally—squeezed into the narrow space at a rakish angle demonstrating indifference, even contempt, for authority and order—that the officer's smile was larger and more self-satisfied than usual as he licked his finger and flipped open the ticket book. The ticket was written and slipped beneath the wiper blade—it was recessed into the engine frame and took a moment to find—with a flourish.

Only now, as the traffic officer moved on, did the man in black get up from his table. Walking off the terrace, he approached the officer, placing himself between the man and the next parked car. Without speaking, he merely extended a finger and pointed at the Lamborghini.

The traffic officer looked from him, to the car, and back. *"Est-ce que cette voiture vous appartient?"* he asked.

The man slowly nodded.

"Monsieur, elle est..."

"In English, if you please," the man said in an American accent Gabler recognized as southern.

As did most Genevans, the traffic officer spoke decent English. With a sigh—as if making a huge sacrifice—the man switched languages. "Very well."

"It appears I have committed a parking transgression of some kind. As you can probably tell, I'm a stranger here. Kindly allow me to remove my car, and let us forget about the ticket."

"I'm very sorry," the officer said, though his tone of voice did not sound at all sorry. "The ticket is written."

"So I've noticed. And what heinous act, pray tell, have I committed?"

"Monsieur, you are parked in a blue zone."

"All these other cars are parked in a blue zone, as well. Hence my assumption that parking in a blue zone was permissible."

"Ah!" said the officer, as if scoring an important point in a philosophic debate. "But your car does not display a *disque de stationnement.*"

"A what?"

"A parking disk. You may not park in a blue zone without displaying a parking disk that indicates the time that you arrived."

"Indeed. A parking disk. How quaint. And how am I, a visitor, expected to know that?"

The traffic officer gave the man a look of bureaucratic disdain. *"Monsieur,* as a visitor to our city, it is you who are expected to understand, and abide by, my rules."

"My rules?"

The officer looked slightly chagrined at this slip. "Our rules."

"I see. Even if such rules are capricious, unnecessary, and, ultimately, pernicious?"

The little traffic officer frowned. He looked confused, uncertain. "The law is the law, *monsieur.* You have broken it, and—"

"Just a minute." The American put a hand on the officer's wrist, effectively stopping his progress. "What is the fine associated with this ticket?"

"Forty-five Swiss francs."

"Forty-five Swiss francs." Still blocking the man's way, the American reached into his suit jacket and—with insolent slowness—removed a wallet and counted out the money.

"I cannot accept the fine, *monsieur*," the officer said. "You must go to the—"

Suddenly, and violently, the American tore up the bills. First once, then twice, then again and again, until nothing was left but tiny squares. He tossed them in the air like so much confetti, so that they fluttered down, landing all over the traffic officer's cap and shoulders. Gabler looked on, agape at this development. Passersby and others sitting on the terrace were equally astounded by this exchange.

"*Monsieur*," the officer said, his face growing still redder. "You are clearly intoxicated. I must ask you not to enter this vehicle or—"

"Or what?" the American said with acid scorn. "You'll write me a ticket for littering while under the influence? Pay attention, sirrah, and I'll cross the street, right here. Then you can write me a ticket for jaywalking under the influence as well. But no, let me guess—you don't have the authority to levy such a weighty punishment. That would take a *real* policeman. How very sad for you! 'Take thy beak from out my heart!'"

Mustering all his dignity, the rotund traffic officer reached for a cell phone at his side and began to dial. As he did so, the American dropped the melodramatic attitude he'd abruptly assumed and reached into his jacket pocket again, this time pulling out a different wallet. This one, Gabler saw, contained a shield of some kind. He showed it to the officer for just a moment, then slipped it back into his jacket.

Immediately the manner of the officer changed. The chest-swelling, officious, bureaucratic behavior faded. "Sir," he said, "you should have told me at first. Had I known that you were here conducting some kind of official business, I would not have issued the ticket. However, that doesn't excuse—"

The American leaned in toward the smaller man. "You misunderstand. I am not conducting any official business. I am merely a traveler stopping off for a stirrup cup on my way to the airport."

The traffic officer shook his head and backpedaled. He turned toward the Lamborghini and the traffic ticket, which flapped slowly back and forth in the breeze floating down the Place du Cirque. "Allow me, *monsieur*, to remove the ticket, but I must ask you—"

"Don't remove that ticket," the American barked. "Don't even touch it!"

The officer turned back, now thoroughly cowed and confused. "*Monsieur?* I don't understand."

"You don't?" returned the voice that grew icier with every word. "Then allow me to explain it in terms that, one would hope, even the meanest intelligence could grasp. I've decided I *want* that ticket, Goodman Lickspittle. I am going to *contest* that ticket, in court. And if I'm not mistaken, that means *you* will have to appear in court, as well. And at such a time I will take the greatest pleasure in pointing out to the judge, the lawyers, and everyone else assembled what a disgraceful shadow of a man you are. A shadow? Perhaps I exaggerate. A shadow, at least, can prove to be tall—tall indeed. But you: you're a homunculus, a dried neat's tongue, a carbuncle on the posterior of humanity." With a sudden movement, the American knocked the officer's cap from his head. "Look at you! You must be sixty if you're a day. And yet here you are, still writing parking tickets, no doubt precisely as you were doing ten years ago, and twenty years ago, and *thirty* years ago. You must be so wonderful at the job, so *singularly* efficient, that your superiors simply don't dare promote you. I salute the remarkable comprehensiveness of your insipidity. What a piece of work is a man, indeed! And yet I sense you aren't *entirely* happy with your position—that gin-blossom I see writ large across your features implies that you frequently drown your sorrows. Do you deny it? I see not! Nor is your wife particularly happy about it, either. Oh, I detect in your hunted features, your bullying swagger that nevertheless yields instantly to superior force, a true Walter Mitty. Well, if it's any consolation, I can at least predict what shall be inscribed upon your tombstone: 'That will be forty-five francs, please.' Now, if you will kindly step away from my vehicle, I'll just head to the nearest police station and ensure . . . and ensure—"

During this rant, the American's face had fallen apart, becoming loose, haggard, and gray. Beads of sweat stood at his temples. He'd hesitated once in his tirade to pass a hand across his forehead; another time to wave the hand in front of his nose, as if to brush away some odor. Gabler noticed that the entire café, in fact the entire street, had gone silent, watching this bizarre drama play out. The man was either drunk or on drugs. Now the man moved unsteadily toward the Lamborghini, the officer quickly giving ground before him. The American reached for the door handle—pawed for it, more exactly, with a blind, flailing gesture—and missed. He took another step forward; swayed; steadied himself; swayed again, and then crumpled to the sidewalk. There were cries for help, and some rose from their tables. Gabler, too, jumped to his feet, the chair tumbling away behind him. In his surprise and consternation, he didn't even realize he had just spilled his half-full glass of Pflümli down one leg of his well-pressed pants.

45

Lieutenant Peter Angler sat behind the desk of his office in the Twenty-Sixth Precinct. All the thick paperwork on the desk had been relegated to its four corners, and the center was bare save for three items: a silver coin, a piece of wood, and a bullet.

There were times in every investigation where he felt that things were about to reach a turning point. At such times, Angler had a little ritual he always went through: he pulled these three relics out of a locked desk drawer and examined them in turn. Each, in its own way, marked a milestone in his life—just as every case he cracked while on the force was its own milestone in miniature—and he enjoyed reflecting on their importance.

First, he picked up the coin. It was an old Roman Imperial denarius, struck in AD 37, with Caligula on its face and Agrippina Sr. on the reverse. Angler had purchased the coin after his thesis on the emperor—with its medical and psychological analysis of the changes wrought on Caligula by his serious illness of that year, and the illness's role in transforming him from a relatively benevolent ruler to an insane tyrant—won first prize at Brown his senior year. The coin had been very expensive, but somehow he felt he had to own it.

Placing the coin back on the table, he picked up the piece of wood. Originally curled and rough, he had sanded and smoothed it himself until it was barely larger than a pencil, then varnished it so that it glowed brilliantly in the fluorescent light of the office. It had come from the first old-growth redwood that he, in his days as an environmental activist, had saved from the logging companies. He had camped in the upper canopy of the tree for almost three weeks, until the loggers finally gave up and moved elsewhere. As he descended the tree, he'd cut off a small dead branch as a memento of the triumph.

Lastly he reached for the bullet. It was bent and misshapen from the impact with his own left tibia. He never discussed, on the Job or off, the fact that he'd taken a bullet; never wore or displayed the Police Combat Cross he'd earned for extraordinary heroism. Few people who worked with him even knew he'd been shot in the line of duty. It didn't matter. Angler turned the bullet over in his hands, then replaced it on the desk. *He* knew, and that was enough.

He put the items carefully back in their drawer, relocked it, then picked up the phone and dialed the number for the departmental secretary. "Have them come in," he said.

A minute later, the door opened and three men stepped in: Sergeant Slade and two desk sergeants assigned to the Alban murder. "Report, please," Angler said.

One stepped forward. "Sir, we've completed our examination of the TSA records."

"Go on."

"As you requested, we went back through all available records for a period of eighteen months, looking for any evidence that the victim might have made trips to the United States other than June fourth of this year. We found such evidence. The victim, using the same false name of Tapanes Landberg, entered the country from Brazil roughly one year previously, on May seventeenth, coming through JFK. Five days later, on May twenty-second, he flew back to Rio."

"Anything else?"

"Yes, sir. Using Homeland Security documentation, we found that a man using the same name and passport took a flight from LaGuardia to Albany on May eighteenth, returning May twenty-first."

"A false Brazilian passport," Angler said. "It would have to be of excellent quality. I wonder where he got it?"

"No doubt such things are easier to obtain in a country like Brazil than they are here," said Slade.

"No doubt. What else?"

"That's it, sir. At Albany, the trail went cold. We checked all available avenues through local law enforcement, travel companies, bus terminals, regional airports and airlines, hotels, and car rental companies. There is no further record of Tapanes Landberg until he boarded the plane back to LaGuardia on May twenty-first, and thence to Brazil the following day."

"Thank you. Excellent work. Dismissed."

Angler waited until the two had left the office. Then he nodded at Slade and motioned the man toward a chair. From one of the piles of paperwork at the edges of his desk, he took a large stack of oversize index cards. They contained information compiled enthusiastically by Sergeant Slade over the past several days.

"Why would our friend *Alban* have gone to *Albany*?" Angler asked.

"No idea," Slade replied. "But I'd lay odds those two trips are linked."

"It's a small town. The airport and central bus terminal would both fit in the Port Authority waiting room. Alban would have a hard time hiding his tracks there."

"How do you know so much about Albany?"

"I have relatives in Colonie, to the northwest." Angler turned his attention to the index cards. "You've been a busy man. In another life, you could have made a superlative muckraking journalist."

Slade smiled.

Angler shuffled slowly through the cards. "Pendergast's tax and property records. I can't imagine they were easy to obtain."

"Pendergast is a rather private individual."

"I see he owns four properties: two in New York, one in New Orleans and another nearby. The one in New Orleans is a parking lot. Odd."

Slade shrugged.

"I wouldn't be surprised if he owned offshore real estate, as well."

"Neither would I. I'm afraid that would resist any further digging on my part, though, sir."

"And it's beside the point." Angler put these cards down, glanced at another set. "His record of arrests made and convictions obtained." He shuffled through them. "Impressive. Very impressive indeed."

"The statistic that I found most interesting was the number of his perps who died in the process of being apprehended."

Angler searched for this statistic, found it, raised his eyebrows in surprise. Then he continued his perusal. "I see that Pendergast has almost as many official censures as he has commendations."

"My friends in the Bureau say he's controversial. A lone wolf. He's independently wealthy, takes a salary of one dollar a year just to keep things official. In recent years the upper echelons of the FBI have tended to take a hands-off approach, given his success rate, so long as he doesn't do anything too egregious. He appears to have at least one powerful, invisible friend high up in the Bureau—maybe more."

"Hmmm." More turning of index cards. "A stint in the special forces. What'd he do?"

"Classified. All I learned was that he earned several medals for bravery under fire and completing certain high-value covert actions."

Angler formed the cards into a pile, then squared them against his desk and put them to one side. "Does all this confuse you, Loomis?"

Slade returned Angler's look. "Yes."

"Me, too. What does it all mean?"

"The whole thing stinks . . . sir."

"Precisely. You know it, and I know it. And we've known it for some time. Hence, all this." And Angler patted the pile of index cards. "Let's break it down. The last time Pendergast saw his son alive— by his own admission—was eighteen months ago, in Brazil. A year ago, Alban returned briefly to the U.S. under an alias, traveled to upstate New York, then returned to Brazil. Around three weeks ago, he returned to New York—and this time, was killed for his pains. In his body was found a piece of turquoise. Agent Pendergast claims that piece of turquoise led him to the Salton Fontainebleau, where he was supposedly assaulted by the same man who pretended to be a scientist and who probably killed a technician at the Museum. All of a sudden, after being uncooperative and evasive, Pendergast becomes forthcoming...that is, once he learned we'd found 'Tapanes Landberg.' But then, after unloading a bunch of questionable information on us, he clams up again, stops cooperating. For example, neither he nor Lieutenant D'Agosta bothered to tell us that the phony professor killed himself in the Indio jail. We had to find that out for ourselves. And when we sent Sergeant Dawkins out to examine the Fontainebleau, he came back reporting that the inside of the place looked as if it had been unvisited for years and could not have been the scene of some extended fight. You're exactly right, Loomis—it stinks. It stinks to high heaven. No matter which way I turn, I find myself being confronted by the same conclusion: Pendergast is sending us on one wild goose chase after another. And I can think of only one reason for that—he himself is complicit in his son's death. And then, there's this." Leaning forward, Angler plucked an article in Portuguese from atop one of the piles on his desk. "A report from a Brazilian newspaper, vague and unsourced, that describes a massacre that took place in the jungle, with the involvement of an unnamed gringo described here as a man '*de rosto pálido.*'"

"*De rosto pálido?* What's that mean?"

"Of pale visage."

"Holy shit."

"And all this took place eighteen months ago—just when Pendergast himself was in Brazil."

Angler put the article down. "This article came to my attention just this morning. It's the key, Loomis—I feel it. The key to the whole mystery." He leaned back in his chair and glanced at the ceiling. "There's one missing piece, I believe. Just one. And when I find that piece...then I'll have him."

46

Constance Greene walked down a gleaming corridor on the fifth and top floor of Geneva's Clinique Privée La Colline, a gowned doctor at her side.

"How would you characterize his condition?" she asked in perfect French.

"It has been very difficult to make a diagnosis, *mademoiselle*," the doctor replied. "It is something foreign to our experience. This is a multidisciplinary clinic. Half a dozen specialists have been called in to examine the patient. The results of the consultations and tests are...baffling. And contradictory. Certain members of the staff believe he is suffering from an unknown genetic disorder. Others think that he has been poisoned, or is suffering withdrawal symptoms from some compound or drug—there are unusual trace elements in the blood work, but nothing that corresponds to any known substance in our databases. Still others consider the problem to be at least partly psychological—yet nobody can deny the acute physical manifestations."

"What medications are you using to treat the condition?"

"We can't treat the actual condition until we have a diagnosis. We're controlling the pain with transdermal fentanyl patches. Soma as a muscle relaxer. And a benzodiazepine for its sedative effect."

"Which benzo?"

"Klonopin."

"That's a rather formidable cocktail, Doctor."

"It is. But until we know what the source is, we can only treat the symptoms—if we didn't, restraints would have been necessary."

The doctor opened a door and ushered Constance in. Beyond lay a modern, spotless, and functional room containing a single bed. Numerous monitors and medical devices surrounded the bed, some flashing complicated readouts on LCD screens, others beeping in steady rhythms. At the far end of the room was an unbroken series of windows, tinted blue, that looked out onto the Avenue de Beau-Séjour.

Lying in the bed was Special Agent Aloysius Pendergast. Leads were attached to his temples; an IV was inserted into the curve of one wrist; a blood pressure cuff was fixed to one arm and a blood-oxygen meter clipped to a fingertip. A privacy screen was bunched together on overhead rings at the foot of the bed.

"He has said very little," the doctor said. "And of that, even less has made sense. If you can get us any information that could be of assistance, we would be grateful."

"Thank you, Doctor," Constance said with a nod. "I'll do my best."

"*Mademoiselle.*" And with that, the doctor gave the briefest of bows, turned, and left the room, closing the door quietly behind him.

Constance stood for a moment, glancing at the closed door. Then, smoothing down her dress with a sweep of her hand, she took a seat at the lone chair placed beside the bed. Although nobody had a cooler head than Constance Greene, what she saw nevertheless deeply disturbed her. The FBI agent's face was a dreadful gray color, and his white-blond hair was disarrayed and darkened with sweat. The chiseled lines of the face were blurred by several days' growth of beard. Fever seemed to radiate from him. His eyes were shut, but she could see the eyeballs moving beneath the bruised-looking lids. As she watched, his body stiffened, as if in pain; spasmed; then relaxed.

She leaned forward, laid a hand over one clenched fist. "Aloysius," she said in a low voice. "It's Constance."

For a moment, no response. Then the fist relaxed. Pendergast's head turned on the pillow. He muttered something incomprehensible.

Constance gave the hand a gentle squeeze. "I'm sorry?"

Pendergast opened his mouth to speak, took a deep, shuddering breath. *"Lasciala, indegno,"* he murmured. *"Battiti meco. L'assassino m'ha ferito."*

Constance released her pressure on the hand.

Another spasm shuddered through Pendergast's frame. "No," he said in a low, strangled voice. "No, you mustn't. The Doorway to Hell...stay back...stay away, *please*...don't look...*the three-lobed burning eye...!*"

His body relaxed and he fell silent for several minutes. Then he stirred again. "It's wrong, Tristram," he said, his voice now clearer and more distinct. *"He* would never change. I fear you were deceived."

This time, the silence was far longer. A nurse came in, checked Pendergast's vitals, replaced the transdermal patch for a fresh one, and left. Constance remained in the chair, still as a statue, her hand on Pendergast's. Finally—at long last—his eyes fluttered open. For a moment, they remained vague, unfocused. Then, blinking, they made a survey of the hospital room. At last, they landed on her.

"Constance," he said in a whisper.

Her response was to squeeze his hand again.

"I've...been having a nightmare. It seems never to end."

His voice was dry and light, like a faint breeze over dead leaves, and she had to lean in closer to catch the words.

"You were quoting the libretto of *Don Giovanni*," she said.

"Yes. I...fancied myself the Commendatore."

"Dreaming of Mozart doesn't sound like a nightmare to me."

"I..." The mouth worked silently for a moment before continuing. "I dislike opera."

"There was something else," Constance said. "Something that did sound like a nightmare. You mentioned a Doorway to Hell."

"Yes. Yes. My nightmares have included memories, as well."

"And then you mentioned Tristram. Some mistake he had made."

To this, Pendergast only shook his head.

Constance waited as he slipped back out of consciousness. Ten minutes later, he moved, opened his eyes again.

"Where am I?" he asked.

"In a hospital in Geneva."

"Geneva." A pause. "Of course."

"From what I can gather, you ruined some meter man's day."

"I remember. He insisted on giving me a ticket. I was dreadful to him. I fear that I...cannot abide petty bureaucrats." Another pause. "It is one of my many bad habits."

When he again fell silent, Constance—confident now that he was lucid—filled him in on recent events, as D'Agosta had informed her: the suicide of his attacker in the Indio jail, the man's face-altering plastic surgery, the reconstruction of his original appearance, and D'Agosta's discovery of his real identity. She also passed on D'Agosta's discovery, from Angler's case file, that when Alban had entered the country under the name Tapanes Landberg a year before, he'd made a brief trip to upstate New York before returning to Brazil. Pendergast listened to it all with interest. Once or twice, his eyes flashed with the old spark she remembered so well. But when she was finished, he closed his eyes, turned his head away, and drifted back into unconsciousness again.

When next he awoke, it was night. Constance, who had not left his side, waited for him to speak.

"Constance," he began, his voice as quiet as before. "You must understand that, at times, it is becoming difficult for me to...maintain my hold on reality. It comes and goes, as does the pain. At present, for instance, just to converse with you in a lucid fashion requires all my concentration. So let me tell you what I have to say, as briefly as possible."

Constance, listening, kept very still.

"I said something unforgivable to you."

"I've forgiven you."

"You are too generous. From almost the beginning, when I scented the lilies in that strange animal gas chamber at the Salton Sea, I sensed what had happened: that my family's past had come back to haunt me. In the form of someone bent on vengeance."

He took a few shallow breaths.

"What my ancestor Hezekiah did was criminal. He created an elixir that was in reality an addictive poison, which killed a great many people and ruined the lives of others. But that was so . . . so far in the past . . ." A pause. "I knew what was happening to me—and you'd guessed it as well. But at the time, I simply couldn't bear your pity. What hope I'd initially held out for reversing the effects quickly faded. I preferred not to even think about it. Hence my appalling remark to you in the music room."

"Please don't dwell on it."

He fell into silence. In the dark room, lit only by the medical instrumentation, Constance was not sure if he was still awake.

"The lilies have begun to suppurate," he said.

"Oh, Aloysius," she said.

"There is something worse than the suffering. It's that I lack answers. This baroque plot at the Salton Sea bears all the hallmarks of something Alban would organize. But who was he working with, and why did they kill him? And . . . how can I bear this slide into madness?"

Now Constance gripped his hand in both of hers. "There has to be a cure, an antidote. We'll conquer this together."

In the dimness, Pendergast shook his head. "No, Constance. There is no cure. You must go away. I'll fly home. I know private doctors who can keep me as comfortable as possible while the end approaches."

"No!" said Constance, her voice louder than she had intended. "I'll never leave you."

"I do not care to have you see me like . . . like this."

She stood up and leaned over him. "I've got no choice."

Pendergast shifted slightly under the covers. "You always have a choice. Please honor my request that you not see me in extremis. Like that man in Indio."

In a languorous movement, she bent over the prostrate sufferer and kissed his brow. "I'm sorry. But my choice is to fight this to the end. Because—"

"But—"

"Because you are the other half of my heart," she murmured. She sat down once more, took up his hand, and did not speak again.

47

The uniformed police officer pulled the squad car over to the curb. "We're here, sir," he said.

"You're sure?" Lieutenant D'Agosta said, peering out the passenger window.

"Forty-One Twenty-Seven Colfax Avenue. Did I get the address wrong?"

"No, that's the one."

D'Agosta was surprised. He'd expected a trailer park or a grim apartment deep in the projects. But this house in the Miller Beach section of Gary, Indiana, was well tended, and—though it might be small—was freshly painted, and the grounds were neatly pruned. Marquette Park was only a few blocks away.

D'Agosta turned to the Gary cop. "Would you mind going over his record again for me? Just so I've got everything in my head."

"Sure thing." The cop unzipped a case, pulled out a computer printout. "It's pretty clean. A couple of traffic tickets, one for doing thirty-eight in a thirty zone, another for passing on the shoulder."

"Passing on the shoulder?" D'Agosta asked. "They give tickets for that here?"

"Under the last chief, we did. He was a hard-ass." The cop looked back at the rap sheet. "Only thing of any substance we have on him was being nabbed during a raid on a known mob hangout. But he was clean—no drugs, no weapons—and since he had no other connections or affiliations we knew of, no charges were pressed. Four months later, his wife reported him missing." The cop returned the rap sheet to the case. "That's it. Given possible ties to the mob, we figured he'd been killed. He never showed up again, alive or dead, no body, nothing. It was eventually shelved as a cold case."

D'Agosta nodded. "Let me do the talking, if you don't mind."

"Be my guest."

D'Agosta glanced at his watch: half past six. Then he opened the door to the cruiser and heaved himself out with a grunt.

He followed the uniformed officer up the walkway and waited while the doorbell was pressed. A few moments later, a woman appeared at the door. With long practice, D'Agosta took in the details: five foot six, 140 pounds, brunette hair. She held a plate in one hand and a dishcloth in the other, and she was dressed for work in a pantsuit that was dated but clean and well pressed. When she saw the officer, a look went across her face: an expression of both anxiety and hope.

D'Agosta stepped forward. "Ma'am, are you Carolyn Rudd?"

The woman nodded.

D'Agosta flashed his badge. "I'm Lieutenant Vincent D'Agosta of the New York Police Department and this is Officer Hektor Ortillo of the Gary police. I was wondering if we could have a few minutes of your time."

There was just the slightest hesitation. "Yes," the woman said. "Yes, of course. Come in." She opened the door and ushered them into a small living room. The furniture was, again, old and functional, but well kept and impeccably clean. Once again D'Agosta got the clear impression of a household in which money had grown tight, but form and civility still mattered.

Ms. Rudd asked them to sit down. "Would you like some lemonade?" she asked. "Coffee?"

Both men shook their heads.

Now there were noises on the stairs leading to the second floor and two curious faces appeared: a boy, maybe twelve, and a girl a few years younger.

"Howie," the woman said. "Jennifer. I'm just going to have a little chat with these gentlemen. Could you please go back upstairs and finish your homework? I'll be up soon."

The two children looked at the cops, silent and wide-eyed. After a few seconds they crept back upstairs and out of sight.

"If you'll excuse me a moment, I'll just put this dish away." The woman retreated to the kitchen, then returned and took a seat across from D'Agosta and the Gary cop.

"What can I do for you?" she asked.

"We've come to talk to you about your husband," D'Agosta said. "Howard Rudd."

The hope he'd seen in her face a few moments earlier returned, much stronger. "Oh!" she said. "Have you ... any new evidence? Is he alive? Where is he?"

The eagerness with which these words tumbled out surprised D'Agosta as much, if not more, than the appearance of the house. Over the last few weeks, he'd developed a distinct portrait of the man who had attacked Agent Pendergast and most likely killed Victor Marsala: a thuggish bastard with no moral code, a venal son of a bitch with few if any redeeming values. When Terry Bonomo and the NYPD facial-detection software identified this man as Howard Rudd, late of Gary, Indiana, D'Agosta had been pretty sure what he'd find when he flew out to speak to the man's wife. But the hope in her eyes was making him rethink his assumptions. He suddenly felt unsure how to go about this.

"No, we haven't 'found' him. Not exactly. The reason I'm here, Mrs. Rudd, is to learn more about your husband."

She looked from D'Agosta to Officer Ortillo and back again. "Are they reopening the case? I felt they shuffled it off way too soon. I want to help you. Just tell me what I can do."

"Well, you can start by telling us what kind of a person he was. As a father and a husband."

"Is," she said.

"Excuse me?"

"What kind of a person he *is*. I know the police think he's dead, but

I'm certain he's alive out there, somewhere. I can feel it. He wouldn't have left if he didn't have a good reason. Someday he'll come back—and he'll explain what happened, and why."

D'Agosta's discomfort increased. The conviction in the woman's voice was unsettling. "If you could just tell us about him, Mrs. Rudd."

"What's there to say?" The woman paused for a moment, reflecting. "He was a good husband, a devoted family man. Hardworking, loyal, a wonderful father. Never went out drinking or gambling, never looked at another woman. His father was a Methodist preacher, and Howard absorbed a lot of his good traits. I've never known anyone as dogged as he was. If he started something, he'd see it through, always. Worked his way through the community college washing dishes. He was a Golden Gloves boxer in his younger days. His word was the most important thing to him, save for his family. He sweated to keep that hardware store of his going, sweated night and day, even when the Home Depot opened up on Route 20 and business dried up. It wasn't his fault he had to borrow money. If only he'd known who..."

The stream of words stopped suddenly, and the woman's eyes widened slightly.

"Please go on," D'Agosta said. "If only he'd known what?"

The woman hesitated. Then she sighed, glanced at the staircase to make sure the children were out of earshot, and continued. "If he'd known the character of those men he borrowed from. You see, the bank felt the store to be a bad risk. They wouldn't give him a loan. Money got tight." She clutched her hands together and looked at the floor. "He borrowed from bad people."

Suddenly she looked up again, directly at D'Agosta, imploringly. "But you can't blame him for that—can you?"

D'Agosta could only shake his head.

"The nights he spent sitting at the kitchen table, looking at the wall, saying nothing...oh, it broke my heart!" The woman wiped away a tear. "And then, one day, he was gone. Just gone. That was over three years ago. And not a word from him since. But there's a reason for it—I know there is." A defiant look came over Mrs. Rudd's face. "I know what the police think. But I don't believe it. I *won't*."

When D'Agosta spoke, it was gently. "Did you have any indication that he was about to leave? Anything at all?"

The woman shook her head. "No. Nothing but the phone call."

"What phone call?"

"It was the night before he went away. There was a phone call, pretty late. He took it in the kitchen. He kept his voice low—I don't think he wanted me to hear him. Afterward, he looked devastated. But he wouldn't talk to me, wouldn't tell me what it was about."

"And you have no idea what could have happened to him or where he's been all this time?"

The woman shook her head again.

"How have you been making ends meet since?"

"I got a job in an advertising company. I do page layout and design work for the firm. It's a decent living."

"And these people your husband borrowed money from. After he disappeared, were there any threats from them? Any reprisals?"

"None."

"Would you happen to have a picture of your husband?"

"Of course. Quite a few." Mrs. Rudd turned, reached toward a small group of framed photographs on a side table, plucked one up, and handed it to D'Agosta. He looked at it. It was a family shot, with parents in the middle, the two children on either side.

Terry Bonomo had nailed it. The man in the photograph was the spitting image of their computer reconstruction, pre-surgery.

As he handed the photograph back, Mrs. Rudd suddenly grasped his wrist. Her grip was surprisingly strong. "Please," she said. "Help me find my husband. *Please*."

D'Agosta couldn't bear it any longer. "Ma'am, I have bad news for you. Earlier, I told you we hadn't found your husband. But we do have a body, and I'm afraid it may be him."

The grip on his wrist tightened.

"But we need a sample of his DNA in order to be sure. Could we borrow a few personal effects of his—a hairbrush, say, or a toothbrush? We'll return them to you, of course."

The woman said nothing.

"Mrs. Rudd," D'Agosta continued, "sometimes not knowing can be a lot worse than knowing—even if knowing proves to be very painful."

For a long moment, the woman did not move. Then, slowly, she released her grip on D'Agosta's wrist. Her hand slumped into her own lap. Her eyes went distant for a moment. Then, pulling herself together, she stood up, walked toward the steps, and mounted them without a word.

Twenty minutes later, in the passenger seat of the police car on the way back to O'Hare, the pocket of his suit jacket containing a hairbrush of Howard Rudd's, carefully sealed in a ziplock bag, D'Agosta pondered ruefully just how wrong one's assumptions could be. The last thing he'd expected was that tidy house on Colfax Avenue, or the fiercely loyal and determined widow who lived inside.

Rudd might be a murderer. But he was also, it seemed, at one time a good man who made a bad call and got himself into trouble. D'Agosta had seen it happen before. Sometimes the more you struggled, the deeper into the shit you sank. D'Agosta was forced to reevaluate Rudd. Now he realized that Rudd's very love of family, and the bind he found himself in—whatever it might have been, exactly—had forced him to do some terrible things, including change his looks and identity. He had little doubt the leverage they had used against him was his little family.

These were some bad motherfuckers.

He glanced over at the Gary policeman. "Thank you, Officer."

"Don't mention it."

D'Agosta returned his gaze to the freeway ahead. It was strange—very strange. They had "Nemo," Marsala's likely killer and Pendergast's attacker, on ice...but with no history, no backstory—except that he had once been a hardworking, decent family man named Howard Rudd. There was a gap of three years between Rudd's disappearance in Gary and his appearance at the Museum, posing as a phony scientist named Waldron.

This left D'Agosta with one big question. What the hell happened in between?

48

Lieutenant Angler sat in the back room of the Republic Rent-a-Car agency at the Albany airport, gloomily twirling a pencil on the desk in front of him, waiting for Mark Mohlman—the manager—to finish with a customer out front and return to the office. Everything had been going so well, it was like a dream. And now, Angler realized, that's probably just what it had been. A dream.

At his request, his team had prepared lists of everyone who'd rented a car in the Albany area during the May window when Alban was in town. Examining the lists himself, Angler got a hit: a certain Abrades Plangent—another anagram for Alban Pendergast—had rented a car from Republic on May 19, the day after he flew to Albany. Angler had made a call to the rental office and got a Mark Mohlman on the line. Yes, they had a record of the rental. Yes, the car was still in active use, and was available, although it was currently at another agency about forty miles away. Yes, Mohlman could arrange to get the vehicle back to Albany. And so Angler and Sergeant Slade got into a pool car and made the three-hour drive from New York City up to the state capital.

Mohlman had proven to be just the man they needed. An ex-marine and a card-carrying member of the NRA, he helped them with all the enthusiasm of a wannabe cop. Tasks that might have taken all sorts of tiresome paperwork, or perhaps even a court order, became cakewalks in Mohlman's efficient hands. He found the records of Alban's rental—a blue Toyota Avalon—and provided them to Angler. Alban had returned the car after three days, having put only 196 miles on the odometer.

It was at this point that Angler began to feel a nagging suspicion. Alban Pendergast had the annoying ability to disappear just about anytime he wanted to. Putting himself in Alban's shoes, he decided that the young man would probably have taken additional steps to cover his movements. He asked Mohlman to double-check the fleet tracking information for the car during the period of Alban's rental. Mohlman was again only too happy to oblige. He logged into Republic's vehicle tracking system and accessed the fleet records of the Avalon. Angler's hunch was correct: the tracking data didn't match the odometer. According to Republic's tracking system, the car had been driven 426 miles during Alban's rental.

And that was when the investigation started to fall apart. All of a sudden, there were too many variables. Alban could have monkeyed with the odometer settings—that was allegedly impossible, but Angler wouldn't put it past Alban to figure out a way. Or he could have removed the car's fleet tracker and put it on another vehicle, swapping it back later, thus furnishing false data. Or maybe he hadn't bothered swapping it back—he'd just left a different tracker on the vehicle to add to the confusion. They needed some way to distinguish among the possibilities, and he didn't have a clue how to do that.

At that point, Mohlman had been forced to leave the office to deal with an irate customer. And so Angler sat morosely, twirling the pencil. Sergeant Slade sat across from him, characteristically silent. As he twirled, Angler wondered exactly what he'd hoped to achieve by coming here. Even if he knew exactly how many miles Alban had traveled and what kind of car he'd rented, so what? Alban could have gone anywhere in those three days. Blue Avalons were legion. And in the tiny towns that dotted upstate New York, traffic cameras were exceedingly rare.

But when Mohlman came into the office, there was a smile on his face. "The black box," he said.

"What's that?"

"The black box. The event data recorder. Every rental car has one."

"They do?" Angler knew about fleet trackers from his own experience with police cruisers, but this was something new to him.

"Sure. For a few years now. Initially, they were used just to provide info on how and why air bags deployed. The boxes were turned off by default; it took a hard jolt to get them to start recording. But recently the rental companies have paid to get cars with special boxes that are a lot more sophisticated. Nobody who rents a car can get away with anything nowadays."

"What information do they collect, exactly?"

"Well, the newest ones record rudimentary location data. Distance driven per day. Average speed. Steering. Braking. Even the use of seat belts. And it's tied into the GPS system. When the engine is turned off, the black box records the vehicle's direction, relative to when the engine was turned on. And, just like with an airplane, a car's black box can't be removed or tampered with. People just haven't realized how much we in the rental business can keep track of what they're doing with our cars."

Can't be removed or tampered with. Hope began to creep back into Angler's soul. "But we're talking about events that happened a year ago. Could this thing still have that data stored inside?"

"That depends. Once its memory is filled up, the device starts overwriting the oldest data. But you may have caught a break there. This Avalon has been assigned to our Tupper Lake office for the last six months—and they don't get many rentals out of there. So, yeah, the data still might be there."

"How do you access it?"

Mohlman shrugged. "You just plug it in. The latest models can even transmit their data wirelessly."

"You can do this?" Angler asked. He couldn't believe his luck. Alban might be smart, but in this he had made a serious mistake. He hoped to hell Mohlman wouldn't need to ask for the approval of a judge.

But Mohlman merely nodded. "The car's still in the garage. I'll have my guys download and print it out for you."

An hour later, Angler was seated at a workstation in Albany's central police headquarters, a map of New York State open on his lap. Sergeant Slade sat at another workstation beside him.

Mohlman had come through. In addition to all sorts of relatively useless information, the Avalon's event data recorder provided them with a key item: on the day Alban rented the car, it was driven eighty-six miles almost due north from the Albany airport.

That put the car square in the tiny town of Adirondack, on the shores of Schroon Lake. Angler had thanked Mohlman effusively, asked him to keep quiet about this, and promised him a ridealong in an NYPD cruiser if he ever found himself in Manhattan.

"Adirondack, New York," Angler said aloud. "Zip code 12808. Population three hundred. What the hell would take Alban all the way from Rio to Adirondack?"

"The view?" Slade asked.

"The view from Sugarloaf's a hell of a lot more dramatic." He accessed the workstation's criminal database and searched the region for the dates in question. "No murders," he said after a minute. "No thefts. No crime at all! Christ, it looks as if all of Warren County was asleep on May nineteenth, twentieth, and twenty-first."

Exiting the system, he began a Google search. "Adirondack," he muttered. "There's nothing there. Except a lot of tall trees. And a single firm: Red Mountain Industries."

"Never heard of it," said Slade.

Red Mountain Industries. It rang a faint bell. Angler searched for it, read over the results quickly. "It's a large, private defense contractor." More reading. "With something of a dubious history, if you can believe these web conspiracy theorists. Secretive, if nothing else. Owned by someone named John Barbeaux."

"I'll check him out." Sergeant Slade turned to his own workstation.

Angler didn't reply for a moment. The right-brained part of him was thinking again—and thinking fast. Pendergast had last seen his son in Brazil, eighteen months ago.

"Sergeant," he said. "Do you remember that newspaper article I told you about? When Pendergast was in Brazil a year and a half ago, there were reports of a massacre, deep in the jungle, spearheaded by a pale gringo."

Slade stopped typing. "Yes, sir."

"A few months later, Alban secretly travels to Adirondack, New York, home of Red Mountain, a private defense contractor."

There was a silence while Slade pondered Angler's words.

"You're thinking that Pendergast was behind that massacre?" Slade said at last. "And that somebody at Red Mountain perhaps assisted him? Financed the project, provided the weapons? Kind of a mercenary action?"

"The thought was crossing my mind."

Slade frowned. "But why would Pendergast be involved in something like that?"

"Who knows? The guy's a cipher. But I bet I know why Alban went to Adirondack. And why he was killed."

Slade went silent again, listening.

"Alban knew about the massacre. There's even a good chance he was there: remember, Pendergast said the only time he met his son was in the *jungles of Brazil*. What if Alban was blackmailing both his father, Pendergast, and his contact at Red Mountain about what he knew? And so together, they engineered his death."

"You're saying Pendergast bumped off his own son?" Slade said. "That's cold, even for Pendergast."

"Blackmailing your father is pretty cold, too. And look at Pendergast's case history—we know what he is capable of. It may be a theory, but it's the only answer that fits."

"Why drop the body off on Pendergast's own doorstep?"

"To throw the police off the real scent. That whole business with the turquoise, the supposed attack on Pendergast in California—another smokescreen. Recall how uncooperative and disinterested

Pendergast was at first. He only warmed up when I began to zero in on Alban's movements."

There was another brief silence.

"If you're right, there's only one thing we can do," Slade said. "Go to Red Mountain. Talk to this Barbeaux directly. If there's a rotten apple in his company, selling arms on the side and pocketing the profits—or perhaps directly involved in mercenary activities—he'd want to know."

"That's risky," Angler replied. "What if Barbeaux's the one who's dirty? That would be like walking right into a lion's den."

"I've just finished checking him out." Slade patted his workstation. "He's as pure as the wind-driven snow. Eagle Scout, decorated Army Ranger, deacon at his church, never a breath of scandal or a rap sheet of any kind."

Angler thought a moment. "He would be the best person to launch a quiet investigation into this. Into his own company. And if he's dirty—despite the Eagle Scout badge—it would put him off guard, smoke him out."

"My thought exactly," Slade replied. "One way or another, we'd learn the truth. As long as our initial approach was kept quiet."

"Okay. We'll offer to keep it quiet if he makes a good-faith effort. Will you put the necessary paperwork through, notify the team of where we're going, who we'll be interviewing, and when we'll be returning?"

"Already on it." And Slade turned back toward his workstation.

Angler put the map aside and stood up. "Next stop," he said in a low voice, "Adirondack, New York."

49

For the second time in less than a week, Lieutenant D'Agosta found himself in the gun room of the mansion on Riverside Drive. Everything was the same: the same rare weaponry on display, the rosewood walls, the coffered ceiling. The other attendees were the same, as well: Constance Greene, dressed in a soft organdy blouse and pleated skirt of dark maroon, and Margo, who gave him a distracted smile. Conspicuous in his absence was the owner of the mansion, Aloysius Pendergast.

Constance took a seat at the head of the table. She seemed even more of a cipher than usual, with her stilted manner and old-fashioned accent. "Thank you both for coming," she said. "I've requested your presence this morning because we have an emergency."

D'Agosta eased into one of the leather chairs that surrounded the table, a sense of foreboding filling his mind.

"My guardian, our friend, is unwell—indeed, he is extremely sick."

D'Agosta leaned forward. "How sick?"

"He is dying."

This was greeted with a shock of silence.

"So he was poisoned, like the guy in Indio?" D'Agosta said. "Son of a bitch. Where's he been?"

"In Brazil and Switzerland, trying to learn what happened to

Alban and why he himself was poisoned. He had a collapse in Switzerland. I found him in a Geneva hospital."

"Where's he now?" D'Agosta asked.

"Upstairs. Under private care."

"My understanding is that it took users of Hezekiah's elixir months, years, to sicken and die," Margo said. "Pendergast must have received an extremely concentrated dose."

Constance nodded. "Yes. His attacker knew he would get only a single chance. It's also a fair assumption—based on his even quicker decline—that the man who assaulted Pendergast in the Salton Fontainebleau, and is now dead in Indio, got an even stronger dose."

"That fits," Margo said. "I got a report from Dr. Samuels in Indio. The dead man's skeleton shows the same unusual compounds I discovered in Mrs. Padgett's skeleton—only in much more concentrated amounts. It's no wonder the elixir killed him so fast."

"If Pendergast is dying," D'Agosta said, rising, "why the heck isn't he in a hospital?"

A narrow stare met his look. "He insisted on leaving the Geneva hospital and flying home via private medical transport. You can't legally hospitalize someone against his will. He insists there's nothing anyone can do for him and he will not die in a hospital."

"Jesus," said D'Agosta. "What can we do?"

"We need an antidote. And to find that antidote, we need information. That's why we're here." She turned to D'Agosta. "Lieutenant, please tell us the results of your recent investigations."

D'Agosta mopped his brow. "I don't know how relevant some of this is, but we traced Pendergast's attacker to Gary, Indiana. Three years ago, he was a guy named Howard Rudd, family man and shop owner. He got into debt with the wrong people and vanished, leaving his wife and kids. He appeared two months ago with a different face. He's the guy who attacked Pendergast and probably killed Victor Marsala. We're trying to account for that gap in his history—where he was, who he was working for. Brick wall so far." D'Agosta glanced at Margo. She had said nothing, but her face was pale.

For a moment, there was silence. Then Constance spoke again. "Not quite."

D'Agosta looked at her.

"I've been compiling a list of Hezekiah's victims, on the assumption that a descendant was responsible for the poisoning. Two victims were Stephen and Ethel Barbeaux, a married couple, who succumbed to the effects of the elixir in 1895, leaving three orphaned children, including a baby who was conceived while Ethel was taking the elixir. The family lived in New Orleans, on Dauphine Street, just two houses down from the Pendergast family mansion."

"Why them, in particular?" said D'Agosta.

"They have a great-grandson, John Barbeaux. He's CEO of a military consulting company called Red Mountain Industries—and a wealthy and reclusive man. Barbeaux had a son—an only child. The youth was a musical prodigy. Always of delicate health, the boy fell ill two years ago. I haven't been able to learn much about the details of the illness, but it apparently baffled an entire corps of doctors and specialists with its unusual symptoms. A titanic medical effort failed to save his life." Constance looked from Margo to D'Agosta and back again. "The case was written up in the British medical journal *Lancet*."

"What are you saying?" D'Agosta asked. "That the poison that killed John Barbeaux's great-grandparents jumped down through the generations to kill his son?"

"Yes. The boy complained of the stink of rotten flowers before he died. And I've found a scattering of other similar deaths in the Barbeaux family, going back generations."

"I don't buy it," said D'Agosta.

"I do," said Margo, speaking for the first time. "What you're suggesting is that Hezekiah's elixir caused epigenetic changes. Such changes can and do get passed down the generations. Environmental poisons are the leading cause of epigenetic changes."

"Thank you," said Constance.

Another brief silence settled over the room.

D'Agosta rose to his feet and began pacing restlessly, his mind racing. "Okay. Let's put this together. You're saying Barbeaux poisoned Pendergast with the elixir as a way of getting revenge, not only for his ancestors, but for his *son*. How did Barbeaux get the idea? I mean, it's unlikely he'd even have known about what happened to his great-grandparents, who died more than a century ago. And this entire revenge plot—killing Alban, sticking a piece of turquoise into him, luring Pendergast all the way across the country—it's baroque in complexity. Why? Who could have dreamed it up?"

"A man named Tapanes Landberg," said Constance.

"Who?" asked Margo.

"Of course!" D'Agosta smacked his palm against the other and turned. "Alban! As I told you, he made a trip to New York—to the Albany area, according to Lieutenant Angler's case file—over a year before he was killed!"

"Red Mountain Industries is located in Adirondack, New York," Constance said. "An hour and a half's drive from Albany."

D'Agosta turned again. "Alban. The crazy fuck. From what Pendergast has told me, this is exactly the kind of game he'd love to play. Of course, brilliant as he was, he'd have known all about Hezekiah's elixir. So he went out, found a descendant of a victim—somebody with both the motive for revenge and the means to carry it out. He hit pay dirt with Barbeaux, whose son died. Alban must have learned something of Barbeaux's personality; he's no doubt the eye-for-an-eye kind of fellow. It would be beautiful in a different context: both Barbeaux and Alban being revenged on Pendergast."

"Yes. The scheme reeks of Alban," said Constance. "He may even have researched the Salton Fontainebleau and the turquoise mine. He could have told Barbeaux: Here's the setup. All you have to do is synthesize the elixir and lure Pendergast to the spot."

"Except that, in the end, Alban got double-crossed," said Margo.

"The big question," D'Agosta went on, "is how the hell will all this help us develop an antidote?"

"We've got to decipher the formula for the elixir before we can reverse its effects. If Barbeaux was able to reconstruct it, then so can we." Constance looked around. "I'll search the basement collections here, the files, the family archives, and the old chemistry laboratory, looking for evidence of Hezekiah's formula. Margo, will you do more work on the bones of Mrs. Padgett? Those bones contain a vital clue—given the great lengths Barbeaux went in getting one."

"Yes," said Margo. "And the coroner's report on Rudd might also help unravel the formula."

"As for me," said D'Agosta, "I'm going to check up on this Barbeaux character. If I find he's responsible, I'll squeeze him so hard the formula will pop out of—"

"*No.*"

This was said by a new and different voice—little more than a cracked whisper, coming from the doorway to the gun room. D'Agosta turned toward it and saw Pendergast. He stood unsteadily, leaning on the door frame, wearing a disordered silk dressing gown. He seemed almost corpse-like, save for the eyes—and these glittered like coins above puffy, blue-black bags of skin.

"Aloysius!" Constance cried, standing up. "What are you doing out of bed?" She hurried around the table toward him. "Where's Dr. Stone?"

"The doctor is useless."

She tried to usher him out of the room, but he pushed her away. "I must speak." He staggered, righted himself. "If you are correct, then the man who did this was able *to kill my son*. He is clearly an extremely powerful and competent adversary." He shook his head as if to clear his mind. "You go after him, you'll place yourselves in mortal danger. This is my fight. I, and I alone . . . will follow through . . . *must* follow through . . ."

A man abruptly appeared in the doorway—tall and thin, wearing tortoiseshell glasses and a chalk-striped suit, a stethoscope around his neck.

"Come, my friend," the doctor said gently. "You must not exert yourself. Let's return upstairs. Here, we can take the elevator."

"No!" Pendergast protested again, more feebly this time—clearly, the effort of leaving his bed had exhausted him. Dr. Stone bore him off, gently but firmly. As they vanished down the hall, D'Agosta heard Pendergast saying: "The light. How glaring it is! Turn it off, I beg you…"

The three remained standing, looking at each other. D'Agosta noticed that Constance, normally remote and unreadable, was now flushed and agitated.

"He's right," D'Agosta said. "This Barbeaux is no ordinary guy. We better think this through. We need to stay in close touch and share information. A single mistake might get us all killed."

"That's why we won't make one," said Margo quietly.

50

The office was spartan, functional, and—as befitted the personality of its occupant—contained more than a hint of military efficiency. The large desk, gleaming with polish, held nothing beyond an old-fashioned blotter, a pen-and-pencil desk set, a phone, and a single photo in a silver frame, arranged in orderly ranks. There was no computer or keyboard. An American flag stood on a wooden stand in a corner. The wall behind contained bookshelves racked with volumes of military history and Jane's yearbooks and annuals: *Armour and Artillery*, *Explosive Ordnance Disposal*, *Military Vehicles and Logistics*. Another wall displayed an array of framed medals, awards, and commendations.

A man sat behind the desk, wearing a business suit, crisp white shirt, and dark-red tie. He sat erect, and he wore the suit as one might wear a uniform. He was writing with a fountain pen, and the scratch of the nib filled the otherwise silent office. Outside the single picture window lay a small campus of similar buildings, clad in black glass, surrounded by a double set of chain-link fences topped with razor wire. Past the outer fence was a line of trees, rich and green, and, in the farther distance, a splash of blue lake.

The phone rang and the man picked it up. "Yes?" he said curtly. His voice was full of gravel, and it seemed to come from deep within his barrel chest.

"Mr. Barbeaux," came the secretary's voice from the outer office. "There are two police officers here to see you."

"Give me sixty seconds," he said. "Then show them in."

"Yes, sir."

The man hung up the phone. He sat at his desk, motionless, for another few seconds. Then, with a single glance at the photograph, he rose from his chair. He was just over sixty years of age, but the motion was made as effortlessly as by a youth of twenty. He turned to examine himself in a small mirror that hung on the wall behind his desk. A large, heavy-boned face stared back: blue eyes, lantern jaw, Roman nose. Although the tie was perfectly knotted, he adjusted it anyway. Then he turned toward the door to his office.

As he did so, it opened and his secretary ushered in two figures.

Barbeaux looked at them in turn. One was tall, with dark-blond hair that was slightly windblown. He moved with authority, and with the grace of a natural athlete. The other was shorter and darker. He returned Barbeaux's look with an expression that betrayed absolutely nothing.

"John Barbeaux?" said the taller man.

Barbeaux nodded.

"I'm Lieutenant Peter Angler of the NYPD, and this is my associate, Sergeant Slade."

Barbeaux shook the proffered hands in turn and returned to his seat. "Please, sit down. Coffee, tea?"

"Nothing, thanks." Angler sat down in one of the chairs ranged before the desk, and Slade followed suit. "This is quite the fortress you have here, Mr. Barbeaux."

Barbeaux smiled at this. "It's mostly show. We're a private military contractor. I've found that it pays to look the part."

"I'm curious, though. Why build such an extensive operation way out here, in the middle of nowhere?"

"Why not?" Barbeaux replied. When Angler said nothing, he added: "My parents used to come up here every summer. I like the Schroon Lake area."

"I see." Angler crossed one leg over the other. "It is very pretty country."

Barbeaux nodded again. "In addition, land is inexpensive. Red Mountain owns more than a thousand acres for use in training, warfare simulations, ordnance testing, and the like." He paused. "So. What brings you gentlemen to upstate New York?"

"Actually, Red Mountain. At least in part."

Barbeaux frowned in surprise. "Really? What possible interest could the NYPD have with my company?"

"Would you mind telling me what it is that Red Mountain Industries does, exactly?" Angler asked. "I poked around a bit on the Internet, but your official site was rather short on hard data."

The surprised look had not left Barbeaux's face. "We provide training and support to law enforcement, security, and military clients. We also do research in advanced weapons systems and cutting-edge tactical and strategic theory."

"Ah. And would that theory extend to counterterrorism?"

"Yes."

"Do you provide on-the-ground as well as back-office support?"

There was a slight pause before Barbeaux answered. "At times, yes. How, exactly, can I be of help to you?"

"I'll tell you in a moment, if you'll permit me just one or two more questions. I assume the U.S. government is your biggest client?"

"It is," said Barbeaux.

"And so it would be fair to say that maintaining your reputation as a security contractor is of great importance to you? I mean, all those congressional oversight committees and that sort of thing."

"It is of paramount importance," replied Barbeaux.

"Of course it is." Angler uncrossed his legs and sat forward. "Mr. Barbeaux, the reason we're here is because we have uncovered evidence of a problem in your organization."

Barbeaux went very still. "Excuse me? What kind of problem?"

"We don't have the details. But we believe there is a person or persons—it might be a small cadre, but it's more likely to be a rogue individual—who has subverted Red Mountain's resources and may be involved in unauthorized doings. Perhaps private arms dealing, training, or mercenary activity."

"But that's simply not possible. We vet all new employees extensively, with the most exhaustive background checks available. And all ongoing employees must submit to yearly lie detector tests."

"I understand it must be hard for you to accept," Angler replied. "Nevertheless, our investigations have led to this conclusion."

Barbeaux was silent for a moment, thinking. "Naturally, I'd like to help you gentlemen. But we are such a scrupulously careful outfit—you have to be, in this business—that I just don't see how what you say could be."

Angler paused briefly before continuing. "Let me put it in a different light. If we're right, wouldn't you agree that—whatever the specifics—it would leave Red Mountain vulnerable?"

Barbeaux nodded. "Yes. Yes, it would."

"And if it were true, and news leaked out . . . well, you can imagine what the fallout would be."

Barbeaux considered this for a moment. Then he slowly released his breath. "You know—" he began, then stopped. And then he stood up and came around the desk. He looked first at Angler, then at Sergeant Slade. The shorter man had been silent throughout the conversation, letting his superior do the talking. Barbeaux looked back at Angler. "You know, I think we should have this conversation someplace else. If I've learned anything in my life, I've learned that walls can have ears—even in a private office such as this."

He walked to the door, led the way through the outer office, to the hallway beyond, and then to the elevator bank. He pressed the DOWN button, and the nearest set of doors whispered open. Ushering the two police officers in ahead of him, Barbeaux stepped in himself and pressed the button marked B3.

"B3?" Angler asked.

"The third level below ground. We have a couple of ordnance proving ranges down there. They are soundproofed and otherwise hardened. There we can talk freely."

The elevator descended to the lowest level, and the doors opened onto a long concrete corridor. Red lightbulbs within metal cages threw a crimson glow over the hallway. Stepping out of the elevator,

Barbeaux walked down the hallway, passing the occasional window-less door of thick steel. At last he stopped before one marked simply PR-D, opened it, flicked on a row of light switches with the back of his palm, then satisfied himself that the room was unoccupied before showing the two officers in.

Lieutenant Angler entered and looked around at the walls, floor, and ceiling, which were all lined with some kind of black, rubberized insulating material. "This looks like a cross between a squash court and a padded cell."

"As I said, we won't be overheard." Barbeaux closed the door and turned to face the officers. "What you say, Lieutenant, is very disturbing. However, I'll cooperate as best I can."

"I felt confident you'd say that," Angler replied. "Sergeant Slade has done a background check on you, and we feel you're the kind of man who would want to do the right thing."

"How can I help, exactly?" Barbeaux asked.

"Launch a private investigation. Let us help you unmask this operative or operatives. Mr. Barbeaux, the fact is we're not interested in prosecuting Red Mountain. We came into this sideways, through a murder investigation. My interest is in a potential suspect, connected to the murder, whom we believe may be involved with rogue elements in your company."

Barbeaux frowned. "And who is this suspect?"

"An FBI agent whom I'd rather not name, for the present. But if you cooperate, I'll see that Red Mountain is kept out of the papers. I'll bring the FBI agent to justice—and you'll see your firm rid of its rotten apple."

"A rogue FBI agent," Barbeaux said, almost to himself. "Interesting." He glanced back at Angler. "But this is all you know? You have no more information on the identity of this rotten apple inside my own company?"

"None. That's why we've come to you."

"I see." Barbeaux turned to Sergeant Slade. "You can shoot him now."

Lieutenant Angler blinked, as if trying to parse this non sequitur. By the time he turned toward his associate, Slade had his service piece out. Raising it calmly, he fired a quick double tap into Angler's head. The lieutenant's head snapped back and his body crumpled to the floor, a fine mist of blood and gray matter settling over it a moment later.

The sound of the shots was strangely muffled by the proving chamber's soundproofing. Slade looked at Barbeaux as he put his weapon away. "Why did you let him go on for so long?" he asked.

"I wanted to find out just how much he knew."

"I could have told you that."

"You did well, Loomis. You'll be compensated accordingly."

"I hope so. The fifty grand a year you've paid me so far doesn't cut it. I've been working overtime, covering your butt on this. You wouldn't believe the strings I had to pull behind the scenes just to make sure that the Alban Pendergast case was assigned to Angler."

"Don't think it isn't appreciated, my friend. But now there's some pressing business to attend to." Barbeaux walked to a phone that hung near the door, picked it up, and dialed a number. "Richard? It's Barbeaux. I'm in Proving Range D. I've made quite a mess. Please send Housekeeping down to deal with it. Then get the Ops Crew assembled. Set up a meeting in my private conference room for one PM. We've got a new priority."

He hung up the phone and carefully stepped over the body, lying in a rapidly spreading pool of blood. "Sergeant," he said, "take care not to get any of that on your shoes."

51

Constance Greene stood in front of a large recessed bookcase in the library at 891 Riverside Drive. A fire was dying on the grate, the lights were low, and the house was finally silent. The low sounds from the upstairs bedroom, so deeply disturbing, had at last ceased. But the turmoil in Constance's mind had not. Dr. Stone was demanding with increasing urgency that Pendergast be taken to the hospital and put in intensive care. Constance had forbidden it. It was clear to her from her visit to Geneva that a hospital could do nothing and might, indeed, precipitate the end.

Her hand stole to an inner pocket of her dress, where a small vial of cyanide pills nestled. If Pendergast died, this was to be her own, personal insurance policy. Never together in life, but perhaps in death their dust would mingle.

But Pendergast would not die. There must be an answer to his sickness. It would be found somewhere in the abandoned laboratories and dusty files in the rambling sub-basements of the Riverside Drive mansion. Her long study of Pendergast's family history—Hezekiah Pendergast, in particular—convinced her of it.

If my ancestor Hezekiah, Pendergast had told her, *whose own wife was dying as a result of his elixir, could not find a cure, could not undo the damage his nostrum had caused . . . then how can I?*

How, indeed.

She slid a heavy tome from the bookshelf. As she did, a muffled click could be heard, and two adjoining bookcases swung out noiselessly on oiled hinges, revealing the brass grille of an old-fashioned elevator. She stepped inside, shut the gate, and turned a brass lever. With a rattle of ancient machinery, the elevator descended. After a moment it jerked to a halt, and Constance stepped out into a dark anteroom. A faint smell of ammonia, dust, and fungus assaulted her nostrils. It was a familiar smell. She knew this basement well—so well that she almost did not need a light to move around. It was, quite literally, a second home to her.

Nevertheless, she removed an electric lantern from its rack on a nearby wall and switched it on. She moved through a maze of corridors, ultimately reaching an old door, heavy with verdigris, which she pushed open to reveal an abandoned operating room. An empty gurney gleamed in the beam of her flashlight, next to an IV rack draped in cobwebs, a bulbous EKG machine, and a stainless-steel tray spread with operating instruments. She crossed the room to the limestone wall at the far end. A quick gesture—the depressing of a stone panel—caused a section of the wall to swivel inward. She stepped into the opening, her light probing down a spiral staircase cut out of the living bedrock of Upper Manhattan.

She descended the staircase, heading for the mansion's subbasement. At the bottom, the staircase debouched into a long, vaulted space with an earthen floor, a brick pathway running ahead through a series of seemingly endless chambers. Constance walked down the pathway, passing storerooms, niches, and burial vaults. As she moved, her flashlight beam revealed row after row of cabinets, filled with bottles of chemicals in every color and hue, glittering like jewels in the light. This was what remained of the chemistry collection of Antoine Pendergast, who had been known to the public at large by his pseudonym, Enoch Leng—Agent Pendergast's great-granduncle and one of Hezekiah Pendergast's sons.

Chemistry ran in the family.

Hezekiah's wife, also named Constance (strange coincidence, she mused—or then again, perhaps not) had died of her own husband's elixir. In those last, desperate weeks of her life, according to family lore, Hezekiah had finally faced the truth about his patent medicine. After his wife's grisly death, he had taken his own life and been buried in the lead-lined family mausoleum in New Orleans, beneath the old family manse known as Rochenoire. That mausoleum had been permanently sealed after the burning of Rochenoire by a mob, and it now lay under the asphalt of a parking lot.

What, then, had happened to Hezekiah's laboratory, his collection of chemical compounds, and his notebooks? Had they perished in the fire? Or had his son, Antoine, inherited things related to his father's chemical researches and carried them here, to New York City? If he had, they would be somewhere in these decrepit labs in the sub-basement. The other three sons of Hezekiah had no interest in chemistry. Comstock had become a magician of some renown. Boethius, Pendergast's great-grandfather, went off to become an explorer and archaeologist. She could never find out what Maurice, the fourth brother, had accomplished, beyond the fact that he sank to an early death from dipsomania.

If Hezekiah had left notes, laboratory equipment, or chemicals behind, Antoine—or as Constance preferred to think of him, *Dr. Enoch*—was the only one who would have taken an interest. And if that was the case, perhaps some remnant of Hezekiah's formula for his deadly elixir might be found in this sub-basement.

Formula first, antidote second. And all this had to happen before Pendergast died.

After passing through several chambers, Constance walked beneath a Romanesque arch, decorated with a faded tapestry, into a room that lay in considerable disarray. Shelves were toppled; the bottles and their contents shattered on the floor—the results of a conflict that had taken place here eighteen months before. She and Proctor had been trying to restore order from the shambles. This was one of the last rooms awaiting restoration; scattered about the floor lay Antoine's entomological collections, with broken bottles full of dried hornet abdomens, dragonfly wings, iridescent beetle thoraxes, and desiccated spiders.

She glided beneath another archway, into a room filled with stuffed

Passeriformes, and from there into the most unusual region of the sub-basement: Antoine's collection of miscellanea. Here were cases full of such odd things as wigs, doorknobs, corsets, busks, shoes, umbrellas and walking sticks, along with bizarre weapons—harquebuses, pikes, shestopyors, bardiches, poleaxes, glaives, bombards, and war hammers. Next, a room full of ancient medical equipment, apparently for both human and veterinary purposes, some of it evidently much used. This was followed, bizarrely, by a collection of military weapons, uniforms, and various kinds of equipment, dating up to approximately the First World War. Constance paused to examine both the medical and the military collections with some interest.

And then came the devices of torture: brazen bulls, racks, thumbscrews, iron maidens, and, ugliest of all, the Pear of Anguish. In the center of the room an executioner's block had been placed, with an ax lying nearby, near a piece of curled human skin and a shock of hair: relics of a certain horrific event that had taken place here five years earlier, around the time that Agent Pendergast had become her guardian. Constance looked on all these devices with detachment. She was not particularly disturbed by this grotesque evidence of human cruelty. On the contrary, it only confirmed that her view of humanity was correct and needed no revision.

Finally, she came to the room she had been seeking: Antoine's chemical laboratory. Pushing open the door, a forest of glassware, columnar distillation equipment, titration arrays, and other late-nineteenth- and early-twentieth-century apparatus greeted her eye. Years ago she had spent some time in this particular room, assisting her first guardian. She had never seen anything suggestive. Nevertheless, she was certain that—if Antoine had inherited anything from his father—it would be found here.

She set down the electric lantern on a soapstone table and looked about. She would begin her search, she decided, at the far end.

The chemical apparatus was set up on long tables, coated for the most part in a thick mantle of dust. She quickly went through the drawers, finding many notes and old papers, but nothing that predated Antoine, and all of it focused on Antoine's own unique researches, mostly dealing with acids and neurotoxins. Having gone through the drawers, finding nothing, Constance started with the old oaken cabinets that lined the walls, still full of working chemicals behind the fronts of rippled glass. She went carefully through the bottles and vials and ampoules and carboys, but they were all labeled in Antoine's neat copperplate hand—nothing in the handwriting of Hezekiah, which, she knew from her research, was spiky and erratic.

Once having searched the contents of the cabinets, she examined the doors, the drawers, the bottoms and tops and hinges, for any hidden compartments. And almost immediately she found one: a large space behind a drawer in one of the soapstone tables.

It took only a moment to find the locking mechanism and spring it open. There, inside the compartment, stood a jeroboam full of liquid, with a label that read:

Triflic Acid
CF_3SO_3H
Sept. 1940

The bottle was well sealed—so much so that the glass stopper had been gently glazed with heat and fused to the glass bottleneck. Nineteen forty—far too late to be something from Hezekiah. But why was it hidden? She made a mental note to look into this acid, which she had never heard of.

She closed the compartment, turned away, and continued her search.

The first pass through the laboratory produced nothing of value. A more intrusive search would be necessary.

Looking around with the lantern, she noted that one of the wall cabinets was fixed to the stone with bolt anchors that had apparently, at one time in the distant past, been removed and re-anchored.

Taking up a long piece of metal, she pried out the bolts, one after another, working them loose from the rotting stone, until the cabinet could be moved away from the wall. Behind, she discovered an ancient, worm-eaten leather valise, the leather moldy and chewed by vermin.

It was a valise of the kind a patent-medicine salesman might have carried with him to hold his samples. As she drew it out and turned it over, she saw the remains of elaborate Victorian gold stamping, forming a large design dense with curlicues and intertwined vines, leaves, and flowers. She could just barely make out the lettering:

HEZEKIAH'S

~COMPOUND~

ELIXIR

and

GLANDULAR

RESTORATIVE

Moving aside some glassware, she laid the valise out on a table and tried to open it. It was locked. A quick tug, however, tore off the old hinges.

The case was empty, save for a desiccated mouse.

She shook out the mouse, picked up the case, and turned it over to inspect the back. Nothing there; not even slots or seams. Turning the case over again, she paused, held it up, hefted it.

There was something heavy concealed beneath a false bottom, it seemed. A quick slash with a knife along the base of the valise exposed a hidden compartment, in which was snugged an old leather notebook. She pulled the notebook out carefully and opened it to the first page. It was covered with crabbed, spiky handwriting.

Constance glanced over the page for a moment. Then she flipped quickly through the journal until she reached the final pages. At this point, she settled down to read—to read about the *other* woman named Constance, known lovingly to the family by her nickname of Stanza . . .

52

6 Sept. 1905

Darkness. I found her in darkness—a state so very unlike my Stanza! She of all people has ever sought out the light. Even in inclement weather, with gloom lowering over the city, she would always be the first to put on her bonnet and shawl, ready to walk along the banks of the Mississippi at any sign of sunlight seeping through clouds. But today I found her half-asleep on the chaise longue in her sitting room, blinds shut fast against the light. She seemed surprised by my presence, starting almost guiltily. No doubt it is some passing fit of nerves, or perhaps a female complaint; she is the strongest of women, and the best, and I will think of it no more. I administered a dose of the Elixir via a Hydrokonium, and that calmed her considerably.

H.C.P.

19 Sept. 1905

I grow concerned about Stanza's state of health. She seems to alternate between fits of euphoria—gay, almost giddy spells, characterized by an antic nature most unlike her—and black moods in which she takes to either her sitting room or her bed. She complains of a smell of lilies—initially pleasant, but now rotten and sickly-sweet. Beyond the mention of the lilies, however, I note that she does not confide in me the way she has always done in the past, and this is perhaps most concerning of all. I would I could spend more time with her, perhaps discern what is troubling her, but, alas, these all-consuming business difficulties of late take up my waking hours. A plague on these meddlesome busybodies and their misinformed attempts to undermine my curative!

H.C.P.

30 Sept. 1905

This *Collier's* article, coming as it does just now, is the most damnably infernal stroke of bad fortune. My Elixir has proven itself time and again to be both rejuvenative and salubrious. It has brought life and vigor to countless thousands. And yet this is forgotten amidst the cries of the ignorant, uneducated "reformers" of patent medicines. Reformers—bah! Envious, meddling pedants. What boots it struggling to better the human condition, if only to be assailed as I am at present?

H.P.

4 Oct. 1905

I believe I have found the cause of Stanza's malaise. Although she has been at pains to hide it, I have learned—from my monthly inventory—that nearly three dozen bottles of the Elixir are missing from the storage cabinets. Only three souls on earth have keys to those cabinets: myself, Stanza, and of course my assistant Edmund, who is at present abroad, collecting and analyzing new botanicals. Just this morning, watching unobserved from the bow window of the library, I saw Stanza slipping out of doors to pass empty bottles to the dustman.

Taken in proper amounts, the Elixir is, of course, the best of remedies. But as with all things, lack of moderation can have serious consequences.

What shall I do? Must I confront her? Our entire relationship has been built on decorum, etiquette, and trust—she abhors scenes of any kind. What shall I do?

H.P.

11 Oct. 1905

Yesterday—after finding another half dozen bottles of the Elixir missing from their cabinets—I felt compelled to confront Stanza on the matter. A scene of the most disagreeable nature ensued. She said things to me uglier than I ever imagined her capable of uttering. She has now taken to her rooms and refuses to come out.

Attacks on my reputation, and on my Elixir in particular, continue in the yellow papers. Normally, I would—as I have always done—repulse them with every fiber of my being. However, I find myself so distraught at my own domestic condition that I cannot concentrate on such matters. Thanks to my diligent efforts, the fiscal stability of the family has been restored beyond any future vicissitudes—and yet I take but little comfort in this, given the more intimate difficulties I now find myself in.

H.P.

13 Oct. 1905

Will she not respond to my pleas? I hear her crying in the night, behind her locked door. What sufferings does she endure, and why will she not accept my ministrations?

H.P.

18 Oct. 1905

Today I at last gained admittance to my wife's rooms. It was only due to the kind offices of Nettie, her faithful lady's maid, who is almost prostrate with worry over Stanza's well-being.

Upon entering the chambers I found Nettie's fears only too well founded. My dearest one is fearfully pale and drawn. She will take no nourishment, and will not leave her bed. She is in constant pain. I have had no doctors in—my own medical knowledge is superior to those New Orleans mountebanks and quacks who pass themselves off as physicians—but I can see in her a wasting and dissipation almost shocking in its rapidity. Was it only two months ago we took a carriage ride along the levee, Stanza smiling and singing and laughing, in the full flush of health and youthful beauty? My one consolation is that Antoine and Comstock, away at school, are spared the sight of their mother's pitiable state. Boethius has his nurse and tutors to occupy his time, and thus far I have been able to deflect his inquiries as to his mother's condition. Maurice, bless him, is too young to understand.

H.

21 Oct. 1905

God forgive me—today, despairing of all other physics, I brought Stanza the Hydrokonium and Elixir she has been begging for. The relief, the almost animal hunger, she showed at its sight was perhaps the worst pang my heart has ever borne. I allowed her but a single deep inhale; her cries and imprecations upon my retiring with bottle in hand are too painful to recall. I find our prior situation now painfully reversed—it is she who must be locked in, rather than herself being the instrument of locking me out.

... What have I done?

26 Oct. 1905

It is very late, and I sit here at my desk, inkstand and writing lamp before me. It is a dirty night; the wind howls and the rain lashes against the mullions.

Stanza is crying in her bedroom. Now and then, from behind the securely locked door, I can hear a stifled groan of pain.

I can no longer deny that which I have for so long refused to accept. I told myself I was working only for the commonweal, for the greater good. I believed it in all sincerity. Talk of my Elixir causing addiction, madness, even birth defects—I ascribed it to the whisperings of the ignorant, or to those chemists and druggists who would benefit from the Elixir's failure. But even my hypocrisy has its limits. It took the sad, indeed grievous, state of my own wife to lift the scales from my eyes. I am responsible. My Elixir is not a cure-all. It treats the symptoms rather than the underlying problem. It is habit forming, and its initially positive effects are finally overwhelmed by mysterious and deadly side effects. And now Stanza, and by extension myself, is paying the cost of my shortsightedness.

1 Nov. 1905

Darkest of all Novembers. Stanza seems to grow weaker by the day. She is now racked with hallucinations and even the occasional seizure. Against my own better judgment, I am attempting to ease her pain with morphine and with additional inhalations of the Elixir, but even these do little good; if anything, they seem to speed her enfeeblement. My God, my God, what am I to do?

5 Nov. 1905

In the blackness that is my present life a ray of light now gleams. I see a desperate possibility—small, but nevertheless existent—that I may effect a cure; an antidote, so to speak, to the Elixir. The idea occurred to me the day before yesterday, and since then I have immersed myself in nothing else.

From my observations of Stanza, it seems that the deleterious effects of the Elixir are caused by its peculiar *combination* of ingredients, in which the conjoined effect of excellent and proven remedies, such as cocaine hydrochloride and acetanilide, are canceled and reversed by the rare botanicals.

The botanicals are what produce the evil effects. Logically, those effects can therefore be reversed by *other* botanicals. If I could block the effects of the botanical extracts, it might thus reverse the wasting physical and mental damage it seems to have caused, much in the way the extract of the Calabar bean will neutralize poisoning by the Bella Donna plant.

With this antidote, I may be able to aid not only my poor ailing Stanza, but those others who, through my greed and shortsightedness, have suffered as well.

...If only Edmund would return! His was a three-year voyage to collect healing herbs and botanicals from the equatorial jungles. I daily await the arrival of his packet steamer. Unlike many of my supposedly learned brethren, I firmly believe the natives of this planet can teach us many things about natural remedies. My own travels amongst the Plains Indians taught me as much. I am making progress, but the plants I have tested so far—save for *Thismia americana,* for which I hold out great hope—do not seem effective in counteracting the wasting effects of my accursed tonic.

8 Nov. 1905

Edmund has returned at last! He has brought dozens of the most interesting plants with him, to which the natives ascribe miraculous healing properties. The spark of hope I barely dared foster a few days ago now burns bright within me. The work consumes all my time; I cannot sleep, I cannot eat—I think of nothing else. To the list of botanicals in the Elixir, I have a number of counter-effectives, including cascara bark, calomel, oil of chenopodium, extract of Hodgson's Sorrow; and extract of *Thismia americana*.

But no time to write—there is much to do. And very little time in which to do it—every day, Stanza fades. She is now a mere shadow of herself. If I do not succeed—and succeed quickly—she will slip into the realm of shadow.

12 Nov. 1905

I have failed.

Up until the last moment I was confident of my success. The chemical synthesis made perfect sense. I was certain I had worked out the precise series, and proportions, of compounds—listed inside the back cover of this journal—that, when boiled, would produce a tincture capable of counteracting the effects of the Elixir. I gave Stanza a series of doses—the poor suffering creature can keep nothing solid on her stomach—but to no avail. Very early this morning, her suffering became so ungovernable that I assisted her into the next world.

I will write no more. I have lost that which was dearest to me. I am no longer in thrall to this earth. I pen these last words, not as a living being, but as one who is already with my own dead wife in spirit, and soon in body, as well.

D'entre les morts,
Hezekiah Comstock Pendergast

Constance's gaze lingered on these last words for a long time. Then, thoughtfully, she turned over the page—and went quite still. There was a complex list of compounds, plants, extraction, and preparation steps, all under the label ET CONTRA ARCANUM:

The antidote formula.

Below the list was another handwritten message, but in another hand altogether and in much fresher ink—a beautiful, flowing script that Constance knew very well indeed.

My dearest Constance,

Knowing your innate curiosity, your interest in Pendergast family history, and your penchant for exploring the basement collections, I have no doubt that—at some point in your long, long life—you will stumble upon these jottings.

Did you find that this journal made for rather disquieting reading? Of course you did. Imagine then, if you can, how much more painful I myself have found it—chronicling as it does my own father's search to cure an affliction *he himself* bestowed upon my mother, Constance. (The fact that your name and hers are the same is not an accident, by the way.)

The greatest irony is that my father came so close to success. You see, according to my own analysis, his antidote *should have worked*. Except that he made a wee mistake. Do you suppose he was simply too blinded by grief and guilt to see his one small oversight? One grows curious.

Be careful.

    I remain, Constance,

        Your devoted, etc.

           Dr. Enoch Leng

53

Vincent D'Agosta sat back in his chair and stared morosely at his computer screen. It was after six. He had canceled a date with Laura at the Korean place around the corner and he was determined not to let up until he'd done all he could. So he sat, staring mulishly at the screen as if trying to force it to yield up something useful.

He'd spent over an hour digging into NYPD files and elsewhere, looking for information on John Barbeaux and Red Mountain Industries, and had come up with precisely squat. NYPD had no files on the man. An online search yielded little more. After a brief but distinguished career in the Marine Corps, Barbeaux—who came from money—had founded Red Mountain as a military consulting company. The firm had grown into one of the country's largest private security contracting organizations. Barbeaux had been born in Charleston; he was sixty-one years old and a widower; his only son had died of an unknown illness not two years before. Beyond that, D'Agosta had learned nothing. Red Mountain was notoriously secretive; its own website gave him little to go on. But secretiveness wasn't a crime. There were also online rumors of the kind that swirled around many military contractors. A few lone voices, crying in the digital wilderness, linked the company to various South American and African coups, mercenary actions, and shadow military ops—but these were the same types of people who claimed Elvis was still alive and living on the International Space Station. With a sigh, D'Agosta reached out to turn off the screen.

Then he remembered something. About six months back, a program had been put in place—spearheaded by a police consultant, formerly of the NSA—to digitize all NYPD documents and run them through OCR software. The idea had been to ultimately cross-link every scrap of information in the department's files, with the goal of looking for patterns that might help solve any number of "cold" cases. But, as with so many other initiatives, this one had gone off the rails. There were cost overruns, the consultant had been fired, and the project was limping along with no completion date in sight.

D'Agosta stared at the computer screen. The team was supposed to start with the newest documents logged into the system and then work backward chronologically through the older ones. But with the size of the team slashed, and the volume of new material that came in every day, the word was they were basically treading water. No one used the database—it was a mess.

Still, a search would take only a moment. Luckily, Barbeaux was not a common name.

He logged back into the departmental network, moused his way through a series of menus, and accessed the project's home page. A spartan-looking screen appeared:

```
New York Police Department I.D.A.R.S.
Integrated Data Analysis and Retrieval System
** NOTE: Beta testing only **
```

Below was a text box. D'Agosta clicked on it to make it active, typed in "Barbeaux," then clicked on the ENTER button beside it.

To his surprise, he got a hit:

```
Accession record 135823_R
Subject: Barbeaux, John
Format:  JPG (lossy)
Metadata: available
```

"I'll be damned," he murmured.

There was an icon of a document next to the text. D'Agosta clicked on it, and the scan of an official document appeared on the screen. It was a memo from the Albany police, sent—as a departmental courtesy—to the NYPD about six months back. It described rumors, from "unnamed third parties," of illicit arms deals being made by Red Mountain Industries in South America. However—the document went on to say—the rumors could not be confirmed, the firm in all other ways had a stellar record, and so instead of bumping the investigation up the hierarchy to federal agencies such as the ATF, the case had been closed.

D'Agosta frowned. Why hadn't he discovered this factoid through normal channels?

He clicked on the screen and examined the attached metadata. It showed that the physical copy of the memo had been filed in the "Barbecci, Albert" folder of the NYPD's archives. The record header showed that the person who had filed it had been Sergeant Loomis Slade.

With a few more mouse clicks, D'Agosta opened up the file on Albert Barbecci. Barbecci had been a small-time mobster who had died seven years ago.

Barbeaux. Barbecci. Misfiled. Sloppy work. D'Agosta shook his head. That sort of sloppiness didn't seem like Slade. Then he picked up his phone, consulted a directory, dialed a number.

"Slade," came the atonal voice on the other end of the line.

"Sergeant? This is Vincent D'Agosta."

"Yes, Lieutenant."

"I've just come across a document on a man named Barbeaux. Heard of him?"

"No."

"You should have. You filed the document yourself—in the wrong folder. Put it under Barbecci."

A pause. "Oh. That. Albany, right? Stupid of me—sorry."

"I was wondering how you happened to be in possession of that memo."

"Angler gave it to me to file. As I recall, it was Albany's case, not ours, and it didn't check out."

"Any idea why it was sent to Angler in the first place? Did he request it?"

"Sorry, Lieutenant. I've got no idea."

"It's all right, I'll ask him myself. Is he around?"

"No. He took a few days off to visit some relatives upstate."

"All right, I'll check in with him later."

"Take care, Lieutenant." There was a click as Slade hung up.

54

Read down the list of ingredients," Margo said to Constance. "We'll take them one by one."

"Aqua vitae," Constance said. She was seated in the library of the Riverside Drive mansion, the old journal in her lap. It was just past eleven in the morning—at Constance's urgent summons, Margo had ducked out of work as quickly as possible. Constance's graceful hands were trembling slightly with agitation, her face flushed. But her expression was under rigid control.

Margo nodded. "That's an old-fashioned name for an aqueous solution of ethanol. Vodka will suffice." She jotted a notation in a small notebook.

Constance turned back to the journal. "Next is laudanum."

"Tincture of opium. Still available by prescription in the United States." Margo made another notation, squinting as she did so—although it was still morning, the library windows were shuttered, and the light was dim. "We'll get Dr. Stone to write us out a prescription."

"Not necessary. There's plenty of laudanum in the basement chemical stores," said Constance.

"Good."

Another pause, and Constance consulted the old journal. "Petroleum jelly. Calomel...Calomel is mercurous chloride, I believe. There are jars of it in the basement, too."

"Petroleum jelly we can get at any drugstore," said Margo. She looked over the list of the dozen-odd compounds she'd jotted down in her notebook. Despite everything, she felt a prickling sensation of hope. At first, Constance's news of Hezekiah's antidote, her showing Margo the old journal, seemed like a long shot. But now . . .

"Cascara bark," Constance said, returning her attention to the journal. "I'm not familiar with that."

"Cascara buckthorn," said Margo. "*Rhamnus purshiana*. Its bark was, and still is, a common ingredient in herbal supplements."

Constance nodded. "Oil of chenopodium."

"That's another name for wormseed oil," said Margo. "It's mildly toxic, but nevertheless was used as a common ingredient in nineteenth-century quack medicines."

"There should be some bottles of both in the basement, then." Constance paused. "Here are the last two ingredients: Hodgson's Sorrow and *Thismia americana*."

"I haven't heard of either of them," Margo said. "But they are obviously botanicals."

Constance rose and retrieved a huge botanical dictionary from the bookshelf. Placing it on a stand, she began leafing through it. "Hodgson's Sorrow. An aquatic, night-blooming water lily of the family Nymphaeaceae, with a spectacular deep-pink color. In addition to its color, it has a most unusual odor. It doesn't say anything here about pharmacological properties."

"Interesting."

There was a silence as Constance continued to read through the entry. "It's native only to Madagascar. Very rare. Prized by collectors of water lilies."

Silence settled over the library. "Madagascar," said Margo. "Damn." Reaching into her bag, she pulled out her tablet, accessed the Internet, and did a quick search for Hodgson's Sorrow. With the flick of a finger, she scrolled quickly down through the entries. "Okay, we've got a break. It seems there's a specimen in the Brooklyn Botanic Garden." She called up the website for the garden, searched through it for a moment. "It's in the Aquatic House, which is part of the main greenhouse complex. But how will we get it?"

"There's only one sure way."

"Which is?"

"Steal it."

After a moment, Margo nodded.

"Now for the final ingredient." Constance consulted the encyclopedia again. "*Thismia americana*...A plant found in the wetlands around Chicago's Lake Calumet. It flowers for less than a month above ground. Of interest to botanists not only because of its very localized habitat, but because it's a mycoheterotroph."

Margo said, "That's a rare kind of plant that parasitizes underground fungi for its nourishment, instead of photosynthesis."

Suddenly Constance froze. A strange expression crept over her face as she stared at the encyclopedia. "According to this," she said, "the plant went extinct around 1916, when its habitat was built over."

"Extinct?"

"Yes." Constance's voice had taken on a dead cast. "A few years ago, a small army of volunteers undertook a careful search of Chicago's Far South Side, with the specific intent of finding a specimen of *Thismia americana*. They were unsuccessful."

She laid the book down, walked to the dying fire. She stopped, staring into it, while twisting a handkerchief between her hands. She said nothing.

"There's a possibility," Margo said, "the Museum might have a specimen in its collections." Using her tablet again, she accessed the Museum's Internet portal, entered her name and password. Opening the online catalog of the Botany Department, she did a search for *Thismia americana*.

Nothing.

Margo let the tablet settle on her lap. Constance continued twisting the handkerchief.

"I can see if there isn't something similar in the Museum's collection," said Margo. "The mycoheterotrophs are all quite similar, and might have similar pharmacological properties."

Constance turned toward her quickly. "Go to the Museum. Retrieve the closest range of specimens you can find."

Of course, thought Margo, *this would also involve stealing*. God, how was that going to work out? But when she thought of Pendergast upstairs, she realized they had no choice. After a silence, she said: "We're also forgetting something."

"Which is?"

"The antidote that Hezekiah wrote down here . . . it didn't work. Hezekiah's wife died anyway."

"Leng's final note said something about a wee mistake. One small oversight. Do you have any idea what the oversight might have been?"

Margo turned again to the formula. It was a simple preparation, really, except for the last two highly unusual botanicals. "It could be anything," she said, shaking her head. "The proportions might be wrong. The preparation could have been botched. A wrong ingredient. An unexpected interaction."

"Think, *please* think!" Margo could hear the handkerchief tear in Constance's hands.

Margo tried to comply, thinking carefully about the ingredients. Again, the last two were the ones that were unique. The rest were more common, their preparations standard. It would have to be in the two rare ingredients where the "oversight" lay.

She scanned the preparation directions. Both plants had been extracted into tinctures using a common method—boiling. Usually that worked, but in some cases boiling denatured certain complex plant proteins. Today the best method of botanical extraction for pharmacological use was via chloroform.

Margo looked up. "A room-temperature extraction of these two botanicals using chloroform would be more efficacious," she said.

"I'm sure I can find chloroform in the collections. Let us proceed with all haste."

"We should test it first. We have no idea what compounds are in these two plants. They could be deadly."

Constance stared at her. "There's no time for a test. Pendergast seemed to rally yesterday evening—but now he's taken a decided turn for the worse. Go to the Museum. Do what you have to do to get the mycoheterotrophs. Meanwhile, I'll collect as many of these other ingredients as I can from the basement, and..." She stopped when she saw the look on Margo's face. "Is there a problem?"

"The Museum," Margo repeated.

"Of course. That's the logical place to find the necessary ingredients."

"But they would be stored in...in the basement."

"You know the Museum better than I," Constance said. When Margo did not reply, she continued: "Those plants are vital if we're to have any hope of saving Pendergast."

"Yes. Yes, I know they are." Margo swallowed, then slipped her tablet back into her bag. "What are we going to do about D'Agosta? We said we'd stay in touch, but I'm not so sure we should mention these...plans."

"He's a police officer. He couldn't help us—and he might stop us."

Margo bowed her head in assent.

Constance nodded. "Good luck."

"You, too." Margo paused. "I'm curious—that note...in the journal. It was written to you. What was that all about?"

A silence. "Before Aloysius, I had another guardian. Dr. Enoch Leng. The man who wrote that final note in the journal."

Margo paused, waiting. Constance never volunteered information about herself; Margo knew virtually nothing about her. Many times she had wondered where she had suddenly come from and what her real relationship was to Pendergast. But now, most uncharacteristically, Constance's voice took on a softer, almost confessional tone.

"Dr. Enoch had a notorious interest in a certain branch of chemistry. I sometimes acted as his lab assistant. I helped him with his experiments."

"When was this?" Margo asked. It seemed strange: Constance

looked to be only in her early twenties, and she had been Pendergast's ward for years.

"Long ago. I was a mere child."

"Oh." Margo paused. "And what branch of chemistry interested this Dr. Enoch?"

"*Acids*." And Constance smiled faintly: a faraway, almost nostalgic smile.

55

For as long as Margo had been associated with the New York Museum of Natural History, Jörgensen had been "retired." And yet every day he continued to occupy the corner office where he had always been, seeming never to go home—if he even had a home—and grumbling at anyone who disturbed him. Margo paused at his half-open door, hesitating to knock. She could see the old man bent over some seedpods, studying them under a glass, his head entirely bald, his bushy eyebrows bristling from his face.

She knocked. "Dr. Jörgensen?" she ventured.

The head rotated and a pair of bleached-blue eyes turned on her. He said nothing but the expression in the eyes was one of annoyance.

"Sorry to bother you."

This was met with a noncommittal grunt. Since no offer to enter seemed forthcoming, Margo went in uninvited.

"I'm Margo Green," she said, offering her hand. "I used to work here."

Another grunt and a withered hand met hers. The eyebrows knitted up. "Margo Green . . . Ah, yes. You were around during the time of those awful killings." He shook his head. "I was a friend of Whittlesey, poor old soul—"

Margo swallowed and hastened to change the subject. "That was a long time ago, I hardly remember the killings," she lied. "I was wondering—"

"But *I* remember," said Jörgensen. "And I remember you. Funny, your name came up recently. Now, where was that...?"

He cast about with his eyes but, finding nothing, looked back at her. "What happened to that tall fellow with the cowlick you used to go around with? You know, the one who loved the sound of his own voice?"

Margo hesitated. "He died."

Jörgensen seemed to contemplate this for a moment. "Died? Those were dark days. So many died. So, you moved on to greener pastures?"

"I did." She hesitated. "There were too many bad memories here. I work for a medical foundation now."

A nod. Margo felt encouraged. "I'm looking for help. Some botanical advice."

"Very well."

"Are you familiar with the mycoheterotrophs?"

"Yes."

"Great. Well, I'm interested in a plant called *Thismia americana*."

"It's extinct."

Margo took a deep breath. "I know. I was hoping... wondering... if there might be a specimen of a similar mycoheterotroph in the Museum's collection."

Jörgensen leaned back in his chair and made a tent with his fingers. Margo could see she was in for a lecture. "*Thismia americana*," he intoned, as if not having heard her last sentence, "was a rather celebrated plant in botanical circles. It's not only extinct, but when it was alive it was one of the rarest plants known. Only one botanist ever saw it and took samples. The plant disappeared around 1916, thanks to the expansion of Chicago. It vanished without a trace."

Margo pretended to be interested in this mini-lecture, even though she already knew every detail. Jörgensen stopped without having answered her question.

"So," she said, "only one botanist took specimens?"

"That is correct."

"And what happened to those samples?"

At this, Jörgensen's ancient face creased into an unusual smile. "They're right here, naturally."

"Here? In the Museum's collection?"

A nod.

"Why isn't it listed in the online catalog?"

Jörgensen waved his hand dismissively. "That's because it's in the Herbarium Vault. There's a separate catalog for those specimens."

Margo was speechless at her good luck. "Um, how can I gain access to it?"

"You can't."

"But I need it for my research."

Jörgensen's face began to take on a pinched look. "My dear girl," he began, "access to the Herbarium Vault is strictly limited to Museum curators, and then only with the written permission of the director himself." His voice took on a schoolmaster's tone. "Those extinct plant specimens are very fragile, and simply can't stand handling by inexperienced laypersons."

"But I'm not an inexperienced layperson. I'm an ethnopharmacologist and I have a good reason, a very good reason, to study that specimen."

The bushy eyebrows raised. "Which is?"

"I'm, ah, doing a study of nineteenth-century medicine—"

"Just a minute," said Jörgensen, interrupting, "*now* I recollect where your name came up!" A withered hand snaked out and extracted a document from atop a pile of paper. "I recently received a memo regarding your status here at the Museum."

Margo was brought up short. "What?"

Jörgensen glanced at it, and then proffered it to her. "See for yourself."

It was a memo from Frisby to all staff in the Department of Botany. It was short.

Please be advised of a status change regarding outside researcher Dr. Margo Green, an ethnopharmacologist employed by the Pearson Institute. Her access privileges to the collections have been downgraded from Level 1 to Level 5, effective immediately.

Margo was well aware how this little bit of bureaucratese translated: "Level 5" access meant no access at all. "When did you get that?"

"This morning."

"Why didn't you mention it before?"

"I don't pay much attention to Museum missives these days. It's a miracle I remembered it at all. At eighty-five, my memory isn't what it used to be."

Margo sat in the seat, trying to get her temper under control. It would do no good to get mad in front of Jörgensen. *Best to be straight*, she thought.

"Dr. Jörgensen, I have a friend who is gravely ill. In fact, he's dying."

A slow nod.

"The only thing that can save him is an extraction from this plant—*Thismia americana*."

Jörgensen frowned. "My dear girl..."

Margo swallowed hard. She was getting awfully tired of this "dear girl" business.

"...You can't be serious. If this plant would truly save his life, may I see a medical statement to that effect, signed by his doctor?"

"Let me explain. My friend was poisoned, and this extract must be part of the antidote. No doctor knows anything about this."

"This sounds like quackery to me."

"I promise you—"

"But even if it were legitimate," he went on, overriding her, "I would never allow the destruction of an *extinct* plant specimen, the last of its kind, for a one-off medicinal treatment. What is the value of an ordinary human life *in the face of the last specimen of an extinct plant in existence*?"

"You..." Margo looked at his face, creased with lines of extreme disapproval. She was flabbergasted by the sentiment he had just expressed: that a scientific specimen was worth more than a human life. She was never going to get through to this man.

She thought fast. She had seen the Herbarium Vault years ago, and recalled that it was essentially a walk-in safe with a keypad lock. The combinations to such locks, for security purposes, were changed on a regular basis. She looked at Jörgensen, who was frowning at her, his arms crossed, waiting for her to finish what she had started to say.

He said his memory wasn't so sharp these days. Now, that was an important fact. She glanced around the office. Where would he write down a combination? In a book? In his desk? She remembered the old Hitchcock film *Marnie*, where a businessman had kept the combination to his safe inside a locked drawer of his secretary's desk. It could be in a thousand places, even in an office this small. Perhaps she could trick him into revealing the location.

"Dr. Green, is there anything else—?"

If she didn't think of something fast, she'd never get in that vault... and Pendergast would die. The stakes were that high.

She looked directly at Jörgensen. "Where do you hide the combination to the vault?"

The briefest flicker of his eyes, and then he locked them back on her. "What an offensive question! I've wasted quite enough time with you already. Good day, Dr. Green."

Margo rose and left. In that brief moment, his eyes had involuntarily flickered to a spot above and behind her head. As she turned to leave, she observed that the space was occupied by a small, framed botanical print.

She felt hopeful that behind that print would be a safe containing the combination. But how to get Jörgensen out of his bloody office? And even if she found a safe, where would she find *its* combination? And, assuming she managed to learn the combination, the Herbarium Vault was located deep within the Museum's basement...

Nevertheless, she had to try.

In the middle of the hallway, she paused. Should she pull a fire alarm? But that would cause the wing to be evacuated and probably get her into trouble.

She continued walking down the hallway, offices and labs on either side. It was still lunch hour, and the place was relatively empty. In one empty lab she spied a Museum phone. She ducked inside, staring at the phone. Could she call him, pretend to be someone's secretary, ask him to come to a meeting? But he didn't look like someone who went to meetings...nor someone who would respond favorably to an unexpected summons. And wouldn't he know most of the secretaries' voices?

There *must* be a way to get him out of the office. And that way would be to get him mad, send him off in a fury to dress down a colleague.

She picked up the phone. Instead of calling Jörgensen, she called Frisby's office. Disguising her voice, she said: "This is the Botany Department office. May I speak with Dr. Frisby? We have a problem."

Frisby came on a moment later, out of breath. "Yes, what is it?"

"We received your memo about that woman, Dr. Green," Margo said, keeping her voice muffled and low.

"What about it? She hasn't been bothering you down there, has she?"

"You know old Dr. Jörgensen? He's a good friend of Dr. Green. I'm afraid he's planning to defy your express wishes and give her access to the collection. He's been railing about your memo all morning. I only mention this because we don't want trouble, and you know how difficult Dr. Jörgensen can be—"

Frisby slammed down the phone. Margo waited in the empty lab, its door partly open. In a few minutes she heard a huffing sound and an enraged Jörgensen came striding past, face red, looking remarkably robust for his age—no doubt heading for Frisby's office to set him straight.

Margo quickly hustled down the hall and, to her relief, found that his office door had been left wide open in his hurried exit. She ducked in, eased the door shut, and lifted the botanical print from the wall.

Nothing. No safe—just a blank wall.

She felt crushed. Why had he looked in that direction? There was nothing else on the wall. Maybe it was just a random glance, or maybe she hadn't gotten a good fix on it. She was about to put the picture back when she noticed a piece of paper taped to the rear of the frame, with a list of numbers on it. All the numbers had been crossed out but the last.

56

Aloysius Pendergast lay in bed, keeping as still as possible. Every movement, even the tiniest, was an agony. Just breathing in enough air to oxygenate his blood sent white-hot needles of pain through the muscles and nerves of his chest. He could feel a dark presence waiting at the foot of his bed, a succubus ready to climb on top and suffocate him. But whenever he tried to look at it, it vanished, only to reappear when he looked away.

He tried to will the pain away, to lose himself in the contents of his bedroom, to focus his concentration on a painting on the opposite wall, one in which he had often taken solace: a late work by Turner, *Schooner off Beachy Head*. He would sometimes lose himself for hours in the painting's many layers of light and shadow, in the way Turner rendered the sheets of spume and the vessel's storm-tossed sails. But the pain, and the vile reek of rotting lilies—cloying, sickly-sweet, like the stench of suppurating flesh—made such mental escape impossible.

All his usual mechanisms for coping with emotional or physical trauma had been taken away by the sickness. And now the morphine drip was exhausted and would not be replenished for another hour. There was nothing but a landscape of pain, stretching away endlessly on all sides.

Even in this extremity of his illness, Pendergast knew that the malady afflicting him had its ebbs and swells. If he could survive this current onslaught of pain, it would—in time—subside to afford temporary relief. He would be able to breathe again, to speak, even to rise from his bed and move about. But then the swell of pain would return, as it always did—and each time it was worse and more prolonged than before. And he sensed that at some point soon, the escalation of pain would stop subsiding, and the end would come.

And now, at the periphery of his consciousness, came the crest of the wave of pain: a creeping blackness at the edges of his vision, a vignetting of sorts. It was a signal that, within minutes, he would lose consciousness. Initially, he had welcomed this release. But in a cruel twist, he had soon learned there was, in fact, no release. Because the blackness led, not to a void, but to a hallucinogenic underworld of his subconscious self that had proven in some ways even worse than the pain.

Moments later the blackness caught him in its grip, tugging him from the bed and the dimly lighted room like an undertow catching an exhausted swimmer. There was a brief, sickening sensation of falling. And then the darkness melted away, revealing the scene like a curtain parting from a stage.

He was standing on a scarified ledge of hardened lava, high on the flanks of an active volcano. It was twilight. To his left, the ribbed flanks of the volcano led down to a distant shore, so far away as to seem a different world, where little clutches of whitewashed buildings huddled at the edge of the spume, their evening lights piercing the gloom. Directly ahead and below him was an immense chasm—a monstrous gash ripped into the very heart of the volcano. He could see the living lava roiling like blood within it, glowing a rich angry red in the shadow of the crater that rose just above. Clouds of sulfur steamed up from the chasm, and black flecks of ash, whipped by a hell-wind, skittered through the air.

Pendergast knew precisely where he was: standing on the Bastimento Ridge of the Stromboli volcano, looking down into the infamous Sciara del Fuoco—the Slope of Fire. He had stood on this same ridge once before, just over three years ago, when he had witnessed one of the most shocking dramas of his life.

Except the place now looked different. Brutal at the best of times, it had become—playing out as it was in the theater of his fevered hallucination—something of pure nightmare. The sky encircling him was not the deep purple of twilight, but rather a sickly green, the color of rotten eggs. Livid flashes of orange and blue lightning seared the heavens. Bloated crimson-colored clouds scudded before a guttering, sallow sun. A ghastly Technicolor hue illuminated the entire scene.

As he took in the hellish vision, he was startled to see a person. Not ten feet in front of him, a man sat on a deck chair set upon a fin of old lava that stood out precariously from the ridge above the smoking Sciara del Fuoco. He was wearing dark glasses, a straw hat, a floral shirt, and Bermuda shorts, and was sipping what looked like lemonade out of a tall glass. Pendergast did not need to draw any closer to recognize, in profile, the aquiline nose, neatly trimmed beard, ginger-colored hair. This was his brother, Diogenes. Diogenes—who had disappeared at this very spot, in the horrific scene that had played out between himself and Constance Greene.

As Pendergast watched, Diogenes took a long, slow sip of the lemonade. He gazed out over the boiling fury of the Sciara del Fuoco with the placid expression of a tourist gazing out at the Mediterranean from the balcony of a Nice hotel. *"Ave, Frater,"* he said without turning toward him.

Pendergast did not reply.

"I would ask after your health, but present circumstances obviate the need for that particular bit of hypocrisy."

Pendergast merely stared at this bizarre materialization: his dead brother, lounging on a beach chair at the edge of an active volcano.

"Do you know," Diogenes went on, "I find the irony—the *fitting* irony—of your present predicament almost overwhelming. After all we've been through, after all my schemes, your end will come at the hands, not of myself, but of your own issue. Your very own son. Think on't, brother! I should have liked to have met him: Alban and I would have had a lot in common. I could have taught him many things."

Pendergast did not respond. There was no point in reacting to a feverish delusion.

Diogenes took another sip of lemonade. "But what makes the irony so deliciously complete is that Alban was merely the precipitant of your undoing. Your *real* killer is our own great-great-grandfather Hezekiah. Talk about the sins of the fathers! Not only is it his own 'elixir' killing you—but it is because of the elixir that an indirect victim of it, this Barbeaux fellow, is now taking his revenge." Diogenes paused. "Hezekiah; Alban; myself. It all makes for a nice family circle."

Pendergast remained silent.

Still offering only his profile, Diogenes stared out over the violent spectacle churning at their feet. "I'd think you would welcome this chance for atonement."

Pendergast, goaded, finally spoke. "Atonement? What for?"

"You, with your prudery, your hidebound sense of morality, your misguided desire to do right in the world—it's always been a mystery to me that you weren't tortured by the fact we've lived comfortably off Hezekiah's fortune all our lives."

"You're talking about something that happened a hundred and twenty-five years ago."

"Does the span of years do anything to lessen the agony of his victims? How long does it take to wash the blood from all that money?"

"It is a false syllogism. Hezekiah profited unscrupulously, but we were the innocent inheritors of that wealth. Money is fungible. We are not guilty."

Diogenes chuckled—barely audible over the roar of the volcano— then shook his head. "How ironic that I, Diogenes, have become your conscience."

The enervating anguish of Pendergast's conscious self began to break through the hallucination. He staggered on the ridge of lava; righted himself. "I..." he began. "I...am *not*...responsible. And I will not argue with a hallucination."

"Hallucination?" And now, finally, Diogenes turned to face his brother. The right side of his face—the side he had been presenting to Pendergast—looked as normal and as finely cast as it always had. But the left side was horribly burned, scar tissue puckering and veining the skin from chin to hairline like the bark of a tree, cheekbone and the orbit of a missing eye exposed and white.

"Just keep telling yourself that, *frater*," he said over the roar of the mountain. And as slowly as he had turned to face Pendergast, Diogenes now turned away once more, hiding the horrible sight, his gaze once again on the Sciara del Fuoco. And as he did so the nightmare scene began to waver, dissolve, and fade away, leaving Pendergast once again in his own bedroom, the lights dim around him, fresh waves of pain surging over him once more.

57

Far below Pendergast's bedroom, Constance stood at one of the last of the long sub-basement rooms, breathing hard. A black nylon bag was slung over her shoulder. Traceries of cobwebs hung from her dress.

She had reached the end of Dr. Enoch's cabinet. It was two thirty PM, and she'd spent hours trying to assemble the necessary compounds for the antidote. Putting the nylon bag down, she consulted her list again, although she knew perfectly well what was still missing. Chloroform and oil of chenopodium.

She had found a large carboy of chloroform, but it hadn't been well sealed and, over the years, had evaporated. She had found no trace of chenopodium. Chloroform was available by prescription, but that would take too long and Constance did not expect that it would be easy to persuade Dr. Stone, upstairs, to write a scrip. But oil of chenopodium was the bigger problem, as it was no longer used in herbal preparations because of its toxic nature. If she couldn't find it down here, she would be out of luck. There had to be some in the collections somewhere, as it had been a common ingredient in patent medicines.

But she had seen none.

She started back through the rooms, sweeping beneath the archways. She had skipped the few remaining ruined storage rooms on her outward exploration. Now she would inspect those, too. Over

the months, she and Proctor had undertaken the painstaking cleaning process—tossing away the piles of broken glass, gingerly clearing
away the crushed artifacts or spilled chemicals.

What if the bottles of oil of chenopodium had been among those
broken and disposed of…?

She paused in the one room they had not yet restored. Toppled
shelves lay strewn about, and millions of fragments of broken glass
winked and glittered on the floor, which was stained with various
colored substances and sticky, dried pools. A vile, moldy smell hung
in the air here like a toxic miasma. But not everything was broken:
many bottles lay on the floor intact, and some shelves still were
upright or leaning, crowded with jars of numerous colors, each with a
label written in Enoch Leng's elegant hand.

She started going through the unbroken bottles on some shelves
that had escaped the general destruction. The bottles rattled under
her fingers as she sorted through them, one Latin name after another,
an endless procession of compounds.

It was maddening. The cataloging system Dr. Enoch had used had
all been in his own head—and after his death she had never been able
to decipher it. She suspected it was random—and that the doctor had
simply recorded the entire library of chemicals in his photographic
memory.

Completing one shelf, she started on the next, and then the next.
A bottle fell and shattered; she kicked the pieces aside. A stench rose
up. She kept going, sorting faster and faster, more bottles dropping in
her haste. She looked at her watch. Three o'clock.

With a hiss of irritation, she moved to the intact bottles lying
about the floor—the ones that hadn't broken. Stooping, her feet
crunching over broken glass, she continued searching, plucking up a
bottle, reading the label, tossing it aside. Here were many oils: calen-
dula, borage seed, primrose, mullein, poke root…but no chenopodium. With sudden frustration she lashed out at one of the shelves
she had already ransacked, sweeping all the bottles to the floor. They
landed with a crashing and popping sound, and now a truly horrific
stench rose up.

She stepped aside. Her loss of control was regrettable. Taking a series of deep breaths, she regained her presence of mind and began searching the last of the shelves. Still nothing.

And suddenly there it was: a big bottle labeled OIL OF CHENOPO-DIUM. Right in front of her.

Scooping up the bottle, she put it in her bag and continued searching for chloroform. Almost the next bottle she picked up turned out to be a small, well-sealed vial of that, too. She stuffed it into the bag, rose, and swept toward the stairs leading to the elevator.

She took this sudden reversal of luck to be a sign. But even as she reached the library, the bookshelves sliding back into place, Mrs. Trask was there, proffering her a phone.

"It's the lieutenant," she said.

"Tell him I'm not in."

With a look of disapproval, Mrs. Trask continued holding out the telephone. "He's most insistent."

Constance took the phone and made an effort to be cordial. "Yes, Lieutenant?"

"I want you and Margo down here, on the double."

"We're rather occupied at the present time," said Constance.

"I've got some vital information. There are some really, *really* bad people involved in this. You and Margo are going to get yourselves killed. I want to help."

"You can't help us," said Constance.

"Why?"

"Because . . ." She went silent.

"Because you're planning some illegal shit?"

No answer.

"Constance, get your ass down here now. Or so help me God I'll come up there with a posse and bring you down myself."

58

Let's go through it," D'Agosta said. It was late afternoon, and Margo and Constance were seated in the lieutenant's office. "You say you've found a cure for what poisoned Pendergast?"

"An antidote," said Constance. "Developed by Hezekiah Pendergast to counteract the effects of his own elixir."

"But you're not sure."

"Not positive," said Margo. "But we've got to try."

D'Agosta sat back. This sounded crazy. "And you've got all the ingredients?"

"All but two," Margo said. "They're plants, and we know where to get them."

"Where?"

Silence.

D'Agosta stared at Margo. "Let me guess: you're going to rob the Museum."

More silence. Margo's face looked white and strained, but there was a hard glitter in her eyes.

D'Agosta smoothed a hand over his balding pate and looked back at the two defiant women sitting across the desk. "Look. I've been a cop for a long time. I'm not an idiot, and I know you're planning something illegal. Frankly, I don't care about that right now. Pendergast is my friend. What I do care about is you being successful in getting those plants. And not being killed in the process. You understand?"

Margo finally nodded.

D'Agosta turned to Constance. "You?"

"I understand," said Constance, but he could tell from her face that she did not agree. "You said you had vital information. What is it?"

"If I'm right, this Barbeaux is a lot more dangerous than anyone imagined. You're going to need backup. Let me help you get those plants, wherever they are."

More silence. Finally, Constance rose. "How can you help us? You yourself pointed out that what we're doing is illegal."

"Constance is right," said Margo. "Can you imagine the red tape? Look. Pendergast—your friend—is dying. We are almost out of time."

D'Agosta felt himself losing his temper. "I'm well aware of that, which is why I'm willing to step over the line. Look, damn it, if you don't let me help you, I'm going to throw you both in the tank. Right now. For your own protection."

"If you do that, Pendergast is sure to die," Constance said.

D'Agosta exhaled. "I'm not going to let you two go running around playing cop. Barbeaux or his men have been a step ahead of us all the way. How do you think I'd feel with three deaths on my head instead of one? Because he may well try to stop you."

"I hope he does," said Constance. "And now I'm afraid we must be going."

"I swear I'm going to have you taken in."

"No, you're not," she said quietly.

D'Agosta rose. "Stay here. Don't go anywhere."

He left his office, closing the door behind him, and went over to Sergeant Josephus, manning the outer desk. "Sergeant? Those two in my office? When they leave, I want them followed. A full tail, twenty-four seven, until further notice."

Josephus glanced back toward D'Agosta's office. D'Agosta followed his gaze. Through the glass of the door, he could see Constance and Margo talking between themselves.

"Yes, sir," Josephus said. He pulled out an official form. "Now, if I could have their names—"

D'Agosta thought a moment, waved his hand. "Scratch that. I've got another idea."

"Sure thing, Loo."

D'Agosta opened the door to his office, stepped inside, and stared at the two women. "If you're planning to go to the Museum to steal some plants, it isn't the guards you need to worry about—it's Barbeaux's men. You got that?"

Both of them nodded.

"Get out of here."

They left.

D'Agosta stared at the empty doorway, full of an impotent anger. Son of a bitch, he had never met two more impossible women in his life. But there was one good way to keep them safe, or at least reduce their chances of tangling with Barbeaux. And that way was to put out a warrant on the man, bring him in for questioning, and keep his ass in the station until the women did what they had to do. But to get the warrant, he would need to work up the evidence he had, put it together, and give it to the DA.

He turned to his computer and began furiously typing.

The departmental offices fell silent. It was a typical late-afternoon lull at the station, while most of the officers were in the field and had yet to return to book perps or file reports. A minute passed, then two. And then steps sounded softly in the hallway outside D'Agosta's office.

A moment later, Sergeant Slade appeared. He'd come from his office, which—if he stood in just the right spot—commanded an excellent view of D'Agosta's own doorway. He continued walking past D'Agosta's office, then stopped at the next door—the door to the empty room in which D'Agosta and others in the department had been keeping overflow files.

Slade glanced casually around. There was nobody in sight. Turning the knob, he opened the door of the empty office, stepped inside, and locked the door behind him. The lights were off, naturally, but he did not turn them on.

Making sure to remain quiet, he walked toward the common wall to D'Agosta's office, from which the sounds of typing continued without relent. A pile of boxes was stacked against the wall, and he knelt, carefully moving them aside. Placing his fingertips against the wall, he felt along it for a few moments until he found what he was searching for: a tiny wire microphone, embedded into the drywall, with a miniaturized, voice-activated digital tape recorder attached.

Rising to his feet and popping a piece of licorice toffee into his mouth, Slade fixed an earbud to the device, then inserted it into one ear and snapped the recorder on. He listened for a moment, nodding slowly to himself. He heard D'Agosta's futile arguing; the opening of the door; and then, the two women talking.

"Where is the plant in the Museum, exactly?"

"In the Herbarium Vault. I know where that is, and I have its combination. What about you?"

"The plant I need is in the Aquatic Hall of the Brooklyn Botanic Garden. Once the garden is closed, and it's completely dark, I'll secure it. We don't dare wait any longer than that."

Slade smiled. He was going to be well rewarded for this.

Slipping the device into his pocket, he carefully pushed the boxes back in place, moved to the office door, unlocked it, and—checking to make sure he remained unobserved—stepped out and began strolling languidly back down the corridor, the sounds of D'Agosta's typing ringing in his ears.

59

The Gates of Heaven Cemetery lay atop a thinly wooded bluff overlooking Schroon Lake. In the green distance to the east lay Fort Ticonderoga, guarding the Hudson approaches. Far to the north rose the bulk of Mount Marcy, tallest mountain in New York State.

John Barbeaux moved pensively through the manicured grass, threading a slow course between the gravestones. The ground rose and fell in slow, graceful curves; here and there a graveled walk curved beneath the trees. The leaves scattered the rays of the afternoon sun and threw dappled shadows over the drowsy pastoral landscape.

At length, Barbeaux arrived at a small, tasteful family plot, consisting of two memorials surrounded by a low iron fence. He stepped inside and approached the larger: a statue of an angel, hands clenched to her breast, tearful eyes glancing heavenward. A name was carved into the base of the monument: FELICITY BARBEAUX. There was no date.

Barbeaux was carrying two cut flowers in his right hand: a long-stemmed red rose and a purple hyacinth. He knelt and laid the rose before the memorial. Then he stood again and contemplated the statue in silence.

His wife had been killed by a drunk driver, not quite ten years ago. The police investigation had been botched—the man, a tele-marketing executive, had not been read his rights, and the chain of custody had been imperfectly established. A shrewd lawyer was able to get the man a one-year suspended sentence.

John Barbeaux was a man who prized family above all else. He was also a man who believed in justice. This was not justice as he understood it.

Although Red Mountain had been a far smaller and less powerful company a decade ago, Barbeaux nevertheless exerted significant influence, and he had many contacts in various obscure walks of life. First, he arranged to have the man arrested again when over one hundred grams of crack cocaine was found in his glove compartment. Although a first offense, this precipitated a five-year mandatory minimum sentence. Six months later, once the telemarketer had begun serving his term at Otisville Federal Correctional Institution, Barbeaux saw to it that—for a onetime payment of ten thousand dollars—the man was shivved with a filed-down screwdriver in the prison shower and left to bleed his life down the drain.

Justice served.

Barbeaux took a last, lingering look at the statue. Then, with a deep breath, he moved toward the second monument. This one was much smaller: a simple cross bearing the name JOHN BARBEAUX JR.

In the years following Felicity's death, Barbeaux had showered affection and attention on his young son. After a childhood beset with health problems, John Jr. had emerged into adolescence as a promising artist. More than promising, in fact: a truly gifted pianist, a prodigy as both a performer and composer. His father lavished everything on him: the best tutors, the best schools. In John Jr., Barbeaux saw great hope for the future of his line.

And then things began to go horribly wrong. It started out innocently enough. John Jr. grew a little moody; his appetite waned; and he seemed increasingly distracted by insomnia. Barbeaux put it off to some adolescent phase. But then it grew worse. The youth began smelling an odor; an odor he was unable to rid himself of. At first, it was sweet, lovely—but over time it slowly changed to the most vile stench of rotting flowers. Barbeaux's son grew weak, febrile;

he was plagued by headaches and joint pains that worsened by the day. He became increasingly delusional, the victim of ungovernable rages interspersed with periods of exhaustion and lethargy. Frantic, Barbeaux sought the aid of the world's greatest doctors, but no one was able to diagnose, let alone treat, the malady. Barbeaux could only watch as his son steadily declined into madness and unbearable pain. At the end, the once-promising boy was little more than a vegetable. The death that ultimately claimed him at sixteen years of age—heart failure, brought on by severe weight loss and exhaustion—had been almost merciful.

That had been less than two years ago. And Barbeaux had retreated into a fog of grief. He had been too unmanned even to select a large, elaborate memorial for the son, as he had for the wife: the very thought was unendurable, and in the end a simple cross became the only testament to so much wasted promise.

But then, almost a year to the day after John Jr.'s death, an event happened that Barbeaux could never have predicted. He had a visitor one evening—a young man that could not have been more than a few years older than Barbeaux's son, but of such a different build, energy, and magnetism as if to have come from another planet. He had a foreign accent, but spoke excellent English. This young man knew a great deal about Barbeaux. In fact, he knew more about Barbeaux's family than Barbeaux did himself. He told Barbeaux the tale of his great-grandparents, Stephen and Ethel, who had lived on Dauphine Street in New Orleans. He told the story of a neighbor of the couple, Hezekiah Pendergast, who had created the nostrum known as Hezekiah's Compound Elixir and Glandular Restorative—a quack patent medicine that was responsible for the suffering, madness, and death of thousands. Among the victims, this young man told the astounded Barbeaux, were Stephen and Ethel Barbeaux, barely in their thirties, who both died of its effects in 1895.

But that wasn't all, the young man said. There was another victim in the family, far closer to Barbeaux. His own son, John Jr.

The young man explained how the elixir had caused epigenetic changes in the Barbeaux family's bloodline—heritable changes to genetic makeup that had, in this case, jumped the generations to kill his son, more than a hundred years later.

Then the young man came to the real point of the meeting. The Pendergast family was still alive, in the form of one Aloysius Pendergast, a special agent with the FBI—and not only alive, but prospering, thanks to the wealth accumulated by Hezekiah and his deadly elixir.

And now the young man revealed just why he had come. He was, he said, named Alban...and he was the son of Special Agent Pendergast. Alban told him a most harrowing tale—and then proposed a complex, curious, but exceedingly satisfying plan.

One last thing, Alban said. The words echoed in Barbeaux's mind. *You might be tempted to hunt me down, as well—and thus eliminate another Pendergast. I warn you against any such attempt. I have remarkable powers beyond your comprehension. Satisfy yourself with my father. He's the one living like a parasite off of Hezekiah's fortune.* And then he left behind an extensive packet of documents backing up his story, and outlining his plan...and vanished into the night.

Barbeaux had dismissed this talk of "powers" as the braggadocio of youth. He sent two men to follow Alban, excellent men, experienced men. One returned with his eye hanging out, and the other was found with his throat cut. All this Alban had done, quite deliberately, in full view of Barbeaux's security cameras.

I have remarkable powers beyond your comprehension. Indeed, he did have remarkable powers. But they were not beyond Barbeaux's comprehension. And that had been Alban's fatal mistake.

The tale Alban had told seemed too strange to be true. But as Barbeaux looked through the packet he'd been given; as he examined his family history and the symptoms of his own son; and especially once he'd had certain blood tests performed—he realized that the story was, in fact, true. This was a revelation; a revelation that turned his grief into hatred and hatred into obsession.

A cell phone rang in the breast pocket of his suit. Gazing off in the direction of Mount Marcy, Barbeaux plucked it from his pocket.

"Yes?" he said.

He listened for a minute. As he did, his knuckles went white grasping the phone. A shocked look came over his face.

"Do you mean to tell me," he interrupted, "that he not only *knows* what has happened, but is taking steps to *stop* it?"

He listened again, longer this time, to the voice on the far end of the line.

"All right," he said at last. "You know what to do. And you'll have to move fast—very fast."

He hung up, then dialed another number. "Richard? Is the Ops Crew standing by? Good. We have a new objective. I want you to prep them for an emergency deployment to New York City. Yes, immediately. They have to be in the air inside of half an hour."

And with that he slipped the phone back into his pocket, turned away, and quickly left the cemetery.

60

It was six o'clock that evening by the time Constance Greene returned from police headquarters and let herself in through the front door of the Riverside Drive mansion, walked down the refectory passage, and crossed the marble-lined expanse of the grand reception hall. All was silent within, save for the soft passage of her feet. The mansion felt deserted. Proctor was still recovering in the hospital, Mrs. Trask was somewhere deep in the kitchen, and Dr. Stone was probably upstairs, sitting in Pendergast's room.

She continued down the tapestried hallway, past the marble niches that interrupted, at regular intervals, the rose-colored wallpaper. Now she mounted a back staircase, easing up the treads to minimize the creaking of the old boards. Once in the long upstairs hallway, she walked down it, past a large and disgusting stuffed polar bear, to reach a door on the left. She placed her hand on the knob. Taking a breath, she turned it, then quietly pushed the door open.

Dr. Stone rose noiselessly from a chair by the door. She felt irritated by his presence, his foppish dress, his yellow ascot and tortoiseshell glasses, and especially his utter inability to do anything beyond palliative care for her guardian. This was unfair, she knew, but Constance was in no mood for fairness.

"I should like a moment alone, Doctor."

"He is sleeping," he said while retreating.

Before Pendergast's condition had grown serious, Constance had rarely set foot inside his private bedroom. Even now, as she paused just within the doorway, she looked around in curiosity. The room was not large. The dim light came from behind recessed molding that ran just below the ceiling, and from a single Tiffany lamp that sat on the bedside table: the room had no windows. The wallpaper was flocked burgundy on red, with a subtle fleur-de-lis pattern. On the walls hung a few works of art: a small Caravaggio study for *Boy with a Basket of Fruit*; a Turner seascape; a Piranesi etching. A bookcase held three rows of old, leather-bound volumes. Scattered around the room were several museum pieces that, instead of being display objects, were put to actual use: a Roman glass urn held mineral water; a Byzantine-era candelabra held six white, unburned tapers. Frankincense smoked in an old Egyptian incense burner made of faience, and the heavy scent of it hung in the room, in a futile attempt to banish the stench that filled Pendergast's nostrils day and night. A stainless-steel IV stand, hung with a saline drip, was in sharp contrast with the rest of the room's elegant furnishings.

Pendergast lay motionless in the bed. His pale hair, now darkened with sweat, made a sharp contrast with the crisp white pillows. The skin of his face was as colorless as porcelain and almost as translucent; she could almost make out the musculature and fine skeletal detail beneath, and even the blue veins in his forehead. His eyes were closed.

Constance approached the bed. The morphine drip had been set to one milligram every fifteen minutes. Dr. Stone, she noted, had set the lock-out dose at six milligrams an hour; since Pendergast refused to permit supervision by a nurse, it was important that he not be allowed to overmedicate himself.

"Constance."

Pendergast's whisper surprised her; he was awake, after all. Or perhaps her movements, quiet as they were, had roused him.

She came around the bed and took a seat at its head. She recalled sitting in just such a position in Pendergast's hospital room in Geneva, just three days before. His rapid decline since then was deeply frightening to her. And yet, despite his weakness, the terrible, constant effort he struggled with remained evident—the fight to keep pain and madness from completely overwhelming him.

She saw his hand move under the covers, then withdraw. It now held a piece of paper. He raised it, shaking.

"What is this?"

She was shocked by the coldness, the anger, in his voice.

She took the paper and recognized it as the list of ingredients she had drawn up. It had been left on the table in the library, which had become a sort of war room for her and Margo. That had obviously been foolish.

"Hezekiah worked out an antidote to try to save his wife. We're going to make it—for you."

"We? Who is *we*?"

"Margo and I."

His eyes narrowed. "I forbid it."

Constance stared back. "You've got no say in the matter."

He raised his head, with effort. "You're being an absolute fool. You have no idea who you're dealing with. Barbeaux was able to kill Alban. He bested me. He will surely kill you."

"He won't have time. I'm going to the Brooklyn Botanic Garden tonight, and Margo is at the Museum right now—gathering the last ingredients."

The eyes seemed to glitter as they bored into her. "Barbeaux, or his men, will be waiting for you at the garden. And waiting for Margo at the Museum."

"Impossible," said Constance. "I just found that list this morning. Margo and I are the only ones who have seen it."

"It was lying in the library, in plain sight."

"Barbeaux can't possibly have gotten into the house."

Pendergast raised himself fully, even as his head seemed unsteady. "Constance, this man is the very devil incarnate. Don't go to the Botanic Garden."

"I'm sorry, Aloysius. I told you—I'm going to fight this thing to the end."

Pendergast blinked. "Then why are you even here?"

"To say good-bye. In case . . ." Constance began to falter.

At this, Pendergast made an effort to rally himself. With a supreme act of will, he rose onto one elbow. His eyes cleared a little, and he held Constance with his gaze. The hand snaked back under the covers and reappeared, this time grasping his .45. He pushed it toward her. "If you refuse to listen to reason, at least take this. It's fully loaded."

Constance took a step back. "No. Recall what happened the last time I tried to fire a gun."

"Then bring me the phone."

"Who are you calling?"

"D'Agosta."

"No. Please don't. He'll interfere."

"Constance, *for the love of God*—!" His voice choked off. Slowly, he sank back onto the white sheets. The effort had exhausted him to a fearsome degree.

Constance hesitated. She was shocked, and deeply moved, that he felt so strongly. She hadn't been handling this correctly. Her stubbornness was making him agitated to the point of danger. She took a deep breath and decided to lie. "You made your point. I won't go to the garden. And I'll call off Margo."

"I hope to God you're not deceiving me." He stared at her, his voice low.

"No."

He leaned forward and whispered, with the last of his strength: *"Do not go to the Botanic Garden."*

Constance left him with the phone and stumbled out into the hall, breathing hard. There she paused, thinking.

She had not considered that Barbeaux might be waiting for her at the Botanic Garden. This was a surprising idea—but not an altogether displeasing one.

She would need a weapon. Not a gun, of course, but something more suited to her . . . style.

Moving quickly now down the hallway, she descended the steps to the reception hall, turned and entered the library, moved the secret book, and slipped into the elevator to the basement. Then she almost ran down the corridor to the rough-hewn basement stairs that spiraled down to even deeper spaces, disappearing into the shadow-haunted, dust-fragrant chambers that lay beyond.

Dr. Stone heard Constance's retreating footsteps from his waiting room next door. He came out and reentered Pendergast's bedroom, with a little shiver at the thought of her. While Constance was certainly a young woman of taste, elegance, and exotic beauty, she was also as cold as dry ice—and there was, on top of that, something not right about her, a certain quality that gave him the absolute creeps.

He found his patient once again asleep. A phone had slipped out of his hands and was lying next to his open hand on the sheets. He picked it up and checked it, wondering whom he had been trying to call, saw that no call had been made, then gently turned it off and placed it back on the bureau. And then he took up once again his position in the chair at the door, waiting for what he was sure would be a long night . . . before the end.

61

Margo realized that getting into the Museum after hours was going to be a major problem. She felt sure Frisby would have put her name on a watch list at the first-floor security entrance—the only way in and out of the Museum after closing time. So she decided to simply hide in the Museum until it closed. She'd get what she came for, then exit the after-hours security station as nonchalantly as possible, with a story about having fallen asleep in a lab.

As closing time neared, Margo, posing as a museumgoer, made her way into the remotest, least-visited halls. Her chest felt tight, her breathing constricted. As the guards were beginning their sweeps, ushering visitors out, she hid in a bathroom and climbed onto a toilet seat to wait, mentally willing herself to relax. Finally, around six o'clock, all was quiet. She crept back out.

The halls were more or less empty, and she could hear the guards' shoes echoing distantly on the marble floors as they made their rounds. It was like an early warning signal, allowing her to evade them as she made her way to the one place she knew the guards would never check—the Gastropod Alcove.

Was she really going to do this? *Could* she follow through? She steadied herself by recalling Constance's words: *Those plants are vital if we're to have any hope of saving Pendergast.*

She ducked into the alcove and hid in the back, in a deeply shad-owed corner. It gave her a shiver to realize this was probably where Marsala's murderer had also hidden. The guards, as she expected, walked past the alcove roughly every half hour, not even bothering to shine their lights inside. No crime would play out twice in the same spot—they had returned to the *status quo ante delicti*. From time to time a staff member would also walk past on his or her way out, but as nine o'clock neared the Museum began to feel completely empty. There were, no doubt, some curators still toiling in their labs and offices, but the chance of running into them was small.

The thought of what she was about to do—*where* she was going to go—made Margo's heart hammer in her chest. She was about to descend into the one place that frightened her more than anything; that woke her in the middle of the night, bathed in a cold sweat; that prompted her never to enter the Museum without a bottle of Xanax in her bag. She thought of popping a Xanax then and there, but decided against it; she needed to stay sharp. She took slow, deep breaths, forc-ing her mind to focus on the small, immediate steps—not on the overall task. She would take it one move at a time.

Another set of long, deep breaths. Time to go.

Sneaking out of the alcove just after a guard passed by on his rounds, she crept down the halls to the nearest freight elevator, inserting her passkey into the slot. Even though it was a low-level-access key, Frisby had already sent her an email asking her to return it; but she had only gotten the memo that afternoon and figured she had at least a day's grace period before the pompous ass made an issue of it.

The elevator groaned and creaked its way down to what was technically known as Building Six basement storage—an anachro-nism, considering all the buildings comprising the Museum were now interconnected into a single, maze-like unit. The doors opened. The familiar smell of mothballs, mold, and old dead things lingered in the air. The scent hit her unexpectedly, spiking her anxiety and reminding her of the time she had been stalked through these same corridors.

But that was a long time ago, and these fears of hers should properly be classified as phobias. There was nothing down here to threaten her now, except perhaps a stray Museum employee demanding to see her ID.

Taking a few more steadying breaths, she stepped out of the elevator. Opening the door into the Building Six basement, she walked quietly through the long, dim passageways hung with caged lightbulbs, making her way toward the Botany collection.

So far, so good. She inserted her key into the dented metal door of the main botanical collection and found it still worked. The door opened on smooth hinges. The room beyond was dark and she took out a powerful LED headlamp she'd stashed in her bag, put it on her head, and stepped inside. The dark cabinets stretched out in front of her, vanishing into the darkness, and the stale air smelled of mothballs.

She paused, her heart thudding so hard in her chest she almost couldn't breathe, fighting down the surge of irrational fear. Despite everything she'd told herself, the smell, the claustrophobic darkness, and the strange noises once again triggered panic and gulping terror. She stopped to take more calming breaths, overcoming the terror with a strong application of reason.

One move at a time. Bracing herself, she took a step forward into the darkness, and then another. Now she had to shut the door behind her; it would be unwise to leave it open. She turned and eased it closed, blocking out what little light came in from the hall.

She relocked the door and peered ahead. The Herbarium Vault lay at the far end of the room. Shelves containing preserved plants in liquid rose up into darkness all around her—the so-called wet collections—as narrow aisles led off in two directions, everything vanishing into murk.

Get going, she told herself. She started down the left-hand aisle. At least these specimens didn't leer at her out of the darkness like the dinosaur skeletons or stuffed animals did in some of the other storage rooms. Botanical specimens weren't scary.

Even so, the monotony of the place, the narrow aisles looking all the same, the gleaming bottles that sometimes looked like so many eyes peering at her from the dark, did little to allay her anxiety.

She walked swiftly down the aisle, took a hard right, walked some more, took a left and then another right, working her way diagonally to the far corner. Why did they design these storage rooms to be so confusing? But after another moment she halted. She had heard something. The echoing sounds of her footfalls had initially obscured it, but she was sure she'd heard something nonetheless.

She waited, listening, trying not to breathe. But the only sounds were the faint creaking and clicking noises that never seemed to go away, probably caused by the building settling or the forced air system.

Her anxiety increased. Which way? The scare had caused her to forget which turn was next in the grid of shelving. If she got disoriented, lost in this labyrinth... Making a quick decision, she went down one aisle until she hit the storage room wall, realized she was indeed going in the right direction, and then followed it to the far corner.

There it was: the vault. It looked like—and probably was—an old bank vault, converted to a different use. It was painted dark green, with a large wheel and a retrofitted keypad, currently blinking red. With a gasp of relief she hustled over and punched in the number sequence she'd memorized from Jörgensen's office.

The keypad light went from red to green. *Thank God.* She turned the wheel and pulled open the heavy door. Leaning in, she flashed her headlamp around. It was a small space, perhaps eight by ten, with steel shelves covering all three walls. She glanced at the heavy door. No way was she going to shut it and risk being locked in. But she would, at least, partially close it. Just in case someone should come into the storage room—which seemed extremely unlikely.

She squeezed inside and eased the door shut to the point where it was open only a few inches.

Forcing down the feeling of panic, remembering to take things one step at a time, Margo turned her attention to the handwritten labels on the drawers, scanning them with her headlamp. They were in various stages of order, some quite ancient, handwritten in faded brown ink, others much newer and laser-printed. In a far corner of the vault, beyond the shelving, she saw a couple of ancient blowpipes—of either Amazonian or Guiana Indian origins, judging by the carved decoration—stacked against the back wall. A small quiver of braided bamboo, containing several darts, hung from one. She wondered what these were doing in here; the payload of most darts came from frogs, not botanicals. She assumed they'd been locked up because of their poisonous nature.

She returned to scanning the labels, quickly found the drawer marked MYCOHETEROTROPHS, and slid it quietly open. It contained racks of specimens, arranged not unlike a traditional hanging file cabinet. The old dried plant specimens, prepared many years before, were affixed to yellowing paper leaves with spidery script indicating what they were. These, in turn, had been sealed between high-tech glass plates. There weren't many, and in less than a minute she had found the *Thismia americana* specimens.

This was going unbelievably well. If she could keep her fear under control, she'd be out of the building in ten minutes. She realized she was covered with a clammy sweat, and she couldn't stop her heart from pounding, but her one-step-at-a-time strategy was, at least, keeping her wits about her.

There were three *Thismia* plates, one containing several underground rhizomes, another with samples of the aboveground plant, and a final one of the blossoms and seeds.

Margo recalled Jörgensen's words. *I would never allow the destruction of an extinct plant specimen, the last of its kind, for a one-off medicinal treatment. What is the value of an ordinary human life in the face of the last specimen of an extinct plant in existence?* She stared at the plant, with its tiny white flower. She couldn't agree less with such a misanthropic worldview. Maybe they wouldn't need all three specimens—but she was taking all of them regardless.

She slipped them carefully into her bag, zipped it up, and slung it over her shoulder. With an excess of caution, she turned off the headlamp and pushed open the door of the vault. She stepped into the darkness, listening intently. When all seemed silent, she stepped out and, feeling with her hands, shut the vault door, then turned the wheel. It locked automatically, and the green light switched back to red.

Done! She turned back around and, reaching up, turned on her headlamp.

The shadowy outline of a man stood there. And then a bright light suddenly flicked on, blinding her.

62

D'Agosta stood up from his desk and stretched. His back ached from hours of sitting in the hard wooden chair, and his right ear throbbed from having a phone receiver pressed against it.

He'd spent hours, it seemed, on the phone with the DA's office, trying to get a subpoena to have John Barbeaux brought in for questioning. But the DA's office wouldn't see it his way and said he hadn't met probable cause—especially for a guy like Barbeaux, who would immediately lawyer up and make their lives hell.

The chain of reasoning seemed obvious to D'Agosta: Barbeaux had hired Howard Rudd to pose as the fake Dr. Jonathan Waldron, who had in turn used Victor Marsala in order to get access to the skeleton of the long-dead Mrs. Padgett. Barbeaux needed a bone from that skeleton in order to reverse-engineer the components of Hezekiah Pendergast's elixir, thus allowing him to resynthesize that elixir and use it on Pendergast. D'Agosta had no doubt that, once Alban was placed on Pendergast's doorstep and the plot was in motion, Rudd killed Marsala as a way of tying up loose ends—he'd no doubt lured the tech to a remote corner of the Museum, under pretext of payment or some such thing. It seemed equally clear that Barbeaux had then used Rudd as bait to lure Pendergast into the animal handling room at the Salton Fontainebleau—and been gassed with the elixir for his trouble. All in seeking revenge for Hezekiah's poisoning of Barbeaux's great-grandparents and the death of his son.

Although he couldn't be sure, D'Agosta was fairly confident that Barbeaux had hired Rudd three years ago, paid off his gambling debts, given him a new face and a new identity, and kept him on as an anonymous enforcer he could use for any number of nefarious jobs—keeping him loyal by threatening his family with harm. It made complete sense.

The DA had dismissed all this with barely concealed contempt, calling it a conspiracy theory of supposition, speculation, and fantasy, and entirely unsupported by hard medical data.

D'Agosta had then spent a good part of the early evening phoning various botanical experts and pharmaceutical specialists, looking for that medical data. But he quickly understood that there would have to be tests, analyses, blind studies, and so on and so forth, before any conclusions could be drawn.

There had to be a way to dig up enough evidence to at least get Barbeaux's ass in his office long enough for Margo and Constance to do their thing.

Probable cause. Son of a bitch. There must be a piece of evidence out there, somewhere, that he'd overlooked, which would suggest Barbeaux was crooked. Frustrated, he got up from his desk. It was nine o'clock; he needed some fresh air; a walk to clear his head. Shrugging into his jacket, D'Agosta strode to the door, snapped off the lights, then began to make his way down the corridor. After a few steps, he paused. Maybe Pendergast would have some ideas on how to squeeze Barbeaux. But no—the agent would be too weak for that conversation. Pendergast's condition filled him with anger and a sick feeling of impotence.

As he exited his office, he paused. The Marsala files were next door: what he really should do is go through them again in case he'd overlooked something. He stepped into the vacant room he was using for overflow storage.

Turning on the lights, D'Agosta began to survey the stacks of folders piled on the conference table and against the walls. He'd take everything related to Howard Rudd. Maybe Barbeaux had a connection to Gary, Indiana, that he could—

At that moment D'Agosta went quite still. His roving eye had stopped at the room's lone garbage can. It contained only one thing: a crumpled-up licorice toffee wrapper.

Slade's ubiquitous toffee. What the hell had he been doing in here?

D'Agosta took a breath, then another. It was only a candy wrapper, and yes, Slade did have access and authority to be in there, looking at these files. D'Agosta wasn't sure why, but all of a sudden his cop instincts were going off. He looked around again, more carefully this time. Boxes and filing cabinets were stacked against the walls. The files were where he remembered leaving them. Slade should have checked with him, that was true, but maybe Angler didn't want D'Agosta to know. After all, the guy was obviously not too keen on Pendergast, and D'Agosta was known to be a friend of the agent.

As he moved to grab the Rudd files, his eye spied a dusting of white plaster on the rug, a spot near the wall that was shared with his own office. D'Agosta approached the wall and moved the boxes away from it. There was a small hole drilled in the wall, just above the baseboard.

He knelt and peered more closely, let his finger drift over the hole. It was about half a millimeter in diameter. He probed it with an unbent paper clip and found it didn't go all the way through.

His gaze went back to the dusting of white plaster. This hole had been made recently.

A candy wrapper, a recently drilled hole... such things weren't necessarily connected. But then he recalled how Slade had misfiled the tip on Barbeaux from the Albany police.

Had it really come from Angler's desk—or had Slade even shown it to Angler before misfiling it?

Albany. That was another thing. Hadn't Slade said Angler was away, visiting relatives upstate?

He trotted back to his office and, without bothering to turn on the lights, typed his password into the computer and accessed the homicide department's personnel records. Locating Peter Angler's file, D'Agosta searched the extensive next-of-kin records all NYPD officers were required to maintain. There it was: his sister, Marjorie Angler, 2007 Rowan Street, Colonie, New York.

He grabbed his phone, dialed the number on his computer screen. It rang three times before it was answered.

"Hello?" came a woman's voice.

"Is this Marjorie Angler? My name is Vincent D'Agosta. I'm a lieutenant with the NYPD. Is Lieutenant Angler there?"

"No. He's not staying with me."

"When did you last speak with him?"

"Let me see—four, five days ago, I think."

"May I ask what you talked about?"

"He said he was coming upstate. Some investigation he was working on. He said he was rushed for time, but that he hoped to stop by to see me on the way back to New York City. But he never did—I imagine he was too busy, as usual."

"Did he say where he was going?"

"Yes. Adirondack. Is there a problem of some sort?"

"Not that I know of. Listen, Ms. Angler, you've been very helpful. Thank you."

"You're welcome—" the voice began again, but D'Agosta was already hanging up.

He was breathing faster now. Adirondack. Home of Red Mountain Industries.

Several days before, Angler had been on his way to Adirondack. Why hadn't he returned to the city? He seemed to have disappeared. Why had Slade lied about his whereabouts? Or was Slade merely mistaken? And the hole: it was exactly the kind of hole you would use to plant a miniature microphone.

Had Slade embedded a wire microphone in the wall of his office? If so, he'd listened in on D'Agosta's phone calls. And he'd no doubt also listened in on his conversation with Margo and Constance.

The hole was empty. The mike was gone. That meant the eavesdropper believed he had all the information he needed.

It seemed too incredible to be true: Slade was dirty. And who was he working for? Only one answer: Barbeaux.

Now D'Agosta's vague concern about Barbeaux somehow threatening or intercepting Margo and Constance became suddenly much more specific. Barbeaux would know all that Slade knew, and that was just about everything. Specifically, he would know Margo and Constance were headed to the Museum to steal plant specimens.

D'Agosta grabbed for the phone again, then hesitated, thinking furiously. This was a tricky situation. Accusing a fellow cop of being dirty—he damn well better be right.

Was he? *Was* Slade dirty? Christ, all he had was a candy wrapper and a misfiled document. Not exactly a lot of evidence for destroying a man's career.

The fact was, he couldn't call in the cavalry. They would think he was crazy—he had less on Slade than what the DA had already rejected on Barbeaux. There was nothing else for it—he'd have to go after Margo and Constance in the Museum by himself. He might be right, and he might be wrong—but he had no choice but to act, and act quickly, because if he *was* right, the consequences were too terrifying to even consider.

He darted out of the office and made for the elevator as quickly as he could.

63

Margo stood there, paralyzed by the blinding light.

"Well, well, why am I not surprised?"

It was Frisby's voice, coming from behind the light.

"Switch off that damned headlamp. You look like a miner."

Margo complied.

"Here you are, on schedule, caught red-handed stealing one of the most valuable items in our entire herbarium." The voice was triumphant. "This is no longer an internal Museum matter, Dr. Green. This is a criminal matter for the police. This will put you away for many years—if not for good."

The light was lowered and Frisby—now visible behind the brilliance—extended a hand. "Give me your bag."

Margo hesitated. What on earth was he doing down here? How had he possibly known?

"Hand me the bag or I will be forced to take it from you."

She looked left and right for an escape route, but Frisby's bulk blocked the way. She would have to knock him over—and he was more than half a foot taller than she.

He took a menacing step forward and, realizing she had no choice, she held out her bag. He opened it, slid out one of the glass plates, and read, in a stentorian tone: "*Thismia americana.*" He carefully replaced it in the bag. "Caught red-handed. You are *finished*, Dr. Green. Let me tell you what is going to happen now." He took out his cell phone and held it up. "I'm going to call the police. They will arrest you. Since the value of these specimens is far in excess of five thousand dollars, you will be charged with a Class C felony, burglary in the second degree, which carries a sentence of up to fifteen years in prison."

Margo listened, only barely comprehending. She was stupefied, because this meant the end of not just her own life—but Pendergast's, as well.

He searched through the rest of the bag, poking around while shining the light inside. "Pity. No weapon."

"Dr. Frisby," Margo said in a wooden tone, "what is it you have against me?"

"Who, me, have something against you?" His eyes widened in mock satire, and then narrowed. "You're a hindrance. You've been a disruption in my department with your incessant comings and goings. You've been meddling in a police investigation, encouraging them to cast suspicion on our staff. And now you've rewarded my generosity in giving you access to the collections with outright thievery. Oh, I have nothing against *you*." With a frosty smile, he punched in 911 on his cell phone, holding it so she could see what he was doing.

He waited a moment, then frowned. "Bloody reception."

"Listen," Margo managed to say. "A man's life—"

"Oh, for God's sake, spare me the pathetic excuses. You played a nasty trick on Jörgensen, got him all riled up. He came boiling into my office and I feared he might have a heart attack. When I heard you'd been in his office asking for access to a rare, extinct plant, I figured you were up to something. What were you planning to do—sell it to the highest bidder? So I came down here, placed a chair in the far corner, and waited for you." His voice swelled with satisfaction. "And here you came, on cue!"

He grinned triumphantly. "Now I'll take you to security to await the police."

A thousand ideas raced through Margo's head. She could run; she could snatch the bag; she could knock Frisby down and escape; she could plead with him, try to talk him out of it; she could try to bribe him...But not a single option had the slightest chance of success. She was busted, and that was that. Pendergast would die.

For a moment the two stared at each other. Margo could see from the expression on Frisby's face that there would be no mercy from this man.

And then his look of triumph suddenly changed: first to one of puzzlement, then to shock. His eyes grew wide and bugged out; his lips contracted. He opened his mouth but no sound came out, save for a strange boiling in the back of his throat. He dropped the flashlight, which hit the stone floor and went out, plunging the room into darkness. Instinctively, Margo reached out and snatched back her bag with nerveless fingers. A moment later she heard the sound of his body hitting the floor.

And then a new light came on, revealing the outline of a man who had been standing behind Frisby. He stepped forward and, in an act of courtesy, shone the light on his own face, revealing a shortish man with a dark face, black eyes, and the very faintest of smiles playing at the corners of his mouth.

At that same exact time, at precisely nine fifteen, a livery cab turned in at 891 Riverside Drive, then circled around the drive and came to a stop beneath the mansion's porte cochere, engine idling.

A minute passed, and then two. The front door opened and Constance Greene stepped out, wearing an ebony-colored pleated dress with ivory accents. A black duffel of ballistic nylon was slung over one shoulder. In the dim glow of moonlight, the formal, even elegant dress acted almost like camouflage.

She leaned in at the driver's window, whispered something inaudible, opened the rear passenger door, placed the duffel carefully on the seat, and then slid in beside it. The door closed; the cab moved back down the drive; and then it merged with the light evening traffic, heading north.

64

Dr. Horace Stone found himself suddenly awake in the room with his patient. He did not care for nursing duties, but his patient was paying him extremely well and the case was most unusual, if not fascinating. There would be an excellent *JAMA* article in this—of course, not until after the patient's demise and postmortem, when they might have at least a better chance of diagnosing this most unusual affliction.

An excellent article indeed.

Now he saw what had awakened him. Pendergast's eyes had opened and were drilling into him with intensity.

"My phone?"

"Yes, sir." Stone fetched the phone from the bureau and handed it to him.

He examined it, his face pale. "Nine twenty. Constance—where is she?"

"I believe she just left."

"You *believe*?"

"Well," said Stone, flustered. "I heard her say good-bye to Mrs. Trask, I heard the door shut, and there was a livery cab outside that took her away."

Stone was shocked when Pendergast rose in his bed. He was clearly coming into the remissive phase of the disease.

"I strongly advise—"

"Be silent," said Pendergast, pushing back the covers and, with difficulty, rising to his feet. He pulled the IV from his arm. "Step aside."

"Mr. Pendergast, I simply cannot allow you to leave your bed."

Pendergast turned his pale, glittering eyes upon Dr. Stone. "If you try to stop me, I will hurt you."

This naked threat stopped Stone's retort. The patient was clearly febrile, delusional, perhaps hallucinating. Stone had asked for a nurse and been denied one. He could not handle this on his own. He retreated from the room as Pendergast began changing out of his bedclothes.

"Mrs. Trask?" he called. The house was so blasted large. "Mrs. Trask!"

He heard the housekeeper bustling around downstairs, calling from the bottom of the stairs.

"Yes, Doctor?"

Pendergast appeared in the bedroom doorway, slipping into his black suit, stuffing a sheet of paper into one pocket, and sliding his gun into an inside holster. Dr. Stone stepped aside to let him pass.

"Mr. Pendergast, I repeat, you are in no condition to leave the house!"

Pendergast ignored him and headed down the stairs, moving slowly, like an old man. Dr. Stone followed in pursuit. A frightened Mrs. Trask hovered at the bottom.

"Please get me a car," Pendergast told the housekeeper.

"Yes, sir."

"You can't get him a car!" Stone expostulated. "Look at his condition!"

Mrs. Trask turned to him. "When Mr. Pendergast asks for something, we do not say no."

Dr. Stone looked from her to Pendergast himself who, despite being obviously debilitated, returned the stare with such an icy look that he was finally silenced. It all happened so quickly. Now Mrs. Trask was hanging up the phone and Pendergast, staggering slightly, made his way to the porte cochere entrance. In a moment he was out the door, and the red taillights of the hired car were turning up the drive.

Stone sat down, breathing hard. He had never quite seen a patient with such steely resolve in the grip of such a fatal illness.

As he reclined in the rear of the car, Pendergast took the piece of paper from his pocket and read it over. It was a note, in Constance's copperplate hand: the list of chemical compounds and other ingredients. Beside some of these ingredients, locales had been listed.

Pendergast read the list over carefully, first once, then twice. And then he folded the page over on itself, tore it into small pieces, lowered the window of the car, and allowed the pieces to float out into the Manhattan night, one by one.

The cab turned onto the entrance ramp for the West Side Highway, heading for the Manhattan Bridge and, ultimately, Flatbush Avenue in Brooklyn.

65

Shaking his head, the man bent down and plucked something from the back of Frisby's neck.

"Interesting collection you've got down here," he said, holding up the object, dripping with Frisby's blood. Margo recognized it as a giant Sumatran buckthorn: six inches long, recurved, razor-sharp—notorious as a weapon in certain parts of Indonesia.

"I'd better introduce myself," the man said. "I'm Sergeant Slade of the NYPD." He reached into the pocket of his suit coat and produced an ID, illuminating it with his flashlight.

Margo peered at it. The shield and identification looked real enough. But who was this man, and what was he doing down here? And hadn't he just...stabbed Frisby? She felt a growing sense of confusion and terror.

"I guess I arrived in the nick of time," said Slade. "This old curator—you called him Frisby, right?—seemed to be getting off on calling the cops on you. Little did he know the cop was already here. And he was all wrong about the rap they'd have hung on you. Take it from me: you'd have pled down to Class E and received nothing more than community service. In New York City, no jury cares about a few moldy plant specimens stolen from a museum."

He bent to examine the body of Frisby, gingerly stepping around the spreading pool of blood under the neck as he did so, and then rose again.

"Well, we'd better get on with it," he said. "Now that I'm here, you don't have much to worry about. Please give me the bag." And he held out his hand.

But Margo just stood there, frozen. Frisby was dead. This man had stabbed him—with a buckthorn, no less. This was nothing less than murder. She remembered D'Agosta's warning and she suddenly understood: cop or no, this man was working for Barbeaux.

Sergeant Slade took a step forward, buckthorn in hand.

"Give me the bag, Dr. Green," he said.

Margo stepped back.

"Don't make things more difficult for yourself than they have to be. Give me the bag and you'll get no more than a slap on the wrist."

Tightening her hand on the bag, Margo took another step back.

Slade sighed. "You're forcing my hand," he said. "If that's the way you want to play it, I'm afraid what's in store for you will be far more extreme than community service." He shifted the thorn into his right hand and gripped it hard, advancing on her. Margo turned and realized she was backed into a cul-de-sac of the botanical collections, with shelving on either side and the vault behind her.

She stared at Sergeant Slade. He may have been short, but he moved with the grace of a lean and powerful man. In addition to the giant thorn in his hand, Margo could see a service belt beneath his suit jacket that held a gun, pepper spray, and cuffs.

She took another step backward and felt her spine contact the metal door of the vault.

"It'll be quick," Slade said, with a note in his voice that sounded almost like regret. "I don't enjoy this—I really don't." The hand with the buckthorn rose into striking position and he loomed forward, bracing himself to swipe the weapon across her throat.

66

"You may pull over here, if you please."

The cabbie nosed his vehicle to the curb. Constance Greene pushed some money through the sliding window, collected the bag, and stepped out onto the sidewalk. She stood for a moment, considering. Across Washington Avenue stood a wrought-iron fence, and beyond that the dark trees of the Brooklyn Botanic Garden. Even though it was nine thirty, the traffic on Washington Avenue was steady and there were pedestrians on the move.

Slinging the bag onto one shoulder by its strap, Constance smoothed down the pleats of her dress and brushed the hair from her face. She walked to the corner, waited at the crosswalk for the light to change, and crossed to the other side.

Here the wrought-iron fence surrounding the garden stood about waist-high and was topped with dull spikes. Casually strolling along the fence, Constance walked to a spot midway between streetlights: a dark zone where overhanging tree limbs cast additional shadows. Setting down her bag, she took out her cell phone on the pretense of checking it and waited until there was no one in view. Then, in one smooth movement, she grasped two of the spikes and swung herself over, dropping down on the far side. Reaching over the fence, she retrieved her bag. A quick jog carried her into the protective darkness of the trees, where she paused to look back to see if her movements had attracted attention.

All seemed normal.

Opening the duffel, she removed a small satchel from it and hid it beneath some ground cover. Then she began moving through the darkness. She had not brought a flashlight: the waxing moon was just rising over the trees, and in any case her eyes were unusually well adapted to darkness from the many years of living in the basement corridors and crawl spaces underneath 891 Riverside Drive.

She had downloaded a map of the Brooklyn Botanic Garden from the institution's website and carefully memorized it. Ahead of her lay a border of dense shrubbery that formed a natural wall. She eased into the shrubbery and pushed her way through, emerging in an isolated corner of the Shakespeare Garden. Trampling through a dense patch of irises, their crushed scent rising around her, she gained a brick path that wound through the plantings. Here she paused again to listen. All was dark and quiet. She had no idea what kind of security might be present in the garden, and she moved with exquisite care, instinctively employing skills sharpened from roaming the New York docks as a child, stealing food and money.

Staying off the main paths, Constance continued past a bed of primroses and another course of shrubbery, followed by a low stone wall. Scaling this, she arrived at the edge of the main pathway leading up to the Palm House, a stately Tuscan Revival building of iron and glass. Beyond it were the greenhouse complexes, including the Aquatic House, home to Hodgson's Sorrow. But the main path was broad and too well lit to make for a good approach. She waited in the shrubbery, watching for security and puzzled to see none. It occurred to her that this might be evidence of Pendergast's claim that Barbeaux would get there before her; if so, he would have neutralized the security.

This was good to know.

Then again, this was a botanical garden, not an art museum. Perhaps there wasn't any night security at all.

Keeping to the shadows of the plantings, she passed between the Fragrance Garden and the Japanese Hill-and-Pond Garden. A night breeze carried the scent of the honeysuckle and peonies toward her. Making her way past a dense planting of azaleas, she could see the Magnolia Plaza ahead, the trees already off their spring bloom. Beyond lay the waters of the Lily Pool, glimmering in the moonlight.

While examining the map of the Botanic Garden, Constance had mentally sketched out a route of approach. The best point of entry would be the elegant Palm House, much of which had been converted from greenhouse into an event space for hosting social functions. The building had large, single-paned glass windows. The newer greenhouses, on the other hand, had smaller windows, some of them with double-paned glass.

She darted across the Magnolia Plaza and regained the shadows along one long wing of the Palm House. The grand old Victorian structure was composed of a central dome and two glass wings. She paused to peer through one of the panes. This wing of the Palm House had been set up for an elegant wedding that was apparently to take place the next day, with long tables covered in white linen, opulent place settings, candelabras, glassware, and unlit candles. There was no obvious sign of a security system. Kneeling, she slid the backpack off her shoulder and onto the ground. She slid a small leather wallet out of one external pocket of the backpack, and from it she extracted a glass cutter and a suction cup. Fixing the cup to the center of the large glass pane, she carefully cut an incision around the pane's periphery. A few sharp taps knocked out the glass, and she carefully laid it aside, pushed the backpack through the opening, then crawled in after it, tucking her dress around her so it would not snag.

Collecting the bag again, she made her way among the silent tables, through the great central glass dome, across a parquet dance floor, toward the far wing. There was a door leading into the next wing that she tested and found to be unlocked. Throughout her passage, she had been prepared to retreat quickly at the first sound of a tripped alarm, but the Palm House remained silent and shadowy.

She pushed the door ajar, listened, looked, then ducked through. This was the Bonsai Museum, supposedly the greatest outside of Japan. Beyond it lay her destination: the Aquatic House and orchid collection.

The Bonsai Museum offered few hiding places, the dwarf trees arranged on pedestals in rows along the front and rear walls, leaving an open central aisle. Crouching behind a pedestal, Constance paused. There remained no evidence of security—or of Barbeaux. It was cooler here in the Bonsai Museum, and there was a soft hum from fans set near the roof.

She moved swiftly past the twisted little trees and paused at the next door. Cracking it open slightly—once again, it wasn't locked—she hesitated. All was silent. She slipped through and found herself in an entrance lobby. To her right rose the Steinhardt greenhouse complex, with its huge Tropical Pavilion, and straight ahead lay the entrance to the Aquatic House.

Creeping across the dark lobby, she advanced to the entrance to the Aquatic House: a pair of glass doors that were shut. She approached the closest one, crouched in the shadows, and peered within.

All was silent. And then, after the most careful scrutiny of the space beyond the doors, her eye began to make out the faintest outline of a man standing perfectly still. She could not see him directly; rather, she saw his reflection off a watery surface glimmering in the moonlight. The outline of a gun was in his hand.

So Pendergast was right after all. That Barbeaux knew about her coming here was startling. As best she knew, she had discussed the location only with Margo. But clearly, their plan had been leaked and there was a traitor in their midst. Barbeaux knew she was coming for the plant in this greenhouse. He was waiting for her.

She thought about Margo, and her own mission within the Museum basement. Was it possible Barbeaux knew about that, as well? Of course it was. She could only hope Margo's vast knowledge of the Museum's secret places would help keep her safe.

Ever so slowly, she shifted her position, and in so doing spied a second dim figure in the Aquatic House. This one had an assault rifle slung over his shoulders.

These men were clearly professional soldiers, and they were heavily armed—alarming, but not surprising, given Red Mountain's stock-in-trade. Barbeaux was leaving nothing to chance.

Constance knew that the greenhouse beyond was large, and even in the dark she could tell it was crowded with vegetation. If she could see two men from her lone vantage point, there would surely be others, perhaps several more, that remained hidden from view. Why were they all concentrated in this location?

Clearly, Barbeaux was set on preventing anyone from getting the plant. He wanted to ensure that Pendergast suffered the longest, most lingering, most painful, most *apt* death possible. But this just raised another question. Why were there men here at all? It would have been far easier to simply remove or destroy the specimen of Hodgson's Sorrow, and then leave. Why the ambush?

There could be only one answer: because they knew what building the plant was in, but they didn't know the name of the plant. Their information, however it had been gained, was incomplete.

Mentally reviewing the map of the garden, she recalled there was a second, higher level to the Aquatic House, gained via a staircase in the lobby, which allowed visitors to gaze out over the swampy jungle. She considered going upstairs to reconnoiter, but realized that surely at least one watcher would be placed on the mezzanine level, as well.

There were too many men. She could never confront them all at once. She would have to sneak in, remove the plant from under their very eyes, and sneak back out. She would deal with Barbeaux later. It was a disagreeable option . . . but it was the only one.

Stealth was now paramount. That meant her backpack had become an impediment. Slipping the glass cutter and suction cup into a pocket of her dress, she secreted the nylon bag underneath a visitor's bench. Then she crept back to the double doors of glass and tried to construct a picture of where Barbeaux's men were hiding. If the men weren't there, she could have found the plant in minutes.

Now it wouldn't be so simple.

She retreated along the inner walls to the lobby. The door to its main entrance was locked. Moving more swiftly, she retraced her steps back through the Bonsai Museum, the main body of the Palm House, the far wing, and then out the missing panel of glass. She circled the Lily Pool, keeping to the darkness of the massive trees in the arboretum beyond. Bypassing the Tropical Pavilion, she approached the rear wall of the Aquatic House, again constructed almost entirely of glass. The panes were smaller here than in the Palm House, but still big enough to crawl through. There was no door in this wall. They would not expect entry here.

She crouched and listened. Nothing. Attaching the suction cup to a nearby pane, she started to cut it free. As she did so, the blade made a sharp noise against the glass. Immediately she paused. There was plenty of Brooklyn background noise: distant cars honking, jets passing overhead, the beating heart of the city. But still, the *scritch* of the cutter had been too prominent—and no doubt sounded even louder inside.

As if in answer, she saw a shadowy figure moving stealthily within, coming to check out the sound. He peered about this way and that, weapon at the ready. She knew he couldn't see her waiting in the darkness outside. After a moment, he melted back into the foliage, satisfied it was nothing.

Constance waited, rethinking how she was going to get in. If she could find a way to do so without breaking or cutting any glass, it would greatly lessen her chances of being discovered.

She crawled along the edge of the long glass wall, her fingers probing against the panes as she moved. Some were a little loose. The bronze frames were corroded, especially where they met the low concrete foundation.

Still crawling, she tried one pane after another until she found a piece of glass that was looser than the rest. Inspecting its frame, she found the bronze almost completely corroded along the bottom edge.

She worked her glass cutter under the thin frame and began to pry outward. The bronze bent readily, its crust of oxidation flaking and falling off. Slowly, careful not to put so much pressure on the glass as to break it, she worked the cutter around the inside of the frame, bending it out. After several minutes the frame had been so thoroughly loosened that she risked applying the suction cup to the pane and pulling gently. It held fast, but now only one area of the frame remained to be bent. A few more seconds with the cutter, and she was able to remove the pane of glass. A stream of humid, flower-scented air flowed over her.

She crawled inside.

A dense wall of hanging orchids separated her from the men. This, she recalled from the map, was the Orchid Collection, which occupied the far end of the Aquatic House. Beyond it lay a curving walkway with a double railing, and beyond that was the large indoor pool in which Hodgson's Sorrow would be found.

Constance paused, thinking. The foliage around and ahead of her was extremely dense. Her choice of a long black dress with white accents had been appropriate for camouflage. However, for the kind of crawling in close quarters that lay ahead, it would prove an obstacle. Worse yet, it might tear on a protruding branch and create unwanted noise. With a frown of displeasure, she worked the dress off her shoulders and slid it from her body. Beneath, she was wearing a black chemise. Then she took off her shoes and stockings, reducing herself to bare feet. Balling the dress up, she stowed it, the stockings, and the shoes behind a bush and crawled forward, slipping a hand into the thick curtain of orchids with infinite slowness and drawing it half an inch aside.

The visitors' path lay bathed in moonlight, but the moon was low and deep shadows stretched across the shrubbery. There was no other way to approach the central pond—she would have to cross this path. As she paused, considering the situation, she was able to identify three additional men, standing in the darkness. They were utterly silent. The only things moving were their heads, which turned first one way and then the other, watching, listening.

These gentlemen were not going to be easily evaded. But evade them she must, or Pendergast would die.

The ground beneath her was wet and muddy. While her chemise was black, the exposed parts of her body were pale and could be easily detected. She scooped up the mud and methodically smeared it over her face, arms, and legs. When she was satisfied that she was fully covered, Constance crept forward again, inch by inch, parting the orchids with infinite caution. The smell of wet soil, flowers, and vegetation was pervasive. She paused after each move. As a little girl, down on the docks by Water Street, she had often stolen fish this way, moving so incrementally that no one noticed her. But back then she had been a waif. Now she was a full-grown woman.

In a few minutes, she had managed to move ten feet ahead and was now lying among a border of tropical ferns. Next, she had to cross a low railing and then the walkway. From her vantage point she could see several of the watchers, but there were no doubt others she could not see. She did have one advantage: they did not know she was already inside and among them. Their attention seemed to be focused on the entrance and an emergency exit in the rear.

More stealthy movement brought her up behind a large plaque, still in deep shadow. Getting across the walkway was going to be the crux. She could not crawl over it in slow motion. She would have to flit across at the moment when no one was looking.

She watched and waited. And then she heard the faint hiss of a radio, a murmured voice. And then another, coming from a different place; and then a third. It was exactly nine forty-five. They were checking in with each other.

In a minute they had revealed their locations—at least, those at the near end of the greenhouse. Constance counted a total of five. But she estimated that only three of them were in a position to notice her scurry across the open walkway.

She rotated her eyes upward. The moon was rising higher, casting a troublesome light into the greenhouse, and it would be most of the night before it finally set behind the trees. But a few clouds were scudding across the sky. As she watched, she could see that one of them would obscure the moon in, perhaps, three minutes.

She closed her eyes—even the whites could give her away—and

waited, counting. Three minutes passed. She opened her eyes again slightly and saw the cloud flaring white as its edge began to move across the face of the moon. A shadow fell over the greenhouse. Darkness descended.

This was her moment. Slowly, she raised her head. The watchers had melted into the darkness, so she had no way of discerning which way they were looking. It was very dark in the greenhouse now, and it would never be darker. She would have to risk it.

In one smooth, easy movement she rose to a crouch, stepped over the railing, darted across the pathway, and lay down beneath a large tropical tree draped in orchids. She remained motionless, hardly daring to breathe. All was silent. A moment later, the moonlight flared back up. Nobody had moved; nobody had seen her.

Now for the pool, and the plant . . .

She felt something cold touch the nape of her neck, ever so lightly. A quiet voice said: "Don't move."

67

Margo threw herself sideways as the buckthorn darted toward her, slicing her jacket and nicking her shoulder. She landed on the floor, jammed up against a stack of shelving, trapped, her headlamp spinning off into darkness. Slade took a step forward. She was now lying on the ground, with the policeman calmly standing over her.

"You're just making things more difficult," Slade said.

Her arm was wedged behind her back and it was making contact with something cold. She realized it was a specimen jar, part of a row of them along the bottom level of shelving.

"Look, all I want is the plant you've got." The man tried to make his voice sound reasonable. "We don't need things to end this way. Give it to me and I'll let you go."

Margo said nothing. The man was a liar. Although her mind was going a mile a minute, she could see no way out.

"There's no chance of your getting away from me, so you might as well cooperate."

She glanced past him, in the direction of the distant door of the botanical collection through which she'd come.

"Don't even think about making a run for it," Slade said. "When I came into Building Six storage, I locked the entryway and jammed the lock with a broken penknife so no one else could enter. We're alone in here—just you and me." An odd smile formed on his thin face.

Margo choked down her fear and thought hard. She vaguely remembered that there was another exit at the far end of the Building Six basement. She racked her brains, trying to recall the corridors that would lead her to it. If she could only get past him, she could head for that back exit and lose him. After all, she knew the byways of the Museum and he did not—

"And don't think about trying for the back exit, either. The truth is, I know these underground corridors almost as well as you do."

She was shocked that he seemed to have divined what was in her mind. But this had to be another lie, his claiming to know the Museum's basements.

"Oh, I know this Museum like the back of my hand," the man said. "I wish to God I didn't—the Museum ruined my life. I wasn't always with the NYPD, you see. I was once an FBI agent. Graduated second in my class from the Academy. My very first assignment as a field agent was to take charge of a forward command post, right here at this Museum, to help make sure the opening of a certain blockbuster exhibition went off without a hitch. Do you know what exhibition that was, Margo? You should—you were there."

Margo stared. Slade ... Slade ... she vaguely remembered hearing that name during the mopping up of that dreadful night twelve years ago, when the Museum had become a slaughterhouse. She'd never seen his face. Could this really be the same man?

"You're ... *that* Slade?"

Slade looked gratified. "That's right. The Superstition exhibition. It was my bad luck that one SAC Spencer Coffey was in charge of the FBI contingent. That exhibition didn't go off too well, did it? How many died—twenty-six? It was one of the biggest screwups in the Bureau's history. So big that they made an example of not just Coffey, but all of us. Coffey was transferred to Waco, and I was cashiered from the FBI with the rest of his team. I was a branded man after that, lucky to get a job with the NYPD as a beat cop. And the brand stayed with me. Why do you think a man with my seniority and experience is still a sergeant?"

This bitter little speech had given Margo time to gather her wits.

She tried to keep him talking. "So the answer for you was to go on the take?" she asked. "Is that how it worked?"

"I had nothing to do with that disaster—I didn't even arrive on the scene until the dust was settling—and yet they threw me to the wolves without a second thought. Things like that can make a man receptive to—shall we say—*better offers*. In time, I got a better offer— and here I am."

Slade leaned forward, gripping the buckthorn, and she realized he was bracing himself to try once again to stab her in the neck with it. Her fingers closed around the specimen jar behind her. As he prepared to stick her, she kicked out hard, striking the inside of his ankle and knocking him off balance. Slade veered sideways momentarily to regain his balance and she swung the bottle up and around, smashing it against the side of his head. It shattered, spraying ethyl alcohol everywhere and knocking Slade to his knees. She scrambled up and leapt over him, running down the aisle, her bag held tight under her arm. Behind her, Slade rose with a howl of anger.

Panic gave Margo strength and clarity of mind. She raced down the aisles, burst out the door of the botanical collection, and took a left down the corridor, heading toward the back exit of Building Six. Because of the ancient layout of the Museum's basement, it wasn't a straight shot. She would have to go through a string of storage rooms in order to reach it. She could hear Slade running behind her now, his breath rasping, his shoes pounding on the cement floor—and growing closer, ever closer.

68

Constance lay in the dirt, unmoving. A dim light played over her, and she could hear faint murmurings as the men communicated with one another. She felt a strange, gathering combination of remorse, chagrin, and particularly anger: not because she was about to be killed—she cared nothing for her own life—but because her discovery meant that Pendergast would die.

She heard faint footfalls, and then a different voice said: "Stand her up."

Her neck was prodded again. "Get up. Slow."

Constance rose to her feet. A tall man with a military bearing stood in front of her, dressed in a dark business suit. His face, dimly illuminated by the moonlight, was large and granitic, with prominent cheekbones and a heavy, over-thrusting jaw.

Barbeaux.

For a moment her concentration narrowed to a fierce pinpoint, so overpowering was her hatred and loathing for this man. She remained motionless while Barbeaux played a light over her.

"What a sight you are," he sneered in a gravelly tone.

Several other men had silently appeared and now took up positions around her. All were heavily armed. Every avenue of escape had been cut off. She considered snatching a firearm, but knew that would be useless; besides, these automatic weapons were foreign to her.

Barbeaux did not look like the kind of man who could be surprised or overcome easily, if at all. He had a calm, intelligent, and alert air of cruelty about him that she had encountered, notably, only twice before: her first guardian, Enoch Leng, and Diogenes Pendergast.

His inspection complete, Barbeaux spoke again. "So this is the operative Pendergast sends as his avenging angel. I didn't believe it when Slade told me about you."

Constance did not react.

"I'd like to know the name of the plant you're looking for."

She continued to stare at him.

"You've come in some last-ditch, desperate attempt to save your precious Pendergast. We were one step ahead of you, as you can see. Nevertheless, I am impressed at how far you managed to get in this fool's errand before we caught you."

Constance let him talk.

"Pendergast is on his deathbed now. You can't imagine the delight I take in his suffering. His malady is unique: unendurable physical pain, mingling with the knowledge that you are losing your mind. I know all about it. I've *seen* it."

Barbeaux paused, his eyes lingering on her mud-smeared form. "I understand that Agent Pendergast is your 'guardian.' What exactly does that mean?"

Silence.

"You don't speak, but your eyes give you away. I can see your hatred of me. The hatred of a woman for her lover's killer. How touching. What is the age gap—twenty, twenty-five years? Disgusting. You could be his daughter."

Constance did not drop her eyes. She continued to stare into his.

"A bold girl." Barbeaux sighed. "I need the name of the plant you seek. But I can see you will require persuading." He reached out, touched her face. She did not flinch or draw away. His hand moved down, smearing the mud on her neck, then descended to her chemise, lightly grazing her breast through the silk.

Fast as a striking snake, Constance slapped him sharply across the face.

Barbeaux stepped back, breathing hard. "Hold her."

Men on either side seized her by the arms. One had a shaved head; the other, hair to his shoulders. She did not struggle. Barbeaux took a step forward and reached out again, his hand closing over her breast. "Too bad Pendergast won't be here to see his little plaything abused. Now tell me the name of the plant." He squeezed her breast, hard.

Constance bit her lip against the pain.

"The *name* of the *plant*."

He hurt her again. She gave a short cry, checking herself immediately.

"Don't annoy us with hysterical outbursts. They won't do you any good. We've neutralized what little security there was here. We have the place to ourselves."

Now Barbeaux's hand descended farther, gathering the material of the chemise. He pulled it up. "Such a young, supple body. I can just imagine Pendergast bending it like a pretzel for his own recreation."

He let go of the chemise and stared at her a moment, appraisingly. Then he stepped back once again, nodded to Shaved Head. The man turned toward Constance, slapped her hard across the face: once, twice.

Constance endured this in silence.

"Bring the prod," Barbeaux ordered.

From a small pack slung over his shoulder, Long Hair removed a villainous-looking device about two feet long with a rubber handle, a spring-like curl of metal encircling its central shaft, and two silvery prongs protruding from the business end. A cattle prod. He waved it under her nose.

"Gag her," said Barbeaux. "You know how I can't stand screaming."

Out of the pack came a wad of cotton and some duct tape. Shaved Head gave her a sudden punch in the stomach and, when she doubled forward, jammed the cotton into her mouth, then wrapped duct tape over it, circling her head. He stepped back while Long Hair readied the prod. The other men had formed a dark, silent ring around the proceedings, watching intently.

While Shaved Head held her by both arms, Long Hair jammed the prod into her stomach. He hesitated a moment, smiling crookedly, and then pressed the button, activating the electric current. Constance jerked in agony, all her muscles constricting, while Shaved Head pinned her in place with his hands. A muffled sound of anguish rushed from her nose, defeating all her efforts to remain silent.

Long Hair pulled the prod away.

"Again," said Barbeaux. "When she's ready to talk, she'll let us know."

Constance tried to straighten herself up. Long Hair waved the prod around teasingly, getting ready for another jolt. Suddenly he darted forward, jabbing it between her breasts and pulling the trigger again. She writhed, driven almost mad by the pain, but this time made no sound. Long Hair withdrew the prod again.

Constance struggled to straighten up again.

"This filly needs breaking hard," said Barbeaux.

"Maybe," said Shaved Head, "she needs stimulation in a more sensitive area."

Barbeaux nodded, reached out, and lifted her chemise. Smiling, Long Hair closed in with the cattle prod.

Just then a shot rang out. At the same moment, the top of Long Hair's head came off in a single piece, spinning, hair flying, blood and brain matter rising in a cloud of pink and gray.

The men reacted instantly, throwing themselves to the ground, Shaved Head yanking Constance to the ground with him. But even as the men took cover, two more shots rang out in close succession. One man doubled up, grabbing his belly with a roar, while another already on the ground was struck in the back. He jerked, letting out a scream of agony.

Constance tried to twist out from under Shaved Head's grip, but her muscles were still convulsing from the electric shocks and he held her fast. She saw that Barbeaux was the only other one to remain standing—he had coolly stepped behind the cover of a massive tree trunk.

"Single shooter," said Barbeaux. "Upper level. Flanking maneuver, both sides." He signaled to three men, who immediately jumped up and disappeared, leaving her with Barbeaux, Shaved Head, a third man, and the three bodies crumpled and bleeding out within the orchids. She heard several more shots and looked up. Plucking a radio from his waistband, Barbeaux issued more orders, apparently to men in place outside the greenhouse. As she listened to the fugue of voices over the radio, Constance estimated Barbeaux must have close to ten men still in place in and around the Aquatic House. She watched him with narrowed eyes. What was happening? Had Lieutenant D'Agosta somehow deduced her location and arrived with the NYPD?

Shaved Head pushed her back down. "Don't fucking move," he said.

From his position behind the tree, Barbeaux continued to issue a calm stream of commands into his radio. For a while, all was silent. And then another series of shots rang out, deeper within the complex of greenhouses, followed by the sound of falling glass. There was excited chatter over Barbeaux's radio.

Constance lay pinned in the muck, gradually recovering her breath. Barbeaux had mentioned a single shooter. But if that shooter was D'Agosta, he would have brought backup. Whatever it meant, Pendergast might not be lost, after all . . .

Another burst of chatter over the radio, and then Barbeaux turned to Shaved Head. "Get her on her feet. You can remove the gag now—they've got the shooter. It's Pendergast."

69

Margo came to the door of the first storage room, jammed her passkey into the lock with a prayer. It turned. She gasped, yanked the door open, rushed in, and slammed it behind her. As she did so Slade crashed into it, forcing it open a crack, but she braced herself and pushed back with all her might. He slammed into it again and she pushed back.

This was not going to last long. She would lose this contest. And he might just shoot through the door.

He slammed into the door again just as she yanked it open, causing him to sprawl onto the floor at her feet. She gave him a hard kick to the side of the head, then sprinted into the darkness of the storage room. Over her shoulders, she could hear him gasp in pain. She had lost her headlamp and he still had his flashlight. Its beam flashed past her as she skidded around one corner of the endless rows of shelves, sprinted first down one aisle, then another. She noted in passing that the shelves were covered with large glass jars, each one holding a glistening, staring, mucilaginous globe as large as a bowling ball: this was the Museum's legendary collection of cetacean eyeballs.

As she ran, she reached into her bag, plucked out her phone, and examined it. As she expected: no bars. The thick walls of the Museum basement effectively blocked all cell phone reception.

She was fast and in good shape, but apparently so was Slade, and as she ran she realized she would lose this running contest, too. She had to find a way to stop him or at least slow him down. Why wasn't he firing his gun? Perhaps he couldn't risk the noise it would make. Slade was obviously a careful man—and one never knew who might be wandering around the basement, even late at night.

Passing a bank of lights at the end of an aisle, Margo snapped them all on—it might make her visible, but if he wasn't using his gun it would also neutralize his advantage with the flashlight. As the fluorescents popped on, she immediately turned and ran in the opposite direction down the next aisle. She could hear Slade, running up the aisle adjacent to hers. She had a sudden idea: pausing before the shelf and thrusting her hands forward, she pushed a group of specimen jars out the far side of the shelf, sending them crashing to the floor just in front of him. But even as she continued running, she could hear him skipping and hopping over the huge, soft, rolling eyeballs. It had only slowed him down a little. Maybe she could push over the entire shelf onto him—but no, the shelves were too massive and bolted to the floor.

There were several doorways leading from the whale eyeball room to other storage areas, but only one of them led to the back exit from Building Six. He was gaining, and she wasn't any closer to that exit. And at this time of night, that exit might well be locked from the inside. As she ran along the shelves she pulled more jars off, letting them crash to the floor. Could she light the ethyl alcohol on fire? But she had no lighter in her bag, and even if she did the entire storage room might go up, taking her with it.

Doubling back at the end of the next aisle, she yanked more jars off a shelf and they crashed to the floor behind her, the huge whale eyeballs rolling about, trailing alcohol and slime. With a curse Slade slipped on one, then grabbed the edge of a shelf to keep from falling, sending more jars crashing to the floor in the process. The fishy reek of eyeballs and alcohol filled the room. He was up again in a flash, but Margo had bought herself a few more seconds. As she reached the end of the next aisle, gasping for air, legs burning, she finally made out the door that, ultimately, led to the exit from Building Six. But he was so close, he'd reach her before she could even get her key in the lock.

Beside the door was a fire extinguisher.

Even as she heard his feet coming up behind her, she yanked the fire extinguisher from its bracket, spun around, and swung it at Slade, hitting him in the solar plexus and sending him to the floor. As he began to rise again with a grunt she pulled the pin and aimed the nozzle at him, spraying the foam into his face at point-blank range. He blindly tried to fend off the spray, futilely grabbing for the extinguisher.

"Bitch!" he screamed as he tried to get up, clawing the foam away as Margo kept blasting the white stream into his face. "I'll kill you for this!" He lunged, slipped, and fell flat again. She saw her opening and hit him over the head with the extinguisher.

With a groan he fell silent: unconscious, half-buried in foam, eyes rolling in his head.

She paused, thinking furiously. Another powerful blow to the head, now that he was immobile, would crush his skull. She raised the extinguisher...only to find herself unable to do it. She tossed it away. She still had her bag—thank God. She should just get the hell out. But which way? If she continued on toward the rear exit, she would have to traverse several more rooms, probably locked, any one of which her passkey might not work on. It would be far faster to retrace her steps, back past the botanical collections to the elevator. What Slade had said about jamming the lock was probably bullshit—how would he get out, then?

She started running back in the direction of the Herbarium Vault. God, she hoped she could get out that way. Otherwise she'd have to return, pass Slade again. Maybe he was already dead.

Moving as quickly as she could in the dim emergency light, she passed the entrance to the botanical collections and made her way down the corridor to the exit from Building Six. If she could get up the elevator, she could head for the security entrance, staffed by armed guards. There she'd be safe. She could tell them about Frisby, dead, the killer cop unconscious in the basement...

She reached the exit door, tried the crash bar. Locked. The door handle didn't yield, either. She tried to fit her key into the lock but saw that, true to his word, Slade had jammed the blade of a penknife into it. She swore aloud. She would have to try the back exit, after all—past him. Now she wished she had bashed his brains out. If only she'd had the presence of mind to take away his gun. She wouldn't make that mistake on her return pass—that is, if he was still unconscious.

Moving fast and silently, Margo retraced her steps. What if he had come to and was awake? She'd better get her hands on a weapon. She cast about. She was now by the entrance to the botanical collections again. She thought for a moment. What kind of plant would be of any use against a gun? None, of course.

Then she remembered something.

Darting into the collections, she ran past the cabinets and shelving—pausing just long enough to retrieve her headlamp—until she reached the Herbarium Vault, the tiny red light on its front panel like a guiding beam. Gasping for breath, she punched in the code, then opened the heavy door.

There they were: in the gleam of her headlamp, she could make out in the far corner the blowpipes—long hollow tubes—and the quiver of little bone darts, each about two inches long, with a tuft of feathers at one end. The tips of the darts were smeared with a sticky black substance.

She grabbed one of the blowpipes, slung the quiver around her free shoulder, and loaded it with a dart, pushing it into the hollow tube, feather tuft rearward. Now, exiting the vault and moving through the collections, she advanced as quickly as possible, snapping off the headlamp and relying on the emergency lighting, through the storage room door and back into the whale eyeball collection. As she entered, the stench hit her with an almost physical blow.

Her heart nearly stopped: there, in the aisle where she had left the cop, was a puddle of foam, but no body. Wet footprints led away.

She froze in terror. He was conscious, on his feet—perhaps lying in wait for her. She cast about but could see nothing. Trying to control her hammering heart, she listened intently. Were those stealthy foot-falls, echoing from some indeterminate direction?

Panic took over and she ran toward the rear exit, only to round a shelf and slam directly into Slade, weapon drawn. He grabbed her, put her in a hammerlock, and threw her to the ground. He stepped over her, gun in hand.

"I've had enough," he said in a low voice. "Give me the fucking bag or I'll put a .45 round in your head."

"Go ahead. The noise will bring security at a run."

He said nothing, and she could see she had guessed right. But then a small smile appeared on his face. "It appears I need a weapons upgrade. Something *silent*." He bent down and picked up the blowgun tube and its quiver of darts, which she had dropped in the collision. He pulled one dart from the quiver, looked at it. "Poisoned. Nice." He examined the tube. "And you conveniently loaded it for me."

He raised it awkwardly, placed it to his lips. Margo threw herself sideways just as he puffed, the dart flashing out and missing her by inches, clattering off a shelf. She scrambled sideways in a crab-like motion, then lunged to her feet as he pulled out another dart and poked it into the tube. She ran desperately as a second dart flashed past her. She heard him coming after her yet again.

Her only chance now was to lose him somewhere in the Museum's endless storage rooms.

She ran around one corner, then another, shelving flashing past. Reaching a door in the nearest wall, she flung it open, passed through another storage room, turned a corner at the rear, and raced for a door at the end of a cul-de-sac. Locked—and this time, her key didn't work. She turned to backtrack, but heard Slade sneer from just around the corner.

"I do believe you're trapped."

She cast about, but there was no way to go. He was right: she really was trapped.

Gasping, heart hammering, Margo saw Slade's shadow against the far wall of the cul-de-sac—black against red in the emergency lighting—creep forward as he approached the corner. And then she saw the blowpipe appear, bobbing slightly, inching forward. Next, Slade's head and hands came into view. He was moving cautiously, blowpipe to his lips, taking his time, aiming carefully, preparing to fire another dart.

He wasn't going to chance missing her again.

Barbeaux led the way, Shaved Head pushing Constance along before him. They passed through the Bonsai Museum and into the far wing of the Palm House, still decorated for a wedding but now looking a little the worse for wear. Four men stood around a figure seated at the table reserved for the bride and groom. A single candle had been placed on it, casting a dim illumination that barely penetrated the murk.

Constance faltered when she saw Pendergast slumped in the chair, handcuffed, his face smeared with dirt, his suit awry. Even his eyes had lost their luster. For an instant, those slitted, leaden eyes flickered toward her, and Constance was horrified by their look of hopelessness.

"Well, what a surprise," said Barbeaux. "Unexpected, but not unwelcome. In fact, I couldn't have planned it better myself. Not only have you delivered into my hands your pretty little ward—but also your own very ill person."

He contemplated Pendergast for a moment with a cold smile, and then turned to two of the men. "Stand him up. I want him attentive."

They pulled Pendergast to his feet. He was so weak he could barely stand; they had to support him, his knees buckling. Constance could hardly bear to look at him. It was she who had drawn him here after her.

"I was planning to pay you a visit at the end," Barbeaux said, "so you'd know who did this to you, and why. And..." Barbeaux smiled again, "especially how the idea for this little scheme originated."

Pendergast's head lolled to one side, and Barbeaux turned to his men. "Wake him up."

One of the men, with a neck so covered in tattoos it was almost completely blue, stepped forward and delivered a stunning, open-handed blow to the side of Pendergast's head.

Constance stared at Tattoo. "You will be the first to die," she said quietly.

The man looked over at her, his lip curling in derision, his eyes wandering lasciviously over her body. He issued a short laugh, then reached out and grasped her hair, pulling her toward him. "What, you gonna take me out with that M16 hidden under your teddy?"

"That's enough," said Barbeaux sharply.

Tattoo backed off with a smirk.

Barbeaux returned his attention to Pendergast. "I suspect you already know the broad outlines of why I poisoned you. And you surely appreciate its poetic justice. Our families were neighbors in New Orleans. My great-grandfather went shooting with *your* great-great-grandfather, Hezekiah, up at his plantation, while he had Hezekiah and his wife to dinner several times. In return, Hezekiah poisoned my great-grandparents with his so-called elixir. They died hellish deaths. But it didn't end there. My great-grandmother took the elixir while pregnant and gave birth before she succumbed to the effects. But as a result, the elixir caused epigenetic changes to her bloodline, to *our family DNA*, casting a blight across the generations. Of course, nobody knew it at the time. But now and again, another family member would die. The doctors were stumped. My ancestors whisperingly called it the 'Family Affliction.' But then it spared my father's generation. And mine. I believed the Family Affliction had burned itself out."

He paused. "How wrong I was. My son was the next victim. He died—slowly and horribly. Again, the doctors were baffled. Again, they said it was some inherited flaw in our genes."

Barbeaux paused, staring calculatingly at Pendergast.

"He was my only son. My wife was already gone. I was left alone in my grief."

A deep breath. "And then I received a visit. From *your* son. Alban."

At this, Barbeaux turned and began pacing, slowly at first, his voice low and tremulous.

"Alban found me. He opened my eyes to the evil your family had perpetrated on mine. He pointed out that the Pendergast family fortune was largely founded on the blood money from Hezekiah's elixir. Your lavish lifestyle—the apartment in the Dakota, a mansion on Riverside Drive, your chauffeured Rolls-Royce, your servants—is based on the suffering of others. He was sickened by your hypocrisy: pretending to bring justice to the world, while all the time being the very image of injustice."

During this speech, Barbeaux's voice had grown louder, and now he halted, face flushed, the blood pulsing visibly in his thick neck. "Your son told me how much he hated you. My God, what a splendid hatred that was! He came to me with a plan of justice. What were his words for it? *Delectably appropriate.*"

He resumed pacing, faster this time.

"I don't need to tell you how much time and money it took to put my plan into action. The greatest challenge was piecing together the original formula of the elixir. Conveniently, there was a skeleton of a woman murdered by the elixir in the New York Museum's collection, and I obtained a bone from it, which provided my scientists with the final chemical formulae. But you know all about that, of course.

"And then there came the challenge of devising and setting the trap out at the Salton Sea—a location Alban had discovered on his own. It was important to me that you suffered the same fate as my son and the others in my family. Alban had anticipated that. And I would never have succeeded had not Alban—before he left me that special evening—warned me in the strongest terms not to underestimate you. Wise counsel indeed. Of course, at the time he warned me against something else, as well: not to send my men after him. Then he left."

Barbeaux halted and leaned toward Pendergast. The agent returned the look, his eyes like glassy slits in his pale face. Blood trickled from his nose, almost purple against the alabaster skin.

"And then, something remarkable happened. Almost a year later, just as my plan was reaching maturity, Alban returned. It seems he'd had a change of heart. In any case, he tried at length to talk me out of my vengeance, and, when I refused, he left in anger."

He took a deep, shuddering breath. "I knew he wouldn't leave it there. I *knew* he would try to kill me. He might have succeeded, too...if I hadn't had those security tapes recording his initial visit. Despite Alban's warning, you see, I'd had my men try to stop him from leaving. But he'd bested them most effectively—and most violently. I watched those fascinating tapes of him in action, over and over again...and in time I figured out the only possible way he'd been able to do the seemingly impossible. He had a kind of sixth sense, didn't he? An ability to envision what was about to happen." Barbeaux looked at Pendergast to gauge the effect his words were having. "Isn't that right? I suppose we all have it to some degree: a primitive, intuitive sense of what's just about to happen. Only in Alban, this sense was more refined. He'd told me, arrogantly, of his 'remarkable powers.' By examining the security tapes frame by frame, I determined your son had the uncanny ability to *anticipate* events; to, in a sense, almost see a few seconds into the future. Not in an absolute way, you understand, but to see the *possibilities*. Again, no doubt you know all this."

Barbeaux's pacing quickened further. He was like a man possessed. "I won't go into all the sordid details of how I bested him. Suffice to say, I turned his own power against him. He was cocky. He had no sense of his vulnerability. And I think he'd grown a little soft between our first meeting and our second. I set up the most elaborate and meticulous plan of attack, briefed my men on it. All was in place. We lured Alban in with the promise of another meeting—one of reconciliation this time. He arrived, knowing all, feeling invincible, certain the meeting was a sham—and I spontaneously strangled him with a shoelace, on the spot. It was a sudden improvisation, with no malice aforethought. I had deliberately avoided thinking about when and how I would *actually* kill him. As such, it short-circuited his extraordinary ability to anticipate. By the way, the look of astonishment on his face was priceless."

He rumbled a laugh, turned.

"And that was the greatest irony of all. I'd been racking my brains about how to lure you—the most suspicious and circumspect of people—into my trap. In the end, it was Alban himself who provided the bait. I put his own corpse into my service. I was out there, by the way, at the Salton Fontainebleau. If you only knew how much time, money, and effort it cost to stage that—right down to the cobwebs, the untouched dust, the rust on the doors. But it was worth it—because that was the cost of fooling you, luring you in. Watching you sneak in like that, thinking you'd gotten the upper hand—I'd have paid ten times as much to witness that! You see, it was I who pressed the button, released the elixir, poisoned you. And now, here we are."

His face broke into another smile as he swung around again. "One other thing. It seems you have another son at school in Switzerland. Tristram, I believe. After you're gone, I'll pay him a little visit. I'm going to scrub the world clean of the Pendergast stain."

Now Barbeaux halted, planting himself in front of Pendergast, massive jaw thrust forward. "Have you anything to say?"

For a moment, Pendergast was silent. Then he said something in a low, indistinct voice.

"What's that?"

"I'm…" Pendergast halted, unable to muster the breath to continue. Barbeaux gave Pendergast a short, brutal slap. "You're what? *Say* it!"

"…Sorry."

Barbeaux stepped back, surprised.

"I'm sorry for what happened to your son…for your loss."

"Sorry?" Barbeaux managed to say. "You're *sorry*? That doesn't begin to cut it."

"I…accept the death that is coming."

Hearing this, Constance froze. An electric silence descended among the group. Barbeaux, clearly astonished, seemed to struggle to recover the momentum of his anger. And in the temporary silence, Pendergast's silvery eye flickered toward Constance—for no more than an instant—and in that momentary look she sensed a message was being sent. But what?

"Sorry..."

Constance could feel, ever so slightly, the slackening of Shaved Head's grip on her arms. He, like everyone else, had been intent on the drama unfolding between Barbeaux and Pendergast.

Suddenly Pendergast collapsed, going limp and dropping like a bag of cement toward the floor. The two men on either side jumped to catch his arms, but they were taken by surprise and thrown off balance as they tried to pull him back to his feet.

And in that instant, Constance knew her moment had come. With sudden violence she twisted free of Shaved Head and leapt into the darkness.

71

Slade held the blowpipe steady. His eyes narrowed slightly as he aimed.

In a sudden moment of desperation, Margo lunged forward, grabbed the end of the blowpipe, and gave a mighty puff of air into it. With a strangled cry Slade dropped the weapon and staggered back, hands at his throat, coughing and choking. As he spat out the two-inch dart, Margo ran past him, out of the cul-de-sac and into the maze of shelving in the storage room.

"Fucking *hell*!" He ran after her, voice strangled. A moment later she heard gunshots ring out, the rounds ricocheting off the concrete walls in front of her with jets of pulverized dust. The gun was incredibly loud in the enclosed space. He had abandoned all caution.

She sprinted back into the room full of whale eyeballs and paused for a second. Slade had cut off the main route out of the basement. The back exit was past a warren of rooms, many of them probably locked. On impulse, she veered off, chose one of the room's other exits, and pulled its door open. As she did so, Slade came into view, swaying slightly in the faint light, then dropping awkwardly into firing position. Had the business end of the dart poisoned him? He looked stricken.

She flung herself sideways as a fusillade of bullets riddled the door. Running through the doorway and down the corridor beyond, she glanced into the offices and storage rooms passing to her left and right, hoping to discover some way to shake him—but the effort was useless as all the rooms were dead ends. Her only hope now was that security had heard the gunshots and would come to investigate, find the jammed door, and break it down.

But even that would take time. She wasn't going to escape the basement. She had to defeat him somehow—or at least keep him at bay long enough for help to arrive.

The corridor ended in a T-intersection and she turned left, Slade's feet pounding loudly behind her. As she made the turn, she glimpsed back and saw him halt, fumbling more rounds into the magazine of his gun.

The main dinosaur lab, she knew, lay just ahead: it was large, with many possible places to hide. And it would have an inter-Museum phone that would allow her to call for help.

She reached the lab door—closed—jammed her key into the lock, and turned it, mumbling a prayer. It opened. She darted in, then slammed and locked the door behind her.

She palmed on the lights to orient herself. At least a dozen worktables were arrayed around the huge room, containing fossils in various stages of restoration or curation. In the center of the room, two huge dinosaur skeletons in the midst of assembly reared up: a famous "dueling dinosaurs" fossil set that, in a highly publicized coup, the Museum had recently acquired—a triceratops and a *T. rex*, locked in a death embrace.

She heard pounding on the door, shouting, and then shots being fired through the lock. She cast about but could see no phone. There had to be one somewhere. Or another exit, at least.

But she could see nothing. There was no phone, no other exit. And the multitude of hiding places she'd hoped for were not to be found.

So much for her plan.

A fusillade of shots punched the lock partway through the door. Slade was going to be inside the lab at any moment. And as soon as he was through, she'd be dead.

She heard him scream in rage...or was it pain? Was the poison working?

The two huge skeletons loomed above her like a grotesque jungle gym. Instinctually, she rushed up to the triceratops, grasped a rib, and began clambering, climbing hand over hand. The mount was far from complete, and the entire setup shivered and shook as she climbed. Her scramble dislodged smaller bones, which fell crashing to the floor. This was crazy; she'd be trapped up there, a sitting duck. But some instinct told her to keep climbing.

Gripping a spinal process, she pulled herself onto the backbone of the triceratops. Another series of shots punched the lock cylinder out entirely, sending it skidding across the floor. She could hear Slade heaving himself against the door, the metal plate that held the lock rattling, its bolts springing out. Another heave against the door and the plate sprang off.

Scrambling in desperation, Margo vaulted from one dinosaur skeleton to the other, climbing onto the higher, steeper backbone of the *T. rex*. Its massive head, the size of a small vehicle and studded with huge teeth, was not yet fully braced and welded into place with iron, and it shook and wobbled terrifyingly.

As she reached it, she saw that it was actually cradled in a metal understructure. Most of the bolt holes that had been drilled into the frame were still empty—no wonder it was shaking so precariously.

She swung her body around and, with her back to a metal girder, braced her feet against the side of the skull. There was always the possibility he might not see her up here.

A final heave on the door and it sprang open with a thud. Slade staggered in. He waved the gun about wildly, his steps uneven, drunken. He swiveled this way and that, and then looked up.

"There you are! Treed like a cat!" He took a few shaky steps and positioned himself underneath her, raising the gun with both hands, taking careful aim.

He looked like he had been poisoned—but not poisoned enough.

She gave a great heave with both feet, rocking the skull out of its cradle. It swayed up and paused at the edge for a moment, then toppled over and came down, crashing through the rib cage of the triceratops. She had a momentary glimpse of Slade, frozen like a deer in a car's headlights, before the huge mass of petrified bones came down on him, knocking him to the ground. A second later the top part of the tyrannosaur skull landed on him, teeth first, with a sickening wet thud.

Margo clung precariously to the shuddering metal frame as more bones unraveled from the mount and fell clattering and tinkling to the floor. She waited, gasping for breath, until the violent rocking of the mount had settled. With infinite care, muscles trembling, she climbed down.

Slade was on the floor, arms flung wide, his eyes bugged open. The upper part of the *T. rex* skull had impaled him with its teeth. It was a horrifying sight. She stumbled backward, away from the carnage. As she did so, she remembered her bag. It had been instinctively clenched tight to her body throughout the ordeal. Now she unzipped it and looked inside. The glass plates holding the plant specimens were shattered.

She stared at the various dried plant remains, mingled with broken glass at the bottom of the bag. *Oh Jesus. Will this suffice?*

She heard a sharp voice and turned. Lieutenant D'Agosta stood in the doorway, two guards behind him, staring at the scene of carnage. "Margo?" he said. "What the hell?"

"Thank God you're here," she choked out.

He continued to stare, his eyes moving from her to the body on the floor. "Slade," he said. It wasn't phrased as a question.

"Yes. He was trying to kill me."

"The son of a bitch."

"He said something about getting a better offer. What the hell was going on?"

D'Agosta nodded grimly. "Working for Barbeaux. Slade listened in on our conversation in my office this afternoon." He looked around. "Where's Constance?"

Margo stared at him. "Not here." She hesitated. "She went to the Brooklyn Botanic Garden."

"What? I thought she was with you!"

"No, no. She went to get a rare plant from there—" She stopped as D'Agosta was already on his police radio, calling in a massive police response and paramedics to the botanic garden.

He turned back to her. "Come on—we've got to hurry. Bring your bag. I hope to hell we're not already too late."

72

Constance sprinted toward the far wall of the Palm House, two men in pursuit. Behind, she could hear Barbeaux shouting orders. It seemed he was sending other men out to encircle her and ensure she didn't escape into the streets of Brooklyn.

But Constance had no intention of escaping.

She raced for the initial hole she had cut in the glass at the end of the hall and launched herself through it, the shrubbery outside checking her headlong fall. She rolled once and was immediately up and running. Behind her, she heard the slamming of a crash bar and glanced back to see two dark figures hurtle out the side entrance to the Palm House and split up, trying to outflank her, while a third figure struggled through the hole she had just come through.

Ahead of her lay the Lily Pool, shimmering peacefully in the moonlight. She took a hard left just before the pool and ran alongside it, heading away from the garden exit—the direction opposite what her pursuers would anticipate. That caused them to pause, reconnoiter, and then veer back toward her—a gain of precious seconds.

Circling around the domes of the Steinhardt Conservatory, Constance headed back toward the Aquatic House. She was making no attempt to hide her movements, speed being of the essence, and the three men could see her and were now swiftly closing in, trapping her against the Aquatic House.

She ran alongside the wall of glass, then slipped back through the second hole she had made, emerging into the flower-choked orchid garden. She ran through the foliage, stepped over the three dead bodies, circled the main pool, and exited the double glass doors and into the lobby. There she paused just long enough to scoop up the duffel she had hidden under a bench before darting into the Tropical Pavilion. This was the largest greenhouse in the garden: a vast space with a soaring, six-story glass dome enclosing a dense, humid jungle.

Slinging the bag over her shoulder, she ran to one of the giant tropical trees in the center of the pavilion, grasped at its lower branches, and then began to climb upward, limb over limb. Even as she climbed, she heard her pursuers enter.

She flattened herself on an upper limb, pulled open the duffel, and removed a small chemical case that lay within. Silently, she unlatched it. Inside were four little flasks of triflic acid—acid she had appropriated earlier that evening from Enoch Leng's cache in the sub-basement of the Riverside Drive mansion. Each flask was nestled within foam rubber protective packing that she had fashioned to size. Now she took out one flask and carefully removed its glass stopper. She was careful to hold the flask away from her—even the fumes were deadly.

She could hear the men spreading out across the pavilion, their flashlight beams playing about, voices murmuring, radios crackling. The beams began to move into the trees. A voice called out: "We know you're in here. Come out now."

Silence.

"We'll kill your pal Pendergast if you don't show yourself."

Cautiously, Constance peered over the edge of the heavy limb she was on. It was perhaps thirty feet from the ground, and the tree rose at least another thirty feet above her.

"If you don't come out," came the voice, "we're going to start shooting."

"You know Barbeaux wants me alive," she said.

Locating her from her voice, the beams immediately flashed up into her tree, probing this way and that. The three men moved through the thick understory until they were under the tree, encircling it.

Time to show her face. She stuck her head out and looked down at them, face expressionless.

"There she is!"

She ducked back.

"Come down now!"

Constance did not reply.

"If we've got to come up and get you, that'll piss us off. You really don't want to piss us off."

"Go to hell," she said.

The men conferred in low, murmuring tones.

"Okay, Goldilocks, here we come."

One grasped the lower branch and hoisted himself up, while another held a flashlight beam to illuminate the climb.

Constance peered over the swell of the branch. The man was climbing quickly, his face upturned, scowling and angry. It was Tattoo.

Good.

She waited until he was less than ten feet below her. Positioning the flask above the climbing man, she tipped it briefly, pouring out a precise stream of triflic acid. The stream struck Tattoo directly in the left eye. She saw, with interest, that the superacid cut into him like boiling water poured onto dry ice, issuing a great hissing cloud of vapor in the process. The man let out a single, gasping cough and then simply vanished from sight in the widening cloud. A moment later she heard his body crash through the branches and hit the ground, followed by the surprised expostulations of his compadres.

Still peering over the edge, she saw him lying on his back in a thicket of crushed vegetation, his body going into a crazy horizontal dance, writhing and convulsing, jittery hands clutching and tearing at random leaves and flowers, until suddenly his entire frame tensed, arching upward like a drawn bow until only the back of his head and his heels were on the ground. He jittered for a moment in that frozen position. Constance fancied she even heard vertebrae snapping before the body collapsed into the bed of disordered vegetation, and his brains slid out of a steaming hole in the back of his head to settle in a greasy gray puddle.

The effect on the two others was gratifying. These were men, Constance surmised, who had fought in war and seen much killing and death. They were, of course, stupid—like many men—but were nonetheless highly trained, dangerous, and good at their job. But they had never seen anything like this. This was not guerrilla warfare; this was not a special op; this was not "shock and awe"—this was something completely outside their training. They stood like statues, flashlights fixed on their dead companion, stunned into paralysis, uncomprehending and therefore unable to react.

With great rapidity, Constance moved out on the limb until she was positioned above one of the two—Shaved Head—and this time she poured out the rest of the bottle's contents, then let it fall, taking care that not a single drop of the acid touched her own skin.

Again, the results were most satisfactory. This dousing was not as precisely aimed as the first, and the acid splattered in a swath across the man's head and one shoulder, as well as the surrounding vegetation. Nevertheless, the consequences were instantaneous. It appeared as if his head melted in on itself, expelling a rush of cloudy, greasy gas. With a shriek of animal horror, Shaved Head sank to his knees, his hands clutching his skull even as it was dissolving, panicked fingers pushing through liquefying bone and brain matter before he keeled over, going into the same peculiar convulsions as Tattoo. As he did so, the vegetation that had been splashed with the acid began to smoke and curl up, bits of it flashing into fire, then quickly flaring out—no fire could sustain itself long in the damp vegetation.

Like all superacids, Constance knew, triflic acid generated a strong exothermic reaction when encountering organic compounds.

The third man was now collecting his wits. He backed away from his convulsing comrade, and then looked up, firing his weapon in a panic. But Constance was already hidden behind a limb and the man was shooting randomly. She used the opportunity to climb higher into the tree's upper limbs. Here the branches knitted together with the surrounding trees, forming a dense canopy. Slowly and deliberately, keeping the duffel close, she moved from one limb to another, while the frantic man below fired ineffectually at the sounds of her movement. Managing to climb onto an adjacent tree, she descended a few feet and concealed herself in the crook of a thick limb covered in leaves.

There was the crackle of a radio. Now the shots stopped and the flashlight beam played about, searching this way and that. In that moment, two more men burst into the Tropical Pavilion.

"What's going on?" one of them cried, pointing to the smoking bodies. "What the hell happened?"

"The crazy bitch poured something on them—acid, maybe. She's up in the trees."

More flashlight beams joined in roaming about among the canopy.

"Who the fuck was firing? The boss says don't kill her."

As she listened to this exchange, Constance took stock of the small chemical case. Three more flasks remained within it, full and carefully stoppered. Then, of course, there were the other contents of her bag to consider. She mentally reviewed the situation. There were, as best she could guess, six or seven men remaining, including Barbeaux.

Barbeaux. She was reminded of Diogenes Pendergast. Brilliant. Formidable. With the kind of sadistic streak reserved only for psychopaths. But Barbeaux was cruder, militaristic, less refined. Her hatred for Barbeaux was now so incandescent she could feel the heat of it warming her vitals.

73

John Barbeaux waited in the darkened space of the Palm House. The two men who stayed with him had stretched Pendergast out on the floor. The handcuffed agent remained unconscious despite being slapped and even shocked with the cattle prod. Barbeaux leaned over and placed two fingers on Pendergast's neck, searching for the carotid pulse. Nothing. He pressed a little harder. There it was: very weak.

He was at death's door.

At this, Barbeaux felt a vague disquiet. The moment of his triumph had come; the moment he had been thinking about for so long, fantasizing over, savoring—the moment when Pendergast would be confronted with the truth. The moment Alban Pendergast had promised. But it hadn't quite played out as he'd imagined. Pendergast had been too weak to appreciate the full flavor of his defeat. And then—to Barbeaux's vast surprise—the man had apologized. He had, essentially, taken responsibility for the sins of the fathers. That shock had taken much of the enjoyment out of his achievement; deprived him of the chance to gloat. At least, he felt fairly certain this was what lay at the heart of his disquietude.

And then, there was the girl...

It was taking his men far longer to retrieve her than he'd anticipated, and he began pacing once again. His movements caused the lone candle on the table to flicker and gutter. He blew it out, leaving the Palm House to the light of the moon.

He heard another fusillade of shots. This time, he pulled out his radio. "Steiner. Report."

"Sir," came the voice of his Ops Crew leader.

"Steiner, what's going on?"

"That bitch took out two of our men. Poured acid on them, or something."

"Stop shooting at her," said Barbeaux. *I want her alive.*

"Yes, sir. But—"

"Where is she now?"

"Up in the treetops of the Tropical Pavilion. She's got a bottle of acid, and she's freaking crazy—"

"Three of you with automatic weapons, against one woman, treed, dressed only in a slip, armed with, what, a bottle of acid? Do I have that right?"

A hesitation. "Yes."

"I'm sorry—what the *fuck* is the problem, exactly?"

Another hesitation. "There is no problem, sir."

"Good. There will be if she's killed. Whoever kills her, dies."

"Sir . . . forgive me, sir, but the target—well, he's either dead or dying. Right?"

"Your point being?"

"So what do we need the girl for? Her retrieval of that plant—it doesn't matter now. It would be much easier to just throw up a screen of bullets, drop her with—"

"Aren't you hearing a word I've said? Steiner, *I want her alive.*"

A pause. "What . . . do we do?"

And this from a professional. Barbeaux couldn't believe what he was hearing. He took a deep breath. "Bring your squad into position. Approach diagonally. Liquid falls vertically."

A silence. "Yes, sir."

He replaced the radio. A lone girl, up against professional mercenaries, some of them ex-special-forces. And yet she had them spooked.

Unbelievable. Only now were his men's limitations becoming obvious. Crazy? Yeah—crazy like a fox. He had underestimated her. That would not happen again.

He leaned down and touched Pendergast's neck. Now he could feel no pulse at all, no matter how he probed or pressed. "God*damn* it," he muttered through clenched teeth. He felt cheated, betrayed, robbed of the victory he had worked so long and hard to achieve. He gave the body a savage kick.

He turned toward the two men who had taken up positions on either side of Pendergast. There was no longer any need to keep vigil over the body; there was something more important to accomplish.

Barbeaux looked at them in turn, then jerked a thumb over his shoulder. "Join the others," he snapped. "Get the girl."

74

The lone survivor of her first attack had been joined by two others. Based on the radio chatter, Constance knew that at least two more were on their way. The men below were rallying, developing a plan. She watched as the three began spreading out in the foliage below. Then they began to climb the trees surrounding her own. Their intention was to come at her from three sides.

She jammed the small chemical case back into the duffel, slung the duffel around her neck to free up both hands, and climbed higher. As she did, the trunk grew thinner and began to sway, the branches feathering out in all directions. Higher and higher she climbed until ultimately the trunk spread out into a mass of slender branches that sagged and swayed with her movements. The glass dome was only about six feet above her head.

As she climbed upward, trying to reach the glass of the ceiling, the entire treetop began swaying. The men had now reached the canopy as well, and were creeping out on lateral branches, boxing her in.

A branch she was grasping broke with a crack and she slipped, stopping her fall only by wrapping her arms around an adjoining group of small branches, leaving her swaying and dangling in space.

"There she is!"

The flashlight beams shone on her as she pulled herself up the slender branches until she found another purchase for her feet.

Every move sent the branches into a fresh paroxysm of swaying and cracking.

Trying not to agitate the canopy, she maneuvered with care, working her way still higher. The tiniest twigs and branches came within a foot or two of the glass ceiling, but they were too slender to support any weight. She was now triangulated in the flashlight beams.

A low laugh. "Hey, little girl. You're surrounded. Climb down."

If any of them came any closer, Constance knew, their combined weight on the network of branches would send them all crashing to the ground. They were stymied.

Through the heavy canopy of branches, she could see that two more men had entered the Tropical Pavilion. One of them removed a pistol and aimed it at her. "Start down or I'll put a bullet in you."

She ignored this, working her way higher with exquisite care and balance.

"Get your ass *down!*"

She was now just below the glass roof. The branches were shaking and swaying, her bare feet slipping. She had nothing to break the glass above her except the bag, and she didn't dare use it for fear of breaking certain of its contents. Steadying herself in the topmost branches as best she could, she removed a cloth from the bag, wrapped it around her fist, and punched out the pane of glass above her with one blow.

This caused violent agitation in the network of branches she was clinging to, and she slipped down a few feet as broken glass rained down around her.

"She's going out the top!" one of the men called.

With a desperate, reckless move she lunged upward, grasping and clawing at the metal frame above her and securing a purchase with one hand, cutting her fingers in the process. Pushing out first the small case, then the bag, she followed these onto the roof, swinging herself up and then climbing out and on top.

Placing her feet on the bronze frames that held the sections of glass in place, not treading on the glass itself, Constance knelt, opened the small chemical case, and took out a second bottle. Two of the men who'd climbed the adjoining trees were directly below her, working their way up toward the hole. The other man was descending fast, no doubt to join up with the two on the ground and prepare to intercept her outside when she climbed down to the ground.

She leaned over the hole she had made in the roof and glanced down at the closer of the two climbers. He was yelling at her and waving his gun. Taking the glass stopper from the bottle, she upended its contents onto the man, then skipped back. The gun went off, blowing out the pane next to her, and then there was a scream; a dull cloud of acrid gas blossomed in the moonlight, followed by a popping of leaves and twigs, to a constellation of flares and gouts of flame. She heard a falling body crash through branch after branch, hitting the ground with a sickening thump.

A fusillade of shots came from the other climber, bursting panes around her, but he was high in the swaying canopy and unable to aim properly. Or perhaps he was not trying to hit her, but rather trying to intimidate her. It made no difference. She plucked the third bottle from the case, skipped along the roof into a fresh position, removed its stopper, and—leaning over one of the skylights blown out by the bullets—doused the remaining climber with it. A horrible gush of steam rose up through the broken glass, gray, shot through with ropy strands of crimson, and Constance reared backward to avoid it. An ululating, throat-shredding cry tore through the broken panes, followed by the sounds of yet another body crashing downward. Taking the final small bottle from the case, she tossed it through one of the other ruined skylights. Perhaps it would act as a grenade, taking out one or more of the men down at the floor level of the pavilion. She heard an odd puffing noise, like the lighting of a gas range, and then a flare of flame shot up from far below, flickering angrily for several seconds before going out.

This was followed by an intense silence.

Abandoning the empty chemical case on the roof, Constance slung the backpack over her shoulder and began moving across the dome, to a ladder that curved down from the top.

She descended just as two men came running out of the green-house complex, followed soon after by a third. She ran into the darkness of the arboretum, its giant trees leaving the ground in almost complete darkness. Making a ninety-degree turn to the right, she headed toward the dense plantings of the Japanese Garden. At the torii gate, she ducked into deep shadow and paused to look back. Her pursuers had lost her in the darkness under the trees, and now they were fanning out in an encircling maneuver, talking to each other via radio. Nobody else had emerged from the nearby buildings.

That, Constance thought, left Barbeaux alone in the Palm House with Pendergast.

The three men spread out farther as they approached the Japanese Garden. She crept through the darkness and skirted the pond, moving along narrow graveled pathways among dense plantings of weeping cherries, willows, yews, and Japanese maples. Partway around the pond stood a rustic pavilion.

Based on the squawk of radios and the whispered murmur of voices, Constance could tell that the three had taken up triangular positions around the Japanese Garden. They would know she was surrounded; they would assume she'd gone to ground.

It was time.

In a thick, dark stand of twisted juniper, Constance knelt, letting her bag slip to the ground. She zipped it open and reached inside. Out came an old bandolier of heavy leather, studded along its length with looped ammunition pockets, which she had appropriated from Enoch Leng's military collections. She fixed it sash-style over one shoulder and belted it at her waist. Reaching into the duffel again, she removed from another ancient case five large, identical syringes and laid them in a row on the soft ground. These were old, handblown glass "balling guns"—catheter-type irrigation syringes used for administering medicine orally to horses and other large animals. These, too, were courtesy of Leng's bizarre cabinet of curiosities, in this case the collection devoted to veterinary curiosa, its contents used by him in experiments best not speculated on. All five syringes were filled with triflic acid and capable of delivering a larger, more directed payload than the flasks had been. Each was nearly a foot long, as thick around as a tube of caulk, and made of borosilicate glass with sodium metasilicate as both lubricant and sealant. These last facts were particularly important: triflic acid, she had learned, would violently attack any substance composed of carbon-hydrogen bonds.

One at a time, Constance slid the oversize syringes into the leather pockets of the bandolier. It had been manufactured to hold fifty-millimeter artillery shells, and the syringes fit well. Each had a glass stopper snugged over its tip, but nevertheless she handled them very gingerly: triflic acid was not just a powerful superacid; it was also a deadly neurotoxin. Ensuring the bandolier was firmly in place, she rose cautiously to her feet, abandoning the now-empty duffel, and glanced around.

Three men.

Leaving the stand of juniper, she moved to the pavilion itself, a wooden structure built out over the pond, with open sides and a low-slung roof of cedar shakes. Climbing onto a nearby railing, she grasped the edge of the roof, pulled herself onto it, and knelt there, peering over the edge. The men were now tightening their noose, creeping into the Japanese Garden, guns drawn. They were moving laterally, flashlight beams probing the vegetation. One of them was approaching the pavilion itself. She crouched lower as the man's light went past.

In utter silence, Constance slid one of the syringes out of the bandolier, slipped off the protective glass tip, aimed at the man as he passed just beneath—and then directed a long, smoking jet of acid over him.

Under the rain of acid, the man's clothes burst into flames and dissolved. His sharp screams were almost immediately cut off by a gargled choking. Windmilling his arms, he staggered first one way, then another—the flesh literally melting from his bones as the stream cut into him—before blindly throwing himself into the pond. As he hit the water, a cloud of vapor rose up and spread slowly over the waters as the man convulsed. Within seconds he had disappeared beneath the surface, leaving behind a surge of bubbles.

The other two men had dived into the brush. Now they knew she was on the pavilion roof.

Without giving them time to recover, Constance tossed the now-empty syringe aside and scuttled across the roofline in the direction of the pond. Keeping the bulk of the pavilion between herself and the remaining two men, she slipped carefully into the water and—keeping below the surface—swam to the far shore, where she emerged. The men fired at her from cover but, crouching in the darkness more than a hundred feet away, their bullets went wide. She crawled into a dense, expansive stand of azaleas that had been planted next to the pond, pushing deep into the shrubbery on hands and knees while additional rounds snipped away the branches over her head. The men were shooting to kill despite Barbeaux's orders. They were angry and panicked. But they were still formidable. She must be ready for what was about to happen.

In her mind, Constance visualized a lioness in the bush: a lioness swollen with hatred and savage thoughts of revenge.

Reaching the center of the azalea cluster, she crouched in the blackness. Silently, she eased another syringe of acid from the bandolier and readied it for use. She tensed, waiting, listening.

She could not see the men, but she could hear their whispered voices. They had come around the pond and seemed to be positioned at the edge of the azaleas, perhaps thirty feet away. Additional whispers betrayed the fact that they were circling around. There was the hiss of a radio; a short conversation. They were not as panicked as she had expected. They were relying on their superior firepower.

Now they picked up her track and started into the patch. The noise they made allowed Constance to better track their approach. She waited, motionless, crouched low in the densest heart of the bushes. Closer and closer they came, pushing through the azalea, moving with extreme caution. Twenty feet, ten...

The lioness would not wait. She would charge.

Constance leapt up and ran straight at them without uttering a sound. The two, taken by surprise, did not have time to react before she was upon them. At a run, turning sideways in order to avoid any backsplash, she emptied the contents of the syringe over one man—a colorless torrent of death—still running, threw aside the empty, slid out another syringe, then turned again to drench the second man. Never faltering, dropping this syringe as it, too, was spent, she burst out the far end of the azalea stand, then stopped, glancing back to examine her handiwork.

A vast swath of the azalea garden, roughly following the course she had just taken, was now aflame: entire bushes exploding like popcorn, gouts of fire flaring up, leaves disintegrating, branches bursting into red-and-orange glow. The men themselves were screaming, one wildly firing his pistol at nothing, the other whirling like a top and clutching his face. Now they sank to their knees, great gushers of gray-and-pink mist roiling violently up from their dissolving flesh. As Constance looked on, what was left of the figures sank to the ground, convulsing as the shrubbery blackened and dissolved.

She watched the ghastly tableau for just a moment longer. Then, turning away, she headed quickly across a dew-heavy lawn and onto the path leading to the Palm House, its panels of glass glittering in the moonlight.

75

I'm back," came the strangely old-fashioned voice from behind Barbeaux.

He whipped around, gazing with astonishment. The petite form of Constance Greene stood there. Somehow, she had managed to approach without making any sound.

Barbeaux gazed at her with astonishment. Her black chemise was torn, her body and face filthy, smeared with mud and bleeding from a dozen cuts. Her hair was caked with dirt, twigs, and leaves. She seemed more feral than human. And yet the voice, the eyes, were cold, unreadable. She was unarmed, empty-handed.

She swayed slightly on her feet, looked at Pendergast—lying motionless at Barbeaux's feet—then returned her gaze to him.

"He's dead," Barbeaux told her.

She did not react. If there was any normal emotion going on in this crazy woman, Barbeaux could not see it, and this unnerved him.

"I want the name of the plant," he said, leveling his gun at her.

Nothing. No recognition that he'd spoken.

"I'll kill you if you don't give it to me. I'll kill you in the most horrific way imaginable. Tell me the name of the plant."

Now she spoke. "You've begun to smell lilies, haven't you?"

She's guessed. "How—?"

"It's obvious. Why else did you want me alive? And why else

would you want the plant, now, when *he* is dead?" She gestured at Pendergast's body.

With self-discipline born of long practice, Barbeaux pulled himself together. "And my men?"

"I killed them all."

Even though, from the radio chatter, he'd surmised that things had gone very badly, Barbeaux could scarcely believe his ears. His eyes roamed over the insane creature that stood before him. "How in the world—?" he began again.

She did not answer the question. "We need to come to an arrangement. You want—*need*—the plant. And I want to collect my guardian's body for a decent burial."

Barbeaux gazed at her for a moment. The young woman waited, head slightly cocked. She swayed on her feet again. She looked like she might collapse at any minute.

"All right," he said, gesturing with the gun. "We'll go to the Aquatic House together. When I'm satisfied you've told me the truth, I'll let you go."

"Is that a promise?"

"Yes."

"I'm not sure I can make it on my own. Hold my arm, please."

"No tricks. You lead the way." He prodded her with the gun. She was smart, but not smart enough. As soon as he'd secured the plant, she would die.

She stumbled over Pendergast's body, then walked along the wing into the Bonsai Museum. There she fell to the ground and was unable to get up without Barbeaux's assistance. They entered the Aquatic House.

"Tell me the name of the plant," Barbeaux demanded.

"*Phragmipedium.* Andean Fire. The active compound is in the underwater rhizome."

"Show me."

Using the railing to support herself, Constance circled the large, central pool, stumbling.

"Hurry up."

At the far end of the main pool were a series of descending, smaller pools. A sign at one of them identified it as containing the aquatic plant called Andean Fire.

She gestured, swaying. "There."

Barbeaux peered into the dark water. "There's nothing in the pool," he said.

Constance sank to her knees. "The plant is dormant this time of year." Her voice was slow, thick. "The root's in the mud underwater."

He waved his gun. "Get up."

She tried to rise. "I can't move."

With a curse, Barbeaux pulled off his jacket, knelt at the pool, and stuck his shirtsleeved arm into the water.

"Don't forget your promise," Constance murmured.

Ignoring this, Barbeaux began rummaging around in the muck at the bottom. In a few seconds he withdrew the arm with a grunt of surprise. Something was odd. No—something was wrong. The cotton material of his shirt was starting to come apart, dissolving and running off his arm in pieces with faint palls of smoke.

The sound of police sirens, shrill and anxious, began rising in the distance.

Barbeaux rose, staggered back with a roar of fury, pulled his gun out with his left hand, raised it—but Constance Greene had disappeared into the riot of growth.

Now pain took hold, excruciating pain, rippling up his arm and into his head, and then Barbeaux felt a jolt in his brain like electricity, followed by another, even worse. He staggered back and forth, swinging his smoking arm around, seeing the skin blacken and curl away to expose the flesh beneath. He began firing the gun crazily into the jungle, his vision fogging, his lungs choking, the shocks in his head and the muscle spasms in his body coming faster and faster until a spasm knocked him to his knees and then threw him down to the ground.

"There's no point in struggling," Constance said. She had reappeared from somewhere, and—out of the corner of his eye—Barbeaux saw her pick up his gun and toss it into the bushes. "Triflic acid, which I have introduced into this secondary pool, is not only highly corrosive, but it's extremely poisonous as well. Once it eats its way through your skin, it starts to affect you systemically. A neurotoxin—you will die convulsing with pain."

She turned and darted away again.

In a paroxysm of rage, Barbeaux managed to rise and stagger in pursuit, but could only make it to the far wing of the Palm House before collapsing again. He tried to rise once more, but found he had lost all control of his muscles.

The sounds of sirens had grown much louder, and in the distance, through his fog of pain, Barbeaux could hear the sounds of shouting, running feet. Constance rushed in the direction of the commotion. Barbeaux hardly noticed. His brain was on fire, screaming even while his twitching mouth could no longer utter a word. His body began to shudder and jump, his stomach muscles clenching so hard he thought they would tear asunder, and he tried to scream but the only sound that emerged was a gasp of air.

Now there was a commotion nearby, and he made out individual words. "... Paddles!" "... Charged!" "... I've got a pulse!" "... Hang some D5W!" "... Get him to the ambulance!"

Hours, or maybe it was just moments, later a police officer and an EMS worker were leaning over him, shocked expressions on their faces. Barbeaux felt himself being lifted onto a stretcher. And then Constance Greene was among them, staring down at him. Through the fog of pain and the racking convulsions, Barbeaux tried to tell her she had lied; that she had welshed on their deal. Not even a gasp escaped his lips.

But she understood anyway. She bent forward and spoke softly, so that only he could hear. "It's true," she said. "I reneged. Just as you would have."

The workers prepared to lift the stretcher, and she spoke more quickly. "One last thing. Your fatal mistake was believing you had—and please forgive the crudeness of today's vernacular—a bigger pair of balls."

And as the unendurable pain overwhelmed him and his vision failed, Barbeaux saw Constance rise, turn, and then race away as Pendergast's stretcher headed toward the ambulance.

76

Within about five minutes, the scene at the Brooklyn Botanic Garden had gone from merely crazy to totally insane. Paramedics, cops, firemen, and EMS workers were everywhere, securing the site, yelling into radios, shouting in surprise and disgust at each fresh and horrifying discovery.

As he jogged toward the central pavilion, a bizarre figure came rushing toward D'Agosta—a woman dressed only in a torn chemise, filthy, her hair full of twig ends and bits of flowers.

"Over here!" the figure cried. With a start, D'Agosta recognized Constance Greene. Automatically, he began to remove his jacket to cover her, but she ran past him to a group of paramedics. "This way!" she cried to them, leading them off in the direction of a huge Victorian structure of metal and glass.

Margo and D'Agosta followed, through a side door and into a long hall, apparently set up for a wedding reception but looking as if it had been raided by a biker gang: tables overturned, glassware shattered, chairs knocked over. At the far end, on the parquet dance floor, lay two bodies. Constance led the paramedics to one of them. When he saw it was Pendergast, D'Agosta staggered, grabbed the back of a chair. He turned on the paramedics and screamed, "Work this one first!"

"Oh no," Margo sobbed, her hand over her mouth. "No."

The paramedics surrounded Pendergast and began a quick ABC assessment: airway, breathing, circulation.

"Paddles!" one of them barked over his shoulder. An EMS worker with defib equipment came up as Pendergast's shirt was ripped away.

"Charged!" the EMS worker cried. The paddles were applied; the body jerked; the paddles reapplied.

"Again!" ordered the paramedic.

Another jolt; another galvanic jerk.

"I've got a pulse!" the paramedic said.

Only now, as Pendergast was placed on a stretcher, did D'Agosta turn his attention to the second supine figure. The body was twitching violently, eyes staring, mouth working soundlessly. It was a man in shirtsleeves, well into middle age, with a solid build. D'Agosta recognized him from pictures on Red Mountain's website as John Barbeaux. One of his arms was blistering and smoking, with bone exposed, as if burned in a fire, the shirt eaten away almost to the shoulder. Several newly arriving paramedics bent over him and began working.

As D'Agosta watched, Constance approached the twitching form of Barbeaux, nudged one of the paramedics aside, and bent in close. He could see her lips move in some whispered message to him. Then she straightened up and turned to the paramedics. "He's all yours."

"You need an assessment, too," said another paramedic, approaching her.

"Don't touch me." She backed up and turned away, disappearing into the dark bowels of the greenhouse complex. The paramedics watched her go, then returned their attention to Barbeaux.

"What the hell happened to her?" D'Agosta asked Margo.

"I have no idea. There are . . . a lot of dead people here."

D'Agosta shook his head. It would all be sorted out later. He turned his attention to Pendergast. The paramedics were now raising his stretcher, one holding an IV bottle up, and they headed toward the ambulances. D'Agosta and Margo followed.

As they were jogging along, Constance reappeared. She had a large pink lily in her hand, dripping wet.

386 DOUGLAS PRESTON & LINCOLN CHILD

"I'll take your jacket now," she said to D'Agosta.

D'Agosta draped his jacket over her shoulders. "Are you all right?"

"No." She turned to Margo. "Did you get it?"

In response, Margo pressed the handbag slung over one shoulder.

A brace of ambulances were parked at the closest corner of visitors' parking, lightbars turning. As they hurried toward them, Constance stopped to retrieve a small satchel, hidden in some bushes. The paramedics opened the rear of the nearest ambulance and rolled in Pendergast's stretcher, climbing in after it. D'Agosta started to get in, followed by Margo and Constance.

The emergency workers looked at the two women. "I'm sorry," one began, "but you're going to have to take separate transportation—"

D'Agosta silenced the man with a flash of his badge.

With a shrug, the paramedic shut the doors; the siren started up. Constance handed Margo the satchel and the lily plant.

"What is this stuff?" one EMT said angrily. "It's not sterile. You can't bring that in here!"

"Move aside," Margo said sharply.

D'Agosta put a hand on the man's shoulder and pointed at Pendergast. "You two focus on the patient. I'll be responsible for the rest."

The EMT frowned, saying nothing.

D'Agosta watched as Margo went to work. She pulled open the ambulance storage compartment in the rear of the vehicle, slid out a shelf, opened Constance's satchel, and began pulling out various things—old bottles filled with liquid, ampoules, envelopes of powder, a jar of emolument. She laid them all out in order. To these, Margo added the lily that Constance had handed her, and then some dried plant specimens from her own handbag, picking them out from among pieces of broken glass. Next to all this she smoothed out a wrinkled piece of paper, grabbing abruptly for a handhold as the ambulance pulled out onto Washington Avenue, its siren shrieking.

"What are you doing?" D'Agosta asked.

"I'm preparing the antidote," Margo replied.

"Shouldn't you do this in a lab or something—?"

"Does it look to you like we have the time?"

"How is the patient?" Constance asked the paramedic.

The paramedic glanced at D'Agosta, then at her. "Not good. B/P low, pulse thready." He pulled open a plastic tray at one side of Pendergast's stretcher. "I'm going to start a lidocaine drip."

As the ambulance careered onto Eastern Parkway, D'Agosta watched Margo grab a bag of saline from a nearby drawer, pluck a tracheotomy scalpel from another drawer, and pull away its protective silver covering. She slashed open the saline bag, poured some into an empty plastic beaker, and dropped the leaking bag on the floor.

"Hey," said the paramedic. "What the hell are you doing—?" Again, he was silenced by a warning gesture from D'Agosta.

The ambulance shrieked its way past Prospect Park, then through Grand Army Plaza. Steadying herself against the movements of the vehicle, Margo took a small glass jar from among the contents of Constance's satchel, warmed it briefly in her hands, then removed its stopper and poured out a measure into the plastic beaker. Immediately the ambulance filled with a sweetish, chemical smell.

"What's that?" D'Agosta asked, waving away the odor.

"Chloroform." Margo re-stoppered the jar. Taking the scalpel, she chopped up the lily Constance had retrieved from the Aquatic House, mashed it, and added the pulp, along with the dried, crushed pieces of plant from her own handbag, into the liquid. She stoppered the beaker and shook it.

"What's going on?" D'Agosta asked.

"The chloroform acts as a solvent. It's used in pharmacology to extract compounds from plant material. Then I have to boil most of it off, as it's poisonous if injected."

"Just a moment," Constance said. "If you boil it, you'll make the same mistake Hezekiah did."

"No, no," Margo replied. "Chloroform boils at a far lower temperature than water—around a hundred forty degrees. It won't denature the proteins or the compounds."

"What compounds are you extracting?" D'Agosta asked.

"I have no idea."

"You don't *know*?"

Margo rounded on him. "*Nobody* knows what the active ingredients in these botanicals are. I'm winging it."

"Jesus," D'Agosta said.

The ambulance turned onto Eighth Avenue, approaching New York Methodist Hospital. As it did, Margo consulted her sheet of paper, added more liquid, broke an ampoule, mixed in two kinds of powder from their glassine envelopes.

"Lieutenant," she said over her shoulder. "When we get to the hospital, I'm going to need some things right away. Ice water. A piece of cloth for straining. A test tube. Half a dozen coffee filters. And a pocket lighter. Okay?"

"Here's the lighter," said D'Agosta, reaching into his pocket. "I'll take care of the rest."

The ambulance came to a halt before the hospital's emergency entrance, the siren cutting off. The paramedics threw open the rear doors and slid the stretcher out to the waiting ER staff. D'Agosta glanced down at Pendergast, covered in a thin blanket. The agent was pale and motionless as a corpse. Constance got out next and followed the stretcher inside, her attire and dirty appearance eliciting strange looks from the hospital staff. Next, D'Agosta hopped down and made his way quickly toward the entrance. As he did so, he looked over his shoulder. He could see Margo in the rear bay of the ambulance, brilliantly illuminated by the emergency lights, still working with single-minded purpose.

77

ICU Bay Three of the emergency room at New York Methodist Hospital resembled a scene of controlled chaos. One intern wheeled in a red crash cart, while a nurse nearby readied an ear, nose, and throat tray. Another nurse was attaching various leads to the motionless figure of Pendergast: a blood pressure cuff, EKG, pulse oximeter, fresh IV line. The paramedic workers from the ambulance had passed off their information on Pendergast's condition to the hospital staff, then left; there was nothing more they could do.

Two doctors in scrubs swept in and quickly began to examine Pendergast, speaking in low tones to the nurses and interns.

D'Agosta took a look around. Constance was seated in a far corner of the bay, her small form now dressed in a hospital gown. It had been five minutes since he'd delivered the requested materials to Margo, back in the ambulance. She was still in there, working like a demon, using his lighter to heat a liquid in the test tube, filling the air with a sweet stench.

"Vitals?" one of the doctors asked.

"BP's at sixty-five over thirty and falling," a nurse replied. "Pulse ox is seventy."

"Prep for endotracheal intubation," the doctor said.

D'Agosta watched as more equipment was wheeled into place. He felt a terrible mixture of rage, despair, and distant hope gnawing at him. Unable to keep still, he began to pace back and forth. One of the doctors, who earlier had tried to throw him and Constance out, shot him a glare, but he ignored it. What was the point of all this? This whole antidote thing seemed far-fetched, if not completely nuts. Pendergast had been dying for days—weeks—and now the final moments had come. All this fuss, this pointless bustle, just made him feel more agitated. There was nothing they could do—nothing anyone could do. Margo, for all her skill, was trying to concoct an elixir whose dosage she could only guess at—and that hadn't worked before. Besides, it was moot now; it was taking her too long. Even these doctors, with all their equipment, couldn't do jack to save Pendergast.

"Getting a lethal rhythm here," an intern said, monitoring one of the screens at the head of Pendergast's bed.

"Stop the lidocaine," the second doctor said, pushing his way between the nurses. "Get a central vein catheter ready. Two milligrams epi, stat."

D'Agosta sat down in the empty chair beside Constance.

"Vitals failing," one of the interns said. "He's coding."

"Get that epi," the doctor barked. "Stat!"

D'Agosta leapt to his feet. *No!* There had to be something he could do, there *had* to . . .

At that moment Margo Green appeared at the entrance of the ICU bay. Flinging the privacy screen wide, she stepped inside. She held a small beaker in one hand, partly full of a watery, greenish-brown liquid. The top of the beaker was covered with alternating layers of coffee filters and the cotton he'd appropriated from an ER gown locker. The entire beaker had then been wrapped in thin clear plastic and sealed with a rubber band.

One of the doctors looked over at her. "Who are you?"

Margo said nothing. Her gaze turned toward the still body on the bed. Then she approached a set of nurses.

"Damn it," a doctor cried. "You can't all be in here! This is a sterile environment."

Margo turned to one of the nurses. "Get me a hypodermic," she said.

The nurse blinked her surprise. "Excuse me?"

"A hypodermic. With a big-bore syringe. *Now.*"

"Do what she says," D'Agosta said, holding out his badge. The nurse looked from Margo, to the doctors, to D'Agosta. Then, silently, she pulled open a drawer, exposing a number of long objects wrapped in sterile paper. Margo grabbed one and tore away the wrapper, exposing a large plastic syringe. Reaching into the same drawer, she selected a needle, fitted its adaptor to the end of the syringe. Then she walked toward D'Agosta and Constance. She was breathing heavily, and beads of sweat stood out on her temples.

"What's going on?" one of the doctors asked, looking up from his work.

Margo looked from Constance to D'Agosta, then back again. The syringe was in one hand; the beaker in the other. Her mute question hung in the air.

Slowly, Constance nodded.

Margo eyed the antidote under the strong light of the ER bay, tore the seal off the beaker, stuck the needle into the liquid, drew up an amount, then pulled it out, holding it up and flicking the end of the syringe to remove extraneous bubbles. Then, taking a deep breath, she approached the bed.

"That's it," the doctor said. "Get the hell away from my patient."

"I'm ordering you to give her access," D'Agosta said. "On my authority as a lieutenant in the NYPD."

"You have no authority here. I've had enough of this meddling. I'm calling security."

D'Agosta planted his hands at his waist. His right hand curled over his holster and, to his great shock, found his service piece missing.

He spun around to see Constance standing there, pointing his .38 at the doctors and nurses. Although she had washed most of the mud from her person, and had exchanged the ragged silk chemise for a long hospital smock, she was still covered in scratches and cuts. Her face bore an expression that was chilling in its singular intensity. A sudden silence fell over the bay, and all work ceased.

"We're going to save your patient's life," she said in a low voice. "Back away from the security alarm."

Her expression, as much as D'Agosta's weapon, caused the hospital staff to shrink back.

Quickly, while the doctors were stunned, Margo inserted the needle into the IV line, just above the drip chamber, and squeezed off about three ccs of liquid.

"You'll kill him!" one of the doctors cried.

"He's dead already," Margo said.

There was a moment of shocked stasis. Pendergast's body lay motionless on the bed. The various bleeps and blips of the monitoring machines formed a kind of funereal fugue. Now, amid the chorus, a low, urgent tone sounded.

"He's coding again!" the first doctor said, leaning in from the far end of the bed.

For a moment, Margo remained still. Then she raised the syringe to the IV line again. "Fuck it," she said, squeezing off a dose doubly large as the last one.

As if with a single movement, the nurses and interns surged around the body, ignoring the gun. Margo was dragged roughly away in the process, the syringe taken from her unresisting hand. There was a flurry of shrill, shouted orders and a security alarm went off. Constance lowered the gun, staring, her face white.

"Pulseless ventricular tachycardia!" one voice rose above the rest.

"We're losing him!" the second doctor cried. "Cardiac compression, *now!*"

D'Agosta, frozen in shock, stared as the gowned figures worked feverishly around the bed. The EKG on the monitor above had flat-lined. He stepped over to Constance, gently took the gun from her hand, and replaced it in the holster. "I'm sorry."

He stared at the useless activity, trying to think of the last time Pendergast had spoken to him. Not the half-raving outburst in the gun room, but really *talked* to him, personally, face-to-face. It seemed very important for D'Agosta to remember those last words. As far as he could remember, it had been outside the jail at Indio, just after they'd finished trying to interrogate Rudd. And what had Pendergast said to him, precisely, as they'd stood on the asphalt of that parking lot, under the hot sun?

Because, my dear Vincent, our prisoner is not the only one who has begun smelling flowers of late.

Pendergast had understood what was happening to him almost from the beginning. God, to think those were to be the agent's last words to him…

Suddenly the sounds around him, the shouted voices, changed in tone and urgency.

"I've got a pulse!" one doctor said. The EKG flatline began flickering, jumping, coming back to life.

"Blood pressure climbing," said a nurse. "Seventy-five over forty."

"Cease cardiac compression," said the other doctor.

A minute passed as the doctors continued their labors, the patient's vitals slowly coming back to life. And then, on the bed, the figure of Pendergast opened one eye, just slightly—a gleaming slit. D'Agosta, shocked, saw the pinpoint pupil rotate about, taking in the room. Constance leaned forward and clasped his hand.

"You're alive!" D'Agosta heard himself say.

Pendergast's lips worked; a short phrase escaped. *"Alban… Goodbye, my son."*

EPILOGUE

Two Months Later

Beau Bartlett guided the silver Lexus off the county road onto white gravel, drove slowly down a long lane framed by black oaks hung with Spanish moss, and emerged onto a circular drive. A large and stately Greek Revival plantation house came into view, and, as usual, it just about took Bartlett's breath away. It was a hot afternoon in St. Charles Parish, and Bartlett had the windows of the sedan closed, the A/C blasting. He killed the engine, opened the door, and bounded out with an excess of good humor. He was dressed in a lime-colored polo shirt, pink pants, and golf shoes.

On the front porch, two figures rose. One he recognized immediately as Pendergast, dressed in his standard black suit, looking his usual pale self. The other was a young woman of singular beauty, slender, with short mahogany hair, wearing a pleated white dress.

Beau Bartlett paused and approached the grand mansion. He felt like an angler hooking the fish of a lifetime. It was all he could do not to rub his hands together. That would be tacky.

"Well, well!" he exclaimed. "Penumbra Plantation!"

"Indeed," murmured Pendergast as he approached, the woman trailing at his side.

"I've always believed it the handsomest estate in all Louisiana," Bartlett said, waiting to be introduced to the lovely young lady. But he was not introduced. Pendergast merely inclined his head.

Bartlett swiped his brow. "I'm curious. My firm's been trying to get you to sell the place for years. And we're not the only ones.

What made you change your mind?" A sudden feeling of anxiety came across the developer's chubby face—even though the initial papers had been signed—as if the very question might cast a shadow of doubt over the transaction. "Of course, we're happy you did, very happy indeed. I'm just... well, curious, that's all."

Pendergast looked slowly around, as if committing the sights to memory: the Grecian columns; the covered porch; the cypress groves and extensive gardens. Then he turned back to Bartlett. "Let us just say that the estate had become a... nuisance."

"No doubt! These old plantation houses are a black hole of maintenance! Well, all of us at Southern Realty Ventures thank you for putting your trust in us." Bartlett fairly burbled. He took a handkerchief from his pocket and wiped his damp face with it. "We've got wonderful plans for the estate—wonderful plans! In twenty-four months or so, all this will have been transformed into Cypress Wynd Estates. Sixty-five large, elegant, custom-built houses—mansionettes we call them—each situated on its own acre of land. Just think!"

"I am thinking of it," Pendergast said. "I am imagining it rather vividly."

"I hope you might even consider picking up a Cypress Wynd mansionette of your own—far more carefree and convenient than this old house here. It comes with a golf membership, too. We'll give you a hell of a deal!" Beau Bartlett gave Pendergast a friendly nudge with his shoulder.

"How generous of you," said Pendergast.

"Of course, of course," Bartlett said. "We'll be good stewards of the land, I promise you. The old house itself can't be touched—being on the National Register of Historic Places and all that. It will make a hell of a fine clubhouse, restaurant, bar, and offices. Cypress Wynd Estates will be developed in an environmentally sound manner—LEED green certified construction throughout! And according to your wishes, of course, the cypress swamp will be preserved as a wildlife refuge. By law, a certain percentage of the development—ah, estate—must be zoned for environmental purposes anyway and as

protection against runoff. The swamp will fit that zoning require-
ment very nicely. And of course, no less than thirty-six holes of golf
will only add to the attractiveness of Cypress Wynd."

"No doubt."

"You shall be my honored guest on the links at any time. So . . .
next week, you'll begin moving the family plot?" asked Bartlett.

"Yes. I will handle all the details. And expenses."

"Very good of you. Respectful of the dead. Commendable.
Christian."

"And then, there's Maurice," said Pendergast.

At the mention of Maurice—the elderly manservant who had
maintained Penumbra for countless years—Bartlett's perpetually
sunny expression fell slightly. This Maurice was as ancient as the hills,
utterly decrepit, not to mention dour and silent. But Pendergast had
proven quite a stickler on this point.

"Yes. Maurice."

"You will keep him on here, in the position of wine steward, for
as long as he desires to stay."

"So we've agreed." The developer looked up again at the massive
façade. "Our attorneys will be in touch with yours about setting the
final date for the closing."

Pendergast nodded.

"Very good. Now, I'll leave you and . . . the lady . . . to pay your
final respects, and please take your time!" Bartlett took a courteous
step away from the house. "Or do you need a ride into town? You
must have come by taxi—I don't see a car."

"A ride won't be necessary, thank you," Pendergast told him.

"Ah. I see. In that case, good afternoon." And Bartlett shook the
hands of Pendergast and the young woman in turn. "Thank you
again." And then, with a final dab of his handkerchief, he returned to
his car, started up the motor, and drove away.

Pendergast and Constance Greene climbed the ancient boards of the
covered porch and stepped inside. Producing a small key ring from
his pocket, Pendergast opened the main door of the mansion and

*   *   *

ushered Constance in before him. The interior smelled of furniture polish, aged wood, and dust. Silently, they walked through the various first-floor spaces—drawing room, saloon, dining room—gazing here and there at the various accoutrements. Everything in view had been tagged with the names of antiques dealers, estate agents, and auction houses, ready to be picked up.

They paused in the library. Here Constance stopped at a glass-fronted bookcase. It contained a king's ransom: a Shakespeare First Folio; an early copy of the Duc de Berry's illuminated *Très Riches Heures*; a first edition of *Don Quixote*. But what Constance was most interested in were the four enormous volumes at the far end of the bookcase. Reverently, she drew one out, opened it, and began slowly turning the pages, admiring the incredibly vivid and life-like depictions of birds they contained.

"Audubon's double elephant folio edition of *The Birds of America*," she murmured. "All four volumes. Which your own great-great-great-grandfather subscribed to from Audubon himself."

"Hezekiah's father," said Pendergast, his voice flat. "As such, that is one edition of books I can keep, along with the Gutenberg Bible, which has been in the family since Henri Prendregast de Mousqueton. Both predate Hezekiah's taint. Everything else here must go."

They retraced their steps to the reception area and mounted the wide stairs to an upper landing. The upstairs parlor lay directly ahead, and they entered it, passing the pair of elephant tusks that framed the doorway. Inside, along with the zebra rug and the half dozen mounted animal heads, was a gun case full of rare and extremely expensive hunting rifles. As with the downstairs possessions, a sales tag had been fixed to each rifle.

Constance stepped up to the case. "Which one was Helen's?" she asked.

Pendergast reached into his pocket, withdrawing the keyring again. He unlocked the case and pulled out a double-barreled rifle, its side plates intricately engraved and inlaid with precious metals. "A

Krieghoff," he said. He gazed at it for some time, his eyes growing distant. Then he took a deep breath. "It was my wedding present to her." He offered it to Constance.

"I'd rather not, if it's all the same to you," she said.

Pendergast returned the gun and relocked the case. "It is past time I let go of this rifle and all associated with it," he said quietly, as if to himself.

They took seats at the parlor's central table. "So you're really selling it all," Constance said.

"Everything that was, either directly or indirectly, acquired with money from Hezekiah's elixir."

"You're not saying you believe Barbeaux was right?"

Pendergast hesitated before answering. "Until my, ah, illness, I never faced the question of Hezekiah's fortune. But Barbeaux or no, it seems that divesting myself of all my Louisiana holdings, purging myself of the fruit of Hezekiah's work, is the right thing to do. All these possessions are now like poison to me. As you know, I'm putting the funds into a new charitable foundation."

"Vita Brevis, Inc. An apt name, I assume?"

"It's quite apt—the foundation has a most unusual, if appropriate, purpose."

"Which is?"

A ghost of a smile appeared on Pendergast's lips. "The world shall see."

Rising, they made a brief tour of the mansion's second story, Pendergast indicating various points of interest. They lingered a little in the room that had been his as a child. Then they descended again to the first floor.

"There's still the wine cellar," Constance said. "You told me it was magnificent—the consolidation of all the cellars from the various family branches, as they died out. Shall we tour it?"

A shadow crossed Pendergast's face. "I don't think I'm quite up to that, if you don't mind."

A knock came at the front door. Pendergast stepped forward,

opened it. In the doorway stood a curious figure: a short, soft man wearing a black cutaway set off by a white carnation. An expensive-looking briefcase was in one hand, and in the other—despite the clear day—a fastidiously rolled umbrella. A bowler hat sat on his head, at an angle just shy of being rakish. He looked like a cross between Hercule Poirot and Charlie Chaplin.

"Ah, Mr. Pendergast!" the man said, beaming. "You're looking well."

"Thank you. Please come in." Pendergast turned to make the introductions. "Constance, this is Horace Ogilby. His firm looks after the Pendergast legal interests here in the New Orleans area. Mr. Ogilby, this is Constance Greene. My ward."

"Charmed!" Mr. Ogilby said. He took Constance's hand and kissed it with a grand gesture.

"I take it all the paperwork is in order?" Pendergast asked.

"Yes." The lawyer moved to a nearby side table, opened his briefcase, and produced a few documents. "Here's the paperwork for resituating the family plot."

"Very good," said Pendergast.

"Sign here, please." The lawyer watched as Pendergast signed. "You do realize that—even though the plot is being relocated—the, ah, requirements of your grandfather's bequest will remain in force."

"I understand."

"That means I can anticipate your presence again at the graveside in—" the lawyer paused a moment to calculate—"another three years."

"I look forward to it." Pendergast turned toward Constance. "My grandfather stipulated in his will that all his surviving beneficiaries—now sadly reduced in number—must make a pilgrimage to his grave site every five years, upon pain of having their trusts revoked."

"He was quite an original gentleman," said Ogilby, shuffling the documents. "Ah, yes. Only one other item of importance for today. It concerns that private parking lot on Dauphine Street you're selling."

Pendergast raised his eyebrows in inquiry.

"In particular, those restrictions you added to the listing contract."

"Yes?"

"Well..." The lawyer briefly hemmed and hawed. "The language you requested is rather, shall we say, unorthodox. Those clauses forbidding any excavation below ground level, for example. That would preclude any development and greatly reduce the price you'll get for the property. Are you sure this is what you want?"

"I am sure."

"Very well, then. On the other hand—" he patted his plump hands together—"we got a spectacular price for the Rolls—I'm almost afraid to tell you how much."

"I'd rather you didn't." Pendergast read over the sheet the lawyer handed him. "Everything seems to be in order, thank you."

"In that case, I'll be on my way—you'd be surprised how much paperwork is generated by the liquidation of assets on such a grand scale."

"We'll see you out," Pendergast said.

They walked down the front steps and stopped beside the lawyer's car. Ogilby put the briefcase and umbrella in the rear seat, then paused to look around. "What's the name of the development again?" he asked.

"Cypress Wynd Estates. Sixty-five mansionettes and thirty-six holes of golf."

"Ghastly. I wonder what the old family ghost is going to say about *that*."

"Indeed," said Pendergast.

Ogilby chuckled. Then, as he opened the driver's door, he looked around. "I'm sorry. Can I give you a lift into town?"

"I've made my own arrangements, thank you."

Pendergast and Constance watched as the lawyer got in, waved, and drove down the lane. And then Pendergast led the way around the side of the house. At the rear was an old stable, painted white, that had been converted into a garage with several bays. To one side, a vintage Rolls-Royce Silver Wraith, polished to a gem-like brilliance, sat on a flatbed trailer, ready to be taken to its new owner.

Constance looked from Pendergast to the Rolls and back again.

"I really don't need two, you know," he said.

"It isn't that," Constance replied. "You made a point of telling both Mr. Bartlett and Mr. Ogilby that you'd made arrangements for our transportation back to New Orleans. We're not going to ride in the tow truck, are we?"

In response, Pendergast stepped toward the garage, unlocked and opened one of the bays, and approached a vehicle covered by a tarp—the only vehicle now remaining in the building. He grasped the tarp, pulled it away.

Beneath lay a red roadster, low to the ground, its top removed. It gleamed faintly in the dim interior.

"Helen bought this before our marriage," Pendergast explained. "A 1954 Porsche 550 Spyder."

He opened the passenger door for Constance, then slid into the driver's seat. He put the key in the ignition, turned it. The vehicle roared to life.

They pulled out of the garage, and Pendergast got out long enough to close and lock the bay behind them.

"Interesting," Constance said.

"What is?" Pendergast asked as he got back behind the wheel.

"You've divested yourself of everything purchased with Hezekiah's money."

"As best I can, yes."

"But you obviously still have a lot left."

"True. Much of it came independently from my grandfather, the one whose grave I must visit every five years. That will allow me to retain the Dakota apartment and, in general, continue living in the style to which I've become accustomed."

"What about the Riverside Drive mansion?"

"I inherited that from my great-uncle Antoine. Your 'Dr. Enoch.' Along with his extensive investments, naturally."

"Naturally. And yet, how curious."

"I wonder, Constance, where this line of questioning is leading."

Constance smiled slyly. "You've rejected the assets of one serial murderer—Hezekiah—while embracing the assets of another: Enoch Leng. No?"

There was a pause while Pendergast considered this. "I prefer hypocrisy to poverty."

"Come to think of it, there is a rationale. Leng didn't make his money from killing. He made it from speculating in railroads, oil, and precious metals."

Pendergast raised his eyebrows. "I did not know that."

"There is much you still don't know about him."

They waited in silence, the engine rumbling. Pendergast hesitated, and then turned toward her, speaking with a certain amount of awkwardness. "I'm not sure that I've thanked you properly—or Dr. Green—for saving my life. And at such terrible risk—"

She stopped him with a finger to his lips. "Please. You know how I feel about you. Don't embarrass me by making me repeat myself."

For a moment, Pendergast seemed on the brink of saying something. But then he merely added: "I shall honor your request."

He nosed the car forward, engine grumbling, onto the white gravel drive. The great mansion slowly fell away behind them.

"It's a beautiful machine, but not particularly comfortable," Constance said, glancing around the cockpit. "Are we going to drive to New Orleans in this, or all the way to New York?"

"Shall we leave that for the car to decide?" And, driving down the shadow-knotted lane of graceful oaks and onto the main road, Pendergast accelerated with a roar that reverberated through the bayous and sleepy mangrove swamps of St. Charles Parish.

Acknowledgments

We'd like to thank the following for their ongoing support and assistance: Mitch Hoffman, Lindsey Rose, Jamie Raab, Kallie Shimek, Eric Simonoff, Claudia Rülke, and Nadine Waddell. And to Edmund Kwan, MD, our deepest appreciation for his expertise.

A letter from the publisher

We hope you enjoyed this book. We are an independent publisher dedicated to discovering brilliant books, new authors and great storytelling. Please join us at www.headofzeus.com and become part of our community of book-lovers.

We will keep you up to date with our latest books, author blogs, special previews, tempting offers, chances to win signed editions and much more.

If you have any questions, feedback or just want to say hi, please drop us a line on hello@headofzeus.com

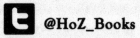 @HoZ_Books

HeadofZeusBooks

www.headofzeus.com

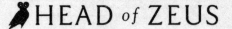 HEAD of ZEUS

The story starts here